CW00821710

Read _Roswell I_
Disclosure, precursor to _Roswell_
Revealed- a World after Disclosure.
Available now from The Aldyth Press!

Review of _Roswell Rising_:

"This month's incredible book!
...I quickly became fascinated,
wanting to know the very next
outcome... Explore the
Roswell Incident from an
alternative angle... This book
would make an excellent movie
and is most certainly
a must-read for any UFO
enthusiast!..."

***** Five stars.
Steve Mera- _Phenomena_ Magazine

Roswell Revealed-
a World After Disclosure

Roswell Revealed- a World After Disclosure
by Ben Emlyn-Jones

The Aldyth Press

Published by
The Aldyth Press

First published in 2017

ISBN: 978-0-9542229-5-6

"The conscious and intelligent manipulation of the organized habits and opinions of the masses is an important element in democratic society. Those who manipulate this unseen mechanism of society constitute an invisible government which is the true ruling power of our country. In almost every act of our daily lives, whether in the sphere of politics or business, in our social conduct or our ethical thinking, we are dominated by a relatively small number of persons who understand the mental processes and social patterns of the masses. It is they who pull the wires which control the public mind."
Edward L Bernays- *Propaganda*, 1928

Chapter 1

The woods were so different to the desert. After a getting used to blazing sunshine, sand, dry cracked earth and hardy cacti, Siobhan Quilley found her current surroundings alien. Water was everywhere. A treacly fog hung over the forest, filling the air with wetness. It soaked the insides of her nose and lungs, and dripped from the tree branches. Muddy leaves stuck to her shoes and the damp leaked in through the holes in them. A stream gurgled downhill ahead. Birds chirruped above and around her invisible in the miasma. The brown cracked faces of tree trunks rose up to meet her and faded behind as she walked along the path. She tightened the collar of her jacket against the chill as she stepped over the low wooden bridge crossing the stream. Its splintery handrails were thick with moss and lichen. A small beetle crawled over the top; she moved her left hand just in time to avoid it. She stopped and watched it clambering over to the underside of the handrail. It was shiny and black; it moved with a purpose and intent that she could never hope to understand. She carried on walking to the other side and looked upwards. The patient sun was still shining somewhere above the fog, somewhere above the low clouds. She didn't really want to go outside, but she had to. She was hungry.

The forest path circuited the edge of the neighbourhood and she followed it precisely. She had more sense than to walk along the highway or traverse the streets of Uniontown. She didn't want to repeat Libby's mistakes; and Siobhan had taken a double precaution. Through the trees she caught glimpses of the deserted houses with their overgrown lawns. There were improvised wind generators, rain butts and barbed wire cordons around the homes of the few remaining residents. Siobhan emerged from the woods and darted over to the mouth of an alleyway, looking around her carefully. There was a shopping centre at the end of Fayette Street, but it was impossible to reach it without using the main road through a residential area to the north of the town. The paving of the road was cracked and long grass was growing through. She didn't see a moving car until she had reached the junction. A low red sedan turned the corner, crawling slowly to save petrol, like all cars did at that time. She ducked behind a hedge and peeked out at it as it drove past. Luckily it didn't stop. The mall was a sprawling battered grey concrete structure surrounded by a car park. The only vehicles there were abandoned ones with flat tyres, covered in rust. She trod carefully over the concrete, avoiding the windblown tree branches and old matchwood boxes. The signboards above the shop fronts were dulled and broken. Many of the windows were glassless or lined by jagged shards. She picked a way through the broken remains of consumerist splendour to a large supermarket at the end of the strip. The sliding doors had come off their runners and a metal shelf lay across the entrance. Siobhan lifted up her skirt and eased herself over it. She took out her torch and switched it on, scanning the darkness. A rat scurried away with a squeak. Then she spotted a chaotic jumble of canned food and smiled. She ran over and crouched down, opening her satchel. She tucked five of the cans into it, not bothering to look at what they contained. Her stomach rumbled at the thought of whatever their contents were. The meagre rations served at Eberly were not enough. She stood up and headed out of the store, anxious not to hang around in the area. Many people raided the forsaken retail sphere of Uniontown and they were not all friendly. What they couldn't find on the derelict shelves they were quite willing to take from others if given a chance.

The wind has risen slightly and because of the noise it made, she never heard the three men approaching. They rounded the corner at the end of the strip beside an old sports shop, just as she was walking diagonally across the car park. They stopped dead in their tracks as they spotted her. She froze in shock. Then one of the men smiled. "Well hello there, young lady." He had ragged clothes, hair and a full brown beard. Some of his teeth were missing. His eyes gleamed dangerously. "Fancy meeting you here. What's your name?" He started walking towards her.

Siobhan edged away.

"Now there's no need to worry your pretty head, baby." he continued. "We ain't gonna hurt you." He was striding faster and his two companions copied him.

Siobhan turned and ran. She heard by their footsteps that the men started running too. She pounded out of the car park and up the road towards the woods. She had sensibly fled before they'd got too close, but her strength was failing. Her heart beat against her ribcage as if it wanted to burst out of her chest, and it thudded painfully in her gullet. She choked and spat as she panted. She was running slower and slower. The men were gaining on her. There was no other choice. She stopped running and turned to face the approaching men. She reached into her jacket pocket and pulled out her revolver. She levelled it at the trio and flicked off the safety catch with her thumb. "Stay back!... Stay back!" she puffed.

The men stood still about twenty feet away, staring at her. Their chests heaved from the exertion. Then the man with the missing teeth grinned again. "Now then, now then. Sweet young gals like you shouldn't be messin' with no guns. Why don't you put that down? We only want to talk..." He lunged forward. Siobhan pulled the trigger and the gun crashed against the ball of her thumb. The report echoed off the walls of the houses on either side of the road. She saw the man lurch backwards and fall. Before he'd hit the ground she was running again. She reached the end of the road by the alleyway and looked back. Nobody was in sight. She made the weapon safe and slid it back into her pocket. Her ears were still ringing from its noise. Then she stood for a moment, bowed with her hands on her knees to recover her breath. She heard a car engine approaching from the junction to her right and reacted immediately, darting into the alley pulling her satchel tight over her shoulder. She peeked out fearfully, but when she saw the approaching vehicle she sighed with relief and ran out to meet it waving. "Hey there!... Hey!" she called. The vehicle was an open-topped Land Rover with four men in it. They were all dressed in identical bright blue baseball caps and their vehicle was crudely sprayed the same colour. Stencilled along the side were the words *ROGER'S*

RAIDERS. The vehicle stopped as the driver saw her. "Hello there." he called back. "You from Eberly?"

"Yes." she replied as she reached the Land Rover.

"Then what are you doing here in town? It's not safe."

"I had to get some food." She tapped her satchel.

"Well jump in; we'll run you home."

"Thanks. Are you Roger?"

"Sure am."

She sat in the back seat between two of the men. They were big and tough-looking, brandishing assault rifles in their arms, at the ready. They wore bandoliers and webbing with ammunition and other weapons. She felt safe and comforted with them on either side of her. She told them about her encounter with the three men at the mall; leaving out part about shooting one of them. Roger met the eyes of his fellows. "OK, we'll check it out after we've dropped you off." His voice was low and businesslike. Then he turned back to Siobhan. "Do you know Libby?"

"Yes, she's a friend of mine."

"How is she?"

She shrugged. "Still a bit shaken."

Roger nodded grimly. "We caught the two guys who did it. We spotted them coming out of the woods at New Salem, near where it happened."

"What did you do with them?"

"Killed them of course." His voice was sing-song and casual.

Siobhan felt a pang of shock. "Are you sure you got the right guys?"

"Oh yeah... well, sure as you can be these days... That saying, we tortured them a bit first and they didn't confess. That's unusual." He drew a combat dagger from a chest-mounted sheath. Its shiny steel blade glinted in the afternoon light; its upper edge was serrated, jagged and regular like a shark's teeth. "It's not often a man can keep a secret when he's on the wrong end of one of these." Roger and his colleagues drove confidently along the highway out of Uniontown. It was a ten minute drive to Mount Braddock on the empty road. It was starting to get dark by then. The vigilantes watched Siobhan dutifully until she was behind the security gate. Then they waved goodbye to her and drove off.

The Eberly campus was one of the few working colleges of Pennsylvania State University left. It had been built as an open-plan institution with a large fenceless lawn facing onto the highway. Today however the lawn was a jungle of long grass and late flowers; and the entire facility was encircled by a high, badly-laid brick wall topped with barbed wire. Siobhan walked into the common room. Ethan looked up from his armchair. "Hi, Vorny."

"Good evening, Ethan." she snapped. "Don't shorten my name please! I've asked you that before."

"Sorry, Sio-*bhan*!" he answered sarcastically. Ethan was a tall and well-built man with a handsome face. Siobhan did fantasize about him occasionally, but he was so arrogant and obnoxious that she had disliked him since she had first met him.

Libby was sitting at the other end of the room reading a book. "Hi, Libby."

She looked up and smiled. Her black eye had almost healed now. "Hi, Siobhan." Her head immediately dropped back into her book.

Siobhan paused and looked at her sadly. Until the previous week Libby and she would have had a longer conversation, but the social and ebullient girl she used to be was now withdrawn and taciturn. It was the previous Monday that she had walked calmly into that same room, holding her torn clothes together with her scuffed hands and explained as best as she could through her swollen and bleeding mouth that she had been raped. There was not much they could do. The college nurse treated her to the extent the college infirmary's resources allowed. The nearest functioning hospital was in Pittsburgh fifty miles away. Ethan drove her there; but, after waiting all night for treatment, the doctors couldn't give her any care that the nurse hadn't already. Of course they had phoned the police immediately. After five minutes of ringing somebody in the Fayette County sheriff's office picked up the phone. The tired-sounding person on the end made a note of the particulars and said: "OK, we'll be in touch." and immediately hung up. "I bet he's the only cop left *in* Fayette County!" hissed Shirley, another student. Then Siobhan remembered the fly-poster that had been pasted to a lamp post just outside the college and they called Roger's Raiders. Roger and his men were the mirror opposite of the police. They turned up at Eberly within fifteen minutes, got the details of the crime from Libby and headed straight off to deal with it; guns in the air, tyres screeching on the road.

Siobhan went straight upstairs to her dormitory and plugged her charger into her roamphone. She wanted to get that done before the electricity went off, as it always did at eight PM. All Eberly's power came from a diesel generator in the back of a lorry parked outside; but the stocks of fuel were dwindling. She knew she'd be getting a call soon and wanted the phone's battery to be up. She got out her can opener and scoffed the contents of the tins in her satchel. They were baked beans, tuna and sweet corn; all uncooked, but she didn't care. Then Siobhan went over to where she had hung up her jacket on the hook on the door and took out her gun. She stared at it in the dim light from the single bulb hanging from the ceiling. Its nickel-plated finish glittered. It was a Smith and Wesson 36 that her father had given her. He'd also taken her to a range and taught her how to use it properly. Most of his lessons were just about safety. She knew never to point the weapon at anything she didn't want to shoot and to "clear" it when she wasn't using it. She did that now, opening the flip-out cylinder and tipping the five rounds onto her bed. The gun took .38 calibre rounds. The bullets were rough lead jacketless ball embedded in a smooth, shiny brass cylindrical casing. One of them was different though. The bullet was gone and the casing was light and empty. Its tapered end was now flared outwards slightly and its interior was caked with black soot. The chamber it had been in was also covered in soot, as was the barrel. She took a handkerchief and a length of wire out of a drawer and cleaned the weapon the way her father had showed her. The soot easily came off on the handkerchief, staining it like oil. "I've just killed somebody." Siobhan said to herself aloud. She stopped and looked up at the window, watching the twilight clouds passing by for a moment. She was surprised at how nonchalant she felt about it. A few years ago her mother had come down with cancer and Siobhan recalled how quickly the shock of the fact had dissolved into a cool acceptance; almost a meaninglessness. Luckily her mother had survived, but for a while she had a terminal prognosis and Siobhan thought her mother was going to die. It was frightening how easily the unthinkable could become normal. Maybe he wasn't dead; maybe he'd survived the shot. She found herself hoping desperately for a moment that this was the case. Then she stopped herself indignantly. Why did she want him to live? He was chasing her, obviously in an attempt to harm her in some way. Maybe in the same way some men had indeed done to Libby the previous week. She killed him in self-defence; she had nothing to feel guilty for. Maybe this trio were in fact Libby's real violators and Roger's men had lynched the wrong suspects. This was shameful on their part; but if Siobhan had in fact killed one of Libby's attackers then this was a good thing. She should feel proud of herself for unknowingly administering folk justice on a cruel and violent abuser. She may well have saved other women from future indignity. But what if she'd made a mistake too? He'd said "*We only want to talk.*" What if that were true? "No!" she told herself aloud. She had seen the aggressive looks on their faces; she had not misjudged them. She had never wanted a gun originally and tried to talk her father out of it; but he had insisted. She shivered as she imagined what might have happened today if she had not been armed. He had been right all along.

Siobhan put aside her ambivalent thoughts as she waited for her roam to ring. She checked the signal and it was only showing one bar, but that was as good as it got in that part of Pennsylvania. She placed the gun and its ammunition in the bottom drawer of her bedside cabinet. She still had enough left for three or four full reloads in a tin box. Hopefully she wouldn't need them. She locked the drawer and tucked the key into her purse. The roam-phone bleeped. She pulled out the charger and pressed the answer button. "Hello?"

"Siobhan!"

"Hi, dad." She rolled her eyes at his abrupt voice.

"Is everything alright?"

"Yes, dad. I'm fine."

"No trouble?"

"No." This was a lie and her voice caught slightly at the end of the word.

Her father detected this. "Really?"

"Really." She paused. "How's mom?"

"Not bad. She missed me a bit while I was in Abyssinia. Wished I hadn't gone. She's still a bit mad at me for it."

"But you came back three weeks ago."

"Do tell!... How's school?"

"OK. I'm still working on that essay about Walter Cronkite. I've even written him a gram; he's not replied, but..." She stopped as the light went off, plunging the room into darkness. The noise of the generator ceased. The sound was so omnipresent that she only noticed it now by its absence.

"What's the matter?" her father barked.

"Nothing, dad. It's just eight PM; lights out time."

"Alright... Now, don't forget..."

"... to be alert at all times." she interrupted, imitating her father's voice. "Keep my gun oiled and loaded. Don't go outside by myself. Keep my roam on at all times. Lock my dorm door at night. Report any suspicious activity to the dean. I know! I know! I'm not a little kid, dad; I'm twenty-three years old!"

"I know, honey; but I care about you. And Pennsylvania is a pretty dark place at the moment."

"Yeah; in more ways than one... How's things at home? Is Brendan OK?" Siobhan regularly felt a lot of concern for her younger brother. He was only six years old and she had always been very protective of him.

"Fine. Enjoying elementary school." He gave a few more details of her brother's life.

"Are you staying in Vegas?"

"I've got a few more days off then I'm going on the new expedition to Area 51. Your mom's not happy about that, but I really need to go. I'm heading up the press corps."

She had a sudden idea. "Why not let me come too, dad? I'm overdue for a field assignment; and, to be honest, Eberly's pissing me off like crazy. I need a break."

"No! Not a chance. It's way too dangerous."

"Oh come on, dad! What's there to make it dangerous? You went there last year after Saucer Day and the folk there had skedaddled."

"Yes, but we only explored a small part of the base; then we left because we weren't sure what else was waiting for us and we didn't have the safety equipment and weapons necessary."

"Well now you do, so what's the problem?"

"The problem is it's still unsafe. We don't know what dangers might still lurk in the darkest recesses of the place."

"Dad, how can I call myself a reporter if I am kept away from stories just because of danger?"

"You're not a reporter, Siobhan! You're a student of journalism."

"Yes, but..."

"No, Siobhan! You are my daughter and it's my duty to keep you out of harm's way. You are *not* coming on the mission to Area 51 and that is final."

The subject changed and Siobhan finished the call with her father a few minutes later. She threw the roamphone down on her bed and growled with frustration. There was no point brooding, she decided; she had far too much else to do. She lit a candle and got to work on her essay. Some of her notes were on her computer and she wouldn't be able to access it until morning when the electricity went on; so she left blank spaces on the handwritten pages. The machine stood still, silent and useless on her desk. She looked at it and sighed. After Saucer Day everybody asked when they were going to be able to purchase their own Digby Carrousel generator from their local hardware shop; indeed Eberly campus needed it more than anybody, but the experts on TV said: "It takes time to adapt the infrastructure". She'd heard the word *infrastructure* a lot lately, but she still didn't know what it meant. What's more that was over a year ago now. By ten PM she felt herself getting drowsy. She undressed for bed and brushed her teeth in the college's permanently cold water. A year ago she would have prayed before bedtime, but she had stopped just before Saucer Day. She still went to mass when she was at home with her family in Nevada, but it had begun to feel more and more like putting on an act. She shrugged as she blew out the candle and settled down on the damp mattress. Her last thought before she drifted off to sleep was about the beetle she'd seen that morning, crawling on the handrail of the bridge crossing the creek. She had moved her hand, careful to avoid harming it; but it was just an insect. Was that normal behaviour?

....

Siobhan awoke slowly with the sunrise. Out of her small window she could see that the murk of the previous day had cleared. She got out of bed and stretched. Her belly was aching slightly; a familiar feeling. She glanced at her calendar. "Damn!" she hissed. The time had passed so quickly. A row of terylene napkins was hanging from a piece of string stretched across her room. She had hung them up to dry last month and forgotten to take them down. She pulled one of them off, knowing she would need it again soon. During her early foraging trips to the derelict grocery shops of Uniontown she had managed to loot a few packets of disposable paper ladies' towels, but such things were a luxury nowadays. All the girls in the college just had to rummage for whatever textile they could find and wash them as best as they could between uses. There was a coughing sound from generator outside the window and it settled into a steady rumble. The lightbulb in the ceiling flickered and then switched on. She smiled to herself and powered up the computer. She gasped as she opened her E-grams. "My God!" There was a reply from Walter Cronkite. She quickly clicked on it. "*Dear Siobhan. It was good to receive your E-gram. I'm pleased you have chosen to pursue a career in journalism...*" He went on for a dozen more sentences. She glowed with pride. She had written to him almost as if to herself, a ritual part of her education procedure, never imagining that one of the greatest reporters in the world would take the time and effort to respond to a mere journalism student at a public college, especially since Saucer Day. After reading the E-gram she called up his meshboard in her browser, wmn.waltercronkite.co.us. The board contained many pages, some of which included embedded vidcasts of his TV news programmes. She watched one of them. Cronkite was a softly spoken man in his early forties with dark hair and a sparse moustache; one of the most famous faces and voices in the world. "...and that's the way it is..." he said at the end of the cast. She raised her eyebrows as she imagined herself sitting beside him in the television studio. "Wow!"

She washed, dressed and went to the refectory for breakfast, which consisted of a single slice of bread and a tangerine. The cook was careful to make sure all the students stamped their ration cards. Siobhan's E-gram from Cronkite had thrilled her and she boasted about it to her friends; some of them didn't believe her. One line of the E-gram in particular reignited a hope that her father's words had extinguished the previous evening. After breakfast she knocked on the door of her tutor's office. Mr Slayman was there and told her to enter. She felt trepidation as she spoke because she needed his permission. She tried to keep calm and not blurt out nervously. He also did not believe her when she told him she'd been in E-gram correspondence with Walter Cronkite. In the end she took him to her dorm and showed it to him on the computer monitor. That clinched it. He printed out the necessary paperwork immediately and Siobhan wrote an E-gram reply to Cronkite.

....

Siobhan's first challenge was how to travel to Washington DC. Of course no buses or trains had arrived or departed at Fayette for months. The only friends she knew with cars, and with whom she had the kind of relationship in which she could ask them to give her a lift, were down to their last few gallons of fuel. They were only willing to use it for emergencies, like when Ethan took Libby to Pittsburgh hospital. This meant Siobhan had to walk back to Uniontown again and do some more looting, except this time for very a different kind of swag. She had already spotted the house she thought gave her the best opportunity; she had become very observant of her shattered environment during the last few months. It was a large isolated property surrounded by a copse of trees just outside town on the western highway to Fairdale. It had a big detached garage and a few broken windows, indicating that there might be at least one vehicle left and nobody around to lay claim to it. She used a large rock to hammer away the glass shards of a window and then found the catch and opened it. It took her twenty minutes searching the lonely house to find the keys to the garage and the car. The residents had not rushed out in a panic. They had abandoned their home in a collected manner, packing as many belongings as they could. The car was old, a pre-Disclosure Ford. It was covered in a layer of dust, but was undamaged. The petrol tank was almost full, easily enough for the journey, and there was good pressure in the tyres. It took a long time to start its cold dry engine, but eventually Siobhan managed to drive the car out of the garage and onto the highway to Mount Braddock. She had no driving licence, but nobody cared about that nowadays. She took the car to Eberly and packed her bags. She bade her fellow students a more heartfelt farewell than she would have in yesteryears. She expected only to be away for a week or two, but things were so uncertain at that time.

It was twilight when Siobhan left the campus and set a course through the eastern hills, sticking to small roads and avoiding the highways where it was not safe. A squadron of military helicopters passed overhead. The government was clearly still very much in control of the country... or at least they wanted the people to think that. However their control was strictly confined to the macro level. Small communities under their sociological radar meant nothing to them. Night fell quickly out in the countryside. The sky was clear and it was a crisp autumnal evening; stars spread out above her. The car was fitted with satellite-director, but she didn't even bother switching it on because she knew it would not be working. Her own roamphone lost its signal within a mile of leaving Fayette County. She had a road atlas with her and stopped every few miles to check her location, switching on the reading light above the windscreen. The landscape became more and more rugged as she climbed through the Ridge and Valley region. There were a few towns marked on the map, but she didn't see them; probably because they were blacked out like most other places. Occasionally a point of yellow light appeared between the trees and bushes; perhaps a farmhouse with its own diesel generator. She had begun to feel calm, even to enjoy the quiet isolation when some people suddenly appeared in her headlights. She slowed the car quickly to avoid getting too close. She stopped twenty feet from them, engaged the handbrake and groped at the catch of the glove compartment where she had put her gun. Then she noticed that the people were steadily walking across the road and they were mostly elderly; however there were a few younger families and even one or two children. A few of them turned and looked at her. They smiled and waved. Siobhan moved the car to the side of the road and decamped, leaving her gun behind. "Hello there." said an old woman with smooth white hair. "What's your name?"

"Siobhan."

"Welcome, Siobhan." she replied. "I'm Ireenee." Some of the others spoke to her. There were about forty of them. Their manner was friendly but unusual, as if they knew her and were expecting her. They all spoke with a strange accent, one that Siobhan had heard a few times since she'd enrolled at Eberly; one that was associated with people who lived in the eastern mountains. "Would you like to come with us, Siobhan?" asked an old man.

"Where are you going?"

"To skywatch."

"Skywatch? What does that mean?"

"Come with us and we'll show you."

She felt inexplicably at ease with these people and followed them as they crossed the road and walked in single file along a narrow footpath; a few of them had torches to light their way. The path led through the dense forest with bushes on either side, so close that twigs tugged at her sleeve. It turned sharply uphill. She had to pant a little with the effort the steepening contours caused. After a few more minutes the trees became sparser and eventually the path opened out into a clearing that covered the peak of the hill. The moon was almost full and the sky clear, lighting up the scene perfectly. The surrounding hills were ash-grey shadows looming in rows to the horizon like desert dunes. The sky was a haze of stars, so many Siobhan had not seen in the glare of her car's headlights. With her eyes adjusted to the night, the moon was almost dazzling to look at. The people spread out in a loose cluster, chattering with excitement. "What are we doing up here?" asked Siobhan.

"You'll see." responded Ireenee.

The people quietened down and looked upwards. They were not completely silent; they muttered quietly to each other. Those with torches began pointing them at the sky. Their beams waved two and fro like spotlights, their ends swallowed up in the infinity of the universe above their heads. Standing still made Siobhan feel cold. It was only October and not frosty, but there was a heavy, damp chill in the air. Then one of the men exclaimed and pointed. Everybody else followed his direction, chattering excitedly. "There!"... "Can you see it?"... "Just over there!"... Siobhan looked and noticed that one of the stars was moving. A medium magnitude point of light was crawling in a straight line across the heavens. There was another gasp from the people as the light suddenly stopped moving and brightened. The people began flicking their torches on and off. The light flicked on and off too. The skywatchers and the light in the sky were soon copying each other. They laughed with delight. "Come closer!... Come closer!" they implored. The light became brighter and brighter until it was more than just a single point. It took on a distinct oval shape.

"My God!" muttered Siobhan. "Is that...?"

"Yes!" the old lady chortled. "It's an MFO. They've come to us again." For the next few minutes the people cheered and laughed with delight. "Come closer! Come closer!" they continued to call. The Mysterious Flying Object remained hovering where it was, at an elevation of about thirty degrees. Its bright egg-shape had an apparent size of about a quarter of a full moon. It scintillated like a diamond, occasionally different colours flickered across it; freckles of red, orange, blue and green. When she had recovered from the surprise, Siobhan took out her roam and switched on its camera to record the scene. A few other people were doing the same, but they were using special cameras with big wide lenses.

"Isn't it beautiful?" Ireenee shone her torch upwards at her own face; it looked very strange lit from underneath. "They used to laugh at us! They called us crazy... Well, they're not laughing any more!"

"I know." Siobhan nodded. "We all know now. My dad..." She stopped herself, deciding it was best not to reveal her family connection to Saucer Day. "How close will it get?"

"It depends. It once landed and we met the guys inside."

"Really?" Siobhan felt her jaw drop. "What are they like?"

"Like the ones you see on TV, except alive. They look so different alive. Their eyes are glowing, full of vitality... I've been seeing them my whole life. Sometimes they come to me and take me away with them, to their ships... Nobody believed me. When I was a little girl they put me in hospital. They thought I was nuts."

Siobhan looked back at her with sympathy. "I'm sorry."

"It's all alright now though, Siobhan. The truth has finally come out and everybody knows it! Isn't it wonderful?" Ireenee grasped her arm joyfully.

A new sound rose in the distance; a low, deep rumble. At first Siobhan thought it was thunder, but it was continuous and growing. The people on the hilltop became alarmed. They turned their heads away from the MFO. "What's going on?" one asked. She soon recognized the sound as the engines of a military combat jet. It grew louder and louder until everybody was covering their ears. The interceptor was invisible, flying without navigation lights, but they all heard it swoop low over the top of the hill. A star blinked as the night-shrouded aircraft briefly eclipsed it. The reaction from the MFO was immediate. It shot upwards instantly like a leaping flea. Siobhan just had time to see it fade out into the distance overhead. The skywatchers groaned and booed in their disappointment. "Get away!... Goddamnit!... Spoilsport!" they yelled at the aircraft as it circled round.

"Sorry about that." said Ireenee to Siobhan. "We didn't expect that to happen. They scared it off."

"They must have picked it up on radar." said a man a few feet away. "Scrambled the air force to tackle it."

"Did they hurt it?" asked Siobhan.

"No. Those MFO's can move faster than anything we've got... Doesn't stop us trying though."

"It would have been cool if the MFO landed." said Siobhan. "I'd like to have seen the guys inside."

The skywatching party lingered on the hilltop for a few more minutes then made their way back down the hill to the road by about eleven PM. They said goodbye to Siobhan in the same strange tone of voice with which they greeted her, as if they had seen her before and they expected to see her again soon. They had wished her a pleasant journey and gone back to their homes.

....

Siobhan sat in the car and watched the video recording she had made on her roamphone. There was nothing there except the audio. Occasionally the camera had picked up the skywatchers' torches, but it was simply not designed for night shots. Her roam was a cheap model, getting old now. Some better and newer roams could have picked up the MFO, but hers couldn't. She deleted the file and put the device down on the passenger seat. She started the engine and sat for a moment, disconcerting thoughts running through her head; then she put the car into gear, switched on the headlamps and continued her journey.

....

She joined the highway just outside Rockville, Maryland. She had once lived in this leafy little town for a few happy years of her life. She was tempted to dip in and have a quick look at the house which had been her home; but it was now almost four AM and she needed to get a move on. She was getting drowsy. She had been tempted to stop the car and cat-nap at the side of the road. "Got to keep going." she told herself. "I'll get plenty of sleep on the plane." The Beltway area looked fairly much as she remembered it. The streetlights were all on and the road paving was in good condition. There were cars and lorries accompanying her, but only one or two at this early hour. She headed west at the intersection, planning to follow the I-four-nine-five to her destination, however something was blocking the road just before she reached the Potomac bridge. At first she thought it was a crashed truck, but as she got closer she saw that it was a wall. It had been built across the road as if it had been thrown there. She got out of the car to have a look at it. It was crudely-laid bare breeze block topped with a roll of razor wire. The tarmac of the road dipped down to meet it at the point it touched the ground, as if it had simply been built over the top without foundations. She got back into the car and retraced her steps, but the wall had blocked off many thoroughfares west of the Capitol. She had to travel all the way back to Frederick to cross the river and it was five-thirty AM when she finally pulled into the car park at Washington International Airport. She assumed she wouldn't be coming back to the car again so she didn't both taking the keys out of the ignition. She carried her bags through the car park to the departure hall.

Siobhan rolled her eyes with frustration when she saw the departures board. There were no flights at all until ten AM and none to Las Vegas until three-thirty PM. There was no alternative but to wait. She went over to the American Airlines ticket desk where a smartly-dressed Latina woman smiled as she saw her approach. However before she could speak to her a policeman standing nearby called her over. "Good morning, ma'am. A moment of your time. Can you tell me where you're going please?" He was a large black man and he wore a blue crowd control helmet above his normal uniform.

"Las Vegas."

He took out a notebook and pen. "Could I take your name please?"

"Siobhan Quilley."

"And your date of birth."

"Twentieth of May 1935." she spat irritably. "Could I go and buy a plane ticket now, officer?"

"I'm afraid you're not authorized to travel from this airport today, ma'am."

She gaped. "What!?"

"Washington International is currently commandeered for official government use only."

"But this is a civil airport!"

"I'm sorry, Miss Quilley. You'll need to take that matter up with the State Department."

"But... Jesus!..."

The policeman raised his head indicating that the matter was not negotiable.

Siobhan's annoyed walk back to the car turned into a panicked dash as she remembered she'd left the keys in it, thinking that she wouldn't be needing it again. Somebody else had thought that too. When she arrived back at the car park there was an empty space where she'd parked it. She dropped her bags and groaned. She felt a bit tearful, but kept her composure. She returned to the terminal and spoke to an assistant at the inquiry desk. Within an hour she was sitting on a coach to Philadelphia International Airport, clutching a folder containing a ticket for a flight to Las Vegas McCarren.

Chapter 2

She relished the warmth of the Nevada sun as she walked out of the arrivals hall at McCarren Field. She'd missed it during her year in college. She hired a car, but did not drive home. It was important that her father did not find out that she was here. She considered asking her mother and brother to keep it a secret, but she didn't like the idea of family secrets. When she was a young girl her mother had asked her to keep a terrible secret from her father and she had been unable to. So she booked herself into a motel and then E-grammed Walter Cronkite from a public Mesh cafe.

She had dinner with the famous reporter and his wife at the Flamingo Hotel down on the Strip. It was a strange feeling to be sitting at a table in the top class restaurant opposite one of the most famous faces in America. For a budding journalist it was a bit like being a school choir member sharing a meal with Elvis Presley. At the same time it felt very ordinary. She did not equate the affable and unassuming gentleman she was talking to with the household name every American TV viewer knew like their own family. His wife Mary was similar in nature. It was quite a funny when other people in the dining room stopped and stared as they walked past their table, first at Cronkite and then at Siobhan, wondering who she was and how she had become best buddies with such a star. Three times somebody approached the table and asked: "Excuse me, are you Walter Cronkite?... It's an honour to meet you, sir!" Cronkite was always very patient and polite with these people, even putting down his cutlery to sign an autograph. "Quilley... Quilley?" he said to Siobhan. "You know I didn't associate your name with the man. I hope you don't think I invited you to assist me just because of your father. I had no idea at the time."

"I'm glad, Mr Cronkite. I want to be more than just my father's daughter."

"And I'm sure you are." He smiled affectionately. "In fact you remind a bit of myself at your age."

"He doesn't know I'm coming; my dad. He doesn't want me to be involved."

"Is he afraid for you?" asked Mary.

Siobhan nodded.

"I know how he feels." She looked at her husband with a grin. He returned it knowingly, as if this were a conversation they had had many times. "I watched Wally go off to war and wondered if I'd ever see him again. When Mars Day went down and everybody was fleeing, first thing he did was jump in his car and drive straight to New York. I'd have stopped him if I could have... if it had been right to have."

"Are you saying I shouldn't be too hard on my dad?" Siobhan asked.

Mary nodded. "When you love somebody, it's easier to be in danger yourself because your heart and soul is being carried around in somebody else's body."

The journalist explained why Siobhan had been blocked from driving on the DC Beltway by a wall. "The entire Capitol zone has been fortified for about two months. Since Saucer Day things have been so unstable that the president decided to ensure continuity of government by physically shutting the federal authorities off from the rest of the country."

Luckily Cronkite managed to pay for the meal for all three out of them out of his expenses budget otherwise she'd never have been able to afford it. Siobhan returned to her motel to get a good night's sleep before it all began the next day.

....

She set her alarm for seven AM; jumped out of bed like a jack-in-the-box and ran to the shower. Within twenty minutes she was on the Interstate north out of Las Vegas in her unfamiliar hire car. The highway ran straight as a dart out of the city; its snow-white chalky pavements and its irrigated copses and gardens giving way to a tabletop of sand and brown balls of scrub. In the distance were tall lilac mountains. The early morning sun shone like a furnace out of a sky that was the deepest blue and she had to put on a pair of sunglasses to see where she was going. She left the I-Fifteen and joined Route Ninety-Three that led uphill into rockier country. There were a few oases by the side of the road, either natural or artificially irrigated. At the town of

27

Crystal Spring there was a crossroads and the route Siobhan took was Highway Three-Seven-Five. An oblong green roadside signboard announced that she was on the right road. After a few more twists and turns the road became ruler straight and the landscape totally flat, allowing her to see the road ahead until it vanished over the horizon. There was nothing out here, just the dry land and the mountains framing the heavens in all directions, and the enormous pure blue sky. She went for half an hour without seeing another vehicle or building. The road was so monotonously, unswervingly straight that she joked to herself that if she wanted to she could lock the steering column and go to sleep for a bit. Yet she knew that just beyond the mountain range to her left was another world, the destination of her quest. Occasionally there were junctions with the roads leading off the Three-Seven-Five, unpaved dusty tracks as straight as the highway. At one of these intersections she saw the only landmark on the route; a black mailbox, just standing all by itself beside the road, as if the house it had once belonged to had been magically dematerialized. After another half an hour she saw some activity ahead; although because of the landscape she noticed it long before she was close enough to identify it.

She passed a sign announcing she was entering the town of Rachel, "population- 54" it declared with some irony in that it called itself a "town". Yet the buildings of the settlement were invisible because of the temporary population that probably exceeded the natives a dozen fold. The area had been converted into a military camp. Tents and temporary buildings lined the roadsides, together with laagers of tanks, jeeps and trucks. Men in uniform strutted around everywhere. A communications antenna towered into the air and a helicopter lifted off the ground with a roar and blast of wind. There was a lot for civilian vehicles and she managed to find a space for her hire car. Then she got out and went looking for familiar a face. She found him in a small bar and grill called *Pat & Joes* that appeared to be the village's communal hub. As she entered the premises she found it packed with military clientele, most of them standing because there weren't enough chairs. The staff

28

looked stressed and overworked as a result of the unusual abundance of customers in what must normally be a quiet and slow-moving hostelry.

He was sitting at the bar sideways, addressing a small but rough-looking man with many rank insignia on his utilities. Clane Quilley was a medium-sized man with a small hunch in his back. His skin was still tanned from his trip to Abyssinia. His hair was still bright ginger, even though it had thinned a bit at the crown over the years and had a few grey streaks. The war had aged him a lot, as well as her mother's betrayal which Siobhan still wondered deep down if she would ever truly forgive. One of her earliest memories had been running her hands through his ruddy locks as he held her in his arms when she must have been about two years old. All her family laughed and smiled as she explored his scalp, fascinated by the scarlet jungle on top of his head. He had protected them both on Saucer Day, hiding them away in a cabin in the woods to keep them safe from the short but destructive war that had ended what the media had dubbed the "ET truth embargo". She and her family had had no idea what was going on. Clane had demanded that they all remain incommunicado from the outside world, removing the batteries from their roams and telling them to keep away from any human contact; therefore they didn't realize that it had even happened until afterwards. It was a few days after Saucer Day that they had been enjoying a picnic by a mountain stream when her father had burst out of the forest yelling at the top of his voice and waving a gun around. When he saw them he wept with relief and told them everything that had been happening. She hadn't believed him until they'd got home and he'd shown them on television. Even in the bedlam of the twelve months since then, as the world reeled around like a drug addict in shock withdrawal, people still remembered him. Now as Siobhan stood in the small diner in a remote Nevada hamlet staring at the side of his head, she felt trepidation. She walked up to the bar. "Hello, dad."

He did a double-take and gawped. "What the *feck* are you doing here!?"

A plume of inward amusement broke through her nervousness. He always sounded more Irish when he was angry. "I'm part of the embedded media corps."

"No you're not! I *told* you! You are *not* coming on this mission!"

"Yes I am, dad. And I don't need your permission to do so." She took her press card out of her pocket and showed it to him.

"CBS!? Where the hell did you get this!?"

"Penn State arranged it."

"But you're only a student!"

"It was a personal request by Walter Cronkite."

"What!?... Don't you dare fool with me, Siobhan!"

"I'm not, dad. Look." She handed him the printout of the most recent E-gram from Cronkite.

Clane read it; then he read it again. A mixture of disbelief and acceptance passed over his face. "Right!" He screwed up the sheet of paper and threw it onto the floor with frustration. "You will stay in the observer pool at all times in the rear echelon. You will obey all instructions from the taskforce press officer. If you deviate from these rules once... just *once*!... I'll have your ass busted back to Tonopah and your materials impounded before your feet touch the ground! Is that understood?"

"Sure, dad; no problem." she replied with a half smile.

Clane calmed down and gestured to the military officer sitting beside him who had been watching the exchange with detached humour. "This is General McCracken of the US Army. He's in command of this operation."

....

At ten AM the forces were called to action. Orders were shouted in hoarse voices and heavy boots pounded on the dry soil. The entire taskforce assembled and stood to attention; and General Bradley K McCracken stepped up onto the back of a jeep so he could survey them. Despite his small stature he radiated confidence and authority, even when standing on the ground, let alone up there. He smoothed his beret down against his short grey hair and delivered a five minute speech about the mission ahead. "...Nobody knows what challenges we might face, what enemy we might have to engage. Expect the unexpected, men! But there is no challenge too great for the US Army! No enemy we cannot defeat! The unexpected is just another expected victory!... Keep your kit in order and remember your training!..."

Just after the troops had been dismissed a bus arrived carrying a group of about twenty men dressed in identical white tailed shirts and trousers. They wore sandals and sported long beards. Some had small round hats. They carried with them rolled up rugs about four feet by three and they laid them in rows on the ground. Then they faced the eastern mountains, knelt down on the rugs and began praying in Arabic, bending over and straightening up in unison. A few people came over to watch, including Siobhan and her father. The ritual lasted about fifteen minutes. Afterwards one of the men explained. "I am Abdul Mohammed Badran of the World Muslim Council and we have come here to pray to *Allah*, the most beneficent, the most merciful, to aid and protect you all on your endeavour. You are in grave danger because you are about to enter the realm of the 'gin'."

"Gin?" said Clane nonplussed. "There's nothing dangerous about gin, so long as you drink it in moderation?"

"No, no, no!" Badran shook his head vigourously making his beard waggle. "D-J-I-N-N... The *Djinn* were created from smokeless fire when God created the earth and man; unlike man and other living things which God made from clay. They have free will like man and God breathed life into them as he did all living things on earth. The *Djinn* are invisible most of the time, but sometimes they can make themselves seen. The MFO's are none other than the invasion of the earth by the *Djinn*. Be careful, all of you. May the hand of *Allah* guide and protect you."

"Thank you." mumbled Clane, looking worried.

At eleven AM the taskforce left Rachel and headed south in single file. Gen. McCracken insisted on riding in the leading tank. He sat on the top of the turret with his brow furrowed; a cigar clenched between his gritted teeth. Behind the tank column came jeeps and lorries. At the very back was the coach containing the press; all of them civilians apart from the driver, crowded together in the hot interior. Siobhan sat beside Walter Cronkite. He had given her a camera and matchbook computer to use in her job of assisting him. They drove south at a steady slow speed, retracing the route Siobhan had driven that morning. They passed the black mailbox at noon, over a hundred vehicles packed in tight formation. Eventually they came to one of the junctions with the unpaved roads and turned sharply right. Because the press bus was at the rear Siobhan saw the convoy moving down the new road from a side angle a mile or so before they reached it themselves. There was a big red "STOP" sign facing south. Eventually they turned the corner and could see ahead. This road ran as straight as an arrow towards the range of peaks to the west. The wheels and caterpillar tracks of the convoy churned up a cloud of dust that spread away northwards on the light breeze. From the end of the road it looked like smoke, as if the track was a line of smouldering fire. The taskforce became more active. Armoured personnel carriers peeled off the carriageway and scurried like beetles over the landscape. Occasionally they stopped and disgorged infantry; men just visible running two and fro. Helicopters flew back and forth overhead; and, higher up, could be heard the roar of an air force jet. This intimidating motorcade crossed the flat landscape. Creosote bushes and Joshua trees lined the road and stretched away into the distance. Siobhan tried to take in as much as she could of the scenery, but most of the time she was focusing on her work. She had the matchbook computer open on her lap and she typed on the keyboard as Cronkite spoke, copying his dictation. "...I asked the lawyer." he said. "'Are you surprised that there are aliens in Area 51?' He replied with only half a raised eyebrow: 'You know I'm not one bit. You must understand that Area 51 is a place where there is no congressional oversight, no executive oversight. Hell, the President of the United States himself would have to ask permission to enter it, if he even knew it exits. It is quite literally a legal black hole. In fact one has to argue if it should even be considered a part of the United States at all, or whether it is instead an enclave of some kind of super-government.'..." Siobhan took photographs with the camera every so often. She then uploaded the text and the images to the social media feed on Cronkite's meshboard. He had somehow managed to allocate a link to one of the few working satellites in orbit; he held the dish antenna in his hands so that Siobhan had hers free. After about half an hour the road rose sharply and became more twisted. Then suddenly the bus jerked to a halt. "What's wrong?" asked one of the reporters.

"Look!" the driver pointed. At both verges of the road stood a pair or signboards saying: *WARNING-RESTRICTED AREA. NO TRESPASSING BEYOND THIS POINT. USE OF DEADLY FORCE IS AUTHORIZED. PHOTOGRAPHY OF THIS AREA IS STRICTLY PROHIBITED.*

"Well it hardly matters now, does it?" said the reporter. "Keep driving!"

"I think we should ask the press officer first..." There followed an argument between the driver and some of the journalists. While this was going on Cronkite and Siobhan stepped outside to take photographs. The signboards were innocuous and unobtrusive. There was no fence or trench physically to prevent people passing through. A hundred yards to their left on the hillside stood a metallic aerial with what looked like a camera on it. A white pickup truck was standing a hundred yards further down the road. Nobody was sitting in it and, even from that distance, they could see that it was sprinkled with desert grit, as if it had been left there long ago. By the oblique angle that it had been parked they could tell that it had been abandoned in haste. "Florenti." said Cronkite. "The contractor that organized security here. The people your dad worked for. That's how they watched for visitors."

"I wonder if anybody still does." added Siobhan.

Eventually the disagreement on the bus was resolved and the passengers reboarded. The bus drove over the invisible cliff between the known and unknown worlds, and accelerated to catch up with the rest of the convoy. The road bent round to the left and climbed a hill; then it came to a small building with more of the pickup trucks parked outside. The bus stopped briefly, allowing the reporters to examine the building. The doors were locked and the windows caked with dust. Siobhan took some photographs. "This is the eastern guard shack." recited Cronkite when they were on the move again. "The Florenti security personnel were based here and carried out patrols in their vehicles along the boundary of Area 51." Siobhan dutifully copied his words on the matchbook. "If we had made this journey thirteen months ago we'd never have gotten this far. The guards would have arrested us within a minute of us crossing the border. They'd probably have just handed us over to the Lincoln County sheriff and we'd have been fined a few hundred bucks, but legally they could shoot you the moment you're inside the compound."

Then Siobhan noticed something. "What's that?" Cronkite followed her gaze. A few hundred yards away was a squat mushroom-shaped structure standing in the middle of the desert on its own like an isolated tree. It was clearly artificial and metallic. It was yellowy grey in colour which helped it to blend in with the background shades. She couldn't be sure at their distance, but she estimated it to be about ten feet high and eight across. The air surrounding it was wrinkled by heat haze. "There's something hot inside it." said Siobhan as she observed this.

"Or under it." added Cronkite. "It looks to me like an air vent or heat extraction duct. This means the underground base is up and running still."

The road ahead was of far better quality; it was paved with new black asphalt. It ran along a ridge for a few miles and then between two bluffs. Then it descended towards a vast flat basin. At the centre was a light-coloured circle of land where a lake had once been many centuries ago when the local climate was wetter and was now an arid salt flat. Beyond it was Area 51.

The press and logistics vehicles were ordered to stop and wait at the edge of the flat land around the lake bed while the vanguard force moved in and secured the closest part of the secret base. The driver spoke on the radio a few times; then, after about an hour, they started moving again. They trundled over the flat valley floor towards the base and the buildings slowly came into clearer view. The first structures visible were large dish antennas and a red and black checked water tower. To their left was a long smooth expanse of square grey ground standing out from the lake bed. "There's the runway." said Cronkite, pointing. "Six miles of it! The longest in the world." As the convoy got closer Siobhan could see that there were aircraft lined up beside rows of large oblong buildings. She took some photos and typed as Cronkite spoke. "I see some fighters, some F2's I think. Next to them are helicopters, perhaps there to assist security." They drove past these and headed south, further into the facility. There were rows of what looked like offices; then they came to far larger buildings. Corrugated steel hangars that towered over a hundred feet high and hundreds of feet long, like airship barns; and blocks with windows in four to five storeys high. Most of the taskforce had established positions here, although smaller hosts were dealing with the other areas of the site. An entire regiment kept moving down the long road to S4, another site about ten miles south; the place where the Saucer Day revelations began. However this time Clane Quilley and his team would be dealing with the main base. The bus stopped and Siobhan stepped out with the rest of the journalists. They were subdued as they stared at these dark silent constructions. They still looked new and undamaged. Thin cloud had covered the sun and a wind was blowing, causing a mild chill in the air. "Do you think there's anybody still here?" Siobhan asked.

Cronkite shook his head weakly after a hesitation. "No... Or at least if they're here they're not a threat, or else the Army boys wouldn't have allowed us to come closer." The soldiers assembled by the nearest large hangar were calling and gesturing for the reporters to come their way. Clane was with them; he had ridden in the forward column, seeing as he was the world's leading authority of MFO's. "Get a load of this, Siobhan!" he yelled and pointed to the hangar doors.

The gaggle of reporters crossed a concrete taxiway towards the open maw of one of the aircraft barns. The interior was filled by a huge black wedge-shaped object

35

propped up by a set of standard aviation wheels. They spread out around it, staring up at it and touching it. It was about the size of a small airliner. "Is this a Martian reproduction vehicle?" asked Siobhan.

"No." answered her father. "It's a jet airplane of some kind. See the intakes at the sides; the tailpipes at the back? Also there are tailfins and a rudder."

"No wings though." said Cronkite.

"I think the whole fuselage is a wing."

"Strange surface." said another newsman running his hands over the aircraft's skin. "It reminds me of a story I once did on a defence project to develop material that wouldn't reflect radio waves. They didn't say what it was for."

"Maybe this was it." said Cronkite. "That could account for its unusual shape. Could it be made to be invisible to radar? An aircraft designed primarily for stealth?"

Another reporter whistled and shook his head grimly. "A warplane you can't detect with radar? Now that would be a formidable weapon indeed."

There was a stepladder at the side of the nose. Siobhan climbed up it. It was about fifteen feet high and she felt slightly vertiginous, but the ladder was stable. At the top was a cockpit very like that of a jet fighter; the pilot entered from above and it was covered by a canopy. It had a yoke, a throttle and what looked like an ejector seat. Its instrument panel was a black screen. She had visited the Martian reproduction vehicle in Washington that her father had flown all the way from Area 51 on Saucer Day. It had been placed in the Smithsonian as a special exhibition. She remembered the sophisticated electronic display it had, that it looked like a sheet of black glass until it was switched on; and this reminded her of that. The voice of one of another reporter registered as she overheard it: "...I was in the Army Air Force for twelve years and I never saw anything close to this. It has limited weaponry that looks purely defensive. I'd say this is built primarily for reconnaissance not combat."

"A spy-plane?" asked somebody else. "How fast is it? How high can it fly?"

"We don't know anything about its performance." said Clane. "We just found it like this."

At the rear of the hangar were some doors that led down corridors. The electricity was off, but the troops had set up portable lanterns inside the building, connected by lines of wire. The passageway led to several nondescript offices and workshops; and it ended in a flight of stairs leading down to a large hall in the upper basement level. It was closed off at one end by a set of giant double doors similar to those Siobhan had once seen in a documentary film about a nuclear bunker. These doors seemed to be the focus of attention for the taskforce's engineers. A group of them were clustered in front of the wall of steel conferring with each other. "What's behind these doors?" Siobhan asked her father after she had pulled him to one side.

"That's a damn good question, Siobhan; and it's what we're trying to find out." he answered. "They must have shut them when we invaded the place last year. When I worked here I was never shown this part of the base so I have no idea what's in there."

"Can we open them?"

Clane shrugged. "The guys from the Corps of Engineers are working on it, but the question is... do we want to?"

"What do you mean, dad?"

"We don't know what's behind them. It could be something dangerous?"

"Like what?"

He shrugged evasively and went back to the group.

....

The press corps were given a meal in a large tent that had been pitched just outside the spy-plane hangar. They sat at tables along with the soldiers, eating ready-to-eat meals in oblong cans, heated over a gas stove. The food was clearly intended for energy and nutrition rather than flavour. It consisted of mincemeat mixed with chopped potatoes and vegetables, washed down with sweet soda and warm water. A row of upright chemical toilet cubicles was set up as well as a washing facility. The sun was setting over the western mountains, as if taking the outside world down with it and leaving them alone at night in universe consisting only of

Area 51. They all slept on collapsible cots in other tents. As one of the few women in the taskforce, Siobhan had her own small tent and a separate ablutions hut in the officers' area. This was close to the open hangar doors. After she went to bed she had trouble sleeping because of the noise. The engineers worked through the night and the sound of hammering, drilling and the rumbling of machinery drifted out as if the armoured doors were a coalface. When she woke up the noise had stopped. After washing and eating breakfast in the mess tent she joined the other journalists and they headed back inside the hangar. The interior of the base had been transformed during the night. The corridor leading to the armoured doors was filled from floor to ceiling with a white fabric lining with a sheet across it. There was a flap open and inside were the taskforce crew. Some were dressed in strange suits made of yellow plastic. These had a large visor and a backpack with an air tank like a deep sea diver's. Clane was rushing around looking busy, barking orders at the men as if he were one of their officers. He saw the reporters approaching and came over. "OK." he said. "We've found a way to open the doors. In a couple of hours we're going to send in a group of scouts and unfortunately there'll only be room for five of you on the mission, so I'm going to throw it open to volunteers."

A dozen of the twenty or so journalists raised their hands. Siobhan's hand rocketed up towards the ceiling.

"I think you should be one of them, Mr Cronkite."

"Dad!" hissed Siobhan.

Clane turned his back and pretended not to see his daughter. "Mr Greencombe... Mrs Spicer... Mr Smith... and you, sorry I've forgotten your name. Something Polish if I recall... OK, you'll need to put on NBC suits so go and see Sergeant McCrae for orientation in thirty minutes sharp."

"But, dad..."

Her father swung round. "No, Siobhan! And this time no means no!"

"I am an accredited member of the press and a personal assistant to Walter Cronkite!" she protested.

"I don't care if you're HL Mencken! We have no idea what lies behind those doors. There could be radiation;

there could be diseases the world has never seen. I will not subject my own daughter to hazards like that. Now go back to the camp and stay there!" He walked off before she had the chance to respond.

She ground her teeth and growled with frustration. Then she noticed that the visors on the protective suits were slightly tinted, and an idea came to her.

Siobhan returned glumly to the mess tent where the press corps were drinking coffee. She poured herself a cup and took a seat next to Annie Spicer, one of the five chosen for the adventure. During the previous evening Siobhan had become especially close to the *Chicago Sun-Times* columnist because their tents were pitched next to each other in the women's area. "Hey, Annie."

"Hi, Siobhan."

"You look cheerful." said Siobhan in a tone that meant her new friend looked the exact opposite.

Annie shrugged. "I'm fine; feeling OK, but..."

"But?"

"I'm just a little nervous about what we're going to face when we go into that underground bit. All part of the excitement I guess. I felt the same way in Korea."

Siobhan nodded. "Yeah, guess so. Mind you, in Korea it was different. You knew more or less what would happen, even if it was the worst thing of all. It was just a war. The troops could protect you because the dangers were all understood. Here it's totally different. It's the complete unknown you're facing. You could meet anything down there! Anything! And there will only be a small team watching your back. It's hit or miss whether you guys will ever come out alive... God, you're so brave, Annie!"

Annie's face blanched and her hand visibly trembled as she held her cup.

"Are you alright, Annie?" asked Siobhan in a concerned tone, encouraged that she had pressed the right buttons.

Annie nodded vigorously. "Yes... Yes. I'm fine. It's just... maybe I shouldn't have volunteered."

"Really?"

She hesitated. "It's just... I've got kids, Siobhan. Two boys. They need me. I hate the thought that their mom wouldn't always be with them."

"I've got no children so I don't know how that feels."

She laughed. "Well you're still young; just wait... At the same time, I don't want anybody thinking I'm a coward."

"You're not a coward, Annie." she soothed putting a hand on Annie's shoulder. "You faced communist guns and bombs in Korea."

"And there are still seldom few women in this business, Siobhan; especially when it comes to perilous assignments. Some of the men think we're just not up to the challenge. That's why I put my hand up."

"An ideal situation would be if there was another woman in that scout party. Then we could prove the point that women can be great reporters too, without you taking the risk personally."

"I'm not afraid of risk, Siobhan." Annie retorted resolutely.

"Of course, Annie. I know that. It's just like you said though, you're a loving mother. You have two growing sons who need their mom and would hate to lose her. What you're feeling is not fear; it's just your maternal sense of responsibility."

There was a long pause. "You know, Siobhan... I shouldn't have stuck my hand up. It was instinctive; impulsive. I should not have volunteered... But I can't back out now. It would be undignified; it would be a professional failure."

"Not necessarily, Annie. I've thought of a plan..."

....

Siobhan lagged behind the other four reporters as they approached the lined corridor again. Walter Cronkite was the only one who had so far acknowledged her presence. He gave her the briefest of sly grins, as if he knew what her plan was and supported her. She lowered her head and turned her face away as they walked past the area where Clane was working. She had changed her clothes as well to make herself less conspicuous. He never even noticed the five journalists as they walked into the dressing room. They were ordered to leave all their belongings in a box. She did so with everything she had, but stopped when her fingers brushed against her gun. The Smith and Wesson revolver was still at the bottom of her handbag. She always kept it with her out of the habit that her father had instilled in her before she went to Pennsylvania State University. She smiled with amusement as she slipped it into her skirt pocket. She had disobeyed one of his orders today; why disobey another? The five selected members of the press corps were then shown how to dress in nuclear-biological-chemical protection suits. These were thick, stuffy one-piece coveralls that stank like old raincoats. The headgear consisted of a helmet with the darkened visor and a radio headset so she could talk to the others through the sealed suit. Once inside she felt safer; her anonymity was assured. When asked her name by the training sergeant she had answered "Annie Spicer" and he ticked the name on a list without a flicker of suspicion. Now nobody would recognize her face through the visor, so long as they didn't get too close to her. Indeed her father walked in afterwards and donned his own NBC suit and didn't give her a second look. She edged away from him, but then realized if she made it too obvious she was avoiding him it might make him wary. The suit was very hot and smothering, but then they attached their backpacks and the trainer connected hoses from them to the suits. A pump started humming and the suit filled with cool fresh air. She breathed deeply and her sweat started to dry. They tested their radio headsets. "Right." said Clane's tinny voice in her earpieces. "Follow me."

Siobhan found it difficult to walk in the suit. The garment was slightly inflated, like a human-shaped balloon. This was so that if there were any leaks they would be from the inside out, the trainer explained. The internal atmosphere was scrubbed and filtered and dehydrated by the system in the backpack and oxygen was added. Her skirt was rucked up around her waist uncomfortably by the garment's trouser crotch. She had surreptitiously moved her gun to an equipment pouch on the outside of the suit, realizing that it would rub her skin painfully once she moved if left inside. Besides, it might come in handy. She put her camera in the same pouch so she could keep taking photographs for Cronkite's report.

"Right, we've got about six hours on the batteries and O-two tanks." said Clane. "Are you all OK?"

The reporters responded affirmative. "Yes." Siobhan replied into her microphone, trying to imitate Annie's voice. She breathed a sigh of relief when her father didn't recognize it.

A second group of a dozen men wearing the suits were assembled ahead; they were armed with assault rifles. There were more introductions then they entered a heavy door attached to a jamb tucked into the fabric liner. Once they were all inside it was ceremoniously shut. "Both ends are hermetically sealed." explained Colonel Davenport, the officer commanding the armed men. He was as anonymous as everybody else behind his reflective visor. There was some discussion on the common radio band not directed at any of the reporters and then a second door opposite opened. They trooped out and Siobhan found herself in the hall they had visited yesterday. This time a massive amount had changed. Some huge machines that resembled lift motors had been installed and round gaping holes had been bored in the wall. More people dressed in orange NBS suits clustered round their handiwork, looking like ladybirds. "We've managed to bypass the servomotors that operate the doors." somebody said on the band. "We cut through the shafts and connected them to these external drives." One of the engineers pointed at their machinery. "It was far more difficult to pull the bolts. Not only did we have to drill laterally into the doors, but there's an electronic lock that we couldn't decrypt. In the end we had to hollow them out, cut them in two and withdraw them manually."

"Can you open the door now?" asked Col. Davenport.

"Yes."

"Very well. Verify the seals on the containment barrier and then do it."

The machinery started humming. There was a pause. Siobhan instinctively took a step back and laid her hand against the wall. The huge steel door jerked apart leaving black crack between them. There was a penetrating high-pitched hissing roar and she felt her suit deflate slightly.

"The pressure's equalizing!" somebody yelled. "Boost the extractor pumps!... Put the filters on a hundred percent."

"Is there any seepage with the outside environment?" another voice asked.

"No."

Other voices came through with expressions of relief.

"It's alright, guys." said Clane, turning to address the reporters. "The area inside those doors has a higher air pressure than the outside so a lot of air has rushed out when we broke the seal, like when you open a soda bottle. We've managed to keep the extra air within the containment system we've set up here."

The noise from the crack faded to nothing. Siobhan's suit blew up again and the motors started again. The crack widened slowly into an oblong of blackness. The motors stopped with it about three feet apart. The people watching became subdued. The unknown space beyond the door appeared to suck at them, like a black hole. The soldiers strode confidently forward and stepped through. "Right." said Clane. "Let's go." He beckoned to the journalists; his voice was breathless and trembling slightly. More people were coming through the airlock to follow them.

"You've been here before, Mr Quilley, haven't you?" asked Cronkite. "I read the stories that came out last year.

"Not here, Mr Cronkite. I only ever worked at S4, and only the top two levels."

Siobhan squeezed her pressure suit through the gap. It was pitch dark beyond it, but the walls and floor were exactly the same as the hall outside. The armed men were a dozen feet ahead; they switched on torches. She then noticed a circular lever on the wall. She went over and turned it. Her pressurized gloves were surprisingly dexterous and she managed it easily. The passageway erupted into light.

Everybody jolted in shock and there were a few expletives from the reporters. The soldiers remained silent; either that or they were talking on a separate radio band.

When they realized that what Siobhan had pulled was just a light switch. They sighed with relief.

Clane turned on her. "What the hell do you think you're doing!?"

"Sorry." she replied in her Annie voice. She rotated her face away so her father couldn't see though her visor.

"Come on, man; she's just found the light." said another reporter.

Clane softened. "Very well. OK, good work, Mrs Spicer; but please be careful what you handle around here. OK?"

"Sure." she answered, pleased that her act was holding up.

"Isn't this place supposed to be abandoned?" asked another reporter. "Then why is the electricity still on? It's not above ground."

"They may have forgotten to turn off the generator when they left." answered Clane. "It's probably similar to the saucers in that it never needs refuelling."

The corridor was wide and lined with grey concrete. It was slightly dusty, perhaps from its year of non-use. It sloped downwards with the same incline as it had above the blast doors for about a hundred yards then it dog-legged to the left before carrying on the same way. "This corner is twice the width of the passage." said Clane. "It's so people outside can't see in. That door marks the edge of a secure area."

"You think there'd be a guard shack." said Col. Davenport.

"They don't need one." Clane pointed to a black plastic hemisphere on the ceiling.

"What's that?"

"CCTV."

"Are you sure. Never seen a security camera like that before."

"I have. They used them at S4."

When they were all round the bend they could see that the corridor opened out into a room across which was a set of security turnstiles with multiple warning notices about how what lay beyond was restricted access to authorized personnel only. These turnstiles were similar to ones found on the New York Subway and other urban railway stations. The engineers cut through them easily with power saws. On the other side of them was a lift bay with a set of four very normal looking lift doors facing them. One of the soldiers pressed a call button. The door made the sound of a bell ringing and the doors slid apart. "Electricity must be on all over the compound." he said and stepped into the lift car.

"No!" yelled Davenport."

"Sir?" The man jumped back out.

"I think we should take the stairs... Just in case."

There was a door next to the lift shafts that opened onto an emergency stairwell of blank walls and conventional steel steps. They were at the top and the only way was down. The soldiers led the way again. It was a good twenty storeys before they came to another door. It would be quite a climb going back and Siobhan hoped they'd be allowed to use the lifts for the return. The bottom door was sealed by another encrypted digital lock. One of the troopers was a sapper and carried a specialized-looking matchbook. He attached an interface cable to the lock which was of a type she'd never seen before. He crouched down and tapped away on the keyboard. "Security is very tight down here." said Cronkite cheerily. A few people turned and looked at him, but nobody responded to his understatement. Siobhan went over and ran her hand along the door's surface. It was solid steel and windowless; not as heavy as the blast doors at the surface, but still very thick, perhaps on the scale of a bank vault.

"OK, I'm almost there." said the sapper. "This lock is part of a network. I've now just accessed the central control station. After this I'll be able to open any door on that network."

Davenport sighed. "Nice work, son."

The door's bolts clacked and it slid to one side with an electric hum. Three soldiers ran forward. "Steady!" barked Davenport. "Let's do this one step at a time. Kovalik, Bergson and Florence! Take point." He turned to the sapper. "Jenkins, you stay here in case we need more hacking done."

"Yes, sir."

The soldiers stepped through the door in single file. The reporters were ordered to stay a safe distance so Siobhan lost sight of them. However she could hear their voices in her earphones. Suddenly there was a roar loud enough to be deafening from inside her suit. The voices of the men yelled and shouted with alarm. A cloud of white smoke or vapour blew out of the door just before it slid shut. Davenport hammered on the door with his fist and yelled at the sapper: "Open it!... Open it!"

"Sir!" Jenkins' fingers danced feverishly on the matchbook.

"Back!" yelled Clane at his charges. "Back, all of you!" The reporters clustered against the far wall in a frightened line. The door slid open. "Medic!" a voice bellowed hoarsely. More people rushed forward and entered the corridor and there was a confused minute of action Siobhan couldn't follow. Then some of the men emerged carrying two of their comrades in their arms. They were placed onto stretchers by the medics and carried up their stairs. As they charged past Siobhan could see that the prone men had had their suits deflated and blood was leaking from holes in the fabric.

....

The corridor beyond the door had been fitted with a booby trap to fend off interlopers. It released a cloud of opaque gas as a smokescreen and then detonated explosive charges that hurled copper darts at anybody not cleared by the security system. The two soldiers affected had survived, but needed emergency field surgery to remove the darts. Their medical care was hampered by the obstacle that they could not be moved out of the airlock without a full biological screening. Davenport and Clane called a pause to the operation and there was a long discussion about what had just happened. Jenkins and some newly arrived engineers examined the corridor and managed to isolate all the power leading to the anti-intruder devices. This made it safe to proceed, at least for a short distance. There was a short corridor beyond the door which ended in a second door through which the engineers cut using a thermite charge. After the soldiers had declared that the area beyond was safe, the reporters were allowed through. Siobhan followed Walter Cronkite along the link corridor. There were some holes on the wall surrounded by black soot, where the projectiles had been fired. Then she stepped through the rough four-foot hole melted through the far door. She could see that it was about an inch and a half thick. The piece cut out lay on the floor on the far side. The corridor carried on beyond the door, but it was surprisingly normal in nature. It had gypsum wallboard panels and linoleum flooring. Notice boards were nailed to the walls and there was a water cooler in a corner. It looked like a passageway from any office building. Indeed there were doors leading off it that opened into fairly ordinary-looking offices, although their desktop computers looked exceptionally modern. The monitors were flat sheets of black glass propped up on plastic stands. A coffee mug stood next to one; its contents had condensed to dry, cracked powder over time. "They must have left in a hurry." said one of the journalists. "Nobody had time to wash up."

Beyond the office block was another security door. Jenkins managed to pick its digital lock within ten minutes and they were all relieved to see that there were no additional automatic defensive measures on the far side. They then came across some rooms that were obviously laboratories. They contained workbenches and stools, cabinets containing bottles of chemicals and industrial refrigerators. There were other devices that Siobhan didn't recognize. There were triangular yellow stickers on many of the items with warning symbols for biohazard, chemical and other less common risks. Each bench had a plastic red box placed on it for storing used disposable sharp tools. She had seen something similar in a hospital. There were clothes pegs in the corridor outside from which hung white laboratory smocks and Wellington boots. At every door were washbasins for decontaminating hands and boxes of rubber gloves. They passed through another security door into a second laboratory that was built for far higher containment capabilities. Each room had a double set of electric doors and a pool on the floor for washing feet. Instead of benches the staff worked behind sealed cabinets with large windows. There were holes in the screens connected to gloves that allowed them to manipulate items inside the cabinet. The furniture in these laboratories had no sharp edges to avoid accidental injury that might lead to infection. The laboratory block was huge. Siobhan and her group walked for over a mile before they came to another lift bay and stairwell leading down. This time Jenkins found it easier to decrypt the lock on the lower security door and neutralize the automatic defence system. There were more laboratories on this level, but they were far better contained. They were sealed chambers behind airtight doors. Access was only via an airlock and rows of hazardous materials suits were hung up ready for use by the staff inside, very similar to the suit Siobhan was wearing. The laboratories themselves were full of locked vacuum cabinets, all plastered with biohazard warning labels. "What do you think they keep in there?" asked Cronkite.

"Don't know, but it's something they're very keen shouldn't get out." replied Clane. "I wouldn't like to catch it, whatever it is."

The underground facility below Area 51 carried on down further. Siobhan estimated that they had to be four to five hundred feet beneath the surface by now. The size of the place took her breath away. The very thought of the amount of rock above her head was smothering. On the floor below the laboratories they found a menagerie of small animals in cages; mostly rodents like rats, rabbits, guinea pigs and mice. The hutches had metal bars and were arranged on shelves like hen batteries. The animals were mostly white and scurried around excitedly as the humans entered their domain.

"They must be used in the laboratories upstairs." said Davenport.

"Strange." said a reporter. "They're all still alive."

"What do you mean?" asked Clane.

"They're alive and well after a whole year since Saucer Day. Their hutches are clean with bowls of food and bottles of water. That means somebody has been looking after them."

Clane stopped and started at him. "You mean...?"

"Yes. We're not alone down here."

The soldiers instinctively raised their heads and shouldered their rifles. Everybody turned and looked around themselves. Nobody was there.

The section beyond the menagerie looked very much like a stable. On both sides of the corridor were heavy mental doors with barred windows at eye level with slots below where food could be passed through to the horses inside. Siobhan peeked through the bars. It was dark within, but she could just see a horse moving around from the corridor lights, just a blank shadow. The horse stopped moving and turned its head to look at her; then it lunged at her, crashing its huge body against the door. It roared with a deafening and very un-equine growl; even inside her suit it made her ears ring. She screamed from shock before she could stop herself. Everybody ran towards the door. "Are you alright, Mrs Spicer?" asked her father.

"Yes." she replied, panting hard. She remembered to impersonate Annie's voice just in time.

The reporters clustered around the bars. "That's not a horse!" one of them yelled.

Siobhan's curiosity overcame her fear. She joined the other reporters at the door. The creature within the supposed stable paced up and down growling. Its brown eyes and huge teeth glinted in the corridor lights; its fur was coarse and matted, almost like a porcupine's needles. "It looks more like some kind of dog." said Cronkite, echoing Siobhan's thoughts.

"I think it is." said another.

"What breed?"

"What do you mean 'what breed'? It's as big as a horse!"

"It looks like a fighting dog, a Pit Bull or a Staffordshire."

"But look at the size! It's ten times as big as any dog I've ever seen."

Clane joined them at the window and looked in. "Maybe it's a product from those laboratories upstairs."

"You mean they've bred it here?"

"Perhaps."

"Why?"

Clane shrugged, a gesture just visible inside his suit. "Who knows? Maybe as a weapon of war."

Cronkite puffed. "I've been on a few battlefields in my time. I've been shot at and stood firm. I've recorded a radio interview from the middle of a minefield. I tell you though; I'd be more scared than I could cope with if I ran into one of those mutts."

There were other oversized canine monsters in the other chambers. They all reacted aggressively to the presence of the humans and the soldiers and journalists moved through the area with caution.

They found the last thing they expected on the floor beneath the giant dog kennels. The corridor opened out onto what looked like a nursery school. The reporters walked around in confusion. The room's floor was covered by a thick carpet. It had shelves of children's books, cuddly toys, shape-sorters and other pre-school games; and brightly-coloured cartoon pictures of people and animals on the wall. "I don't believe it!" exclaimed Cronkite. "We're deep underground in the heart of a secret military base and we come across a goddamn kindergarten? What the hell is going on down here?"

"Where are the children?" asked Siobhan. It was the first time she'd spoken apart from brief acknowledgements and she used her normal voice. She cursed herself for her blunder and looked at her father in alarm, but fortunately he appeared not to notice.

"Why would there be children in this place at all?" asked another reporter.

The incongruous children's playroom ended with another armoured security door of which Jenkins' matchbook made short work. On the other side was what appeared to be a fairly normal hospital ward. Rows of beds lined up along each wall and there was a nurses' station, a storeroom of standard clinical drugs and a treatment room. However, like the rest of the underground facility, it was empty, abandoned; the beds were all neatly made with fresh sheets, as if awaiting admissions from the emergency department at any moment, but there were no existing patients and no staff to look after them. The wards went on for many hundreds of yards. In the surface world this would clearly be the equivalent of a very large and busy hospital. There was a suite of fully-equipped operating theatres as well, all more modern and technologically advanced than anything they'd seen before.

Siobhan entered the stairwell at the far end of the hospital. She followed the soldiers down another flight of steps to another security door. She wondered again how much deeper this subterranean establishment went. Their pumps and oxygen tanks would only last another two hours and then they would have to return. Jenkins set up his matchbook, plugged it into the lock and worked at undoing the seal on the door and the defensive systems beyond. When they reached the laboratory at the other end of the passageway they all stopped dead in their tracks. A few people yelled in shock and revulsion; not just the reporters, but some of the soldiers too. One or two collapsed and had to be carried away by the medics. Walter Cronkite put a hand on Siobhan's shoulder. He didn't say a word, knowing that their voices would be heard on the common band, but he gazed into her visor and their eyes met. His look said that he knew who she was and would not divulge her presence. Siobhan nodded at him in thanks. She was also grateful for his stabilizing influence because of the need to quench her own rising panic and disgust at the extraordinary and obscene spectacle that lay in front of them.

This section of the underground base at Area 51 was a laboratory and storage area of vats containing biological specimens. Some of them were in refrigerated containers, like the ones containing the S4 aliens that Siobhan's father had become famous for talking about in the media. Others were in tanks of preserving liquid. They were of very different species to those even seen in the aftermath of Saucer Day. Most were unrecognisable, just misshapen globs of flesh. Some were clearly animals of some kind; with a vertebra, four limbs and a head, but like nothing ever imagined by the most fevered imagination. Even the giant dogs on the floors above now seemed commonplace in comparison. Some of the embalmed creatures looked vaguely human. She wondered if they might be human hybrids. She had learned from a biology tutor at college that humans could theoretically have offspring with other apes. Were these the offspring? Or had the laboratories at Area 51 found a way to cross *Homo sapiens* with less related clades and phyla? She averted her eyes and her thoughts as much as she could from the aberrations inside the vats. She got the impression that this wasn't just a storage vault. The way the deviant specimens had been arranged, in glass containers with a lot of space in between, made her think this was designed for show. It was some kind of sordid museum; but intended for viewings by whom? The section beyond contained different exhibits. These were obviously natural humans; hundreds of them. There were men, women, boys and girls of all races; black, white, brown and oriental. Their eyes were closed and their hands clenched in death. Some were newborn infants. Others looked like premature babies and aborted foetuses. The reporters who had not already been evacuated from shock exclaimed in outrage. "Holy shit!" yelled Clane. "What's going on here? Who would do such a thing?... What kind of bastards created this place?"

Immediately adjacent to this section was a laboratory with tanks of liquid also containing what looked like foetuses of various animals, except these were still alive. They had umbilical cords that fed into machinery on the walls of the canisters and liquid was visibly flowing along transparent pipes leading to and from these artificial placentas. "Get evidence!" Clane's voice was hoarse and breathy. "Take photographs!" he instructed the reporters.

"Jenkins." said Col. Davenport. "Can you get the hard drives out of these computers?" He pointed at the equipment on nearby lab benches.

"Not sure, sir." replied the sapper. "They're not like any kind of computer I'm familiar with."

The neighbouring laboratory contained rows of large rectangular tanks. They looked like aquariums for fish, except the fish inside were extremely outlandish. They were bright pink, as if filleted, except they were obviously alive. They swam around by rippling fins on their flanks like flatfish. They were about the size of a salmon and also resembled octopuses because they had short tentacles emerging from different parts of their bodies. The opened and closed their mouths as they moved; their maw was circular and lined by small white fangs. They breathed through gills but their eyes were not like a fish's; they had eyelids. "Anybody know what these are?" Clane asked in a rhetorical tone.

"Not a known species I'm guessing." said Cronkite. "Some other mutant they've created."

"Probably like those giant dogs; bred for war." said another reporter. "Look at the teeth on them! One of those would certainly spell curtains for a navy diver. And maybe they could lay mines. I heard the US Navy tried to train dolphins to do that during the war, but the project was cancelled. Basically the crews didn't have the heart for it. Well these critters are far less cute."

Clane was in a frenzy. He ran forward up the aisle between the tanks. "Where are you!?" he bellowed at the ceiling. "Come out and show yourselves!" Then he turned and addressed the others. "When we finally catch these scumbags we should show them no mercy!... Just shoot them here and now! It's the best way."

Siobhan noticed that one of the "fish" in the tank closest to Clane had become very agitated, as if it could understand what her father was saying. It paddled back and forth whipping its tentacles around. Then it placed its snout against the glass wall of its tank directly next to where Clane was standing and braced itself against the far side with its rear tentacles. It trembled as it stiffened and pushed. There was a snapping sound as the glass cracked. Clane's back was less than a foot away from the aquarium. "Dad, watch out!" yelled Siobhan.

Everything happened very quickly. The glass wall of the tank shattered spilling its contents onto Clane's back. When the rush of water had dissipated, the fish-like fiend was clinging to Clane's back; it tentacles grasped his oxygen tank and it was reaching for the seal of his faceplate. It was obviously very strong, having just broken out of its own aquarium, and it had taken a mouthful of suit material at

Clane's nape and was biting hard. He screamed in terror, whiting out Siobhan's earpieces. The others stood completely still, mesmerized with horror. Even the soldiers didn't move; their rifles slung across their chests as if on parade. Siobhan darted forward before she knew what she was doing and reached into the equipment pouch for her revolver. She flicked off the safety catch with her thumb and raised it towards the dripping pink obscenity that was tightening its grip on her father's shoulders. She paused for a second as Clane wheeled around in panic, continuing to scream. "HELP ME!"

"Keep still, dad!" she yelled. She eventually managed to jam the muzzle right against the squishy skin of the beast and train it so that she hoped she would not also shoot her father. The gunshot was just a flash of light and an infrasonic thump from inside her suit. A fountain of dark blood spurted from the creature and mixed with the spilled water on the floor to make a huge pink puddle. The pseudo-fish immediately released its grip and fell to the floor where it thrashed around like a landed squid. Then the spell broke at the same time for the whole group. Everybody rushed forward to help Clane. He was on his knees panting and groaning.

"Look!" shouted Cronkite. The fish in the other tanks were doing the same as their fellow, pushing themselves against their glass prisons to break out; as if they were all following its example together.

"Everybody out!" roared Col. Davenport. "Stay away from the tanks!" The entire entourage lined up in the centre of the aisle to be as far away from the glass walls as possible and fled in single file. Siobhan and Cronkite assisted Clane, who was still semi-conscious with shock. The aquariums all cracked and gave way within two seconds of each other. The floor was inundated with tepid water. The people cried out in alarm as the fish leapt out of their glass prisons and reached for the humans. Luckily everybody was much further away from the tanks than Clane had been and the beasts landed on the floor. Some of them reached out their tentacles and tried to seize passing feet. The people jumped in the air to avoid them. There was more gunfire as the soldiers shot the monsters lying on the floor until what the people left behind was a room spattered with blood, water and glass shards.

The group gathered in the corridor to recover, panting and gasping. Medics ran forward in case they were needed. Clane was now compos mentis. The engineers examined his suit and it was found to be intact. The bite-marks of the bizarre beast had only penetrated the outer later of the material. He looked up at his daughter. The tinted face-shield prevented her from seeing his whole expression, but his eyes were wide in astonishment and anger. "Mrs Spicer?" he asked sarcastically.

Siobhan felt herself quake at her father's glare. "I'm sorry, dad."

His eyes softened. He paused and then placed a hand on her shoulder. "Good shooting." He chuckled weakly.

....

They returned to the surface. The rule Col. Davenport had imposed about not using the lifts was still in place so they climbed the tower of stairs out of the underground lair. Before they could leave the tented cordon and remove their NBC suits they had to be washed down with a disinfecting spray. After they doffed their suits they had to strip naked and have a normal shower. This they did together in a single compartment. Safety outweighed modesty and Siobhan was not allowed a separate facility just because she was a woman. Everybody washed their bodies methodically, respectfully averting their gaze from each other. The detergent made her eyes sting and her skin dry. It was dark and cold outside when they returned to the tent. She sat opposite her father as they ate their dinner. They hardly spoke, but every so often he would look at her and smile knowingly. Clane Quilley was a household name, at least he would have been if everything had not broken down and the world had not gone mad after Saucer Day. For a while it looked as if the structure of society would hold together; it reeled and teetered under the impact, but appeared to steady itself. Then, just as it looked as if it would remain upright permanently, it disintegrated into a cloud of dust exactly as the Empire State Building had on

Mars Day a decade earlier. During the thirteen months since, the people of America lived by hand to mouth to gun. She'd heard rumours that many other nations had fared somewhat better, but international news was sketchy, consisting mostly of rather dubious announcements on highly questionable meshboards. It had been an ordinary day for everybody, Wednesday September the 11th 1957. Then that afternoon a flying saucer had burst out from beneath the sea in Chesapeake Bay and flew towards Washington DC. People thought it was the "Martians attacking again", but it was a man. He landed the craft on the White House lawn and stuck his head out to talk to the people. It was her father, Clane Quilley. Unknown to everybody, even his family, he had worked here at Area 51 on the programme of secretly back-engineering alien spacecraft. Also the fake "Mars vs. Venus" scenario that had seen the world gripped for ten years in a complete delusion. He told them everything, confessing completely, holding nothing back. Siobhan, her mother and brother had known nothing about it until that day when he leapt out of the undergrowth like a madman, gun levelled, ready to kill. Since then he'd hardly been back home. He had travelled everywhere attempting to keep the electricity, gas and water supplies going all over the United States and abroad. He'd most famously helped with the installation of a Digby-powered irrigation system in eastern Africa; a region that had been hit with years of drought and a terrible famine. Siobhan had also been away, determined to study and become the world's greatest roving news reporter. This was partly out of a subconscious admiration for her father; she had the introspection to realize that. However, it was more than that. It was something she had dreamed of even when she was a small girl and he had been away at war.

They all went to bed early, physically and emotionally exhausted. Nightmares haunted Siobhan's sleep, mostly of the day's events. In the morning after breakfast Clane announced a press corps meeting in the base, just outside the cordon. "Right." he began. "There will be another scouting sortie today into the underground facility we explored yesterday. Because of the unexpected and extreme events of yesterday I insist, for health and safety reasons, that only the staff who came with us then should attend today. However because of the... er... distressing experiences we had, this will again be strictly volunteers only. So, hands up who wants to go."

Cronkite, Siobhan and the other three who had come with them before raised their hands.

"Right, that's settled. We're taking Mr Cronkite, Mr Greencombe, Mr Smith, Mr Kolinsky and...erm..." He gave his daughter a sideways glance and a sly grin. "... Miss Quilley."

....

A clean-up team had been working all through the night to make the upper five levels of the subterranean base that had already been explored secure, while they waited for the expeditionary force before venturing deeper. Col. Davenport and Clane Quilley led the military and embedded press contingencies of the unit down the stairs they had traversed the day before and to the place they had ended their previous adventure. They still wore pressurized NBC suits even though the biological research technicians had so far found no trace of any dangerous pathogens. This was no guarantee that such pathogens might not still be lurking in some chamber waiting for the door to open, or some bottle waiting to be smashed. The sixth level down gave them another surprise. It appeared to be a series of accommodation blocks, like a hotel or apartments. Each door along the corridor opened out into a comfortable and spacious flat. They were all different in their style of furnishings and decorations giving the impression that these were permanent homes or else long term residences, not just intended for short stays. They looked inconsistently conventional in such a bizarre location. These were comfortable and unique inner sanctums. They had lounges with settees and armchairs with a TV screen facing them, a very large flat one just like the computer monitors upstairs. A newspaper lay on a coffee table, a copy of the *New York Times* dated September the 11th last year; today's paper on Saucer Day. There were kitchens with refrigerators, hobs and ovens. A calendar for 1957 hung on one fridge door.

There were bathrooms with water closets and showers. Most rooms had a large sheet of glass on a wall that released a glow very similar to sunlight. Siobhan imagined it helped relieve the feeling of claustrophobia that might well have come from living for long periods underground. She also knew that one's health could suffer if one were kept away from sunlight for too long. Her father had once told her this was becoming a major problem on nuclear-powered submarines. There were lots of pictures in most of the apartments too, of landscapes, blues skies, the seaside and big cities which must also have eased the discomfort of living seven hundred feet below the Nevada desert. All the ceilings had grilles from which wafted air. The first flats were clearly intended for groups of single people, but then they came to some that only had one bedroom with a double bed; married quarters. The next question that rose in Siobhan's mind was answered in the following section of flats. There were some bedrooms that were manifestly intended for children. They had toys and books very like those in the out-of-place nursery school they had found on the levels above. There was an infant's crib beside a double bed in one flat. Davenport and Clane allowed the reporters a freer rein in this part of the facility because it looked fairly benign and it was awkward shepherding everybody together from one home to the next, so they were allowed to explore each flat independently. Siobhan's ears had become used to the sounds from inside the suit; the crackled conversation in her earpieces, the hiss of the ventilation system, the creak of the rubbery material as she moved. However, she somehow became alert to a very different noise long before she heard it consciously, as soon as she opened the door to the flat in fact. This was clearly one of the family accommodation units. The lounge had some children's comics on the table, but something was amiss. She stopped for a moment, staring and listening, wondering if she should go on. She decided to venture further in without alerting anybody else; she was probably imagining things anyway. However when she reached the corridor to the bedrooms she stopped again. She could now definitely hear a voice. It was coming from one of the children's bedrooms. She tiptoed as best she could in the cumbersome suit towards the open door where the voice was coming from. It was a child's voice singing quietly. Her heart thumped as she peeked around the frame and looked inside. A young girl was sitting on 'a chair at a table beside a bed with a colourful quilt. She was humming to herself randomly as she drew a picture on a sheet of paper with a felt-tipped pen. On a TV screen nearby a Walt Disney cartoon was playing with the volume turned right down. She stopped and looked up at Siobhan. She showed no surprise; maybe just a little curiosity. Her eyes were an incredible sight, deep blue and very large. Her skin was pale and her hair golden blonde. She put down her pen and stood up. "Hello." she said.

Siobhan stood in the doorway staring at the girl. Her throat stuck as she replied. "Hello." She wondered momentarily if she were seeing a ghost.

"What's your name?" The girl smiled showing clean white teeth. Her lips were thin and hardly coloured at all.

"Siobhan."

"I'm Kerry... Why are you wearing a hazmat suit on this level, Siobhan?"

"I... er... I have to; for protection."

"There's no need." Kerry said confidently. Her accent sounded British with a touch of something else that Siobhan couldn't identify.

Clane's voice broke into her earphones. "Siobhan, who are you talking to?"

"Erm... There's somebody here, dad."

She heard a gasp. "OK, maintain the situation. We're coming over!" A moment later feet pounded in the corridor outside and a dozen of her colleagues crowded around the bedroom door to try and see the girl. Kerry looked around eleven or twelve. She was fairly tall and there was a swelling around her nipples indicating that she was in early puberty. She smiled calmly at the others and introduced herself politely, asking their names.

"How did you get here, Kerry?" asked Siobhan. "Where do you come from?"

She looked nonplussed. "I come from... here."

"Where are your mom and dad?"

A wave of sadness passed over her gaze. "They... I think they've gone. They left with the others."

"Kerry." asked Clane. "Have you been feeding the animals upstairs?"

"Of course." she replied. "Nobody else is here to do it?"

"Are you alone, Kerry?" asked Walter Cronkite.

"No, I'll show you to the others." She ran out of the room and off down the corridor, beckoning them to follow.

There were about a dozen children living in the accommodation sector. They were all about the same age as Kerry and with a similar complexion. They were busy playing football on a small sports court adjacent to the flats and they stopped and came over when the reporters and soldiers arrived. Davenport immediately got on the radio and summoned a full medical team to come and evacuate them. "Colonel." said Siobhan. "Maybe that's not a good idea."

"What ever do you mean, Miss Quilley? They're abandoned children! They need to be taken care of."

"It's just..." She wondered why she was saying this. An inexplicable urge had come over her. She remembered the genetic laboratories on the floors above and especially the foetuses being decanted in the artificial wombs. "Are they... normal children?"

He chuckled. "What's a 'normal child'? My kids are real tearaways."

"No, Colonel. It's just... have you looked into their eyes? They're... they're not really human... at least not in the usual sense."

"What are you talking about, Miss Quilley? How many senses of being human are there?... Don't worry; they'll be in safe hands. Right now we need to get them out of here and to safety. That is normal procedure for children found in combat zones, OK?"

The children were luckily quite happy to cooperate with the medical corps and followed them out of the facility fearlessly and willingly. Kerry waved goodbye to Siobhan as she was escorted down the passageway to the stairwell.

Then a thought occurred to Siobhan as she remembered. She turned to her father. "Dad?"

"Yes?"

"How come they can hear our voices when we're inside these suits?"

"What do you mean?"

"I heard somebody speaking in a suit once when I didn't have one on. Their voice was muffled, almost inaudible. That's why we have our radios."

He shrugged. "Maybe they've got good hearing."

"Maybe."

....

They finally reached the lowest known level of the secret underground base. It was much taller than the others and consisted of a single arched chamber about five hundred feet long by three hundred wide and ninety high. The interior of the chamber resembled a railway station. There was a line of tracks passing from one end to the other and both ends consisted of a circular steel door, clearly these covered tunnels through which the railways ran. The tracks themselves were not normal railway lines. Each one consisted of three rails that were as smooth as mirrors and much wider than normal. The platforms were fairly nondescript, very similar to those on the New York City Subway, with tiled surfaces and benches to sit on while waiting for trains. There was even a notice board which would normally give details of arrivals and departures; although this was now blank. There were three lines passing through the station and on the middle one sat a train. The team of reporters and their associates crossed over a footbridge to the platform by the middle track and descended a flight of stairs. The train was completely circular in cross-section, clearly intended to travel along a tubular tunnel. Despite this it had large clear windows. The interior had rows of seats like an airliner, but there was no drivers' cab. The front of the train was a blunt hemisphere and the passenger cabin ran right up to a circular window on the nose. It was split into four coaches, each about eighty feet long with a segmented link between them so it could traverse bends. A faint whine came from it, indicating its engine was working; whatever kind of engine it had. The interior lights of the cabin were also glowing as if it had just pulled up to the platform a minute ago to pick up some passengers and that it planned to depart within another minute. "So this is how they got away." said Clane through gritted teeth.

"When the Saucer Day invasion began they must have jumped aboard these trains and bolted." added Davenport.

"Why did they leave the children behind?" asked Siobhan.

"How do these trains work?" asked another reporter. Everybody had ignored Siobhan's question.

"Magnetic levitation is my guess." said one of the engineers. "I've seen experimental vehicles like this in Japan. The two side rails are for the levitation and the middle one is a Laithwaite piste."

"Translation please." asked the reporter sharply.

"The train has no wheels and does not touch the track. It floats above it using the homopole magnetic repulsion effect; like when you try to force two fridge magnets together when they're both north or both south pole. They don't stick together, they repeal each other." There's a second set of magnets on the middle rail that pole-phase in order to generate thrust. It's like a standard electric motor except it runs in a line and not as a rotation system creating torque."

"Why no driver?" asked Cronkite.

"Its navigation is automated."

"Is that possible?"

"Sure; an elevator doesn't need a driver to reach the top of a tall building does it?"

"But this is a train."

The engineer shrugged. "What's that except an elevator that runs horizontally? Especially as this is clearly an underground railroad. All it has to do is move down a tunnel. There's talk of making some subway networks run with automatic trains even in the public world."

"Why is the entrance to the tunnel behind those doors?" asked Clane.

The engineer paused then gasped and chuckled with excitement. "This could be a pneumotrain!"

"A what?"

"The reason the tunnel is sealed off is because there's a vacuum inside it. My guess is that there's a second set of doors further down the track making this an entrance to an airlock... A pneumotrain runs in a tunnel that is partly or fully evacuated of its atmosphere. That means it is very efficient and can achieve very high speeds because it's not afflicted by drag from the air, like normal trains are. It's possible they might slightly increase the pressure behind the train too to assist propulsion, like a blow-dart."

Siobhan walked over to the sidewall of the train. The vehicle was accessed by a sliding door and a button next to it had the word *press* on it. She pressed it and the door slid open with a hiss. Everybody swung round and gasped. "What are you doing, Siobhan?" demanded her father. "Be careful!"

"I just wanted to see if it was still working, dad. Don't get your pants in a twist." She was annoyed at the others for ignoring her question about the children just now and wanted to get their attention. She felt Annie was right about male journalists thinking women couldn't cope with hazardous assignments.

"Well it is; so stay away from that door! For all we know there could be a function in it that activates the thing when somebody steps aboard."

"Well perhaps that's good. You said it yourself earlier; we've got to catch the bastards who did all that stuff upstairs. This is obviously how the bastards got away. Why don't we use this train to follow them and apprehend them?"

"That would be extremely reckless at this point in our expedition. We need armed reinforcements, a mission plan and a proper reconnaissance report before any kind of venture like that... Now, can we please get back to the business at hand?" He turned away and addressed the others.

Siobhan amused herself with how funny it would be if she boarded the train alone. She knew her father was right, but his dismissive tone still irked her. However, as the thrill of the idea rose within her, a part of her started goading herself to do it. She looked at Walter Cronkite; her hero, the kind of reporter she most longed to be. He caught her gaze and gave her a supportive smile through his visor. He had picked up on her feelings and clearly sympathized. Walter Cronkite had written many of her favourite journalistic essays. He had spoken about when to take risks and when not. One line stood out in her memory like a motto: *"I pity the reporter who takes a risk to get a story and fails... but not as much as I pity the reporter who declines to take a risk to get a story and thereby fails a hundred times worse."* As those words passed though her mind she found herself walking towards the open door of the train. It was if her body were no longer under her control. She was now inside the carriage. "What the hell are you doing, Siobhan?" she asked herself out loud. Terror mixed with excitement in perfect proportions to make the most ecstatic cocktail.

"SIOBHAN!" She heard her father's yell in her earpiece. He was right. The doors slid shut by themselves and the humming of the engine grew louder. The train began to move, so slowly and smoothly that it was imperceptible. Her father was now banging his fists manically against the windows of the carriage. "SIOBHAN!" his voice was hoarse with fear inside her helmet.

She tried to reply, but her throat was numb. She turned and looked at him. She gave him a confident thumbs up. She didn't want to frighten him.

Clane ran along beside the accelerating train, continuing to call out her name. Some of the others ran up to him and held him back as the platform fell away to the track. Ahead the circular doors to the tunnel were sliding apart. As the train passed through them her father's voice was abruptly cut off, presumably because the radio connection was lost. He continued to gesture pitifully until the doors closed and the station was severed from sight. Siobhan stood alone on the unknown underground train. The enormity of her folly crashed down on her like a tsunami, but it was too late to turn back. She walked towards the front of the train and stared out of the oval nosecone at the immaculate blackness of the tunnel ahead.

Chapter 3

Siobhan sat up. It wasn't like slowly regaining consciousness after sleep or a stupor; she was instantly wide awake and it felt like the next moment. A penetrating baritone buzzing noise came from above her, like a giant beehive. She looked up and saw a grey metallic circle. It was retreating away upwards, getting smaller and smaller and the sound got fainter and fainter. Then with a flick it darted away to the horizon, like a swift on the breeze, leaving a pewter overcast sky. She looked around herself. She was sitting in a patch of bracken in an open glade in a forest. Golden autumnal trees surrounded her on all sides. She stood up gasping, feeling like she was being suffocated. Then she realized why; she was still wearing her hazmat suit and the compressor had stopped working. The material was ragged and flaccid against her body and she had no air supply. She fiddled with the seals until they came loose, then she ripped off her helmet and took a deep breath. The air in the woodland was chilled, but dry; it smelled of soil and mould. She shivered slightly as she took the suit off completely and her sweaty skin was exposed to the light breeze. She took the gun out of the pouch on her suit and slipped it into the waistband of her skirt. "Hello?" she yelled. "Is anybody there?" A trio of startled birds flapped out of the closest tree. She plodded over to the tree-line, trampling the bracken beneath her boots to make a path. As she reached the first trunks she saw light in one direction and headed there through the woods, pushing aside the bare twigs of undergrowth. The forest opened out onto a field; a rusty barbed wire fence blocked her way. The field had clearly once been an arable farmer's field, but the crops had overgrown since Saucer Day and were now mixed with tall grass. Over the tops of the plants Siobhan saw down a gentle slope to a farmhouse. Smoke was issuing from its chimney so somebody was living there. In the distance were soft grassy hills. She pushed along the edge of the woods beside the fence until she came to a cracked tarmac road. She turned left and followed it in the direction of the house. There were no vehicles or other pedestrians; the only sound was the wind and birdsong.

The farmhouse was accessed via a neglected barnyard. In a decrepit old barn Siobhan saw a pile of dry grey animal bones; cattle and horses she guessed from the shape of the skulls. The windows of the house were small and dirty, but she could see light inside. She knocked on the ancient wooden plank door. The door was wrenched open as soon as her knuckles left it and a thin old man leapt out at her brandishing a shotgun. "Who are you!?" he roared, his face stretched with outrage and fear. "What do you want!?"

Siobhan jerked back in alarm.

The man's gaze moved lower and he saw the butt of her pistol at her waist. "Drop the gun!" he ordered. A misshapen short-haired old woman appeared behind the man's shoulder.

Siobhan gently placed her Smith and Wesson on the dried mud at her feet. "I don't want any trouble." She said. "My name's Siobhan and I'm lost."

The man's ire eased and he lowered the gun slightly. "We're all lost these days... I promise you we've got no food in the house and we wouldn't let you take it if we did!" He spoke with a Canadian accent.

"Where am I?"

"Longview."

"Where's that?"

"Alberta."

"Alberta in Canada?

"Have you heard of any other?"

"My word." said the old woman with a cracked voice. "You really are lost aren't you?"

There was a pause. "Could I possibly use your phone?"

....

The elderly couple were named Mr and Mrs Fitzallan. They had run the farm their whole lives until Saucer Day. There was no telephone in the house and no electricity. A television set sat useless in the corner of the lounge like an embalmed corpse. Their home's only source of heat and light was a wood fire in the hearth. Despite what Mr Fitzallan had told her there was enough food in the house for them all to have a meal of beans and mince. There were only about three mouthfuls each and Mrs Fitzallan served it in teacups. "The meat comes from Irwin, our carthorse." she explained.

Siobhan gagged.

She shrugged sadly. "I'll miss the old feller, but we've got to eat."

"So, how did you end up here?" asked Mr Fitzallan. The farmer and his wife raised their eyebrows as she explained. When they told her the day and date Siobhan felt a chill. "It's been four days!" She hissed.

"And you don't remember nothing?"

"I got aboard the underground train... the next thing I know I'm waking up in those woods up the hill. My dad was shouting at me to get out... Oh, my mom and dad! They must be so worried. I need to contact them. To tell them I'm alright."

"There's no way to do that from here. You'll have to go to Calgary; there are telephones there. We can take you."

She jumped to her feet. "When do we leave?"

"Not now. It's too late for today and it ain't safe to wander about at night. We'll drive you up there in the morning."

Siobhan spent a sleepless night in a damp and dirty bed upstairs and in the morning Mr and Mrs Fitzallan wheeled out a low four-wheeled buggy and harnessed it to a tired and flea-bitten stallion called Clyde. "We had a truck but it broke down and we couldn't fix it." explained the farmer's wife. Clyde pulled as hard as he could against the harness as the couple guided the buggy out into the road. Siobhan wondered if he realized that his usefulness in this role was probably the only thing that kept him from following Irwin into the teacups.

The couple both carried weapons and were continuously looking of their shoulder as Clyde trotted along the potholed road. "There are rough folks in these parts." said Mr Fitzallan. "They roam the land looking for plunder; food, water... and women. Even old ladies like Mrs Fitzallan ain't safe from them." He chuckled.

His wife elbowed him in the ribs with a scowl.

As they approached the city of Calgary the atmosphere changed to something approaching normal life in the time before Saucer Day. The quality of the road surfaces improved and a few cars drove along the bigger thoroughfares. Siobhan had noticed the same pattern in Pennsylvania as she went in and out of Pittsburgh. In the city centre there were tall and well-kept buildings and buses ran between them. About half the shops and offices were open. She had left her roamphone behind in the press pool at Area 51 and none of the public payphones worked. Eventually a fireman who was a friend of the Fitzallans allowed her to make a call from their fire station's landline. Her parents' home phone in Nevada rang and rang; nobody was there. She tried Eberly, but they were disconnected again. In the end she had to call the Penn State dean's office. When she told him who she was the dean gasped. "Siobhan Quilley!?"

"Yes, sir."

"Where in God's name are you, girl!?"

"Calgary in Canada, sir."

"How did you get there?"

"I don't know... Look, Prof. Kramer, I need to get hold of my mom and dad..."

"Of course, Siobhan.... Listen; give me the number you're calling from and stay where you are. I'll call you back in a few minutes."

As she waited she realized that the dean probably felt guilty for the university allowing her to go on the trip to Area 51. She sat by the phone for about fifteen minutes. The firemen in the room politely ignored her. The phone rang; she picked it up. "Siobhan." The dean didn't wait for her to answer. "Can you get to McCall Field? There's an aircraft on its way to pick you up."

....

The Fitzallans drove her to the airport in their buggy pulled by Clyde. There she bade them a fond and grateful farewell. McCall Field was a medium-sized airport within the limits of Calgary itself that still had one of its three terminals open. The staff had been informed that a charter flight was on its way to collect her and they showed her to a comfortable waiting room where they served her with tea and coffee. She found a working payphone and tried to call home again a few times but still got no answer. She tried her father's roam, but it wouldn't connect. She growled with frustration. Her conscience niggled her as she imagined how worried he must have been for these last four days. "I hope somebody's told them I'm alright." she muttered to herself. Two hours later her flight arrived. She was surprised to see that it was a US Army Air Force Boeing 407. She had been expecting a light aircraft of some kind. The air crew were brusque and dispassionate. Three of them walked swiftly over to the terminal to meet her as soon as the jetway was in place and they marched her to the aircraft with two on each side and one behind, escorting her as if they were concerned for her safety. They were polite and helpful but wouldn't answer her questions about Area 51 and her father. Once they were in the air they served her a tasty meal and then she reclined her seat and fell asleep, feeling very tired after her rough night in the Fitzallans' spare room. One of the cabin crew woke her up as the aircraft was descending to land. "Seatbelt on please, Miss Quilley. We'll be touching down in WIA shortly."

"Where?"

"Washington International."

"Washington DC?"

"Yes."

"But I live in Nevada. I thought we were going to Las Vegas."

"Not yet, Miss Quilley."

"But why are you taking me to Washington?"

"I don't know... Please raise your seat now, miss." The woman walked off without another word.

Siobhan watched as the flat rooftops of DC solidified out of the cloud and the aircraft rammed into the tarmac at Washington International Airport. The plane stopped before the terminal and another welcoming committee was there. Like the aircrew they were firm and reserved. A car was parked at the end of the jetway and they insisted Siobhan climbed immediately onto the back seat. As they pulled out of the airport two police cruisers joined them and accompanied them through the streets, lights flickering. Siobhan started to feel intensely nervous, as if she were going for a dental appointment. The motorcade turned onto the Beltway and headed north. It was early evening by now and lights were coming on. The convoy turned off at Bethesda and she guessed where they were going before the cars entered the rainbow drive of the Walter Reed National Military Medical Centre. Here was where her father's friend and colleague, James Forrestal, had committed suicide, allegedly, nine years earlier. A shiver ran through her.

She was taken from the car into the hospital and left alone in a white-walled room with an examination couch. The place stank of disinfectant. The door opened and three women entered, all wearing identical white coats. One of them was a dumpy blonde with short spiky hair and excessive lipstick and she introduced herself as Dr Shawcrane. "We have to carry out a complete toxicology examination on you, Miss Quilley." she said.

"Why?"

"Because we don't know where you've been for the last four days."

Siobhan gulped. She hadn't thought of that. She had no memory of the incident so she had stopped actively worrying. However the doctor was right; could she have picked up some disease? Dr Shawcrane took out a syringe and needle from an equipment cupboard and jabbed the inside of her elbow painfully. A column of her blood rose into the syringe. The doctor weighed her on some scales, wiped the inside of her cheek with a cotton bud and took her blood pressure. She used an otoscope to look in her ears. "Say 'ah'." she said as she shoved a wooden ice-lolly stick down Siobhan's throat, making her gag. Then she said: "Right, could you take your clothes off now please, Miss Quilley?"

"Do I have to?"

Dr Shawcrane nodded. "It's necessary."

Siobhan hesitated and then removed her skirt, blouse and stockings. She laid them on a chair next to the couch and smiled.

The doctor raised her eyebrows. "*All* your clothes, Miss Quilley."

Siobhan looked into her hard eyes, as well of those of the other two doctors who had not yet said a word. She undid her bra with a trembling hand and slid her panties down her legs.

The doctor then whipped on a pair of pink rubber gloves with a snap. "Now please bend over the couch and spread your legs, Miss Quilley."

Siobhan obeyed, leaning her elbows on the couch's padded surface, which was covered by a wide strip of tissue paper. She yelped as she felt Shawcrane's hand thrusting into her vagina. "Ow! Stop that!"

"It's necessary, Miss Quilley." the medic repeated.

Shawcrane then poked her finger up Siobhan's bottom and waggled it around as if beckoning to her intestines. Siobhan looked over her shoulder. The two other women were standing against the wall with their arms crossed; their sour faces were watching Shawcrane's examination intently. Siobhan felt her cheeks flush. She turned back to face the wall, squeezed her eyes shut and gritted her teeth.

After that she was allowed to get dressed and was taken to a different room. This one was completely bare apart from a table and two chairs. It had a small window that gave a view of the drive from the ground floor. She took a seat at the same time as a door opened and a man in a dark suit entered. "Good evening, Miss Quilley." he said formally and gravely. She had yet to see anybody smile in Bethesda. "My name is Sandley and I'm with internal affairs." He left a very slight pause before the words *internal affairs*, enough to indicate considerable implications from those words. "I need to talk to you about your recent experience." He opened a briefcase he had brought with him and placed a tape recorder and a notebook on the table. "It won't take long, but..."

She butted in. "Actually, Mr Sandley, before you begin, it is very important I contact my parents."

"This is somewhat more urgent I'm afraid."

"No, it's not!" Siobhan's patience ran out suddenly and without warning. "I live in Boulder City, Nevada yet I've been brought without my consent to Washington DC. I've been poked and prodded from head to toe in the most undignified manner by a trio of perverted harpies! I've had blood sucked out of me! And nobody has told me a damn thing! My mom and dad haven't seen me for five days! For all they know, I'm dead! Now, I'm not cooperating with you people at all for one more second until I speak to my parents; understood?"

Sandley smiled thinly. His face was broad and all his features were narrow. "Your mother and father know you're safe. They know you're in DC; in fact they're hot-tailing it here as we speak."

Siobhan opened her mouth to reply and hesitated. "Thank you." she whispered.

"Would you like a cup of coffee or tea?" Sandley's voice had softened, but he still didn't smile.

She nodded. He left and came back with two steaming mugs. She sipped with relish. "You guys should have offered me one when I arrived."

"We needed the report on your toxicology tests before giving you food and drink."

"And?"

"You're clean. No pathogens, no chemicals, no foreign bodies, no abnormal cell counts."

Siobhan sighed, suddenly understanding that she should feel relieved.

He started the tape recorder. "We need to know what happened to you."

"I can't remember."

"Let's go through what you do remember."

Siobhan outlined the turn of events at Area 51.

"So, what happened after the train entered the tunnel?" asked Sandley.

She rolled her eyes. "I just told you. I can't remember."

"Are you sure?"

"Positive. As far as I was concerned, I just woke up in that forest in Canada and that strange vehicle was flying away."

The government agent ran his hand through his thin black hair. "And so you have no recall at all of what happened to you between the train entering the tunnel and regaining consciousness in Canada four days later?"

She paused. "Why do you keep making me repeat everything?"

He grinned playfully and sighed, placing his hands flat on the table. "It's alright, Miss Quilley. We're almost done." He then looked down at his notebook. "Just one further question." His smile took on a crafty glint. "If you were a packet of crisps, what flavour would you be?"

Siobhan wondered if she'd misheard him. "I beg your pardon."

He repeated the question.

She gasped. "You expect a serious answer to that question?"

He repeated the question again, his tone of voice and facial expression remaining exactly the same.

"Mr Sandley, you can waste your own time if you like, but I'd prefer it if you didn't waste any more of mine."

He shrugged. "No problem, Miss Quilley, we appreciate your assistance... Would you be willing to come back another day? Perhaps we could help recover some of your memory using hypnosis."

She stood up. "The crisps question was the second stupidest you've asked me. Good evening."

....

It was dark outside when Siobhan was discharged from the secure care unit at Bethesda. She went to the hospital cafeteria where she drank coffee and read newspapers as she waited for her parents to arrive. They turned up just before ten PM.

"SIOBHAN!" She looked up to see her father sprinting down the corridor towards her. She just had time to get to her feet before he thundered into her and crushed her in a manic bear-hug. "Siobhan! My baby!... My sweet little baby!" Clane Quilley wept uncontrollably into her hair and repeatedly kissed her ears and temple. "I thought I'd lost you!... I thought I'd lost you!... Thank you, God! Thank you, blessed Mary ever virgin, mother of God!"

Siobhan gasped as she struggled for breath. The next moment her father grasped her shoulder like an eagle and began shaking her violently. His face transformed instantly from tears of loving relief to flushed, creased outrage. "You

73

stupid stupid dumb little bitch!... WHY!? What the fuck were you thinking of!? I thought you were dead you reckless, irresponsible little minx! I thought you were dead and it was all my fault!"

"Clane! That's enough!" Siobhan's mother pushed herself between them and forced him to let go.

Her father continued to cry with anger. "I thought you were dead and it was my fault! I thought I'd killed my own daughter!"

Brendan, her six-year-old brother, stood to one side with a confused look on his face.

"Siobhan!" said her mother, who was also weeping, but was far more in control of herself. "That was a truly foolish thing you did down there!"

"I'm sorry, mom." Siobhan replied.

"Do you know what you've put us all through for the last five days?"

"Sorry, mom."

"What did you think you were doing? Why did you do it?"

"I wanted a story."

"And what good is a story if you don't survive to write it?"

"Reporters sometimes have to take risks."

"Calculated risks, Siobhan!" bellowed her father. "Calculated risks! Not mindless acts of attempted suicide!"

Eventually they all calmed down somewhat and the family wanted a coffee after their long and unplanned plane flight. Brendan was also getting sleepy. They moved to the cafeteria and sat down. "How is it going at Area 51, dad?" asked Siobhan, anxious to change the subject.

Clane Quilley glared at her balefully as he sipped from his cardboard cup. "We broke off the operation to search for *you*."

She looked down, shrugging with embarrassment. "Did anybody else follow me down the tunnel?"

"We couldn't get the door open. There's a vacuum behind it. We tried to find an alternative route and couldn't."

"How is Kerry?"

"Who?"

"That young girl we found in the accommodation area."

"They moved her here."

"Really? Whereabouts?"

"In the secure section I imagine."

Siobhan looked out of the window at the walls of the central tower at Walter Reed. "I'd like to see her again."

"Not likely, Siobhan." Her father smiled for the first time since their reunion. "She's going to be very carefully monitored. She's not human you know. She and those other kids are the product of some kind of hybrid experiment involving extraterrestrial genetics."

"I know... I want to go back there."

Quilley replied by narrowing his eyes.

"Don't look that way at me, dad! Do you think Cronkite won't let me?"

"Oh, I'm sure he will; but what about the college, Siobhan?"

"Of course; they'll never allow it." She sighed. "They'll have to when I graduate."

Her father replied neutrally, without any tone of regret. "What makes you think they won't send you down for what you've done before you graduate?"

There was a long pause. She changed the subject. "Somebody is still alive in Area 51, and they're still holding out at the end of that tunnel. They took me."

"You gave yourself to them." corrected her father deadpan.

"Maybe, but they gave me back. They returned me unharmed. Why? I remember nothing. They must have had some way of making me forget."

Chapter 4

The hall was covered with ribbons and posies; it was like a wedding. Siobhan adjusted her clothing. As unfamiliar as it was, she loved how she looked in her gown and mortarboard. She had picked it up from the tailor just a few days earlier with all the other students and couldn't keep away from any mirror since. It was light blue with a dark blue hem, the traditional colours of Pennsylvania State University. The gold tassel hanging from her mortarboard tickled her nose. She blew against it to move it into a more comfortable place. She looked to either side of herself and caught her friends' eyes. They were all grinning and laughing. The students walked through the doors of the hall in a line and took their seats in the stalls. She looked up at the terrace where the students' families sat and saw her parents and Brendan staring down at her. She waved and they returned the gesture. Classical music played quietly on the loudspeakers. When everybody was seated the faculty entered from another doorway and took their place on a row of chairs on a stage facing the hall floor. They wore similar academic gowns and headgear. Coloured stripes and badges indicated their position and status. An old man with a white beard stood up and went to a speakers' podium. "Good morning, ladies and gentlemen, students and graduates, fellows and associates, friends and relatives." he announced in a gravely cracked voice. "My name is Professor Walter Kramer and I am acting president of this institution. It's a pleasure to welcome you today to Pennsylvania State University New Main. This is one of the happiest times that it is possible to experience here because, on this day, Saturday April fifth 1959, four hundred and seventy young men and women from all across the Penn Sate community, will undergo their commencement..." He went on for a minute or two about how proud and joyous it made him feel. For him commencement days were the whole reason the university existed. "... to send our youths back out into the world forever bettered and strengthened by their time at Penn State, loaded with the knowledge necessary to achieve and to develop..." He spoke of his own memories as a student and included a humorous anecdote about his own commencement. "...The world today is a very different one to the world I grew up in, the one I studied and graduated in. Enormous change has shaken our very civilization to its foundations. We have to face hardships today that make the past seem carefree and stable. Yet through it all, Penn State has endured. We have continued to build and enrich the minds of young Americans..."

The students all lined up along the aisles in careful order. Ushers made sure they weren't out of place otherwise they would be misidentified by the elderly acting president. One by one, they all stepped up onto the stage and applause echoed across the great hall. It was Siobhan's turn. She mounted the steps at the side of the stage, her heart pounding and waited for her name to be called.

"Siobhan Marianne Quilley. B.Sc.J Journalism honours. BA English language and literature two-one." As she walked forward she looked at the audience. She could make out her parents and brother waving manically. She was given her certificate rolled up and tied with blue ribbon. Then she walked over and shook the president's hand. He smiled affectionately and said fervently: "Well done, Siobhan!" It took over two hours to decorate every student in the room. Once back in their seats there was a great cheer and they threw their mortarboards into the air. Siobhan caught one as it came back down; she didn't know if it was her own. After that they left the hall and walked out onto the lawn and the families were allowed to join them. Her mother and father were both dewy-eyed with pride and even Brendan gave her a waist-high hug. There was the constant sound of cameras bleeping as families took photographs in the spring sunshine. Then it was time for the dinner. They had a luxurious banquet in a white canvass marquee in the college grounds that led down to the banks of the river Schuylkill. The air was full of joy and confidence. Clane Quilley was overwhelmed by the infinite supply of fine wine and quickly became tipsy. Silver forks clattered on bone china. Silk sashes fluttered in the light breeze.

After dinner the families retired and the furniture was cleared for the party. Siobhan's parents took Brendan back to their hotel. A rock and roll quartet set up their instruments and began playing; four men in white lounge suits, one of whom played a big acoustic double bass. The students jived and twisted. Bottles of beer, champagne and spirits lined up behind the bar. The general level of drunkenness rose steadily as the afternoon wore on. Play-fights broke out on the lawn and raucous laughter filled the air. Siobhan was sitting at a table with Libby and Ellen when Shirley, another Eberly student, came running up to them. "Hey, girls! Come and look at this!" she bubbled excitedly. She beckoned them out of the marquee. They went outside. It was a balmy afternoon with hazy sunshine. The lawn was an immaculate lush green. There was a commotion over by the old stone bridge that crossed the river. A row of four men stood on the parapet facing away from the onlookers; by the way they wheeled and teetered it was obvious they were badly drunk. They were all naked and their skin was smooth and pale. Their young physiques were firm and shapely. The sight made Siobhan blush; her heart thudded against her chest and her body tingled.

"Gee whiz!" growled Ellen. "I want the one on the left."

"I saw them first; I get first pick!" Shirley laughed with mock protest.

The men leapt off the parapet in unison with a whoop of exhilaration and there was a wet thump of water as they plunged into the river. Everybody roared with laughter.

At that moment Siobhan's eyes were drawn to a nearby tree. Somebody was not participating in the hilarity. A young man sat against the trunk facing away from the party. He was reading a book. "Who's that?" she pointed.

Libby chuckled. "Siobhan, trust you to look at the one guy here with his clothes on!"

"I don't know him. He looks boring anyhow." said Shirley.

"I've seen him before somewhere." answered Siobhan. She left her group of friends and walked over to the tree. The young man looked up as he heard her approach. He smiled nervously. "Hello?" he said.

"Hi." she grinned back.

"Siobhan isn't it?"

78

She laughed. "You remember me from the line-up?"

"No... It's just we met the year before last; end-of-semester party at State Park. It was your freshman wasn't it?"

"Oh yes!" Her memory was jogged.

"You're at Eberly aren't you?"

"Yes... Is your name Julian or have I misremembered?"

"No, that is my name. Good to see you again." He held out his hand.

She took it. He had a single bottle of beer embedded in a tuft of grass next to him. "Can I get you another?"

He nodded. "Sure."

She returned to the marquee and picked up two bottles of beer from the marquee. Her friends gave her an inquisitive look; she ignored them. She was brimming over with excitement for a reason she couldn't fathom. She recalled that she had danced with Julian and they'd talked for a while at the party at the main Penn State campus to celebrate the end of the autumn term. That was just after Saucer Day when her mind had been occupied with that. She sat down beside him and handed him his bottle. He had dark features, thick wavy hair, chestnut eyes and neat white teeth. She was struck by his beauty which was so intense it almost took on quality beyond the sexual. "Your accent; are you from England?"

"Yes, although I've been living in America for so long I've forgotten the old place."

"How long have you been over here?"

"Since fifty-three. We had to leave the country because of Oswald Mosley." He took a gulp of his beer.

She copied his action. "Really? I'm sorry... Are you Jewish?"

"No, but my dad was a leading member of the New Liberals, the opposition to the National Liberals. Mosley outlawed the party and ordered that my dad be fired from his job even though he was a tenured professor at Goldsmiths- University of London... He lost everything. We had no choice but to emigrate."

"Sorry to hear." she said again. "Mosley had a habit of doing nasty things to people who disagreed with him."

"I know. We're definitely not alone. And now all of Britain's gone to pot so nobody can go back." He looked over at her and smiled warmly. "How are things at Eberly?"

"Rudimentary, but we're sticking together."

"I hear it's pretty rough out there."

She shrugged. "So is most of the country." She pointed at Julian's book that he had laid down on the grass with a paper bookmark in it. It was an old hardback volume with a tattered brown paper spine. "What are you reading?"

He held it up for her to see.

"'*Unto This Last* by John Ruskin'." she read aloud. "Is that interesting?"

He guffawed. "It's not bad."

"Is it a schoolbook?"

"Kind of. I've been doing history, economics and political science at Brandywine. I picked up my Masters today." He said it with utmost modesty; verging on neutrality.

"Congratulations." she said echoing his tone to the extent that she could; it defying her instincts. She wondered why he was so lacking in the pride and elation all the other students were feeling.

He signed and rubbed his face with his hands, as if also realizing the contradiction of his behaviour. Then he turned his head and looked at her. "Shall we have another beer?"

She nodded. "Yes please." Her voice was slightly hoarse.

....

Siobhan woke early; the generator had yet to start. The sun was shining brightly on this May morning. She jumped out of bed like a spring, as had become her habit during this, her last week on the Eberly campus. Unusually the water was lukewarm at least, warm enough for her to take a shower. As she sprayed her skin she felt a pain on her arm. She winced and looked down. There was a red mark on the skin of her upper left arm, like a burn or rash. It was circular in shape, about an inch across and there were two oval blotches inside it. She wondered how it had happened. She dried herself off and switched on her roamphone; it beeped straight away. She smiled; it was another text message from Julian: "*Morning S. Sleep well? J. xxx.*" She thumbed a response: "*Dreamed about you again. S. xxx.*" Her father had gasped when she had told him the news. "What do you mean you've got a boyfriend!?" he bellowed. She explained and he demanded to know everything about Julian. He relaxed after a while. "Okay, so when am I going to meet this Julian fellow?" It was not possible until the end of the term. It wasn't easy even for her and Julian. He was at Brandywine college which was in a town just outside Philadelphia; the opposite end of the state from Fayette County. He had driven to Eberly twice and she had driven to Brandywine twice, meeting every weekend during the month since they'd met at the commencement. He worried about her making the long dangerous journey and she worried about him too. However the infrastructure at Brandywine was far more intact and so their get-togethers were more pleasant when she took the risk. They headed into Philadelphia on the Saturday evening, taking in a movie, eating at a restaurant or just walking quietly along the waterfront. He was not her first boyfriend; she had had two other relationships with men that were short-lived and casual and she'd never told her parents about those. This was the first time she felt she was truly in love.

She lay back on her bed smiling as she thought about Julian. She glanced at her bedside clock; it was eighteen minutes past nine. She sat up in alarm. The generator wasn't on yet. She got up and went out into the corridor. She stopped and gasped; the lights were on. She went back into her room and flicked the switch on the wall; her light came on. She dashed back out into the corridor and hammered on the other doors of the dorms. "Ellen! Libby! Look!"

"What is it?" Libby stuck her hear out.

"The mains electric is back on!"

"Really?"

"Yes, try it!"

The entire hall of residence was soon echoing with excited voices. They went to the dean's office and he happily explained that the local power station had just started running again. The state and federal government had started some development schemes to help bring the country back to life after Saucer Day and the restart of the power station was a part of that. They had yet to rebuild the national grid, but local grids were being arranged around each charging node. Electricity! Unlimited and unrationed, twenty-four hours a day; seven days a week. The prospect was delicious.

After breakfast Siobhan went to her room and booted up her computer. She gasped. There was an E-gram from Walter Cronkite. "*Dear Siobhan. I hope you have recovered from your frightening experience at Area 51. Congratulations on your graduation. The reason I'm writing was to ask what thought you have given to your future...*" She read it again, and again. She felt a grin break out on her face. She got up and knocked on the door opposite. "Libby! Libby!"

Libby opened it. "What is it, Siobhan?"

"Cronkite's offered me a job!"

Her mouth formed a cross between a gape and a smile. "Really?"

"Yes!"

Walter Cronkite was offering her a place on his team. Her job would be to act as a researcher, scriptwriter and programme designer. He said that if she did well in this job he would consider making her a director or even get her some on-screen work as an anchorwoman, interviewer and reporter. It was everything she'd dreamed of. The day then took on a surreal synchronicity. The post van called for the first time in over a month and the students all skipped eagerly to their pigeonholes. A bulky brown envelope was waiting in Siobhan's. Its frank was dated a month earlier, but that was about average for post at that time. She took it to the common room, opened it and read. She sighed. "I don't believe this."

"What's up?" asked Ethan.

"I've been offered a scholarship for a masters in English."

"Already?" he asked sceptically. "Where?"

"Harvard."

Ethan spat out his mouthful of coffee. "Harvard!?"

Siobhan went up to her room and looked the definition of *dilemma* on WorldMesh; it said: "*A situation in which an unwelcome and difficult choice has to be made between two*

82

or more undesirable alternatives." She signed and wondered if there was a similar word for an unwelcome and difficult choice between two or more *desirable* alternatives. She called her parents and they were overjoyed. "Take the Harvard scholarship." advised her father. "A job at CBS can be here today- gone tomorrow. You'll be out in the next round of redundancies; that's what the *New York Times* did to me. But a place at Harvard will have you set up for life."

"No, dad!" she heard Brendan say in the background. "I want to see Siobhan on TV."

"Do what you think is best, dear." pacified her mother. "You don't have to decide straight away. Sleep on it."

"Damn!" Siobhan seethed. She stomped down to the common room and collapsed into an armchair. Libby came and sat beside her. "Decisions, decisions!"

"What am I going to do, Lib?"

"I don't know. I can't imagine what it must be like to receive either opportunity let alone both at the same time. I thought you needed an honours degree to get into Harvard."

"Mine's two-one and that's as good as... My dad's right about Harvard. It's the Ivy League."

"So are we." Libby protested.

"Technically, but we're not on the same level as Harvard. The only equivalent would be... What?"

"Oxford? Cambridge?"

"Which have closed. Even in today's world Harvard is an accolade everybody respects, but..."

"But?"

Siobhan rubbed her face with her hands. "Next week is my birthday. I'll be twenty-four. I'm looking at another three goddamn years at college studying fucking English! I only minored in it to get into journalism school. I'll be approaching thirty the next time I get to do anything interesting with my life. And there's Julian. He's two years older than me and he's finished college altogether. He's about to go out into the world. How will he feel about me hanging round in education for another three years? How will we even see each other?"

"So, take the job at CBS."

"That would be a big risk. My dad's right. There's almost no security, no assurance of promotion. No guarantees I won't just end up manning the gallery coffee stall till they kick my ass onto the street. I know Cronkite likes me and his name carries some weight, but he doesn't own the company. Then again, it's still a journalist's dream job... Oh why couldn't just *one* of these opportunities have come my way instead of *both*?" Her attention was drawn to the television set in the corner. It had been playing some commercials well below her attention threshold. Now a new programme started that crossed over it. One of the students lifted the remote control and flicked it to another station.

"No wait, Sandy! Switch it back."

The television programme was a documentary about Area 51. "*The Secret military base in Nevada is secret no longer.*" the commentator said in dramatic tones. "*Last year a combined taskforce of over a thousand troops invaded and captured the hidden outpost. Many of its secrets still are waiting to be unveiled, but now, for the first time on network television, what has been discovered during the seven months of exploration can be...*"

The TV went off with a click, as did the lights and the ceiling fan. The drinks cooler in the kitchenette rattled into silence. The students all exclaimed in frustration. "Oh shit!" "Damn it!" "Jesus!" "The electric's gone off."

Siobhan got to her feet. "Never mind, let's start the generator." She jogged out into the courtyard and approached the parked lorry with the two thick cables snaking from it into the college building. A few of her classmates followed her. She muttered in irritation: "What is it the electric company commercials call it? 'Energy for life'? We only got five goddamn hours!" She clambered up the tailgate and examined the huge yellow cylinder of the dynamo connected to a group of yellow boxes. Thick rubber wires ran everywhere. "Now, how does this work?" Luckily its controls were very comprehensive. There was a switch that simply said *ON-OFF*. She turned the switch. The machine coughed a few times and then returned to silence. "Fuck it!" She walked round it, looking for a source for the problem. There was a tank on one side of the machine with a gauge on it that read zero. She rapped the tank with her knuckles and its hollow interior bonged. It had letters stencilled on it that read *DIESEL ONLY*. "What's up?" asked one of her college mates.

"The fuel's run out. Empty as the Tin Man. We can't start it." There was a chorus of groans outside. "Are there any new drums?"

"No." said Ellen. "They're all gone."

Siobhan jumped out of the lorry. "I'm tired of this! Can I borrow somebody's car?"

She did not make the decision to act consciously; it was just instinctive, like stepping aboard the train in Area 51. She travelled with her friend Jayne who owned the car and also had one of the new roams that give limited Mesh access, including the WorldMesh map applications. They looked up the location and drove there directly. The power station was in Masontown, just a twenty-minute drive from Eberly. It stood on the banks of the river Monongahela; an ugly set of grey structures. Three cooling towers dominated the facility behind its chain-link fence. There was a block that looked half-finished; its external framework resembled permanent scaffolding. Coal chutes and conveyers ran between the buildings and tall pylons stood at the edge waiting in vain to carry electricity to their hungry customers. A smokeless cylindrical chimney oversaw the whole area and a black pyramid of coal poked its top over from behind. When Jayne's car pulled up at the gate a group of about fifty men were standing or sitting loosely, as if not expecting or planning to go anywhere or do anything. Siobhan jumped out of the car feeling galvanized. It was as if her body was being moved for her like a puppet. "What's going on here? Why aren't you guys working?"

The men stared at her indignantly. They were rough-looking, unshaven, wearing coal-stained boiler suits and hardhats. "Who are you, lady?" asked one.

"Somebody without an electricity supply; like most people in this area."

"Well you ain't our boss!"

"Who is?"

"I am." A man stepped forward dressed as the others except his clothes were cleaner. "I'm the manager of this plant and I completely support the actions of my staff. We have been working flat-out for a fortnight to get this baby running again. It's been shut down since Saucer Day; do you know how much repair work we had to do? The FDRA has not paid us a cent. We were promised full pay plus a bonus three weeks ago. We were told it would be delivered up top once the current was flowing. We're tired, we're hungry, we've had to leave our families at home and in danger... So we are not generating one more kilowatt until we get the pay promised to us."

"What's the FDRA?"

He rolled his eyes. "Federal Disclosure and Reconstruction Agency."

"Do you have their phone number?"

The manager looked at her curiously. He reached into his pocket and handed her a slip of paper.

"Can I borrow your roam?" Siobhan asked Jayne, snatched it from her hand before she could answer and dialled the number.

"Hello, FDRA." said a cheery feminine voice on the end.

"Good afternoon, this is Siobhan Quilley of CBS News. I'm at the..." She glanced up at the signboard by the gate. "...the Hatfield Power Plant in Pennsylvania. It has been shut down by its workforce just a few hours after restarting because the FDRA has failed to pay them as it promised to. Would you care to comment?"

The woman on the end of phone chucked. "Is this a joke?"

"No, ma'am. I am Siobhan Quilley of CBS News. I covered the invasion of Area 51 last year. Ask Walter Cronkite. I work closely with him."

"Walter Cronkite!?" The woman paused. "Wait one moment." She put her on hold.

Siobhan looked at Jayne and chuckled. "Amazing how many doors that name opens."

A different voice, a gruff male voice, came on the line. "Hello, Miss Quilley. This is Henry Dealey, director of the FDRA. Could you please pass on my apologies to the men at the Hatfield plant? We do appreciate their dedicated and important work. We have allocated funds to reimburse them for their efforts, for which we are very grateful. Obviously the present lack of banking facilities in west Pennsylvania means we will have to deliver their payment in cash. This is a situation we are aiming to amend soon, but in the meantime it involves arranging secure transport; we hope to do that by early next week."

"Thank you, Mr Dealey. I will tell them."

"You're welcome. Please pass on my regards to Mr Cronkite as well."

When Siobhan related the message to the power plant workers they groaned. "No way! We've heard that before! It's always 'next week' or 'in a few days' every goddamn time. We will start the plant again when the money arrives and not one moment sooner!"

Siobhan paused, rehearsing her words. "Please, give them one more chance. I will call them every hour of every day until that cash delivery arrives at these gates; I promise!... Just *please* restart the plant. We need electricity! Everybody does, including your own families. It will keep them safe. If we have mains electricity restored then we're ninety percent of the way to restoring our community in full. Our economy. Our public services. Don't you realize how important you guys are?... I swear, if the government lets you down again and doesn't deliver the cash, I will support your strike. I will be with you when you down tools and I will join you on the picket line... but please! Just give us the sparks now!"

The men looked at each other. They never said a word, but their meeting eyes delivered speeches. "Alright." said the manager. The workers left the gate and walked back into their ugly but essential facility.

"Thank you!" Siobhan yelled at their departing backs. As she and Jayne drove home Siobhan looked over her shoulder. Smoke began to issue from the power station's chimney.

Sure enough, the mains electricity supply was back on at Eberly. Siobhan fired up her desktop and used WorldMesh to find all the other power stations nearby. She called them up to see if they were working. Three of the five she called were also out of commission. She then looked up water and sewage treatment works and other essential services. After spending two hours on the phone talking to various people she had the idea to write a news story about what she was doing and send it to Walter Cronkite. This took until ten PM. After she sent the story to him in a WordPad file she looked down at her bed. She'd left her letter from Harvard University lying there in its headed envelope. She pulled out the letter and read it again. She screwed it up and threw it into her waste paper basket.

....

Her roam beeped. It was a text message from her father: "*Happy birthday*." Another came in two hours later: "*S. Happy birthday. J xxx.*" Then a third followed after just twenty minutes: "*Many happy returns, Siobhan. Walter Cronkite.*" Siobhan composed brief replies each time as she looked out of the toughened glass window of the security van. This was the first birthday she'd had when she was too busy to celebrate at all. The driver sitting beside her was armed. He looked nervous and drove slowly. There were two armoured cars from the National Guard escorting them. Siobhan was mostly kept busy typing on her matchbook computer, sending progress E-grams and writing notes. These she would adapt into full scripts afterwards and send them to Walter Cronkite. There was a large crowd waiting to meet the security van at the gates of the Hatfield Power Plant. Not only were the workers themselves there, but a number of women and children who must have been their families. They smiled and waved as the convoy stopped. Siobhan and the driver got out and greeted the men. "Siobhan!" The manager came up and shook her hand. "You did great! They may not have listened to us, but they sure as hell listened to you."

"I'll say anything to make sure you and your men get the pay you deserve, Larry." she replied. The guards in the back of the van opened the doors at the back and started reading out names off a list. Each man came forward when his name was called and was given a brown paper packet containing banknotes. "Nine hundred dollars each, Larry."

The manager gasped. "We're only owed seven-fifty, Siobhan."

"The FDRA director decided you were worth another bonus."

"Did you persuade him?"

She just winked in reply.

He laughed. "I don't know how you do it!"

They left the Hatfield power station and drove on to the East Drunkard Water Treatment Works, a name that made Siobhan giggle. They dropped off more packets of cash there then moved on to another power station. They passed a food distribution centre in the town of Waynesburg. A huge crowd of people milled round it. Siobhan found it difficult to type in a moving vehicle, especially since the roads were in poor condition, but she made steady progress with her news story. "*Power, food and water are what the FDRA calls 'level one' priorities.*" she wrote. "*Pennsylvania is now almost ready to tick off all of level one and move onto level two. This involves healthcare, transport and communications. Without level two complete after an estimated period of ten days, the level one progress will be wasted because it needs level two to be maintained.*" She gazed out of the window and contemplated her next words. "*I have lived in eastern Pennsylvania for the last two years and the transformation has been incredible. I've seen shops open, factories working, even a few things on the 'level three' list like a school. After Saucer Day everything fell apart. It was if...*" She paused, wondering how to put it. "*...civilization itself lost its nerve the moment it realized the truth. But like even the worse shocks, it wears off after a while. Now our nation is recovering. The news from other states is equally positive. Some people now have electricity and a water supply for the first time in over a year. Getting the electricity running again; that was the moment. Once we have regular and reliable power, other things can follow.*" She stopped and thought about her trip to Area 51 last year. She pondered for a moment then she E-grammed the document to Cronkite and then drafted a new E-gram.

Chapter 5

The Groom Lake Road looked similar to how it was when she'd seen it in September except there was a lot more activity there. Vehicles of all kinds traversed the long, straight, dusty track levelled towards the distant mountains that used to shield Area 51 from the public gaze. Some temporary buildings had been set up including a small accommodation block for the press. She was staying with her parents in Boulder City so didn't need it even though CBS offered her a room there. The road itself had not been altered; even the warning signs at the edge of the formerly-restricted zone were still there, as if somebody had decided to turn Area 51 into an enormous outdoor museum piece, as her father had suggested it might become one day. The base itself was as busy as it had ever been. People were everywhere, mostly Federal Disclosure and Reconstruction Agency personnel. There was a press contingent based in a series of large caravans. As Siobhan parked her car a number of the reporters came over to introduce themselves, including her CBS team. It was hot and the sun shone with typical flaming summer brightness. As she walked to the caravans she looked over at the FDRA agents. "Michael, why are they armed?" She pointed. Some of the FDRA men were kitted up like fully-armed soldiers with helmets and rifles.

Her guide, a freckly-faced youth even younger than herself, shrugged. "Not sure. We've been told that the place is safe."

"How much of it has been explored so far?"

"All of it up to the railroad tunnels, the one... you disappeared into..." he pulled up nervously, as if worried he had tactlessly raised a sensitive subject; but she just smiled slightly and he went on: "... and a second one at the north end of the base."

"Does anybody have any idea where they go?"

He shrugged expansively like a Frenchman and blew out his cheeks. "God knows. The FDRA are working on that."

She watched the FDRA troops strutting about. They looked no different to the descriptions her father had given her of the armed security present when it had been a working shadow government facility. When she was inside the caravan she found a private spot to plug in her matchbook and look up the FDRA on "Meshpedia", the massive online knowledge resource. She read the entry. It was black text on a white background to give it a bookish ambiance: "*The United States Federal Disclosure and Reconstruction Agency is a United States federal executive administration established by the executive order of President Barry Goldwater on the tenth of March 1958 in order to direct relief efforts throughout the United States and its territories following the generalize breakdown of social cohesion after Saucer Day. Its first and current director is Henry Austin Dealey...*" *Saucer Day* was highlighted, indicating that it was a hyperlink. She glanced briefly at that page and then clicked back. Her report was all about the reconstruction effort, but she had not yet read this page. "Can't see the wood for the trees." she muttered to herself. There was a section of the article entitled "*Armed Operations*", but somebody came into the room and disturbed her privacy before she had a chance to read it.

Siobhan was keen to proceed down into the depths of the base and see the progress that had been made. Michael escorted her through the same entrance she had passed through all those months ago only this time there was no need for protective clothing and the lifts were safe to use. In every room scientists and engineers were hard at work, unpicking the vast previously secret infrastructure. Men and women in lab-coats, looking and pointing, talking animatedly. They fiddled with open electronics cabinets, flicked through documents and analyzed chemicals in test tubes. She walked through the biology section and caught a glimpse of a post-mortem being carried out on one of the genetic monsters that had tried to kill her father. "What would you like to see first?" asked Michael.

She hesitated. "The place I vanished."

The deep cavern containing the railway station looked exactly as she'd left it, except the train wasn't there. She shivered. "What happened to me in there?"

Michael shrugged again. "Nobody knows what's through that door. There's an evacuated tunnel, but we've not found a way to explore it yet.

"They're still down there, Michael. The people who used to run this place."

"That's likely."

Why did they let me go? She thought to herself.

She then asked, somewhat rhetorically: "I'm glad there's electricity down here. How did you get this place back on the grid?"

Michael grinned with excitement. "This place has its own power plant and it's like nothing you've ever seen."

"Well then I'd like to see it."

Michael led her along a corridor that exited on the far side of the station concourse. It was metallic, like the passageway on a ship. A few hundred yards along they passed through a door into a chamber almost as big as the station. It was packed with machinery that she couldn't possibly identify. Cables and conduits ran along the walls like cobwebs. Everything was painted battleship grey and the air reeked of oil and ozone. "Dr Bulstrode?" called Michael.

A number of people were in the room, walking normally or crawling on all fours under floor level spaces, up on ladders examining high panels. They were all clad in white plastic overalls with a hood, like police forensic investigators. One of them looked down from a ladder. "Ahoy, Michael." she called and waved, looking a bit precarious as she let go with one hand. She came down the ladder steadily and approached them with a warm grin. Light brown hair poked out from the sides of her hood and thick spectacles distorted her eyes. When Michael introduced Siobhan she raised her eyebrows. "Siobhan Quilley? Are you Clane Quilley's daughter? It's good to meet you. Dr Jenny Bulstrode." She shook her hand.

"Of course." replied Siobhan. "My dad has told me all about you and what you both did on Saucer Day. It's great to meet you at last."

"Your dad was here only yesterday. He's told me a bit about you."

"He said he had been to Area 51, but he didn't mention you." replied Siobhan.

Dr Bulstrode chuckled. "I'm surprised. He was most interested in my role here." The scientist had a lilting voice. "I hear you're with CBS."

"Yes, I'm working on a story about the Disclosure and reconstruction effort."

"Well you've sure come to the right place. Let me show you Spinning Suzie."

"Who's she?"

Dr Bulstrode pointed to the largest machine in the room. "That's just what we call it." It was a white painted flat cylinder, like a huge drum. It filled half the entire room. It was completely silent yet gave off a sense of deafening supremacy. She mounted the ladder and yelled down a long explanation to Siobhan.

"Doctor." Siobhan called up to her, shuffling her feet with embarrassment. "I'm terribly sorry, but I don't understand."

She smiled thinly down at her. "I'll try to make it simpler."

Dr Bulstrode led Siobhan to a neighbouring room that had been converted into an engineering workshop. A row of benches were covered with all kinds of fragments, wires, screws, nuts, overlaying sheets of papers depicting diagrams and formulae. It was illuminated by a bright white light. Dr Bulstrode pointed at one of the desks. "This is the smallest one we could find." The device looked like a metal doughnut about two feet across. Leading off from it were four truncated pipes and a mycelium of wires. "Even so, it seemed to be successfully feeding an entire floor."

"What is it?"

"Some kind of generator, but not like one anybody has ever heard of before, apart from the people who owned this place. Take a look." She pointed to a transparent panel on the side of the machine just big enough for a human eye. Siobhan peeked in. A dark grey circular plate filled her view; on the edge of it were what looked like horseshoe magnets. She removed her eye from the peephole. "What am I meant to be looking at?"

"Did you see the disk?"

"I think so."

"Did you see any movement?"

"No."

"What if I were to tell you that that disk is actually spinning at over three quarters of a million revolutions per minute?"

"No, it's completely still."

"It's very smooth so you can't perceive the movement, but I assure you it is far from still."

"That's not possible surely."

Dr Bulstrode shook her head sardonically. "It ought not to be."

"How did they get it to do that?"

"We don't know." she answered immediately and completely deadpan. "It makes the mind boggle! The centrifugal effect alone should shatter the disk to pieces, no matter how strong it is made. Then there's friction with the atmosphere. I know it's evacuated, but even a molecule or two... We're examining their blueprints and textbooks in an effort to find out how it was designed and built. Based on what we've read so far it appears it was adapted from the propulsion system used for their flying disk airships. That operates by a spinning mercury vapour and generates antigravity lift. This uses a solid metal disk to create an artificial gravitational field too, only a very different kind of one. It appears to cause local ninety degree inversions in the direction of the gravity flux on the edge of the disk that emerges from these four outlets here." She pointed. "It appears they back-engineered the technology from the extraterrestrial spacecraft that they've been secretly salvaging over the years; have you seen their full collection?"

Siobhan shook her head.

"The mechanism isn't yet fully understood; nevertheless the process can generate a lot of force."

"What for?"

"In the case of this unit, conversion to electrical power. The flux produces torque in a dynamo shaft."

Siobhan knew little about this field, but she ransacked her memory for discussions she'd had with science and engineering students. "How much electricity?"

"Oh, fifty to sixty megawatts easily. Remember this thing powered an entire floor level down here."

Siobhan laid her hand on the top of the machine. Its metal casing was hard and cold. "How can something so small generate that much electricity?"

"Nobody knows."

"What sort of fuel do you put into it?"

Dr Bulstrode lowered her gaze and stared at Siobhan over the tops of her glasses.

"What? You mean...?"

"It requires no fuel. No more than the force of gravity requires any energy input when generated naturally by mass. It seems to have some kind of electromagnetic start-up system, but once it's running at gravity-generating speed the process is internally sustainable."

"So this is one of those free energy devices I've been hearing about in the news."

"Yes, it's the most efficient we've found. It has an over-unity factor of fifty-seven percent. Compared to that, the Digby..."

"Ahem!" Dr Bulstrode broke off as a man entered the room. "Hello there."

"Prof. Pickup." Dr Bulstrode nodded without smiling.

"Dr Bulstrode." he responded in the same icy fashion. He was a large elderly man with a thick white beard and head of hair. He wore the same overalls as everybody else. "I see you've found Miss Quilley, our resident newshound." He had a deep, penetrating voice and spoke with a strong Scottish accent.

"Yes, Professor, I've been showing her around."

He glared at her over the tops of his half-moon glasses. "Well, I'm sure you're very busy carrying out your regular duties, so why don't you let me complete Miss Quilley's tour?"

Dr Bulstrode bowed her head and gave a slight nod. Her cheeks flushed slightly and she walked out of the room. Siobhan gazed at her departing back.

"Prof. Angus Pickup. How do you do." He held out his hand. He grinned in a forced manner.

Siobhan took his hand, but let go quickly. She resented his dismissive manner towards Dr Bulstrode. Her father had regaled her with tales about how Dr Jenny Bulstrode had helped him save the world. It was her investigation into the false flag Martian attack on the Empire State Building that had led to the exposure of the criminals that had taken over the government. Her book *Where Did the Tower Go?* was now an international bestseller. She had very little contact with the media, preferring to concentrate completely on her work in education and engineering.

"I'm leading the FDRA scientific mission here at Area 51. I was appointed personally by Director Dealey." He puffed out his chest as he spoke.

"You must be a very important person then, Prof. Pickup." Siobhan skilfully injected just the right amount of sarcasm into her statement.

He raised his eyebrows in response. "It appears so... Now, come over here and I'll show you something else interesting." He pointed at a bench opposite where some more paraphernalia was arranged. This machine was disassembled and consisted of a set of wheels with flat spokes of multicoloured material. "Do you know what this is?"

"Is it a Digby Carrousel?"

He hesitated. "Yes." His tone indicated he was disappointed that she knew. "Unlike our other discoveries, this piece comes straight from the ingenious mind of man; or should I say woman. No little grey men helped this time. It was invented in 1915 by Jemima Digby, a farmer's wife from Nova Scotia. She and her husband built a tractor powered by one. Word got around of course. Who wouldn't want a tractor you didn't need to pay to fuel? Then some gentlemen in suits from General Electric and Westinghouse arrived. They offered the Digbys a massive amount of money for a 'development license'. Jemima and her husband were struggling farmers; how could they refuse? Of course they had to sign non-disclosure and exclusivity contracts.

The men in suits left saying: 'thanks, we'll be in touch' and the Digby Carrousel was never heard of again."

Siobhan picked up one of the wheels. It had eight spokes with some oblong slats attached. "All those years, decades, they let people starve and live in squalor, when they could have prevented it all. All the trees they've cut down, all the rivers they've poisoned. Suffering and death could have ended in one moment."

"Those days are over now." responded the professor impatiently. "We can only move forward. Mrs Digby is an elderly lady today, but she has been informed of our work. She knows her marvellous endeavour was not in vain."

Siobhan continued to stare at the wheel. It was flimsy in construction and the slats were coloured black and blue in alternating bands. She chuckled. "It's ironic you know. I've spent the whole previous month travelling from one conventional coal-fired power plant to the next working from dawn till dusk to get them all up and running again. What was the point? I was just perpetuating obsolete technology."

"No, Miss Quilley!"

Siobhan started at the unexpected vehemence in his voice.

"You have done exactly the right thing. The FDRA is very clear about this. The first priority in the post-Saucer Day reconstruction programme is to get the existing infrastructure back first. That is all that matters in the initial phase of recovery. The existing systems must be restored to full functionality. Then, and *only* then, can we permit ourselves the luxury of considering replacement innovation... Understood?"

Siobhan looked at him and didn't reply. He seemed to be scolding her, as if she'd committed some kind of misdemeanour; but she couldn't work out what it was. "Sure, but we must not delay that innovation any longer than is necessary. We have to save the world, and the system we had before Saucer Day is part of the problem, not the solution."

Pickup softened. "Naturally. We have already carried out limited trials in Abyssinia and it has been effective in relieving the famine caused by the drought. Your father was a part of that project. What you're holding in your hand right now is that solution."

She looked over her shoulder at the rotating disk device. "Not to mention that thing as well..."

"No!" Pickup yelled again. "The spinning disk is going to take too long to develop. In fact many many years of work will have to be done before we can even duplicate the thing. We don't have that long. The Digby Carrousel is our future; the spinning disk is nothing more than a curiosity."

"Dr Bulstrode seemed very interested in it."

"Dr Bulstrode is an outstanding researcher and a passionate scientist, but she lacks pragmatic awareness. She is a freelancer, not part of the FDRA. She has no authority in this project. We just use her expertise."

Siobhan frowned. "If it wasn't for Dr Jenny Bulstrode, Saucer Day would have ended in the massacre of us all."

He frowned back. "Does that mean we have to abandon objective progress out of a sense of sentimental gratitude?"

"It means we should trust her judgement."

"I do; but I don't obey it uncritically. To do that would be most... unscientific."

There was a pause. "How long will it take to get these Digby things into commercial mass-production?"

He shrugged. "We're working on it."

Chapter 6

There was a knock at the door. The director stuck his head in and smiled. "We're in commercials. Five minutes."

"OK." Siobhan adjusted the collar of her blouse. The makeup lady put the finishing touches to her eye-shadow then she mustered her courage and walked out of the door, heading for the studio. Walter Cronkite was waiting by the entrance. "Siobhan." He shook her hand warmly. "Break a leg out there."

"Thank you for this, Wally." she smiled. She stepped out in front of the dusky eyes of the camera lenses and took her place at the desk.

"Standby, Siobhan!" yelled Bill, the director, from behind the hot glare of the arc lights. "One minute."

"Ready."

"Siobhan, can you give me a mic test please?" asked the sound recorder.

"One two. One two."

"That's fine."

She adjusted her smile, feeling as if she were in a surreal dream. She had rehearsed this moment so many times and couldn't quite believe it was really happening. The first words of her script appeared on the teleprompter.

The director's voice cut in one last time. "Five... four... three..."

"Good afternoon, this is CBS News, going live on the CBS national network and online at wmn.cbs.tv.us." Siobhan's voice was smooth and unblemished. "I'm Siobhan Quilley and here are the latest headlines for Thursday August twentieth 1959. The Federal Disclosure and Reconstruction Agency has announced a 2% rise on regeneration tax. This was passed into law by Congress yesterday and will come into effect on September 11th, the second anniversary of Saucer Day. California Congressman Clyde Doyle today called it the 'anniversary tax'. Henry Dealey, director of the FDRA, said that the tax rise was 'justified due to the increasing demands on rural service communications restoration'. House Majority Leader Charles Halleck called it 'penny-pinching' and asked 'how many more times will the American taxpayer be pillaged

before we can all agree things have gone back to normal?'...
The controversy over the development contract for the
Digby Carrousel continues with a new company,
Consolidated and Marsh, contesting the award of the
contract to General Dynamics. The FDRA announced the
tendering of the development rights for the new free energy
generator at the end of June and the contract winner was
announced two weeks ago. C and M have now submitted a
challenge to be pursued through the courts when the
cooling-off period expires next Friday. President Barry
Goldwater has declared his desire to see the Digby moved
into a state of mass-production as soon as possible... The
twenty-second session of the League of the World today
passed a resolution to hold an international conference on
Disclosure and reconstruction no later than next August.
With the success of domestic projects in the United States,
Ireland and several other countries, 'it is now time', as the
LoW Secretary-General put it: 'to give planet earth back its
legs'... A tornado has damaged over fifty buildings in
Grovespring, Missouri and three people have reportedly
been killed. Emergency responders are in the area and are
searching the damaged buildings for survivors. Twenty
people are currently listed as missing... Staying in Missouri,
Revd. William Huffman, a Baptist minister from Cape
Girardeau has launched a campaign for information over
what he claims was an MFO experience in 1941. He is
being supported by his granddaughter, Charlette. According
to Revd. Huffman there was a Roswell-like event that
happened near the town in 1941 at which he had to attend to
administer last rites to an extraterrestrial being. What
followed was a covert crash-retrieval by the military. The
Department of Defence has so far declined to comment...
The New York Stock Exchange reopened today for the
eighteenth day of trading since Saucer Day. The dollar lost
three points against the Emirati Dirham but gained four
against the Irish Pound and two against the Saudi Riyal.
The price of gold has remained steady at twenty-three
dollars forty-five cents per ounce... And now it's time for
the news, travel and weather where you live." Siobhan held
her grin as if posing for a photograph.

"And... cut!" called the director. Everybody is the room cheered.

Siobhan broke her closing pose, leaned back in her chair and let out a deep sigh of relief. Cronkite ran forward applauding with everybody else. "Well done, Siobhan! That's my girl!" he said and embraced her warmly. "That has to be the best screen debut I've seen in years."

One of her colleagues came forward with a bottle of champagne. The cork popped into the air and bounced off a spotlight. Glasses appeared and everybody toasted Siobhan's initiation into the exclusive club of CBS TV presenters. Siobhan went back to the dressing room and switched on her roam. A text from her family appeared immediately: "*We saw it! Well done, love! xxx.*" There were similar ones from Julian, Libby and Ellen. Siobhan went to the recording department and watched the video of her programme over and over again. She headed home from the CBS studio in Midtown Manhattan to her New York apartment in Greenwich Village and continued to watch it on her matchbook while sitting on the subway. She decided to enjoy anonymity while it lasted; in a few months she'd be too famous to ride public transport without being hassled by fans. She chuckled at the thought. She gave the vidcast a play in all her separate Mesh browsers just to boost the viewing figures and then did the same on her home desktop personal computer. She downloaded the file and stored it in a special folder for posterity. She glowed with pride.

The next morning she took the subway to LaGuardia Field and caught a plane to Las Vegas. She enjoyed a happy reunion with her family; then the following morning she sent an E-gram to Julian: "*All ready to face the enemy? LOL.*"

He replied: "*About to take off xxx.*" Siobhan could sense the unease in his text. She went online and found a meshboard for plane-spotters that tracked air traffic in real time. An aircraft icon appeared above Wold-Chamberlain Field, the airport serving the twin cities of Minneapolis and St Paul. She clicked on it and the correct flight number appeared, including the aircraft's speed, altitude and other statistics. She watched the little yellow aeroplane on the monitor as it traversed the continent at forty-one thousand feet. When it crossed the Colorado- Utah border she left the computer, went to her car and drove into Las Vegas. She timed it well. As soon as she parked up at McCarran Field and entered the arrivals hall Julian's flight flicked up on the board. She sat and waited by the entrance where the passengers came out. People walked out in knots and waves as flights landed, pushing trolleys full of luggage. There they were embraced by loved ones. Julian didn't have a trolley. He travelled light; just a single bag over his shoulder. He was dressed in black jeans that had become fashionable at that time. He had tennis shoes on his feet and a light cotton jersey with a hood. They embraced and kissed as they always did when first reunited. Siobhan missed him terribly when they were apart, but felt that this added spice to their relationship when they were together. They never had any major arguments; they never got on each others' nervcs. They simply didn't have time. Every second they shared was a precious joy. "Hi, Jules." she smiled at him.

"Hi, Siobhan." he smiled back. She started abbreviating his name after their third meeting when it was clear they were going steady. She tried *Ju* and *Jules* and settled on the latter because he responded to it more favourably. There is no diminutive form of *Siobhan*; Ethan's annoying attempt "Vorny" was simply his own idiotic and provocative invention. However she had noticed that when he uttered her name Julian was shortening the first vowel. By now he was almost swallowing it completely and pronounced her name as a single syllable: "*shvorn*". "I loved your TV appearance." he said as they walked to the car park. "I'm really proud of you."

They drove south out of Las Vegas. Julian gazed in wonder at the dusty brown mountains and the sparse vegetation. "It's so dry here! It was raining when I left Minnesota. I can hardly believe we're in the same country."

"Well the United States is a big and varied country. It's not as bleak as it looks; there's a lot to see around here. I'll show you the Hoover Dam later, and we've got to take you into the Las Vegas casinos."

"I've never gambled before."

She frowned with mock reproach. "Jules, you *cannot* visit Vegas and not put on a bet. It's against the laws of *physics*!"

He wiped his brow. "It's so hot here."

She turned up the car's air conditioning without being asked. Julian became quieter as they approached Boulder City. "How much have you told your mum and dad about me?" he asked. "What did they say when you told them?" He sat upright in the passenger seat, his body tight.

"Don't worry. My family are lovely people." She gave his wrist a reassuring squeeze. She pulled up in the drive next to Clane Quilley's new Chevrolet saloon and they got out. The front door opened and three figures appeared in it. Five forced smiles came together on the threshold. "Hello there." Clane called.

"Hi, dad. This is Julian... Julian, this is my dad, mom and little brother Brendan." There were handshakes in every combination.

"Come on in and make yourselves comfortable." said Gina Quilley, Siobhan's mother. The air conditioned house was deliciously cool after the desert heat and Gina served them all cold drinks and biscuits. "Nice place you've got here." said Julian.

"Well technically it's not ours." said Clane. "It actually belongs to my former employers Florenti Inc, but they kind of... went into liquidation after Saucer Day and our home is one of the many things they left for open appropriation, so we appropriated it." He laughed. This led to a discussion about Saucer Day. Julian recognized Clane from the media stories at the time. "I've been spared the goldfish bowl of fame." said Clane. "After everything broke down people forgot how it started. We were all just concerned about where the next meal was coming from. How many cans of water could we fill before the faucets ran dry, would the electricity keep going for the rest of the day. Now things have picked up everybody is just focusing on returning to normal."

Julian caught Siobhan's eye. "The goldfish bowl of fame is something your daughter now has to face." He had relaxed since arriving.

"Of course!" Clane laughed. "My little girl the TV star." Siobhan realized that her father had been equally nervous about this meeting.

"Tell us about your own family, Julian." said her mother.

"Well, my dad is a history professor at Minnesota Duluth and my mum teaches psychology for a private institute. We live in French River, a little town overlooking Lake Superior."

"Sounds lovely." said Gina.

"We've been there since we left London." He gave a brief history of his family's exodus and their arrival in America as asylum-seekers from the Mosley regime.

"I met Mosley once." Clane looked thoughtful. "When I was with the embassy in Ireland we paid a state visit to the UK. A very genial English gentleman, or so he seemed."

"The man's scum!" spat Julian with a passion that made everybody at the table jump.

There was a long silence. "Right." said Gina. "I have to prepare dinner."

Siobhan followed her father as he showed Julian to where the bedrooms were; like most houses in Boulder City, theirs was a bungalow. He led their guest into the spare room. "This is your room, Julian. Hope it's OK for you. Do you need a hand unpacking?" Siobhan waited down the hallway. Her father shut the door and came out alone. She approached him and said in a low voice: "Dad, is this strictly necessary?"

"Is what?" he answered in similar voice, understanding that this conversation was private.

"Putting Julian in the spare room. Can't we sleep together?"

"Sleep together?" He frowned. "Do you mean...?"

"Yes, dad. We do so normally you know. We have reached that stage in our relationship."

Clane gasped. "You mean that boy has been...!? With my daughter!?"

"Dad, keep your voice down!" she gestured to the bedroom door. "We have both been doing it with each other. He didn't tie me down and force me you know."

"But, Siobhan, you're just a..."

Annoyance rose within her. "Just a little girl?"

Her father's face took on a plaintive expression. "Siobhan, you're my sweet baby. I held you in my arms. You're my little sweetness and light. You're my little bundle of joy..."

"I'm twenty-four years old, dad!" she hissed. "I have a bachelors degree in journalistic studies. I am a highly-trained and accomplished journalist and now I'm a TV anchor for CBS... I'm a grown woman, goddamnit!"

He nodded reluctantly.

"Had you made love by the time you were my age?"

He paused. "Yes."

"And what did grandma and grandpa think?"

"I... didn't tell them. They've always thought your mom was my first."

"And I haven't told you. It's something children naturally keep secret from their parents... I love Julian, dad; and he loves me. Would you prefer it if it was somebody else I did it with; a random stranger or even a bad guy?"

"No, of course not."

"Then you should be happy for me."

Her father sighed and ran a hand through his red hair; it had visibly thinned and greyed lately. "Fair enough, Siobhan... I'll keep Julian in the back room, but if you want to join each other... alright. But please be discreet."

She smiled. "Agreed."

"I still don't approve. I know I was an offender here myself, but you should be joined together in holy matrimony before you consummate your relationship."

She hesitated. "Dad... I'm not sure I believe in God anymore."

The look he returned started off as shock, then confusion and finally settled down as understanding. "Well... I did have a feeling about you, that you didn't. A lot of people don't these days." He gave an easygoing grin and patted her on the shoulder. "Don't worry; you'll find Him again one day." He walked off.

Siobhan chuckled to herself with amusement as she walked towards the spare room. To get there she had to pass Brendan's bedroom on the other side of the passageway. His door was wide open and she could hear her young brother's voice: "No, he's a very nice man. I think he is anyway... Julian... He's Siobhan's boyfriend... Of course I know what a boyfriend is... No, I don't like girls... Only at school... Well I guess so; I am seven now..."

Siobhan stopped, curious, and poked her head into the room. Brendan's room was typical for a boy of his age; piles of comic books laid in a mess across the shelves, prints of cartoon characters covered the wall, toy cars were strewn around the floor like an effigy of a motorway pile-up. Brendan sat on his bed cross-legged with his back to the door. He was facing the wall. He was alone in the room and did not have a telephone. "Bren?"

He started and swung round. "Hi, Siobhan."

"Who are you talking to, Bren?"

He paused. "Nobody." As he spoke he covered the lower half of his face with his hands.

"But I just heard you talking. Have you got a roam there?"

"No, mommy says I can't have one till I'm ten."

"Well then there's nobody here, so who were you talking to?"

Brendan squirmed. "Please! He said I'm not allowed to tell you about him?"

"Who?"

"Boggin."

"Who's Boggin?"

He pointed at the wall. "It's him."

"Bren, there's nobody there."

He looked at her with genuine surprise. "There!" He pointed more vigorously. "There! Can't you see him?"

Siobhan sighed. "No, I'm sorry, Bren. I can't."

Her brother looked confused; then he turned to the wall and nodded his head. "OK." He looked back at Siobhan. "Siobhan, Boggin says you might not be able to see him and that's OK..." He paused and looked back again as if hearing some more speech. "He also asks, can you please not tell mom and dad about him."

Siobhan nodded and backed out of the room. "Sure, no problem."

....

Three days later Julian went home. The whole family came to the airport to see him off and they all hugged him. They also had the sensitivity to leave him and Siobhan alone to say a private farewell. She and Julian made plans for her to come and meet his parents at the New Year. The long-awaited and dreaded debriefing took place in the car afterwards. "A very nice boy." said her mother. "A very nice boy indeed. I'm happy for you, Siobhan."

"Yes." chimed in her father. "A decent upstanding lad. I'm glad you've got yourself somebody like him. A girl these days can't be too careful. You can end up with any old Tom, Dick or Harry." It was Saturday so they dropped Brendan off at a leisure centre to play softball with his friends and then drove home. Once the subject of Julian had been exhausted Siobhan spoke up: "Mom, dad; there's something I should tell you about Brendan."

They turned to look at her in the back seat, alarmed by her tone. "What is it, honey?" asked her mother.

"Last week I found him in his room talking to himself. I asked him what he was doing and he said he was talking to somebody. He even pointed at the person, but there was nobody there. He said this person was called 'Boggin' and swore he really was there."

Gina turned white and her lips quivered. "Oh my God, no!... He's got an imaginary friend."

"What's that?"

Gina shivered and replied in hushed tones: "Some children do this, talk to thin air and pretend they have a friend there... Oh no!" Tears budded in her eyes. She opened her handbag and pulled out a tissue paper.

"What did this 'Boggin' look like?" asked her father.

His wife started at him in disbelief. "What?"

"I was just wondering, did Brendan describe this friend?"
"Clane!"

Her father shrugged defensively. "I was just wondering, Gina. After all, there are things in this universe that are mysterious. We all know that now. What if Brendan has simply made contact with some... being from another world?"

"No, Clane!" his wife interjected. "An imaginary friend is a sign of illnesses. Our son is sick!..."

"But..."

The argument continued after they arrived back at home and became more raucous as Siobhan's mother and father persisted in their conflicting positions. Siobhan retreated to her bedroom, but her parents' voices rose to such a volume that she could easily hear them through the walls, and indeed began to worry that the neighbours might as well. Her mother was very worried about Brendan's mental health and insisted that he be taken to see a doctor as soon as possible. Her father didn't want Brendan to be treated medically when his son's behaviour was not in itself a symptom of anything being wrong with him. Clane explained that it was possible that Brendan was simply able to see parts of reality normally beyond the perception of others "...like what I saw in Prague!" he yelled. Siobhan didn't know what this referred to; it was obviously something known only to his parents, although her father had travelled to the European city of Prague the year before last. After about fifteen minutes the quarrel reached its raging climax. "You *want* Brendan to be ill!" shrieked Gina. "You actually prefer him that way because it gives you power over this family!"

Clane roared in the strongest brogue he had spoken in years: "No feckin' quack is going to fill my son with feckin' chemicals just 'cos he's gifted enough to see things the rest of you feckers laugh at! Now I'm off to the feckin' pub!" The front door slammed; a moment later the engine of Clane's Chevrolet roared and its tyres screeched loudly on the street outside.

Siobhan's mother sobbed obtrusively for a few minutes. She was quiet for a while then Siobhan heard a knock at her door. "Come in."

"Siobhan?" Her mother entered. Her face was ruddy and tear-stained; her eyes were bloodshot. "I'm sorry about what just happened. We're both just worried about Brendan."

"It's OK, mom."

"What do you think is wrong with Brendan?"

"I don't know. This is not something I know very much about; imaginary friends."

"There was a movie about it a few years ago. It had James Stewart in it. He played a man who was followed everywhere by an invisible giant rabbit."

"*Harvey*?"

"That's it. That's how I feel now with Brendan. He's like that man."

"But in the movie, didn't the rabbit turn out to be real in the end?"

She shrugged. "I guess so, if memory serves." They were silent for a while. "What we should do when your dad gets home is have a long talk about it, with the *three* of us." She grinned. "He won't be long. After his fourth or fifth Guinness he usually feels more diplomatic."

Her mother then went to the kitchen to cook and Siobhan took a shower. The mark on her arm was hurting again. She looked at it in the mirror. She thought that it vaguely resembled a face, but one with very large eyes. Julian had asked her about it and she told him it was a birthmark. This was a lie, but she didn't want to try and explain how it had suddenly appeared on her when she knew she could not. There might have been a question mark over whether or not to take Brendan to the doctors; but for herself she was certain.

She made an appointment over the phone and went to Dr Simon's surgery the next day. "Hmm." he said as he palpated the discoloured skin of her arm. He gave a very medical pause. "Is it hurting now at all?"

"No. It twinged a bit yesterday though."

"How long have you had it?"

"Just over two months."

He sighed and stood up. "I'm sorry, Miss Quilley. I don't know what that is. It looks to me like a scar; a very old first or second degree burn, but it can't be that... I can refer you to a dermatologist if you like."

She received an appointment by E-gram that afternoon for the following week. The dermatologist was a thin-faced greasy-haired man with a pointed beard like the devil, named Dr Kortz. He examined the mark and scraped off some of the top layer of her skin for tests. However he seemed as nonplussed as Siobhan's general practitioner. "Very strange... Very strange..." He kept repeating. He gazed out of the window of his office in a Las Vegas hospital, lost in thought. "The odd thing, Miss Quilley, is that you're not the first patient I've had with a mark like this."

"Really?"

"Yes. I think I've had three or four; and all within the last year, all living in this region."

"That's very odd. Who are they?"

He raised his hand. "You know I can't give out names, Miss Quilley."

"Of course; I'm sorry. I just wondered what's going on if more than one person has this mark on their arm. Is there some kind of new disease spreading?"

"That is one possibility... Do you mind if I ask you a few questions? This is not my field, but it's just my other patients with this mark reported other symptoms."

"Like what?"

"May I ask you?"

"By all means."

Dr Kortz took a seat at his desk. "Have you ever suffered from missing time?"

"What's that?"

"A lacuna in your memory. For example, you look at the clock and it is one o'clock and then you look again in what feels like just a few seconds and it's two o'clock."

"No, that's never happened to me."

"Do animals behave strangely around? Dogs bark, cat's hiss?"

"No."

"Do you ever experience very intense emotions at things you normally wouldn't be affected by?"

"No."

"Have you..." he spoke slowly for emphasis. "...ever seen an MFO?"

"Apart from the ones on TV the government has? No."

"Very well, Miss Quilley."

He refused to clarify the meaning of his list of questions. As she travelled home from the hospital she pulled herself up. The answer she gave to the first question was not accurate. She *had* had missing time, *four days* of missing time. She had also seen an MFO flying away from where she had woken up in that forest in Canada. What had happened to her during that time she vanished at Area 51? Did it have anything to do with the mark on her arm?

Chapter 7

The plane dropped out of the clouds and Siobhan's eyes were filled with white. It was such an unfamiliar colour that it made her jump. The captain's voice entered her ears: "*Ladies and gentlemen, we are about to land at Chamberlain Field...*" Julian was not waiting for her in the arrivals hall. She switched on her roam and a text immediately appeared: "*Sorry, stuck in traffic. Wait at arrivals. Will be there soon. J xxx.*" She decided to go outside for some fresh air, but the moment the sliding doors to the terminal parted she reeled back gasping. It was like opening the door to a deepfreeze. She quickly unpacked the warm jacket Julian warned her she would need. Everything was upholstered with snow. Of course Siobhan knew what snow was like; she had seen it in New York, but never as deep or thick as this. Great fluffy dollops lay on the tops of rubbish bins. Rows of footprints intermingled with each other; the compacted snow inside them was fresh and white. The cloudy sky was still moulting tiny powered flakes that stuck to the terminal window, fused by the heat from inside. She stepped outside, now wrapped in her anorak, blinking to shake the flakes from her eyelashes. Her nose felt as if it had been pinched and her earlobes stung where they poked out from her hood. She deliberately walked where nobody else had yet, feeling a bit guilty; the snow was pleasant to look at and it seemed bad to deface the virgin fall with her footprints. She became hypnotized as she looked down at the plain of ice dust. There were four lines of compressed opaque ice on the roads of the carpark, stained a patchy brown by the gritters so it resembled chocolate ripple ice-cream. Inside them, car tyres ran like trains on rails. The vehicles were great mounds of snow on wheels which crawled slowly along. They had patches brushed clean over their headlights and windscreens, with just a light sprinkling left behind on the glass like icing sugar. Their radiator grilles were great molten lacerations. The thaw refroze as it trickled down onto the bumpers and number-plates forming icicles. The white velvet shroud over the street changed the acoustics, making car engines, voices and everything else sound fuzzy and muted.

"Siobhan?"

She jumped at the sound of her name and swung round. "Julian!" She ran forward and embraced him.

He chuckled. "I wasn't sure if it was you. I'm not used to seeing you wrapped up like this."

"I'm not used to being wrapped up. I can't believe this place! It was seventy-three degrees in Vegas when I got on the plane."

"It's about eighteen here."

"I can well believe it. I keep thinking I'm at the North Pole and need to find Santa Claus."

The streets of Minneapolis were well-swept, the city being used to heavy snowfall. People hurried along the pavements, their faces swathed in scarves and with woolly hats perched on their heads. Exhaust pipes of vehicles smoked as if fires were burning inside them. Christmas decorations still hung from shop windows, although Christmas was over and so they had a different feeling to them. It was that strange week between Christmas and the New Year which seems disconnected from the rest of the cycles of the calendar. "I'm so sorry I wasn't there to meet you." said Julian.

"It's alright." replied Siobhan. She began to think for the first time about his family. She now knew how Julian had felt back in July when he had visited her own parents. She began asking the same kinds of questions and he gave similar reassurances.

They drove north out of Minneapolis on a major highway, but the view from the road was obscured by two huge berms of dirty snow. With the pale overcast above and snow falling more thickly, the different shades of white blended in with each other. The only spots of colour were other vehicles. Their rear lights were blobs of cherry red in the continuum of whites, creams and light greys. The highway ended at the city of Duluth and the road rose on a flyover giving Siobhan her first look at the landscape. The snow-muffled port was below her, steam and smoke everywhere exacerbated by the cold. Behind that was a plain of white ice stretching to the horizon like a polar cap. "That's Lake Superior." said Julian. "It's frozen over."

They left Duluth by a small road that led through forested land beside the greatest of the Great Lakes. Snow-latticed trees blocked the view of the white expanse. "This must be a nice place in summer." said Siobhan. "A place to go swimming, sailing."

"Yeah whatever." he answered in a dull voice. Julian's mood had changed since they had left the highway. He had become taciturn and a little sullen. Siobhan felt worried; she had never known him to be like this before. She wondered why.

They eventually passed a sign saying *French River* and she lurched with renewed apprehension. Then she saw the last thing she expected on the road ahead, what looked like the entrance to a military base. A lattice blockade of multi-layered barbed wire rose as high as the treetops. There was an opening blocked by a barrier similar to that at a railway level crossing. There was a small hut beside it and as they approached a security guard came out. He was insulted by a winter jacked and hat, yet she could see the holster at his waist outside his clothing. He ginned politely. "Hello, Mr Spencer." He pressed a button on the gate and it swung upwards. Julian waved evasively to him and drove through. "What was that all about?" asked Siobhan.

"French River is a gated community." Julian responded. "The residents bought up the land and put the fence in after Saucer Day." The car turned off the road onto a drive that disappeared into the dense forest. They arced round a bend and were faced with a huge mansion. Siobhan couldn't hold back a gasp. Julian remained unmoved. The house's facade was a flat two-storey row of snow-covered granite with a heavy roof and dormer windows. There were spacious balconies on each corner. By the shape of the snowscape around the building it was obvious that there was a well-designed garden with terraces and lawns. "Good grief!" exclaimed Siobhan. "Is this your home?"

"Yeah." he replied darkly.

They got out of the car and trudged up to the grand portico entrance. Julian rang the doorbell beside the polished oak door and it was opened by a small young black woman in a blue dress with many pockets, making it look like a domestic servant's outfit. Siobhan wondered why he didn't use a key. The maid smiled. "Come on in quickly, Master Spencer; you'll freeze yourself out there."

"Thank you, Selly. It is a bit chilly out here." He turned to Siobhan. "Selly, this is Siobhan. She'll be staying with us. Siobhan, this is Selly."

"Howdy do, Miss Siobhan. I'll make sure everything's ready for you." She gave a slight curtsy. She had a Deep South accent and Siobhan instinctively pictured her strolling along the banks of the Mississippi watching riverboats sail past. She looked incongruous in Minnesota, surrounded by so much snow and ice.

"Hello." replied Siobhan, unsure of what else to say. The maid led them into a vestibule glowing with warmth. It was sumptuous with wooden wall panelling and spotless velvet chairs. A grandfather clock ticked in the corner.

"Julian, you've brought Siobhan!" said a new voice. A woman was standing there. "Hello, Siobhan. It's good to meet you." The woman was in her late forties or early fifties, but had worked hard to make herself look younger. She was tall and slim with blonde hair that was obtrusively dyed. She had expensive jewellery on and too much makeup. "Selly, bring us tea." She addressed the maid without looking at her.

"Yes, Mrs Spencer." The maid replied and obediently padded off.

The woman continued to grin warmly at Siobhan. "Julian has told me so much about you." She leaned forward and kissed her cheek, filling Siobhan's nostrils with the scent of Yardley's. "Albert and I have been pestering him to bring you to us for months." Her accent was English like Julian's.

A large round man about the same age as the woman appeared. He was also well-dressed and well spoken. He greeted Siobhan as warmly as the woman had. "Mr and Mrs Spencer." said Siobhan. "It's good to meet you too. Thank you for inviting me here to share your New Year."

"You're very welcome, Siobhan; but enough of the 'Mr and Mrs'. Call me Tanya and my husband's name is Albert. Julian should have told you, we don't stand on formalities in our family. Silly of him to forget." She glanced at her son briefly.

Julian didn't respond.

They moved to an opulent lounge. Siobhan was almost smothered as she sank into the cushion-covered settee. Julian's older brother Toby came downstairs and joined them; he was a lawyer with a thriving practice in Milwaukee, Wisconsin. Selly the maid dutifully served them all tea and coffee in china cups. "Thank you, Selly." Julian smiled up at her sincerely.

"You welcome, Master Spencer." she answered. "Hope you enjoys it now."

The look they exchanged gave Siobhan a pang of uneasiness.

"How's the job hunting going, Julian dear?" asked Tanya.

"Not bad, mum. I've had an offer of a tutoring position from San Diego."

"History?"

"No, political science."

"Sounds interesting." guffawed his father. "Seems to be the way of the academic world. You learn and learn; and when you've stopped learning, you teach. Unless you're like Toby, in which case you put that knowledge into practical use."

"I'm sure I'll find practical use for my knowledge too, dad," replied Julian in an acidic tone. Siobhan glanced at him with concern. He was still not his usual self. He looked at the floor and sipped his tea with rigid tense lips. He looked demoralized and insecure. She wanted to reach out and hold his hand, but wasn't sure if that was the proper thing to do in the presence of his family.

"I've taught and taught and taught." continued his father. "Would have probably spent the rest of my life doing it in London if Mosley hadn't destroyed me, the bastard."

"What's your subject, Albert?" asked Siobhan.

"History, primarily British history. Kings and queens and all that jazz. That's what I tech now at Duluth."

"I teach as well." said Tanya. "I'm into something different though; psychology."

Albert laughed. "Mumbo jumbo if you ask me!" He shared a look with his wife that indicated that this was an old friendly rivalry they shared. Then he continued. "I must say I love America. Your country has been very kind to me. We're actually part of an English community here; expats. We're not unlike those in India during the Raj except we're not in charge here." In fact you'll meet a few of them tomorrow night." He rolled onto his feet. "Come here, Siobhan. Take a look at these pictures." He led her over to a wall where there was a row of gilt-framed photographs. One was himself dressed in a Masonic apron and he explained that this was after his initiation into the local lodge. There were rows of photographs of Tanya at various events for the Women's Institute that she helped organize. Almost all members of the local chapter were British refugees. "We also host the bridge circle." he said proudly and showed her some more photos of its members. "And this is our summer party at the Beaver Bay tennis club." There was also a photo of Albert skiing. "I try to hit the slopes every year in Colorado; Aspen and Glenwood Springs."

It grew dark earlier than Siobhan was accustomed, due to the latitude of Minnesota and the cloud-covered skies. Despite the informality of the house, dinner was a grand affair. They sat round a table laid with a white cloth and candlesticks. The food was served by Selly, but was cooked by another older local white woman who sang loudly, and not terribly well, as she stirred the gravy and cracked the eggs. Her grating voice was easily audible from the kitchen. This mannerism was tolerated by the Spencers; they even seemed to enjoy it, as if it were a tradition of the home. It was an odd contradiction that Julian's parents appeared more at ease with her than her own did with him. Siobhan was immediately installed into Julian's bedroom and they had not even asked whether or not she needed a room of her own, let alone felt any objections to the unmarried couple sharing a bed. However Julian remained uncomfortable. When he took a bath in the room's en suite tub Siobhan got in with him and washed his back. "Jules, what's wrong?"

"Nothing." he muttered.

"Something's needling you. I can tell."

"It's nothing!" He rose abruptly and stepped out of the bath, spilling water onto the floor. Siobhan sat back stunned as the disturbed bathwater sloshed back and forth along the length of the tub. They went to bed in silence and Siobhan lay awake for hours, staring at the high ceiling.

....

She awoke later than usual, probably because she's fallen asleep late. Julian had already got up and was nowhere to be seen. She showered and dressed then looked out of the bedroom window. It was New Year's Eve and fresh snow had fallen during the night. There was a row of neat round spoors running in a straight line across the flat area of the garden, a cat or fox probably. She went down to the dining room to try and find Julian. She heard his voice coming from the kitchen; he was talking to Selly. Siobhan was about to walk in and greet them both, but some instinct made her wait outside and eavesdrop. "I wish you would call me 'Julian', Selly." he said.

"It wouldn't be fitting, Master Spencer." she replied.

"You're worth more than this, you know. You deserve better."

"I's perfectly happy, Master Spencer. Ain't no complainin' comin' from me."

"Why not? Why don't you complain?... I'd like to help you. You and I together can be so good. We can do so much here to make things better."

Selly paused and then retorted in an irritable tone: "You mustn't go talkin' like that now, Master Spencer. Ain't fitting for you! Now, if you excuse me there; I's busy."

Siobhan heard Julian approach the door. She shrank back behind it and hid as he walked past. He was muttering in frustration. She waited until he was gone and then she peeked into the kitchen. Selly was sweeping the floor with a broom; her face was turned downwards, her arms moving rhythmically. Siobhan glared at her hatefully for a moment and then slipped into the empty lounge. The feeling rising within her now was one she had never experienced before and she was terrified and repulsed almost as much by having the feeling as the feeling itself terrified and repulsed

118

her. It was anger, betrayal, jealousy, hurt. She wasn't sure what to do. Part of her wanted simply to dash out of the house right now and go home; never even say goodbye. She knew she had to confront him. Could she bear to look at him, knowing the truth? She also needed to pack her luggage. What about Selly? She felt the urge to run into the kitchen and slap the little black maid over and over again until she fell to the floor and then kick her and kick her repeatedly. She pulled some tissue papers out of a dispenser and wiped the tears away from her eyes. She stumbled as she mounted the stairs. Her head was spinning and her hands trembled. Julian was sitting on the bed hunched over with his chin on his hand like the statue of The Thinker. He turned and looked at her as she entered the room. He looked shocked by her expression. "Siobhan... What's wrong?"

"That's the question I asked you yesterday and you never replied. I wanted to help you... but now I know what it is I feel like a fool."

He frowned. "What are you talking about?"

"I heard you, you son of a bitch. I heard you in the kitchen talking to that housegirl."

He growled: "Don't call her that!"

She imitated his voice: "'Call me Julian, Selly. We could be so good together.' You're screwing the little nigger whore aren't you!?"

"Oh dear." Julian groaned and facepalmed.

"You're not even going to try and deny it?... How long's it been going on, Julian? Were you with her before we met?"

"I *am* denying it, Siobhan. I am not screwing Selly, I promise you."

"And you expect me to believe that after what I just heard?"

Julian chuckled ironically and angrily at her.

"Don't laugh!... You think this is a big joke!? You think *I* am just a big joke, do you!?"

"Alright, Siobhan. Do you want to know the truth about what I was talking to Selly about?"

Now it was Siobhan's turn to feel confused. "What truth?"

He stood up. "Come with me."

....

They had to wait until the transit of the next snowplough and then curved in behind it along the road out of French River. After they had crossed the cordon and on the highway Siobhan finally asked: "Jules, where are you taking me?"

"On a journey to open your eyes." He kept his gaze dead ahead.

"Do your mom and dad know where you're going?"

"Fuck mum and dad!" He had an expression of vehement hatred on his face when he said those words that Siobhan had never imagined him sporting. They didn't speak after that for the entire journey. They entered Minneapolis and St Paul and Julian negotiated the cryopreserved city streets with familiarity as if he knew where he was going. He flicked his right indicator and turned off the main road. They entered a residential district of squat and box-like houses with flat, undecorated facades of grey breezeblocks and shallow roofs. In some cases snow had fallen off then to reveal worn creosote. Julian slowed down as he negotiated the narrow, labyrinthine streets. The roads had just been ploughed and Siobhan could see they were made of crumbling concrete slabs and the car bumped regularly as its tyres ran over the tar-filled expansion gaps between the slabs. The pavements were cracked and bare frosty earth poked through the gaps. Every few yards there were splashes of broken auto-glass and piles of dog excrement. The houses were surrounded by bare wire fences suspended between off-kilter cement gateposts; their tops were curled over, rusty and ragged. Broken, cannibalized cars sat on piles of bricks in driveways and heaps of sand and gravel were piled up against walls. Toddlers played in sandy patches in gardens while paunchy men shovelled snow from their front paths. Women in jeans chatted to each other over fences and old women dragged shopping bags on sledges down the alleyways that ran between the streets. A Christmas tree, bare of needles and wrapped with damp ribbon, stood defiantly in a gravel driveway. They reached a circus of roads with a row of small grocery shops in the middle surmounted by two-storey flats. A posse of mean-looking young boys in baggy trousers and baseball caps with angry faces stood or sat outside one of the shops with bicycles idling in their hands. They stared at Julian's car with analytic and dispassionate hostility, as if sensing instantly that it came from outside their dominions. In a small rec children played on swings and roundabouts in the shadow of three storey maisonettes. They threw snowballs and slid down slopes on improvised sledges. Everywhere there was refuse; overflowing dustbins, broken glass, crisp packets, old newspapers, discarded children's hats. A dog picked at a broken dustbin bag. They parked outside a maisonette; it was one of a long series of them set at ninety degree angles to each other so their plan resembled a row of chevrons. It was a three-floor pebbledash pastel box with balconies taken up by satellite dishes. A cat tiptoed along a low wall beside it. As Julian stopped the engine, the discordant far-off melody of the children's voices came in through the car's windows. "Do you see?" he asked.

"See what?"

"This place!" Julian leaned forward on the steering wheel and shook his head.

"What about it?"

"This is how most of the proletariat live."

"The proly-what?"

"The working class." He chuckled scornfully. "My family!... They know nothing, Siobhan. Nothing! For them, life is just dad's skiing holidays in Colorado, mum's Women's Institute meetings, the Bridge circles, dad and his Masonic lodge, the tennis club..." his voice rose to an angry shout. "The whole north shore fucking, grand, leafy, English, socially-inbred, petit-bourgeois, self-congratulatory, obtuse, fucking privilege fortress!" Julian thumped the steering wheel with his fist. "The whole place is a dreamland, Siobhan." he hissed. "It's a cotton wool-wrapped sanatorium for people in permanent denial; people who suckle from the capitalist teat and want to pretend that they don't; they want to kid themselves that shit-holes like this don't exist!" He waved his hand in a circle to indicate their surroundings.

"Julian, what do you mean? I don't understand."

"What I'm talking about is this place we're in now. That's why I brought you here, Siobhan. You needed to see it for yourself. I need to show you what my parents never see, what they choose not to see and don't even know it." He sighed and looked hard at Siobhan with more sadness than rancour. "Do you realize that for the people who live here, dad's skiing in fucking Colorado and all that other fucking crap is another world? It's like life on Mars! For these people there's only one vacation, only one circle, only one club, only one lodge, only one institute... survival. They get paid the minimum wage for the crappiest slave-labour jobs going and thank their lucky stars when they can afford the rent at the end of the month. They spend hours and hours going through every shop in town to find the cheapest groceries, all the reduced brands, all the two-for-the-price-of-one deals. They try to keep their kids out of the gangs, away from drugs, away from crime, in school and education; but they find it harder and harder to come up with a justifiable reason to convince them. The mother puts up with being groped by the boss because she fears unemployment more than rape. The father falls asleep early every night knowing that he has to choose between spending time playing soccer with his son, being a proper dad to him, and working that little bit of overtime in the evening to give that same son food on his plate." Julian looked at his lover and his eyes were dewy with anguish. "Could my mum and dad begin to imagine what that's like, Siobhan? Could they?"

She took a deep breath. "You know, it's not as simple as that, Jules. My mom and dad were never as poor as these folk, but they weren't anywhere nearly as rich as yours. But we knew people on both the poorer and richer sides and it wasn't as bad as you make out..."

"Don't make excuses for them!" spat Julian.

His tone annoyed her. "OK, Jules; then there's no point just complaining about it, why not do something positive? Do something to help these people become less poor."

"I am." he responded quietly.

"How are you doing anything positive?"

"I've joined a political party."

"Which one?"

"None of the regular ones of course; they're all the same deep down. The people who've lived for five generations in this crap-dump believed the false promises of all the social democratic liberal reformist politicians, and look where it's got them! No, I've joined a *really* alternative party; I'm now a member of the Workers Revolutionary Socialist League."

"The what?... Are you saying you're a commie?"

He laughed dryly. "That's just a buzz-word from Cold War propaganda."

"But you are, aren't you?"

He nodded. "Yes, but it's not a bad thing. You've been brought up to believe it makes me some kind of monster. It doesn't. It simply means that I think poor people like these should take the means of production into their own hands..."

"I don't believe communists are monsters because of what I've been brought up to believe, Jules. I believe it because communists once kidnapped my dad and tortured him. We thought they'd killed him. They almost did." She felt no anger with him as she spoke these words.

"When was this?"

"When we lived in Ireland."

He paused. "I would never hurt your dad."

"I know... I'm just worried about what you're getting involved in. I don't want people to be poor any more than you do... Look, Jules; I've seen things that could lift these people out of poverty without the need for communism. Things you wouldn't believe. Machines that produce infinite energy without fuel. Generators made from parts of extraterrestrial spacecraft..."

"LIES!" he yelled in his loudest voice yet. He covered his ears with his hands. "LIES!... Bullshit science fiction stories! A bourgeois utopian smokescreen to distract the proletariat from genuine progressive activism! Fascist anti-Semitic crap!"

Siobhan was frightened by his outrage and did not reply.

There was a long silence; then he spoke in a much softer voice: "That's what I was talking about with Selly when you overheard us. I wanted her to join me in the party. I was trying to recruit her."

"Why her?"

"Because of the way my family treat her." He turned and looked at her. There were tears in his eyes again. "Did you know her parents were the first generation of her family who were never slaves? Her grandparents were *owned* human beings. They were small children themselves when they were emancipated after the Civil War; born to parents who had been born slaves too; born slaves and died slaves. And now Selly is treated as if she were a slave by my cruel, pampered, heartless, gutless, brainless, fucking parents!... They dress her up like a china doll and order her about, snapping their fingers at her without even looking at her!"

"Selly is not a slave, Jules. Your family employs her. She can quit if she doesn't like it?"

"An empty purse is a strong incentive not to quit." he retorted. "What's she meant to do? Go back to Alabama and find a job *there*? Do you know how high unemployment is in that part of the country? She has a sick mother whom she sends money home to..." He leaned on the steering wheel, buried his face in his forearm and cried. "I can't bear it, Siobhan... Little children are dying, right now, in this country. They're dying because they're not fed properly. Old men and women are dying. They're dying right now, in this very city. They're freezing to death because they can't afford to heat their homes. They're dying without dignity, alone and forgotten. They're dying in *this* country, the richest nation on earth... and they're dying because they're poor. Because they're poor and for no other reason." He continued to weep. "I hate it, Siobhan! I hate this world for being like that. I hate the people who have made it that way and I hate the people who keep it that way... I can't live in this world! I simply *can't*! I'll do anything to change it. Anything!"

She laid a supportive hand on his sleeve and said nothing.

....

"Ladies and gentlemen." slurred Albert Spencer. "May I have your attention please!... It is now five minutes to midnight."

"Oooooh!" the party-goers whooped.

"I will now switch on the television and we will watch the live broadcast from Times Square." He pressed a button on and the sliding doors of an oak-panelled cabinet slid aside to expose a huge flat-screen high-definition television. "Wait for the ball to drop." The TV showed a huge crowd in the New York plaza. The surrounding buildings were glittering with lights. A singer was performing on a stage in one corner of the square. It looked spectacular on the TV's cinematic display. "Charge your glasses please!"

Selly circulated holding an open bottle of Champagne, pouring a generous glassful for each guest. Siobhan was feeling very tipsy, but held her glass out to allow the maid to fill it. Along with her and Julian's family, there were about fifteen people in the room, all drunk and all jovial.

"Are you ready?... Ten... nine... eight..." the guests all chanted in unison as the clock on the television checked off the seconds. "...four... three... two... one... ZERO! Happy New Year!" Fireworks cracked and flashed on the screen. The illuminated numbers "*1960*" lit up above the stage. Outside the window Siobhan heard more fireworks from nearby houses, booming like distant gunfire. They all linked arms and sang *Auld Lang Syne*.

After the singing Siobhan and Julian went to the kitchen door and forced it open against the snowdrift that had gathered there. They stepped outside sinking into the fall up to their ankles. The clouds had gone and the sky was lit up by a million stars, far more than was visible in the skies above Boulder City. The air was as cold as liquid nitrogen. "I love New Year." said Siobhan. "It's like a new beginning for us all; a time when we can look back, look forward and start again. It's a time to make decisions, to plan change."

"Yes, I know what you mean." He was smiling in the light from the house. His disposition had improved since that afternoon, as if his outburst had relieved a lot of internal pressure from his mind.

"And it's a new decade not just a new year. 1960! Funny to realize from now on we'll have to think of the years as nineteen sixty-something and not nineteen fifty-something. I just got used to it. There will never be another nineteen fifty-something year again. They're over for good; we've exhausted them all."

"The 1950's were a bad decade." said Julian blankly. "Let's hope the 1960's are better."

Julian's mother yelled at them from the back door: "Come on in, you two! You'll catch your death. And the guests are leaving soon; come and say goodbye."

Of the fifteen other guests, all but two had been English and one of those two was clearly Scottish. A number of them were Jews, refugees who had fled Britain after Oswald Mosley took power in 1949. They were a cheerful bunch, all close friends of the Spencers. There had been a happy atmosphere in the spacious lounge, made happier by the copious supply of beers, wines and spirits, glasses of which Selly kept up an effective relay. The person Siobhan had talked to the most to begin with was the Scottish guest. She was a very elderly woman with a sunken wrinkled face with loose saggy skin at her neck, making her chin look like a chicken's crop. She drank none of the intoxicating beverages on offer, but downed numerous cups of coffee. She insisted that these cups had to be filled exactly half-full and on two occasions when Selly over or under-filled them the old crone thrust them back into the maid's hands with an angry exclamation like: "I said I wanted it *half*-full! Is that really so difficult!? Bring me another and this time get it right!... Stupid girl!"

Selly stiffened slightly but did not object. She tottered back the kitchen to carry out her orders. Needless to say Julian and the Scottish lady did not interact at all. Her name was Dr Millicent Arbroath-Laird and along with her coffee she chain-smoked her way through several packets of king size cigarettes which were unfiltered and filled with very dark-coloured tobacco. These gave off a thick noxious fume. Siobhan was a non-smoker and pretty soon she was coughing continuously and her eyes streamed. She wasn't the only one. However Dr Millicent Arbroath-Laird was oblivious to the discomfort her habit was causing other people. She talked normally from within the nicotine miasma that constantly surrounded her. "So how long has your brother being experiencing these hallucinations?" She asked in her husky burr.

Siobhan was on her fourth glass of Bordeaux and the alcohol has loosened her tongue. She ended up telling the old lady about Brendan and his imaginary friend. "It began in July."

"That's six months, a long time; the medication should have worked by now. What treatment did the child psychiatrist give him?"

"Brendan hasn't seen a child psychiatrist yet."

"What!?" Dr Arbroath-Laird shrilled in the same tone she used to rebuke Selly. "You mean your parents have not submitted their son for treatment?"

"No, they can't agree on what action to take."

The old crone stubbed out her cigarette and leaned forward. The action made her break wind noisily; something else she appeared not to notice. "It is very obvious what action they should take. Their child is mentally ill and they have a moral and, I should add, *legal* responsibility to put him into the care of the psychiatric system."

"Well... My mom wants to do just that, but it's my dad who's against it." Siobhan realized that it had been a mistake to divulge Brendan's condition to Dr Arbroath-Laird. "He thinks Brendan is not ill and might simply be seeing... kind of... ghosts or whatnot."

The old lady gasped and then shook her head angrily, pulling another cigarette from the packet and lighting it. "There are no such things as ghosts. That is the kind of dangerous fantasy spread by that odious quack Wilhelm Reich! You're father is completely divorced from reality and he should be ashamed of himself!... I think social services should be informed. Where is it you live in Nevada?"

"Laughlin." She lied instantly and instinctively.

"Right, I shall be on the phone to your local social services department on Monday morning. Action needs to be taken against your father for his foolish superstition and irresponsible neglect. With any luck they will immediately issue an interim care order enabling the medical authorities to administer treatment to your brother by force of law." She puffed deeply on her cigarette filling the room's atmosphere with another bolus of caustic vapour. "My organization has recently marketed a very effective paediatric antipsychotic called 'Taniflen'. It has shown particularly good results in combating the 'imaginary friend' syndrome. Don't worry, Siobhan, I'll make sure your brother is soon sectioned and on a full intravenous three-week course. He'll be as right as rain in no time; a sane, normal, well-adjusted young boy." She smiled benevolently at Siobhan as if she expected thanks.

Siobhan was overcome by revulsion for the old woman. She wanted to grab her by her dry, gelatinous jowls and yell at her to mind her own damn business, and what a great man her father really was. Siobhan got up and moved to another room. Julian's mother came up to her. "Are you enjoying your evening, Siobhan?"

She nodded nervously. "I am thanks, Tanya. I appreciate you inviting me here for New Year."

"You're very welcome. Albert and I are very pleased Julian has found himself a nice girl... I saw you were caught in the corner by old Milly. I hope she wasn't too in-your-face."

Siobhan laughed. "I did find her a bit... overpowering."

"Don't take her too seriously. It's just her way."

Siobhan nodded. She suddenly remembered Prof Pickup, the rather abrasive scientist she'd met at Area 51 back in the summer. He was Scottish too. "I've never been to Scotland, Tanya, so I don't know; are all people from Scotland like that?"

"No, only the shrinks... There I go! I'm one myself, only I'm English so it doesn't count." She winked with humour.

"I knew a few psychology students at Penn State. What's the subject like?"

"Like a lobster pot; easy to get into, but once you're in it's impossible to get out. You just have to keep going deeper

128

and deeper in. Milly and I have gone about as far in as it's possible to go."

"You work with that lady?"

"Yes, we're lifelong colleagues; in fact I was originally her student. We're both founder-members of the Brentwood Institute of Human Relations. Have you heard of it?"

"No."

"We established it in London a few years before the war and relocated to America because of Mosley."

"So, is it a clinic or something?"

She chuckled again. "Not exactly, although we were to begin with. Today we do mainly consultancy work for state and private sector institutions. Our job is to apply social science to contemporary issues. We're engaged in evaluation and action research, organisational development and change management. We have executive coaching and professional development programmes, all in service of supporting sustainable change and ongoing learning. We're dedicated to the study of human relations for the purpose of bettering working conditions and home life for all individuals and organisations, communities and broader society. We seek to influence the environment in all its aspects on the formation or development of human character and capacity; to conduct research and provide opportunities for learning through experience for this purpose. We publish the results of study and research. We train students in or for any branches of the study. We have a proud history of working with organisations within the public, private or charity sectors that are required to look at systemic questions to achieve greater and more effective change. We operate as a bridge between policy and research. We seek to apply that research and make sense of it in a way that will serve the purpose for which we work. We work nationally and internationally to promote a learning culture in organisations and communities through developing individuals, groups and organisations in their capacity to think through actions, to change and put into practice new insights and in accompanying a process of change of quality of conversations and engagement." Tanya panted; she was slightly out of breath at the end of that monologue.

Siobhan nodded politely and said: "Very interesting." This was a lie because Siobhan didn't have the slightest clue what Tanya had been talking about.

....

By one o'clock in the morning the last guest had left and the family went to bed. Selly did a bit more work afterwards and then retired to her small flat in the basement below the stairs. Julian and Siobhan had become much closer over the course of the day following Julian's revelations. During the afternoon before the party he gave her some more information about the organization that he had joined. The Workers Revolutionary Socialist League described itself as a political party; however it seemed to Siobhan that it was merely a very loose tendency of individuals from all over the world with a lot of differing ideas. Its presence was mostly online and it centred around a network of three or four meshboards. Julian was active on the adjoining forums, but admitted that most of the people he interacted with he had never met. None of the community had ever stood for Congress or even for their local council. "We do street activism." Julian assured her. "That's much more important." There were some photographs on the meshboard of Julian standing at a crossroads in Minneapolis in summertime selling copies of a newspaper called *The Socialist Times* to passers by. He showed Siobhan a few back copies he kept in his room tucked under his bed. It was a crudely-printed tabloid with about twenty pages. "How did you get involved in all this?" asked Siobhan.

"At college. I did a module on Karl Marx and it changed my life." He showed her his bookshelf where there were rows of dumpy volumes on arcane economics including a series called *Capital* by Marx himself. The books were dog-eared and had creases on their spine indicating they had been read several times.

"You didn't steal these from Brandywine did you?" asked Siobhan.

He chuckled. "No, but I went out and bought my own copies after I returned the textbooks when I finished the module."

After the party Siobhan and Julian were much happier. They went to bed together, kissed and made love. Siobhan was still worried about her boyfriend, but was confident that now he had confided in her she could help him through whatever hardships he was suffering.

Chapter 8

"Five... four... three..."

The camera light came on. "Good afternoon, this is CBS News, going live on the CBS national network and online at wmn.cbs.tv.us. I'm Siobhan Quilley and here are the latest headlines for Tuesday March eighth 1960." These news broadcasts had become as everyday as brushing her teeth. She was doing three shows a week now and was amusing to remember the thrill and worry she had felt when she made her first foray in front of the camera the previous August. "In a press conference today, Henry A Dealey, director of the Federal Disclosure and Reconstruction Agency announced that he will be running for President and has submitted his nomination as an independent candidate. At the same time he resigned as FDRA director. The first polls are in for the Democratic primaries with a narrow lead for Senator John F Kennedy over his main rival Adlai Stevenson, former Governor of Illinois. Lyndon B Johnson and Senator Hubert Humphrey gained only three points putting them both on fifteen percent. Following last week's surprise withdrawal of the California Senator Richard M Nixon from the presidential race the favourite for the Republican nominee is now the Governor of New York, Nelson A Rockefeller. Vice President Storm Thurmond is still the only candidate the Southern Democrats have tabled with only a few days to go before the deadline... The League of the World has passed a resolution ratifying the much anticipated World Disclosure and Reconstruction Summit. The event will take place in the city of Dubai in the United Gulf Emirates in mid-August. The United States' ambassador to the League, Walter Burgwyn-Jones, called this 'an essential step forward in the advancement of humanity in the post-Disclosure world'. President Goldwater said he 'looked forward to the United States playing a key role in the rebirth of civilization in this new era. Disclosure will give every person in every nation on earth a "new New Deal".'... The FDRA has held a celebration at its headquarters in Washington DC after the arrival in San Francisco station of the first ever Northern Star express, the first successful transcontinental railroad service since Saucer Day. Director Dealey said: 'the reestablishment of railroad transport across the nation is a major milestone in the restoration of the American order'... Latest figures from the New York Stock Exchange. Another bad day for the dollar. It crossed the four Emirati Dirham mark for the third time this year and fell below eighty-five Irish pence. The Saudi Riyal is currently selling at one dollar ten. The price of gold is up to twenty-seven dollars and forty-nine cents per ounce... And now it's time for the news, travel and weather where you live."

After work she drove to her parent's house. This was possible because she had moved to the new CBS studio in Los Angeles, California. This meant she wouldn't be able to work directly with Walter Cronkite anymore and she was sad about that, but the two of them still exchanged E-grams almost daily and spoke on the phone every few days. Besides she disliked New York City now; it had lost something essential since her childhood there. She felt she had grown older quickly, even though she was still two months short of twenty-five. She had rented an apartment in Los Angeles, almost out of a sense of duty to the adult world, but whenever she had the time and energy she would drive up the old Interstate Fifteen through the beautiful mountain-framed Mojave Desert to Las Vegas and stay at her parent's house. Sometimes she would even do this on a weekday night when she was working again in the morning, despite it being almost a four-hour drive. She'd arrive in Boulder City at ten PM, say goodnight to her mother and father, then wake at four-thirty and drive back to LA. "You feel the need to touch base." her mother told her. There was an air service that flew to McCarran in an hour, but flying was stressful and only knocked about thirty minutes off the journey after adding on the time for check-in, boarding and the still frequent delays. It was far less bother to drive. This time she had finished work early and was on the I-Fifteen by three PM. She had just passed Barstow when she received a call on her roam. Her car was an upmarket model thanks to her hefty CBS salary and it had a hands-free and eyes-free system. She heard the ringtone and saw the words: "*Incoming call from Julian*" on her windscreen head-up display. "Accept." she said with a grin to the voice recognition system.

"Hi, Siobhan."

"Hi, Jules."

"How come you're on the road?"

"I finished work early today."

"I had a dream about you last night."

"Likewise."

"What was it like?"

She winked. "I'll tell you when I see you."

He laughed. "You've got your camera on. I can see you now."

She waved. "I'm not putting mine on now; don't want a ticket from the cops... How's things in Granite Land?"

"Not bad. And Silver Land?"

"Same as always."

"OK, talk later. Love you."

"Love you too, Jules." Julian was lecturing in history at Durham, New Hampshire; almost as far away as he could be in the United States. His position in San Diego didn't work out and he was dropped after a term. This was a blow to their relationship because of San Diego's proximity. Nevertheless they continued to hold themselves together as well as possible in a long-distance way. Things had become a bit tense in February when Siobhan had brought up the subject of marriage. This was not because of pressure from her father either. She'd been having dreams at night in which she saw herself as a mother. She could feel the shape and weight of a baby in her arms, her baby. Julian was there; the father. She became saturated with emotion after she woke up. She wept, almost grieving for the child; not one who had died, but one who was not yet born. She told Julian about her feelings and he was deeply uncomfortable. This worried Siobhan. He later explained that he was concerned about getting married because Clane had told him a few times about how he'd love to see them "walking down the aisle." Julian was a staunch atheist and felt uneasy even setting foot inside a church, let alone being wed in one. He had a particular aversion to Roman Catholicism, the Quilley family's faith. Siobhan was an agnostic and shared a lot of his views on religion, but still was willing to go through the motions of a Catholic nuptial mass. Julian was not; he couldn't. They discussed a civil wedding, but Siobhan doubted if her parents would bless that. So they decided simply to carry on as they were; they still loved each other after all.

It was seven PM and twilight when she arrived home. Her father and Brendan were there, but her mother was out. "Where's mom?"

"At her class again." Clane Quilley rolled his eyes slightly. "She'll be home soon." Gina Quilley had announced a few weeks ago that she was going to attend an adult education centre. She'd chosen to do a foundation course in psychology. "So she can finally work me out?" her husband quipped. Clane took a rather amused but slightly disapproving attitude to his wife's new vocation in life.

Brendan gave her a hug. "Hi Siobhan." he said.

"Howdy, Bren." she replied. "How's Boggin?"

"Not here at the moment, but I saw him down the park this morning."

"Now remember, Brendan." warned Clane. "Not a word about Boggin when your mom comes home. OK?"

The boy smiled and nodded.

"Now off you go to bed, there's a good lad."

When Siobhan and her father were alone she asked: "Is it a good idea, getting him to keep secrets from mom? It's teaching him bad habits."

Clane sighed. "It's not something I like doing, but what other choice do we have? She was determined to drop him into the clutches of a child psychiatrist and I can't bear that... I've told him why we're keeping this from his mom. I've been sure to tell him that I still love his mom very much and so should he. He understands. As far as your mom is concerned, Brendan's imaginary friend was just a phase and now it's past... She need never know any different."

Siobhan nodded.

He changed the subject. "I caught your show."

"I know, dad."

"Never miss it." He held up his roam; it was one of the new smart-roams like her Eberly friend Jayne's that allowed portable access to WorldMesh, a thin black oblong slab, bigger than normal roams. "I catch it on the Mesh if I'm not near the TV... What's all this about Dealey running for president?"

"Not sure, dad. It's completely out of the blue. Maybe he's just an opportunist. He does appear to be one of the most popular people in the country. He probably won't get far. Independents never do."

"There's a first time for everything." Clane looked grim.

"Does that bother you?"

"There's something about him, Siobhan... I get a bad feeling. He reminds me of... somebody else I once knew."

"Who?"

"Gerald Caxton."

"Gerald? I thought he was your friend. He used to come and visit us back in Ireland."

Her father shook his head. "There's more to that guy than I thought... than I ever guessed." His face twisted as if he were recalling a painful memory.

"I interviewed Dealey for *Politics of the Day*, back in the New Year."

"What was he like?" Clane asked in an alarmed voice.

"An intelligent and charismatic man, well-spoken, very charming and persuasive; the perfect politician."

"Did he... change in any way while you were talking to him?"

"Change? In what way?"

"Like... get bigger? Turn a different colour?"

She chuckled. "What are you talking about, dad?"

He gave an embarrassed grin. "Nothing... I'm making coffee; would you like one?" He abruptly turned away and headed for the kitchen.

"Yeah, sure." she replied with a quizzical frown.

"As far as the presidency goes, my man's Kennedy." he called as he boiled the kettle.

"Why? Because he's a paddy?"

He laughed. "Inevitably that's a factor. He's ex-Navy too; but I like the guy anyway. He seems decent. He's got a brain, a heart and a pair of balls. Getting into politics these days usually involves the amputation of all those organs."

"He'll probably win. The bookmakers and polls agree he's their favourite."

"Hope so." He brought out two mugs of coffee and handed one to his daughter.

"What do you think of the Dubai conference, dad?"

"It's long overdue. I've been invited."

"I should damn well hope so. Are you going?"

"Oh yeah."

"You should be treated as the keynote speaker. You did save the world."

"Well, me and a few others. Actually I'm a bit pissed off Jenny and Gordon have not been asked. I've written to complain."

"I met Jenny at Area 51 last year. There was this arrogant Scottish prick in charge, bossing her around like she was a piece of nothing."

"Pickup? Yeah, he's a dickhead. He's with the FDRA; he's Dealey's man, running the entire Area 51 science project..."

Father and daughter looked hard at each other and realized that they were both thinking the same uncomfortable thought, one that neither of them could quite put into words.

Chapter 9

"How do you feel?" asked Siobhan.

"Excited." her father replied.

The atmosphere in the airport was one of a package holiday about to depart. They were all congregated in the VIP lounge at Idlewild Airport in New York City. A large number of reporters were there, of which Siobhan was one. The airport staff served the passengers breakfasts, but she didn't have time to eat. This was a working holiday and she was accompanied by her camera crew. Every half hour they did a location broadcast for CBS; sometimes live, sometimes pre-recorded. At the same time she was assisting another team who were making a TV documentary. "Nobody knows yet what will happen during this coming week in Dubai." she said to the camera. "All the most powerful and respected people on earth will be gathering there to talk and decide, decide the fate of the whole planet earth..."

The aircraft was a Boeing 447 Sky-Cat, the largest airliner ever built. Its twin fuselages were on two floors; two rows of windows ran along the sides of both. They looked like two aircraft joined together by a third wing that resembled a continuation of the two on either side, as if both bodies had been impaled by a single wing. Typically a commercial Sky-Cat could carry over a thousand passengers, but this model had been adapted for VIP's. The name of the carrier: "Emirates", was stencilled on the hull. Because she was daughter of Clane Quilley she was allowed to join the dignitaries in the first class cabin instead of roughing it with the press corps in economy, or what could be called "economy" by comparison; the seats there were as good as business class on a standard airline. Siobhan's seat was almost as big as the sofa in Julian's parents' house. Her father sat to her right and John F Kennedy sat by the window to her left. "Does this apply to our politics too?" joked her father quietly. He was in a jovial mood. The five specially-designed Rolls Royce jet engines spooled up to a roar, audible even in the soundproofed interior. Aviation fuel flowed from the airliners capacious tanks to feed the combustion inside them; hydrocarbons became soot and carbon dioxide. Because of the aircraft's size, takeoff was a laborious process. There were still many airports in the world whose runways were too short to service the Sky-Cat. The plane ascended as it headed north towards the Canadian border; soon they reached their cruising altitude of forty-five thousand feet and the clouds were far below them. The cabin crew served them a champagne breakfast, a luxury Siobhan enjoyed rarely, even as a television star. Her father was blown away by it. After his third glass he was drunk. Perhaps the altitude sent it to his head quicker. Because this was a special aircraft, the passengers were not confined to their takeoff seats. They had a large open area to wander with settees and armchairs. There was a circular bar in the middle of the floor behind which stood a slim and pretty dark-skinned woman with a round hat and headscarf, which seemed to be the stewardess' uniform for the Emirates airline. All three presidential candidates were on board and President Goldwater himself was flying to Dubai too on Air Force One. The primaries and caucuses had whittled the race down to the three nominations: John F Kennedy, Henry Dealey and Nelson Rockefeller. The polls were split into fairly equal thirds for each of them and this resulted in frantic campaigning in which the three men bellowed all kinds of insults at each other on television and in debates. However, here on board the flight they were all chatting genially on a corner settee in front of the bar sipping cocktails. Siobhan couldn't imagine how they were able switch attitudes so easily. Part of her programme plan was to interview all the candidates during the flight. This was not easy because when they were not relaxing in the lounge they were hard at work in their seats tickling their matchbooks and talking on their roams. This was August and the election was only three months away so their struggle to seduce the American voter could not let up for a moment, even high in the sky as the Atlantic Ocean rolled beneath them. She eventually managed to corner Kennedy on the seat near the bar. Her notepad hastily arranged their camera tripod and microphones. "Senator Kennedy, thank you for taking the time to talk to CBS."

He nodded with a polite smile. He was a good-looking man who radiated warmth. She had reported on some of his public speeches and admired his oratory skill. Siobhan instinctively felt comfortable with him. "You're very welcome, ma'am." he said.

"What do you hope to achieve this week at the World Disclosure and Reconstruction Summit?"

"Well, the world has entered a new era, one in which we have had to face many uncomfortable facts, but also some thrilling opportunities. We now know that we are not alone in this vast universe. This was something people have always suspected, but to have it confirmed has been traumatic for all peoples of the world. We cannot go back to blissful ignorance, and it would be shameful to wish to. Change is never comfortable, nor is it safe. There are no guarantees. However the world we are leaving behind is one filled with suffering, destruction, global war, the threat of the atomic bomb, poverty and misery. The one ahead of us has the potential to solve those problems and heal the injury caused by them. The future we could create, the one we have the ability to create, is more happy and plentiful than we can currently imagine. Are we the generation that will create that world? Maybe. I can think of no more exciting and joyful time to be alive. The United States of America can be at the vanguard of this magnificent adventure. If the American people choose me to be the thirty-seventh President of the United States I swear to you, it will be."

"How do you think we should interact with the intelligent beings that we now know live out in space?"

Kennedy shrugged. "MFOlogists used to be laughed at as eccentrics on the fringes of society; well, now their time is come. He who laughs last definitely last loudest. According to them the behaviour of the space beings has changed little since Saucer Day. We don't know who they are or what they want. Are they even all the same species? How do we communicate when we can't speak each other's languages? Communicating with a dog or a cat is hard enough; now we're dealing with creatures that are not even from our planet. They appear to exhibit a wide range of behaviour

140

and profess a number of different agendas. This is something we will have to take one step at a time."

"Thank you, Senator." She then tracked down Henry Dealey. "Hello again, Miss Quilley." he grinned playfully. "It's good to talk to you again."

This was the second time Siobhan had interviewed Dealey. The previous time she had not planned on reminding him about their telephone conversation the year before when she was trying to arrange the restoration of electricity supplies to Pennsylvania. She was surprised that he remembered her. "I suppose I should thank you for your agency's prompt response to the deprivation in many parts of the country. You've done a lot of good."

"So have you." He gave her a look that was outwardly friendly, but it caused Siobhan to feel a chilled shiver. He was an overweight man in his early fifties with greasy black hair and a bulbous nose. His eyes were small and very close together. They were light brown and he never seemed to blink, like a snake's. His lips were so thin as to be almost non-existent; his mouth was a knife-slash across his lover face. He was dressed in dark blue suit that was open at the front and with a loose shirt collar like a TV detective.

She grimaced back as sweetly as she could. "So, Mr Dealey, what do you hope to achieve this week at the World Disclosure and Reconstruction Summit?"

He answered after an arrogant pause: "A reality check... The state of the world today has ruined the lives of many decent hardworking citizens. These are people who need urgent action to save them. The same goes on a larger level for entire states. Action means pragmatism. Of course, idealism has a place and a time; indeed it is an essential mindset for progress and innovation. However Senator Kennedy and many others have become intoxicated with idealism to the point where they have begun to regard our global predicament as some kind of fairytale." He sneered. "Try telling that to Mr and Mrs Upstate New York who have been without electricity, water or work for two years! Is some handsome prince going to come and rescue them on a white horse? No! What will rescue them is a sound and rational reconstruction policy that has its head out of the clouds and its feet firmly on the ground. If... *when* I am President I will implement a healthy dose of good old fashioned expediency to repair this planet on a grass roots level. This was my fundamental policy strategy in my management of the FDRA and it will remain so in the White House."

"What about the knowledge that we are not alone in the universe? What action should we take on that?"

Dealey made a dismissive sweeping gesture with his hand. "None whatsoever. It is a complete irrelevance in comparison to the day-to-day lives of ordinary Americans and people in the rest of the world. When the world is back on its feet and running smoothly; then and *only* then shall we have the luxury to indulge ourselves with frivolities and abstract philosophical dissensions."

Siobhan was disliking Dealey more every second. "However, as the exploration of covert government facilities has revealed, the Disclosure issue is far from abstract. In fact the technology discovered there will play an essential role in getting the planet back on its feet."

"No no! It will play an essential role in theoretical long term future advancements. The reconstruction effort must focus on the regeneration of the existing infrastructure. These are two totally different concepts and for practical purposes they must be kept separate. Confusing the two will threaten a breakdown of our carefully-rebuilt current order and a return to chaos." He grinned like a crocodile. "Now I'm sure nobody wants that do they?"

Siobhan felt very tired after her interview with Henry Dealey. She recorded a discussion with Nelson Rockefeller, but it was so nondescript that she quickly forgot it as soon as she'd E-grammed it to the editor. After that she ended up interviewing a few congressmen, including an articulate black man from Alabama with dark penetrating eyes named Martin Luther King. He said: "I'm pleased that since Saucer Day everybody understands the way the black man has felt since he was forced here to these shores; as outsiders, just a part of creation and not the whole. Disclosure has done a lot of good for the cause of black liberation across the nation."

....

The giant airliner had full-sized cabins for the dignitaries, but Siobhan had to make do with her seat as night fell and it was time to sleep. Luckily the seat reclined all the way flat so she slept fairly normally. When she woke up, sunlight was glowing in the windows. The passengers joined her in the daylight world one by one and the stewards and stewardesses served them breakfast. The plane began to descend and they all returned to their seats and fastened their belts. The sea of the Persian Gulf was vanilla blue in the morning sun. Siobhan yawned. It was only just after three AM Eastern Standard Time, but was almost midday local time. The aircraft was gliding down towards a coastline, but it was a very strange one. There were some islands and peninsulas along the coast, but they were an unusually regular shape. Three of them looked like palm trees surrounded by a circular sandbank resembling an atoll. Further out to sea was an archipelago resembling a map of the world and another looked like a dolphin. She realized she was leaning over Kennedy's lap to stare so she backed off and apologized. He chuckled amiably. "They're the World Islands and Palm Islands; man-made land reclaimed from the sea. Quite a spectacle aren't they?" The aircraft banked sharply to the left and the city of Dubai came into view. It seemed to consist mostly of tall buildings and tower cranes. The captain's voice came over the public address informing them that they were about to land at Dubai International Airport and the runway scrolled into view on the ground. With a thud the massive aircraft came down onto the shiny grey runway.

The airport jetway led directly to another VIP lounge inside the sausage-shaped terminal with a view over the airport where a squad of polite staff tended to them for twenty minutes or so; then they were ushered as a group out into the arrivals hall, a cavernous chamber with rows of white pillars stretching as far as the eye could see. A large crowd was there to see them arrive including hundreds of reporters. Camera bulbs flashed. The documentary director wanted to do a shoot with Siobhan at the entrance to the airport, but it just wasn't possible. More staff arrived immediately and led them through a set of sliding doors.

There was a hot air blower in the ceiling that made Siobhan gasp. Then she realized that there was no hot air blower; the heat was coming from the open air. The airport interior was so well air-conditioned that she hadn't realized how warm it was in the Arabian Desert environment outside. A row of big clean cars with tinted windows were picking up the VIP's and driving off with them. Siobhan climbed into the back of one and returned to the lush coolness of leather-scented conditioned air. "Where are we going?" she asked the driver as he pulled away.

"To your hotel first, madam." the driver replied in an unfamiliar accent.

Dubai looked to Siobhan like a giant building site. Both sides of the long wide road were lined by massive construction projects. The cranes she'd seen from the plane were mostly the tallest objects in the city. The bases of what would one day be huge skyscrapers rose from the chaos of scaffolding, pile drivers and cement plants. The sky above was cloudless blue. They passed one of a few completed buildings, a beautiful mosque with walls of pure white stucco; looking like a decorated cake covered in icing. A crowd of people were walking in; all dressed in white like the men who had prayed for them before the Area 51 invasion. The car turned off onto an avenue lined with well-mowed and well-sprinkled verges and small trees, behind which were large boxy houses with pastel-coloured walls, small windows and shallow roofs. Big artificial ponds of smooth turquoise water stretched between the roads and pieces of land were linked together by elegant footbridges. The car pulled up underneath a parapet and Siobhan got out, thanking the driver. Glass door slid apart and she entered an airy reception lounge. A porter wheeled her luggage on a trolley and she walked across a courtyard to a crescent of chalets. The sun felt like a brazier above her head and she sweated from every pore. Even Las Vegas was cold compared to this. Her chalet was more window than wall. Darkened plate glass panes surrounded every room. There was a narrow terrace on one side overlooking one of the artificial pools. Waterfowl of a species she didn't recognize paddled up and down on it. Once inside she was again bathed in the tonic of chilled air-conditioning; this seemed to be an everyday contrast of Dubai. She only had US dollars to tip the porter with, but he didn't seem to mind. She had a shower in the chalet's sumptuous wetroom, spending longer than usual so she could try out all the different soaps and shampoos. She dried herself off using one of the hotel's enormous fluffy towels that went all the way around her three times and then put on a dressing gown. When she switched on her matchbook she had an E-gram from Kennedy. "*Hi, Siobhan. Enjoying Dubai? I'm at staying at the Burj Jumeirah Hotel. Would you care to join me for dinner tonight? JFK?*" Siobhan sat back in shock. Reading these lines and recalling the tone of their conversations on the plane the subtext of his words was blatant. Of course John Kennedy had something a reputation when it came to women that the right-wing popular newspapers relished publishing. However her personal investigations had discovered some truth behind the propaganda. She had interviewed the actress Marilyn Monroe a few months ago and she had spoken for over an hour about the details of the affair she and Kennedy had enjoyed, on and off, for the previous year. This included discussions with Jackie, Kennedy's wife. Monroe was just one of several high society ladies Kennedy had engaged in liaisons with. When Siobhan had presented the interviews to Walter Cronkite he had advised her not to broadcast them. On reflection, Kennedy's manner on the plane during the interview and their many informal conversations was definitely flirtatious. She closed her matchbook and paced up and down the room a few times. Unfamiliar and uncomfortable thoughts ran through her head. She walked over to a full-length mirror and looked at her own reflection. Her hair was damp from the shower and clung to her scalp, but normally it was brown and lush. It fell to her shoulders in healthy waves. She had inherited her mother's chestnut locks, unlike Brendan who sported their father's ginger curls. However her mother's hair was thin and patchy and stuck to the sides of her head; now it was going grey with age too. Siobhan's was thick and moist, easy to brush and wash. Her eyes were wide and blue, her lips full. She pulled apart the sash of her robe and let it fall to the ground. She had a curvaceous and well-proportioned figure. A fellow student had compared her to the actress Mae West. She was, in summation, a very pretty young woman. She was younger than Kennedy's usual mistresses, who tended to be closer to his own age of forty-three. She was also rather lowly by comparison; a *mere* daytime television journalist. However, Kennedy was very attractive. He was handsome, strong, attentive, intelligent and eloquent. His voice was sensual and warm. She understood why women were drawn to him. She went back to her matchbook and searched for Kennedy's meshboard. He had an official dot-gov congressional board, but she was more interested in his personal ones: wmn.johnfkennedy.bod.us and wmn.kennedy4president.co.us. These were both upmarket and well-designed meshboards with segueing graphics and filtered images. She flicked through a number of the pages, reading posts from his blog, watching videos and viewing images. Her heart raced and adrenalin surged. There was a blipping noise and a popup appeared on top of the browser. It said: "*You have a new E-gram from Julian.*" She clicked it: "*Hi S. Hope things are going well at the conference. Thinking of you. Love you xx.*" The E-gram was illustrated by a photo of his smiling face. As she read the message a wave of guilt washed through her. The lustful thoughts she'd just had about Kennedy now felt cheap, dirty and adolescent. There were tears in her eyes as she replied: "*I love you too, J. See you soon xx.*" She then composed a reply to Kennedy. "*Hello, Senator. Thanks for the offer but I'm a too busy tonight with work so am eating at my own hotel. See you tomorrow. Siobhan Quilley.*" She sent it and snapped her matchbook shut.

....

Siobhan awoke with the blazing Emirati sun peeking between the slats of her blind. Her matchbook was still open where she had been working on her news report the previous evening. She had eaten a good dinner in the hotel's adjoining restaurant. All the other guests were delegates like her, but she didn't know any of them except her father who had a chalet of his own on the far side of the hotel. The waiter gave her a flummoxed look when she asked to see the wine list and her father informed her quietly that alcoholic beverages were forbidden in Dubai by law. She was served breakfast on a trolley in her room; grapefruit, cereal and scalding black coffee. Cars came to pick up the delegates and ten AM. The World Disclosure and Reconstruction Summit, dubbed in the media simply as "the Dubai Summit", was held in the centre of the city at the Sheikh Zayed bin Khalifa Al Nahyan Conference Centre, a dome-shaped white-tiled concrete structure the size of a sports stadium that stood surrounded by skyscrapers, some of them almost completely built. Everywhere there were reporters, TV cameras, telephoto lenses, satellite dishes, antennae, studio vans. The entire focus of the world was on this building in this hot little desert country. "Reminds me of the Dublin Treaty." said Clane. "Was that really only ten years ago?"

"The weather is a bit warmer this time though, dad." she said with a half-mile.

"Slightly." He mopped his brow.

"CLANE!"

Clane and Siobhan swung round to see two people rushing towards them. One of them was Dr Jenny Bulstrode and the other was Gordon Stephens, the pilot who had helped Clane save the world on Saucer Day. Clane's face lit up with delight. "Jenny! Gordy!" The three of them embraced affectionately in a group hug. Then they greeted Siobhan. She knew Gordon Stephens quite well as he was a friend of the family and, of course, had met Dr Jenny Bulstrode once.

"How the hell did you get here?" asked Clane.

"We were added to the delegation just yesterday. We got on the first plane we could."

"They must have listened to my complaint."

"Your words have tipped a balance before." said Stephens with a wink.

The ceiling of the conference auditorium towered over the floor in a cave-like hemisphere that was so high that it made Siobhan feel dizzy looking up at it. It was lit by a row of slits that let just the right amount of sunlight into the interior. The echoes of voices were an underlying murmur that reverberated around the chamber. At the front was a huge light blue League of the World flag and arranged along the walls were the flags of all the nations. Everybody had been issued identity badges at reception with their name on it and numerous ushers stood on the aisles to guide the delegates to their seats. There were over five hundred people on the list. Siobhan, as one of the minor attendees, was in a seat in the middle. It was a spacious one though with plenty of legroom and a desk in front of her to work on, like a more comfortable version of the lecture theatre at Eberly. The stage at the front had a panel table for the senior dignitaries. As she sat and watched, Kennedy, Dealey, President Goldwater and Martin Luther King all took their places there along with many other famous names that she recognized. The auditorium had been specially designed for this event with a large photograph from space of the planet earth showing on the display screen. Words in many languages could be heard over the loudspeaker. There was a gallery above the main auditorium for the press and TV cameras. The event was being shown live across the world on TV and streamed on WorldMesh. On the desk in front of her was a glass, a bottle of water and a folder containing paperwork; including an introduction to the conference and agenda, a speakers' bio list, the smaller optional workshops and many other details. When everybody had taken their seats the first session began. The display screen played a short film consisting entirely of emotional vignettes and music depicting scenes from across the world. Fishermen in Bali casting nets, suited men in New York talking on roamphones, Eskimos in Greenland, Bedouin in the Sahara, Aborigines in Australia. Then a voice announced the arrival on stage of the mistress-of-ceremonies, a young woman with the dark skin of a local Middle Easterner; she wore a traditional Arabian dress with an ankle-length skirt, full sleeves and a headscarf or *hijab*. However she spoke perfect English with an educated British accent and her bio said she had been one of the top graduates at Oxford the last year before Saucer Day closed all British universities. "Welcome, ladies and gentlemen; and welcome, all the people of planet earth!" she began dramatically raising her hands in the air. She did a six minute speech in Arabic and then switched to English. She spoke poetically and persuasively about how the world was emerging from a crisis caused by the impact of Disclosure. "Now we are experiencing the most terrible crisis the world has faced for a millennium!" she announced. "But in Chinese there is a word that translates as both 'crisis' and 'opportunity'. Yes, we face dangers, uncertainties for the future; we are forced to take action to prevent this world ceasing to exist... but at the same time, we know so much more about how our world works on a human level and a political level. We know we are not alone in this universe. We may even live in a galaxy teaming with life. For the first time ever we have the means to transform the planet for the benefit of all its people..." She went on for about half an hour, introducing the speakers and giving a rundown of the conference's structure. She got a thunderous round of applause at the end of her speech. She bowed gracefully then retired to her chairwoman's seat. Three more people came up and gave an introductory statement for the summit who were all far less interesting and erudite than the MC; Siobhan daydreamed through their addresses. Then the MC announced: "Thank you to all the speakers for their introductions. Now we will begin the first specialized session; it is on the subject of nature and the environment. Could Prof. Alexandra Maine please take the floor?... Thank you." The MC then gave an introduction to the first speaker and the audience gave her a polite round of applause.

Prof Maine was a thin woman with long straight hair dressed in a colourful tie-dyed two-piece suit. She was blanched and her bony hands were shaking, as if with stage fright. However when she started talking it became clear that the subject matter of her speech was what caused her unease. She had a thick wad of papers with her and most of her speech consisted of her reading out a list of statistics. "It is only now that the true scale of the damage to the earth's biosphere has become apparent. The pre-Saucer authorities kept the truth from the people to avoid mass global panic.

Half the entire biomass of the oceans has disappeared within the last decade. Some species, such as the scrombrid family that include tuna, mackerel and most other edible fish, have depleted by ninety percent. Coral reefs are now approaching the fifty percent mark compared to what they were in pre-industrial times. Over twenty percent of the Amazon rainforest has been destroyed and this pattern is reflected in rainforests across Africa, the Far East and Australia. Topsoil erosion has reached epidemic proportions. The world's population has recently passed three billion and we have less than sixty percent of the arable land left to feed them when the world's population was below one billion. The temperature in the atmosphere and oceans are rising fast and carbon emissions are increasing exponentially. In 1955 humanity's total gross carbon emissions were less than two billion tons; in 1958 they were five point eight billion and last year they came out at fifteen billion..."

"What does she mean by 'carbon'?" Siobhan whispered to her father who was sitting next to her.

"Carbon dioxide. It's recently been rebranded." He rolled his eyes.

"But isn't that a natural part of the air?"

"It's plant food. But there's a new idea that it causes the earth's temperature to rise due to the greenhouse effect..." He cut off as somebody in the row behind him shushed them.

"The ice caps are melting!" continued Prof. Maine. "The Arctic sea ice is half what it was during the war and half of Greenland is paused to slide into the sea. If this happens the sea level will rise by twenty feet. This would inundate millions of square miles of coastline and drown over thirty cities, including Dubai. The refugee crisis from such a disaster..."

Siobhan's heart sank. All this talk of catastrophe was depressing. She opened her matchbook and logged in to the conference centre's wireless network. She searched *global warming* and *climate change* and was relieved to find that climate scientists were not one hundred percent certain that what Prof Maine was saying regarding temperature rise was correct. The dissenters were a minority, but they were a sizeable one. What's more the tone of Prof. Maine's lecture changed very suddenly. She paused and looked up from her papers. This got everybody's attention because she'd hardly stopped to draw breath during the last forty minutes. She smiled. "But, it's not too late... We can reverse this damage, all of it. We've come pretty close to the point of no return, but we have not passed it. Now, for the first time ever we have removed the individuals from power who have been the enablers of the system that caused this destruction. Don't get me wrong; we should not be complacent. The pan is still hot, it is very very hot; but the flame has turned off and maybe it can now cool."

"It's not too late." somebody in the row in front muttered. Somebody else copied them a few seats along. "It's not too late."

"Immediate action is essential." stressed the professor. "We must begin the introduction of the new tech as soon as possible. Fossil fuel use must be eliminated, or at least reduced to minimal levels, as a matter of the utmost urgency. If we delay we may cross the line, the point of no return. Then the frozen methane hydrate deposits on the sea bed will thaw and evaporate, filling the atmosphere with a greenhouse gas ten times more absorbent than carbon. If that happens it's all over. We can never bring the earth's climate back to normal no matter what we do. It's a race against time!" She ended her speech a few minutes later to enthusiastic but perturbed applause.

The conference took a break for twenty minutes and Siobhan went to the leisure areas of the facility and was served some dark and strong local coffee. After that a former US Navy admiral did a speech about marine litter. In the middle of the Atlantic and Pacific oceans there were huge patches of floating debris, mostly plastic shopping bags; millions of tons of them. He suggested specially-designed ships be built to clear up that debris. He displayed his own design for one on the giant wall screen at the front. It showed a ship with two armatures protruding from the bow with a special net to push through the water filtering out the litter. Discarded fishing nets were even more dangerous because they could entangle whales and dolphins. After he had finished a man came on stage to draw on the point made by Prof Maine about topsoil erosion. He was an agricultural scientist who had spent years working in Brazil and had made a remarkable discovery about a substance called *Terra Preta*, "black soil" in Portuguese. This was a man-made self-reproducing medium that provided a very fertile growing matrix for all kinds of crops. It was invented by the Amazon Indians centuries ago to produce enough food to survive in the Amazon basin where the natural soil is very poor for farming. Much of the destruction of the Amazon was due to the rainforest being continuously cleared for farmland and then only used once because of the poor soil quality before the farmers moved on to burn more forest. *Terra Preta* increased the yield of farmland a dozen times. The scientist wanted to mass produce *Terra Preta* all over the world to solve the planet's food shortage and environmental problems. "With *Terra Preta*," he said. "you could feed your family from a window box. No need to plough up the countryside and fill it with chemicals." The rest of the day was devoted to discussions on climate change. Sometimes dialogue would be in foreign languages and Siobhan had to put on a set of earphones where live English translation came through. Several of the speakers disagreed with Prof. Maine and thought that it *was* too late; humans had passed the point of no return already and active steps would need to be taken to mitigate the effects of climate change. Their ideas were collectively christened "geoengineering".

The day's proceedings ended at six PM and Siobhan spent another two hours filming with the documentary producers and broadcasting a summery for CBS News. She felt like a mobile mouth, reciting the words almost subconsciously. She then went back to her hotel totally fatigued. It was odd that she was so tired when she's spent the whole day sitting down. It was nervous exhaustion, she realized. She had found the themes of that first day's sessions very grim. It was twilight when she'd finished dinner without it feeling much less hot and humid, but the chilled air of her bedroom sent her off to sleep within minutes.

....

She looked forward to the following day a lot more because her friends would be speaking. She sat down eagerly in her seat and opened the agenda. The MC gave an opening address and introduced the first speaker. "Ladies and gentlemen, this session is now in progress and I'd like to introduce the first speaker. We are honoured to have on this stage the candidate for President of the United States and former director of the US Federal Disclosure and Reconstruction Agency, Henry Dealey. Mr Dealey, please take the floor."

Dealey wore a same dark suit he had on the plane. He appeared to be sweating despite the cool atmosphere in the auditorium. "Ladies and gentlemen, people of the world." He had a snide voice and spoke with a light urban Midwestern accent. "In 1895 Rudyard Kipling wrote a poem simply called *If*. It includes the line: *'If you can watch the things you gave your life to broken. And stoop and build them up with worn-out tools'*. That is what we, the human race, the citizens of this planet, have had to endure. Our entire civilization has fallen apart. Why? Because we were faced with the reality of what our society was built upon; a corrupt and manipulative clique of crooks who used, abused and lied to us! That revelation is inevitably a shock, but a shock cannot last forever and it has not. We humans have given our lives to build our civilization. Over thousands of years we created it out of nothing. We lifted ourselves out of a primitive past into a superb modern world of genius. All that was broken." His voice rose. "However we are picking up our worn out tools! We are stooping down and we are building it up again!"

The audience clapped.

Dealey then gave a litany of the successes the FDRA had achieved. All the power stations it had got working again, the railways now running, the schools that were open to pupils. "We have done much good work, but we still have much more to do. That duty is being carried out by my successor and former deputy John Crawley. My duty is no longer to lead the FDRA; my duty is now to lead the United States of America!"

There was a muttering from the front row of the audience. The MC gave Dealey a sharp look. Siobhan guessed he had been told not to use this platform for his presidential campaign.

"To get the job done we're going to have to be tough. We're going to have to be hard. We're going to have to be willing to concentrate one hundred percent! Concentrate on nothing else but taking our world by the scruff of its neck and dragging it back onto its feet; shoving our fist into the small of its back and pushing it on down the trail!" He paused, as if anticipating applause. None came so he continued. "Yesterday we heard a lot of idle talk about 'new tech'. I appreciate the good work being done by scientists and innovators; but, quite frankly, deviations and distractions like that are the absolute *last* thing we need in this world right now. It is futile and counter-productive to plan the new house unless you have repaired the existing foundations. We're in a situation in which the foundation blocks are teetering in unstable equilibrium. We are walking the narrow path to reconstruction along the edge of a precipice at the bottom of which lies the turmoil and barbarism we have just escaped from. Ladies and gentlemen, our infrastructure is in disarray!"

"Is it?" whispered Clane to his daughter.

She shook her head. "Not anymore."

Dealey was sweating profusely. His collar and armpits had damp patches on them. He began shouting. "To put it bluntly, we don't have time to putz around with gravity star-drives and witches broomsticks made of time-warp fairy dust! We have real, solid, material problems to deal with! If we're going to save this planet then we are going to have to introduce a regime of the most ruthless pragmatism the world has ever seen! From this day forward, everybody walks hard! Everybody gets down! Everybody does double duty!... At the end of Kipling's poem he says: *'If you can fill the unforgiving minute with sixty seconds' worth of distance run, yours is the Earth and everything that's in it.'* I swear to you, if I have my way we will fill every unforgiving *milli*second! The earth, and everything that's in it, shall be ours!... Thank you!"

Most of the delegation leapt to their feet and roared their approval. There were a few exceptions including Siobhan and her father. They stayed in their seats with their arms folded, staring at the backs and bottoms in front of them.

....

The mood in the leisure room was bleak. Siobhan sat at a table with Dr Jenny Bulstrode and Gordon Stephens. Siobhan was checking social media on her matchbook. The forums were buzzing over Dealey's speech and the news networks were reporting that "#DealeyForPresident" was now trending ahead of "#It'sNotTooLate", the previous phrase that had hit the top of the list yesterday. Clane sipped his coffee quietly and Gordon scratched the bald patch on his scalp thoughtfully.

Dr Bulstrode broke the silence. "I'm speaking today."

Clane looked up. "Today?"

"Yes. Didn't you know?" She spoke very casually about it.

"No, I never checked. I thought they'd moved you down to the Q and A."

"Senator Kennedy organized it."

He smiled. "I'm even surer he's got my vote now."

"There's only one problem." said Siobhan, looking at her guidebook. "Angus Pickup is here and he's on stage right after Jenny."

Dr Bulstrode frowned. "Damn it!... He must have been brought over with Dealey's delegation."

"Well, he is the FDRA's top scientist."

"He's the FDRA's top asshole."

Siobhan did a location broadcast for CBS outside the arena in the baking heat of the late morning: "After that unexpected rousing address by Henry Dealey, independent presidential candidate, the mood of the summit has changed. An energy has built among the people here that we are facing the need for genuine work and not just discussing abstract principles. What will happen this afternoon is anybody's guess, but I predict some controversy ahead as the meeting moves on to discuss the progress of scientific analysis of the secret technology that was hidden by those who have been called the keepers of the Truth Embargo..." After they cut she went to the restroom and washed her face. She was finding it difficult to wear her TV smile and talk in her TV tone of voice. "I'm tired of reporting the news." she told Gordon Stephens. "I want to start making it."

"That's what your boyfriend is doing?" he replied.

"What?"

He showed her his matchbook. It was a news story on one of the meshboards of Julian's organization about a protest in Washington DC in support of Henry Dealey. It primarily consisted of civil rights activists and libertarians, but it also included Marxists and other leftists. Julian's photo was there. It was taken on the street with large buildings behind him. The protest had broken up when the internal factions began fighting each other.

"Oh God, I hope he's OK." She E-grammed him and had to wait a tense thirty-five minutes before he replied in the affirmative.

....

"... and Dr Bulstrode stepped in to provide essential assistance to the United States in defeating the keepers of the Truth Embargo. We're very honoured to have her with us in Dubai today. Dr Jenny Bulstrode, please take the floor." The MC clapped professionally while everybody else cheered. Siobhan and Clane jumped up and down clapping with their hands in the air. Dr Bulstrode stepped shyly onto the stage. She was wearing her lab coat; she saw no need to dress differently just because she was speaking at an international political conference. She began: "When a crime is committed, the first step to working out who did it is to find out how it happened. If you have a body, are there bullet holes in it, poison in the bloodstream or a stab wound in the chest?" She displayed the Danlue film, the famous amateur footage of the destruction of the Empire State Building on Mars Day in 1947. "Look. It doesn't burn up, nor does it collapse and fall to the ground. It turns to dust in midair." She went on to detail the evidence she had gathered which inspired her book. Her tone was matter-of-fact, knowledgeable and calm; a remarkable contrast to Dealey's zealous rhetoric. "Who has built a weapon like this? Where did they get the technology? You realize this kind of destructive power exceeds even that of the hydrogen bomb." She spent forty-five minutes showing some diagrams, graphs and photographs from her work at Area 51 and explaining what they were. "The spinning disk generator is probably the most exciting discovery because of the practical applications possible from it. We believe this is an adaptation of the back-engineered extraterrestrial technology captured during the Roswell incident and many others. There is a vast amount of material to examine and our work has only just begun, but I believe that the development of the spinning disk should be prioritized, for the reasons mentioned yesterday related to the earth's economic, social and environmental problems. We are on the brink of obtaining access to an energy supply that is clean, free, safe and limitless, both in power and endurance. It has already been used to destroy, now let us use it to create. The world needs this technology and it needs it now. Thank you."

Siobhan was on her feet before Dr Jenny Bulstrode's voice had stopped echoing around the chamber. As she hoped, others followed her lead and Dr Bulstrode received an even bigger standing ovation than Henry Dealey had. Dr Bulstrode smiled modestly and bowed her head as she walked off stage.

After the break, the summit reconvened. The MC leaned towards her microphone. "Ladies and gentlemen, the next speaker is the chief research officer of the US Federal Disclosure and Reconstruction Agency. He has been leading the scientific mission at Area 51 for over a year. He is the former professor of mechanical engineering at the University of Glasgow in Scotland and was also the head of applied physics at the Massachusetts Institute of Technology. He has done consultancy work for the Battelle Memorial Institute and has sat on the board of the National Science Foundation. Today he dedicates all his time to his government work. Prof. Angus Pickup, please take the floor."

The tall, bulky old Scotsman stepped slowly and carefully, one step at a time, up onto the stage and towards the podium. His white fluffy hair and beard made his head look like a dandelion. He faced the audience and put his spectacles on dramatically. "Good afternoon, conference. I'd like to begin by paying homage to a brilliant scientist, a genius; somebody without whom my project at Area 51 could never succeed. I am talking about the previous speaker, Dr Jenny Bulstrode. Without her, we would have achieved nothing. She is the kind of engineer I would like to be, the kind I wish I could be; but I will never reach her standards... The world will need idealists like her in future times. It is the visionaries and neophiles who embrace innovation and create new golden ages. It is a tragedy for Dr Bulstrode, simply because she was born fifty years too soon. There will be a time in the future for romantics and dreamers, a day when we will need Don Quixote to ride his horse towards the windmill; we will need Water Mitty to drive his seaplane into the teeth of the storm. But that time is not now... For this reason I speak against the proposal made by Dr Bulstrode. The crisis caused by Saucer Day and the global effort to recover from it requires policy made by people with their focus firmly directed towards the *real* world." He described the repair of the social and industrial network. "I must congratulate most of all Siobhan Quilley whom I had the pleasure of meeting at Area 51 last year and whom I believe is in the room right now." He did not look at where Siobhan was sitting, if he even knew. He talked for a few minutes about the same subjects as Dealey had the previous day, trains and aircraft services resuming; hydroelectric dams and nuclear power stations up and running. He then explained in detail, for over an hour, about how the direction Dr Bulstrode had chosen was, in his opinion, a dead end. "We don't have the time or resources to indulge in fantasy!" he said slowly and emphatically. "Everything Dr Bulstrode has talked to you about is nothing more than woolly frivolity... You may wonder if therefore I am totally opposed to all scientific creativity; no I am not. On the contrary, I am a keen supporter of the irrigation project in Abyssinia, which was started and organized primarily by Clane Quilley, father of Siobhan. This operation employed a new tech system I feel could be very beneficial in the immediate post-reconstruction era, the Digby Carrousel." He described the history and function of the machine. "But even the Digby has to wait. As Director Dealey said yesterday, we need the existing infrastructure working first. Therefore the timeline of my own proposal comes in three stages: reconstruction, reconstruction and reconstruction. It is on the support of these three pillars, that we can develop the Digby Carrousel and build the future world that humanity wants, needs and deserves. Thank you."

....

"An asshole!" Dr Jenny Bulstrode repeated in the leisure room afterwards. She was scowling and her face was pink with frustration. "A lying, patronizing, condescending, arrogant prick!"

"Why's he doing it, Jenny?" asked Clane.

"I don't know." she shrugged. "Workshop politics was never my best subject."

"Is that all it is?" asked Gordon. "Some kind of personal rivalry?"

"It has to be!" she yelled; then lowered her voice, remembering she was in a public place. "You've read my paper on the spinning disk. You've read my book on the Empire State Building; you've seen my talks... My conclusion is irrefutable! I've reached it through science that is absolutely watertight. I am honestly and absolutely my own worst critic and my peers are almost as bad. How can old Pick-Nose possibly stand there and trash me like that? How dare he!?"

Clane nodded. "He's up to something."

"Yes." Siobhan nodded. "But what is it?"

....

The day's proceedings ended on a low note. The delegates filed through to the foyer where the cars queued up. An usher held open the back door of one for Siobhan. "Thank you." she said and got in. As the door was closing another hand grabbed it and forced it back open. "Mind if I join

159

you?" A man climbed in and suddenly filled the space on the seat beside her. He flashed his gorgeous smile at her.

"Senator Kennedy." She shrunk back from him, moving to the far side of the seat, feeling embarrassed.

"Call me 'Jack'. It's a shame you never took me up on my offer of dinner the other night. Perhaps now would be more convenient for you."

"Er..." she found herself nodding.

He leaned forward and spoke to the driver. "The Palm Jebel Ali Hotel please." They drove away from the Downtown area along a wide motorway for over half an hour until they came to another island of working buildings amidst the construction site. They crossed a bridge over a stretch of water; the setting sun glistened on the shallow waves. Ahead was a huge building that was clearly modern, but had been influenced by Middle Eastern architectural styles and had the aura of a medieval caliph's castle. The two never spoke during the journey and Kennedy kept his eyes fixed on the view, but Siobhan began to relax. At the hotel entrance a porter held the car door for them as they stepped out and another usher greeted Kennedy by name. They went up in a lift many floors; Siobhan forced a yawn to equalize the pressure on her eardrums. The restaurant was on an upper floor with a huge window all along one wall giving a spectacular view over the semi-formed Dubai skyline. The skyscrapers and pinnacles of Downtown gleamed in the ruddy evening sunlight. A man in a tuxedo played a white grand piano on a dais in the corner. The tables were covered in white cloths and the chairs were red velvet. A waiter showed them to their seats. Kennedy opened the menu. "Would you like some wine?" he asked.

"In Dubai? I thought there was Prohibition here."

"Some hotels hold special licenses."

When Siobhan saw the prices on the menu she felt a mixture of relief and guilt that her meals were all covered by her delegation expenses account. She felt quite happy because the earlier confusion in her mind was now gone. After they had ordered she decided to make her dinner companion aware of the ground rules. "You know, Jack... you're quite a guy. I understand why women like to be around you. When I received your invitation Sunday night it did make me feel... excited. The fact is though, I'm not on the market. I have a man in my life whom I love and I would never cheat on. Understood?"

Kennedy paused, then he laughed. "Goodness me, has my public persona really run that deep? Believe me, Siobhan, when I invited you out Sunday night I didn't have the slightest thought about adding you to my famous 'list'. I asked you out because I needed to talk to you urgently on a strictly business-related matter."

She looked into his face and saw not one hint of sexual intention in his expression. "I see." She felt foolish. "Apologies."

He smiled sympathetically. "No problem... I wanted to confide in you some information that I would appreciate it if you would keep confidential."

"Agreed."

"I'm going to lose the presidential election."

She jolted from shock as soon as he'd said these words. His voice was completely deadpan; the easy smile on his face didn't even twitch. "What?"

He sighed. "I've found out what's going on through a contact in the CSA. Dealey's campaign has been taken over by some very important people. They're currently schmoozing the Electoral College, trying to make them become faithless. They've also been hanging out with the committee at IBM that are designing these new electronic voting machines. It's clear they want them to be sabotaged so that a vote for me turns into a vote for Dealey. It won't need much nudging because the polls are all in equal thirds and the popular vote will probably go the same way. Dealey's accomplices are also getting involved with the NAACP, the National Association for the Advancement of Coloured People. Why? Because this is only the second election since Negroes became eligible to vote. They're an important sector for any Democratic candidate, but many are becoming sympathetic to Dealey, mostly thanks to his persuasion machine; even Dr King who will be speaking tomorrow."

"Who are they? These 'important people'?"

"It's better that you don't know at this stage, Siobhan. It could be dangerous for you if you did." He glanced nervously over his shoulder as if worried that there were eavesdroppers.

"But what they're doing is a conspiracy to commit electoral fraud! You need to call the FBI, Jack!"

He shook his head. "Goldwater's FBI director is Mason Grumman... Well, he's also a consultant to the FDRA."

She shook her head in disbelief. "Jack, you can't just give up."

"I'm not. However, I have to face facts."

"Let me do an expose on it! I'll produce a goddamn documentary."

"Siobhan." He lowered his eyebrows and looked at her hard. "Who is your current head of programmes?"

"James Aubrey of course."

"Who spoke last week in Memphis... at a Henry Dealey rally, and has received a twenty thousand dollar honorarium from the FDRA."

"Then he'll never agree to it... My God! What's going on?"

"What's going on is that Dealey is being given the Oval Office by corruption."

"But he can't win; he's an independent candidate."

"So was George Washington."

There was a pause as their food arrived with the wine. They kept silent until they were alone again at the table. "Why is this happening, Jack?" she asked. Siobhan sipped her wine. It was a fine old red, a pre-Disclosure Shiraz from California; but it tasted insipid.

"Difficult to tell. However, he seems very keen that things should stay as they are. Notice how he and that Scottish scientist spent a lot of time speaking out against the use of the new tech."

"Not completely. They were all in favour of the Digby Carrousel."

"In favour? Not really. I would say they gave it the requisite airing. They can't state publicly that they are completely against the new tech can they?"

"What do you mean, Jack?"

"Dr Bulstrode's spinning disk looks far more promising to me. Why are they so opposed to it?"

"Because it doesn't work?"

Kennedy hesitated and gave a grimace. "What if they're opposed to it because it *does* work?"

....

Siobhan had a mild hangover when she awoke the following morning. This was strange because she and Kennedy had shared just one bottle of wine between them and he'd had three glasses while she had two. It was as if the forbidden infamy of alcohol in the UGE had poisoned the drink itself. She showered down and had breakfast. When she felt better she stepped out onto her chalet's patio. The sun was up and the heat of the day was already fierce compared to the cooled indoors. She gazed up at the clean blue cloudless sky and thought about the conversation she'd had over dinner. She wasn't sure what to think; and she wasn't obliged to for a while because today's proceedings were on an entirely different subject; what was the intelligence that was engaging the human race. The first to speak was a young American academic who had been a keen student of the extraterrestrial phenomenon ever since Disclosure Day in 1947 and had written several books about it. He looked nervous as he stood at the podium and read from a script: "Who are they?... That is the first question everybody is going to ask. There are a number of possibilities that we can immediately consider. Extraterrestrial beings are just one of them; there are many others. Could they be intelligent machines, supercomputers beyond anything humanity can manufacture? Maybe they actually live right here on earth, but we've simply never crossed paths with them. They could come from deep below the oceans in the unknown world of the seabed. It could be they travel from parallel universes, other worlds like our own that exist in the fourth dimension of space. More and more cosmologists tell us such worlds actually exist. The same experts claim time travel is impossible, at least when going backwards. But what if they're wrong? What if these beings are genuine time-travellers? Alternatively, and most extremely, they could be angels from heaven, or demons from hell!" He widened his eyes for shock effect. "Then again perhaps they are all of the above, or some of the above, acting together on our planet... But what if they are *none* of the above? Something else that we haven't thought of or maybe even have no conception of?" After him came the congressman from Alabama, Dr Martin Luther King, who Siobhan had interviewed on the plane. The smartly-dressed black man stepped regally up to the microphone and the moment he started speaking everybody sat up. Dr King was the greatest orator that Siobhan had ever heard. He made many of the same points he had brought up during her interview on the plane, about the plight of black people in America being similar to that of the extraterrestrials who came to the Earth at Roswell; but he did it with so much grandeur, so much wit, so much poignancy that his voice was the only sound in existence for all the hundreds of delegates in the room. Take it away and a pin dropping would be have been audible. Millions more across the world must have been similarly rapt. An hour passed before anybody had known it and he built up to a verbal crescendo like no other. The round of applause following it may have been lower on volume that previous ovations, but the passion behind it was unprecedented. Siobhan stopped clapping early to dab the tears of emotion from her eyes and she saw others doing the same. "And America needs an exceptional man at this exceptional time!" continued King. "Cometh the hour! Cometh the man! There is only one man the nation and the world and all people of all colours, creeds and tongues can look to lead them to the Promised Land! And that man is Henry Austin Dealey, the future President of the United States!..."

Siobhan gasped. She could almost feel the magic instantly dissipate like a deflating balloon. It was as if, at the moment of his most magnificent words, King has suddenly stuck out his tongue and blown a raspberry or put a clowns' red nose on. He spoke for another ten minutes and then finished his speech, but it was the most monumental anticlimax. She looked around her at the faces of her fellow delegates as they filed out of the room. Most were trying to hide it, but the baffled frowns and disappointed scowls were clear that she wasn't the only one who felt let down. In the leisure room she caught John Kennedy's eyes across the chamber. His expression was unreadable. Siobhan and her allies didn't talk much as they sipped coffee. She saw Dr King walk into the room and felt a plume of anger. She had liked and admired him from when she'd first met him. His speech could have been one of the greatest in history. How could he make such a mistake? However she still wasn't exactly sure what that mistake was.

....

The next day was the fourth and penultimate day of the World Disclosure and Reconstruction Summit. Siobhan had a lot of TV work to do when she arrived at the Sheikh Al Nahyan Conference Centre. She had so far managed to avoid having to speak to Henry Dealey again, but a curt E-gram from Cronkite that morning left her no choice. She asked him the perfunctory questions and he gave his usual answers, his voice dripping with his requisite slippery confidence. Siobhan knew that if she dared to ask him questions based on the accusations John Kennedy made he would see to it that she never hosted a programme on CBS ever again. She knew she had to do something, but she wasn't sure what. She went and washed in the bathroom as soon as the director had yelled "cut!" Her period had started and she felt ill; her belly ached and she lacked energy. She was also, for the first time ever, feeling a dislike for her job. She longed to go back to her hotel and lie in bed all day. The first session of the day was a discussion about the parts of the world known as the "Dark Zone" where recovery from Saucer Day was much slower; in fact in some places it had hardly progressed at all. This included most of Europe, Africa and Australia. Several senior military officers spoke unapologetically about the possible need for a bombing campaign. Siobhan found it hard to concentrate and tuned out every so often. After lunch there was a question and answer session where all the speakers lined up on the stage and were allowed to take questions from the floor, and also from each other. As one could easily predict, a heated argument broke out between Prof. Angus Pickup and Dr Jenny Bulstrode. "Dr Bulstrode has made a total fool of herself." began Pickup, raising his eyebrows and shaking his head as he stood at the podium. "Her book is nothing more than a five hundred-page comic. There are more pictures in it than a kindergarten scribbler and that's no surprise; it has nothing useful to say in terms of its words. If I were in her place I would be utterly ashamed of my work. I would immediately recall the title from press and pulp all the copies in stock! She posits garbled incoherencies about laser beams from space zapping the Empire State Building into dust... and she expects to be taken seriously as a scientist? She totally ignores the evidence my team have gathered that prove the ESB was brought down by a controlled demolition involving thermite, a conventional method that was already in use by the industry. No need to invoke mystical weaponry from Flash Gordon's starship."

Dr Jenny Bulstrode had been sitting hunched on her chair with a purple face and gritted teeth the whole time Pickup had been talking. At this point she exploded like an overfilled balloon and leaped to her feet. "What evidence!?" she yelled.

"Quiet please!" scolded the MC.

"You have no evidence and you insult me!..."

"Quiet please!" she repeated.

"Sit down, Dr Bulstrode." said Pickup. "You may not have the floor."

"I demand the right to reply to that!..." yelled Dr Bulstrode at the chairwoman.

"You may not have the floor." His voice was calm and superior, as if he were advising a teenage girl.

"Dr Bulstrode, you will have a chance to speak after Prof. Pickup has finished." said the chair in a cool professional tone. "Until then please do not interrupt. Prof. Pickup, that interjection will not be taken from your allotted time."

Dr Bulstrode thumped back down into her chair folding her arms and staring at the floor.

"Thank you!... If I may continue... Thermite is a mixture of powdered aluminium and ferrous oxide; rust in layman's terms. It is a pyrotechnic used in welding and cutting. When ignited it produces intense heat that can melt metals in a localized area, cutting through a steel beam for example.

My team found tiny red-grey coloured chips in the debris. Their chemical composition matched exactly that of melted and unburned thermite mixed with molten iron. This is smoking gun evidence that thermite was used to demolish the Empire State Building." He spoke for another fifteen minutes giving details.

The moment he had finished Dr Jenny Bulstrode jumped to her feet and the MC invited her to the podium. "Thermite residue in the debris shower? Where's your evidence, Prof. Pickup? None of the demolition experts nor the FBI reports mention any other evidence of thermite cuts on any of the structures remaining after the attack. You think somebody else would have noticed other things like the welds and scorch marks. And what about all the fuses and wiring? If ESB was a controlled demolition then it is the biggest the world has ever seen. It can take weeks to rig even a small and empty building for explosive demolition. How on earth did they manage one over twelve hundred feet tall under the noses of all the busy office staff? A verified chain of possession needs to be established before those chips you found can be linked to thermite used in your hypothetical controlled demolition. Thousands of tons of thermite would have been needed to achieve what we saw. Inside that building is there even an adequate air supply for the detonation?..."

"Ther*mate*!" Pickup butted in from his chair. "It must have been thermate! With an oxidizer mixed in!"

"Now you're speculating!" she retorted. "How do you know these chips didn't come from something else. Aluminum? Iron? There was tons of it in the ESB; in the furniture, in the gypsum wall panels, in the plumbing. And how are you supposed to cut through a vertical beam? That would have been necessary for collapse. Thermite can only burn downwards; the reacting material falls down by gravity..."

"Containment pads!" Pickup was wearing the same angry expression Dr Bulstrode had previously.

"Quite please!" interjected the chairwoman.

Dr Bulstrode snorted. "And where are the remains of these containment pads, Professor? You see how your theory needs a higher and higher pile of speculation and assumption at every turn?"

On the floor Clane turned to his daughter and they exchanged amused grins.

"Where were the visible flames?" the engineer continued. "With a thousand tons of thermite detonating all at once the ESB should have blazed like a lit firework as it went down. Yet there was no light or thermal signature at all."

At the next break the leisure room was far livelier than before. It rang with triumphant laughter. Everybody praised the tenacity of Dr Jenny Bulstrode.

....

League of the World Declaration 1749

Adopted and opened for signature, ratification and accession by LoW General Assembly resolution 1749 on Friday 19th August 1960. Entry into force Monday 12th September 1960 in accordance with Article 18 of the LoW Constitution.

Agreed Resolutions of the Treaty of Dubai-for Global Disclosure and Reconstruction following Saucer Day (Tuesday 11th September 1957)

Article 1: Repair of the pre-Saucer Day infrastructure on a local, national and international basis is the top priority and will be the first stage of reconstruction.

Article 2: The introduction of the new technology must be achieved as soon as possible after full completion of the first stage. The focus will be on the Digby Carrousel as it is generally accepted to be the most promising method for development.

Article 3: Plans will be put in motion to restore the planet earth's natural environment to a pre-civilization natural state by any means necessary.

Article 4. The regions of the world known as the "Dark Zone" will be explored and assessed and if necessary occupied by an LoW restoration and peacekeeping mission until infrastructure can be restored.

....

The closing day of the Dubai Summit was more light-hearted and relaxed than the previous ones. There was almost a party atmosphere as the delegates and panel read through the text of the draft treaty and voted on its points. Most points were decided by a show of hands and on only two occasions was it necessary to hold a formal poll. This process took the whole morning because there were dozens of subsections and footnotes to all four articles. After lunch there was another panel discussion and Clane Quilley took part. He received a warm round of applause as he stepped up onto the stage and the panellists asked him a series of questions about his world-changing adventure on Saucer Day. The story was, of course, well-known to everybody, it was one of the most famous tales in the world; but to hear the classic story from the central character himself was an exclusive treat. At the end of his speech Henry Austin Dealey got to his feet, still clapping. He approached the podium. "Thank you, Mr Quilley... And now, as we leave the past behind us and look forward to the future, we need to think of the future generation. Clane Quilley has contributed to building that first new generation himself because he has two children and one of them is here, in this room today."

Siobhan shrank back into her seat, wondering what was coming next.

"Last year western Pennsylvania was a part of the Dark Zone. There was no electricity, no running water, no law and order. Some people fled to the cities, others stayed and got on with their lives as best as they could, accepting their terrible new situation. However, one gutsy and ingenious student journalist decided to single-handedly pick her community up and drag it back into the civilized world. That brave and invincible young woman is now the face and voice of daytime news on CBS; she is also bringing the world news of this very conference. I am talking of course about Siobhan Quilley!"

At his cue, a round of applause broke out in the room. Siobhan blushed. Everything happened very quickly. A steward closed on her seat and gestured at her to stand. Smiling faces passed her dazed eyes as she walked along the aisle between the rows of seats. She was now climbing up the steps onto the stage and being blinded by a row of arc-lights. The sudden emergence into open space made her feel agoraphobic and vulnerable. She felt her cheeks radiate as she surveyed the sea of people in the audience. She was hit by a pang of dizziness and stumbled slightly. She was led to the podium and an acrid-smelling microphone was pushed into her face. She felt Henry Dealey lightly touching her shoulder. "Siobhan, welcome."

She regained her broadcasting poise. "Thank you."

"Now, we've known each other probably for longer than anybody else here. The first time we spoke was last May when you called the office of the FDRA and I happened to be there to take your call."

This was not an accurate rendition; the person Siobhan had initially talked to had only alerted Dealey when Siobhan had bluffed her status as a reporter. However this was not the place where she could tactfully correct him. "I remember, yes."

"At the time you were at the gates of a power plant trying to persuade the staff to return to work. Why did you decide to take the bull by the horns the way you did and restore your local community to full functionality?"

"I was tired of living without the usual amenities. The services broke down just hours after they were restored and I acted out of frustration." She spent about twenty minutes on stage in public conversation with Henry Dealey. She kept up her professional manner, "TV Siobhan" as she called that broadcasting alter-ego. She felt annoyed with him for ambushing her the way he did. She had not been told in advance by anybody that she was going to be called to speak on stage at the conference. She had interviewed Dealey twice in Dubai following her initial recording with him on the plane during their journey and whenever she ended the discussion she felt drained. He was like a black hole, sucking the energy out of her as she sat beside him talking to him. Every time he answered one of her questions she braced herself. Even his most innocuous words felt like accusations or insults. It was strange because he was always polite, calm and statesmanlike towards her, more so than some others she had dealt with during the week; but she couldn't stand to be near him. As she stepped down from the stage at the end of her impromptu address she quietly sighed with relief.

She was very busy during the last session of the conference because this was the highlight of the entire event, the official signing of the Dubai Treaty. She provided a live running commentary as the panel area filled up with the signatories including President Goldwater, the Taoiseach of Ireland, Caliph Al Nahyan of the UGE, King Abdulaziz al Saud of Saudi Arabia, the Secretary-General of the League of the World and several others. The men were all handed copies of the finished Treaty document and gold barrelled fountain pens. Shutters clicked and camera flash bulbs flickered as they solemnly added their signatures on the correct dotted lines. After that there was a great cheer from the entire assembly and the world leaders all walked round to the front and held hands together in the air like a triumphant sports team as the room reverberated to the sound of revelry, as did the whole world. "The world is now free and safe." said Siobhan emphatically, staring into the camera lens. "This is the moment it happened, right here, right now... This is the moment we begin again, a new world, a new people and a new era."

....

The atmosphere on the plane home was far more subdued than the journey there. Everybody was exhausted by the week-long summit and there were more than a few first to second degree hangovers among the passengers as a result of the party to celebrate the signing of the Dubai Treaty the previous evening in one of the licensed hotels. Siobhan had polished off a good few glasses of pre-Disclosure Beaujolais and could still feel it. The heavy meal of exotic food that she'd chased down with the wine had not helped her condition. She spent the first few hours of the flight lying in her seat with a wet flannel over her eyes. At about midday she got up she decided to have a hair of the dog that bit her, and ordered a light beer from the bar. The space was empty apart from the stewardess. As soon as Siobhan had her drink she sat on one of the cushioned benches and sipped slowly, letting her fuzzy mind drift.

"Mind if I join you?"

She started, almost spilling her beer. Henry Dealey had walked in quietly without her noticing and was now standing over her. She gestured to the bench next to her.

He sat opposite her and leaned his arms on the table, gazing at her in a friendly but intense way. "Apologies if I made you jump, Siobhan."

She shrugged and smiled thinly.

"You did a great job at the summit, you know that? I've been watching some of the recordings of your live feeds and I am very impressed."

"Thank you, Mr Dealey. I'm glad you appreciate my contribution to the proceedings."

"Call me Henry."

"OK... Henry."

He paused. "A woman with your skills and position has a lot of influence on public opinion."

She shrugged again. "I guess so."

He chuckled. "Skip the false modesty, Siobhan. It's a fact... And it makes you a powerful individual in society."

"Powerful?"

"Like your father, your words could change the world."

"What do you mean?"

"July the 8th 1947, 'RAAF captures Flying Disk'."

"That was my dad's article, it's true."

"And if he had been less proficient writer imagine how different the world would be?"

She frowned. "What do you mean?"

He moved back slightly and his facial expression changed, as if he realized that he had said something he shouldn't have. He resumed on a different track: "The world needs powerful and influential people who care about the fate of the world. The world needs you." He levelled his index finger at her like Lord Kitchener.

She sighed and rubbed her aching forehead. "What's your point, Henry?"

"My point is I need your help. At the summit I've presented proof that I am the best candidate for President of the United States and that anybody who cares about the future of the nation and the planet earth beyond it *must* elect me. There is no other option. What about you Siobhan? Are you in favour of saving the world or not?"

"That should be obvious." she answered quickly. She resented the moral blackmail in his words. "What are you asking me to do?"

"Support me publicly. Attend my rallies, give interviews to my media service, write for my meshboard journal... You'll be very well-paid."

She stared at him in disbelief. His lizard-like eyes were glinting. His pasty white lower face was making an imitation of a smile. "I'm going to destroy you!" she hissed. She hadn't meant to say it. The words had issued from her mouth almost subconsciously; as if she was a tape recorder and somebody had pressed play.

Dealey didn't flinch. "No you won't, Siobhan. Even if you could you would not. You know that I hold they key to the future, the only proper future the world has. You are *going* to play a part in that future whether you want to or not."

Chapter 10

The train braked hard, waking Siobhan up. She shook her head and pressed her nose to the window as they slowly drifted along the tracks towards the railway terminal. The doors of the train swished open, she alighted and ran her ticket through the turnstile then headed out of the concourse into the street. She was looking forward to seeing him, but still felt a little apprehensive. Julian had been acting strangely during her last few Mesh and telephone conversations. There he was, standing outside the station entrance waiting for her with his usual smile. She did a double-take; but no, it was him. His hair had grown somewhat. His brown curly locks were now thick and spherical, surrounding his head like an afro. His chin was covered by a sparse, patchy beard that felt odd against her own chin as she kissed him. He wore small round sunglasses and denims with a white T-shirt peeking between the seams of the jacket. His car was a mid-range hatchback, neither smart nor dirty. The back seat was covered with the standard university shambles of folders and books dumped on top of a matchbook computer. "You look more like a student than a tutor." Siobhan remarked as they drove out of the station carpark.

Julian shrugged and tittered. "Do you like it? It makes me feel more liberated, more of an individual."

"I don't think Durham would approve."

"Fuck Durham! I don't give a shit what they think!" he spat with a vehemence that shocked Siobhan into silence.

They drove to the town of Concord about thirty miles away. "Where are you taking me?" Siobhan asked.

"A meeting. Is that OK?"

"What kind of meeting?"

"A political meeting."

"Er... I'm not sure; I've never been to a political meeting before."

"If you don't want to, that's fine." Julian was speaking to her a gentler tone now. "You can just go to a bar or stay in my digs and watch TV if you'd rather."

"No, that's OK. I don't mind tagging along."

When they reached Concord they drove to a boxy wooden house in a residential district of well-spaced blocks. Siobhan had expected a political meeting to be held in some official location like an office or city hall, but instead it was in the lounge of the house. The residents of the house were all students. There were three men and three women, all a few years younger than her. They were all dressed differently and none were related or in a relationship with each other. One of the men had long, straight feminine hair reaching down to his shoulders and one of the women had her hair cut very short and gelled into even spikes. She wore a lurid pink T-shirt with rips in it that looked as if they were made on purpose. Another of the men had on a rainbow-striped polo shirt and shiny silver trousers with blue sequins along the hems. Siobhan gazed at them in wonder, feeling old for the first time in her life. The doorbell rang every few minutes as more similar people turned up until there were about twenty in the lounge. The people in the house all shared similar political views and took them very seriously. They were not all members of Julian's Workers' Revolutionary Socialist League, but those outside the party were all sympathizers and fellow travellers to a greater or lesser degree. There were posters on every bare space of the wall. These were well-designed and drew the eye in. They had on slogans such as: "AID TO RUSSIA NOW!", "STOP THE HOUSING ACTION TRUST!-HOMES FOR PEOPLE NOT PROFIT!", "BRING BACK THE STUDENT GRANT!" and: " NO MORE CUTS-FAIR PAY FOR ALL HOSPITAL WORKERS!" Dotted in between the posters were a set of old black-and-white photographs depicting men in dark suits sitting in heroic portrait poses. Some of them Siobhan recognized, for instance there was Karl Marx and Vladimir Lenin. There were several portraits of a thinner, younger man with a bookish appearance, thick and neatly-trimmed semi-Mohican hair and a goatee beard. A pair of small reading glasses were perched on his nose. Julian noticed her looking at it and tapped her shoulder. "That's Trotsky."

"Who?"

"Leon Trotsky. The most brilliant man who ever lived." Julian shuddered with a frisson of emotion as he spoke these words.

One half of the room had been converted into an office, full of a chaotic scattering of papers, folders, computer screens and keyboards. There was large printer on top of a cabinet and piles of *Socialist Times* issues wrapped in plastic coverings. The people spoke to Julian warmly and informally even though, as Siobhan later found out, some of them were his own pupils. They greeted him with phrases like: "Hey Jules, how's it going, man?" She was astounded; never under any circumstances would she think of addressing any of her own tutors as anything other than "Professor" or "Doctor". Cups of coffee and cans of beer were passed round. Extra chairs were brought in from the kitchen to give everybody a seat and the meeting was brought to order. "Welcome, comrades." said the chairman. "Welcome to this meeting of the New Hampshire branch of the WRSL. Seeing as we have a few new faces at this meeting I'll give a brief introduction to the WRSL and what we stand for..." Siobhan learned how the Workers Revolutionary Socialist League had been formed in 1923 after it split from the Progressive Socialist Workers Party and merged with Workers Action International. The chairman gave a run-down of the various campaigns that the League had been involved with, its successes and achievements. Siobhan struggled to assimilate this completely new brand of information. She felt she was being watched and sized up by the others in the room; eyes kept turning her way. The chairman clarified some of the in-terminology for her benefit. Then a plump black woman began what they called a "lead-off" where she talked for twenty minutes or so about a pending bus drivers' strike in New Hampshire over the loss of their pension scheme. After she'd finished other members put their hands up and were called to speak by the chairman, in a similar manner to the way teachers did at school. After that the "paper organizer" gave a report on the sales of the *Socialist Times*. There were reports from the fundraiser, the student group organizer, the branch meshmaster, the secretary and finally there was any-other-business. Several hours had passed and Siobhan had understood very little of what had been discussed. She was bored and still drowsy following her delayed, sleepless flight from Las Vegas and it was now dark outside. She felt her eyelids drooping. She was also slightly tipsy from the two cans of cheap lager she'd drunk and needed the toilet. After the formal meeting ended the students hung around for while longer drinking more beers and then finally the gathering broke up. She and Julian drove through the night to Julian's accommodation at the Durham campus. Julian was in a manically energized mood and talked continuously the whole way about what was discussed at the meeting. Siobhan nodded her head and responded politely, but every so often she yawned and rubbed her eyes, dropping hints to her boyfriend that she was tired. To her annoyance he didn't seem to notice and only stopped talking when they got to bed and she could finally sleep. Normally on the first night when they were reunited she and Julian made love, but tonight he showed no interest. Neither did she, so they both just went to sleep.

....

She woke feeling refreshed and comfortable. She stretched her arm out to touch her lover on the other side of the bed and felt only empty sheets. Julian had already got up without waking her. The sheets were cold; he had been gone a long time. She sat up. "Jules?" There was no answer.

She eventually found him in the college refectory. He had just finished breakfast and was sipping a cup of coffee. His face lit up when he saw her, making her feel a bit better. "Morning, Siobhan." They kissed. He ordered another coffee while she ate breakfast. To her dismay, he still wanted to talk politics in a very single-minded way. She tried to change the subject, but to no avail. She was surprised how doctrinaire he had become. The refectory was the main common room for students, but tutors had their own separate dining area; however Julian told her that he rarely used it. "I don't like them and they don't like me."

"Who, Jules?"

He shrugged. "The others in the faculty."

"Why?"

"They're a bunch of rednecks."

She paused, surprised at his severity. "You mean they're conservatives?... What, all of them?"

"Pretty much."

"Well... just because you disagree on political matters doesn't mean you can't get along personally does it?"

He stared at her with an exasperated frown, as if she'd just said something obviously foolish to everybody. "Didn't you listen to a word that was said at the meeting last night? We're fighting a war here! They are our enemy!"

"A war?" Siobhan noticed that he had said "we" and "our" as if he automatically included her.

"Yes! And that makes me *persona non grata* up there." He jerked his thumb over his shoulder to indicate the tutor's private dining area.

"Are you sure? Did they tell you so straight out?"

"They didn't need to... Maybe if Dealey gets in things will change in academia; but until then I'm a fish out of water here."

"Dealey isn't a socialist." She was grateful for at least a partial change of subject.

"No, but his liberal democratic reformism will hopefully act as a trigger for a more revolutionary programme."

She nodded, failing to understand again.

He seemed to guess that and softened. "I'm sorry, Siobhan. This must be all very new to you." They went back to his flat and he gave her three books to read; two of which were just thin home-printed pamphlets: *A Modern Introduction to Marxism-Leninism*, *Communism and America*, and *Everyday Socialist Ideas*. She was surprised to find that Julian's own name was listed as the author for the last title. He had to go and teach a few classes and said before he left: "Have a read of those. They're a good way to jumping into the subject. We can talk about them when I come back."

Siobhan took Julian's literature down to the library where it was cool and quiet. She felt slightly guilty because of her father's own experience of being indoctrinated by a leftist terror group when they kidnapped him in Ireland some years ago. They also gave him books to read and talked to him about them... after they had tortured him and threatened him with death. At the same time she laughed scornfully at herself for interpreting this as any kind of comparison. Here she was, sitting in a comfortable chair at a desk at an institution of higher education in New Hampshire. The books had been given to her by the man she loved. The books outlined the ideas of Karl Marx in language a layman could understand; very different to the highbrow babble of Julian and his acquaintances. Marx had written over a century ago that human society was in a continuous struggle between the rich and poor classes. This included his conflict theory of economics, that capitalism arose out of the private ownership of the means of production by a "bourgeoisie", a group of people who run the factories, farms and other industries. The books gave explanatory examples like: "Supposing a worker produces the equivalent value of twenty dollars for a day's work. He won't get paid twenty dollars; he might get eight dollars and the factory owner keeps the twelve dollar difference. This is the owner's profit, the surplus value. Therefore it is in the interest of the factory owner to pay the worker as little as he can possibly get away with. This is essentially a form of theft and that is why there are rich and poor in society. This is also why there is economic stagnation, 'boom and bust' cycles and depressions. The 1929 stock market crash and the economic collapse that followed were caused by the runaway accumulation of capital in too few hands..." Therefore, said the books, capitalism was unsustainable, both practically and morally. The only solution was for the working classes to take control of the means of production and run it themselves through a "worker's state". This would result in a classless society based on common ownership. After a certain amount of time even that state would wither away and create the society Marx christened "communism". As she read on Siobhan became more and more interested. She was an American and had lived through the Cold War. For a whole decade the socialist east and the capitalist west had stared each other out across the two hemispheres. They even threatened each other with annihilation using nuclear bombs. The very word "communism" had been a dirty one. However she never really understood what it meant.

She and Julian met each other later and he pointed at the books in her hands and asked: "What do you think?"

"Erm... It seems to make sense."

He grinned. "It *does* make sense. *Every* sense."

....

The following day was a Saturday and so Julian went to Portsmouth, a small harbour town near the border with Maine, to do a "paper sale", as he did most Saturdays. Siobhan accompanied him. He parked in the centre of town and walked to a crossroads where there were lots of shops. The weather was fine on this September day and people enjoying a good day out. Four people who had been at the meeting on Thursday night were already there and they had a bag full of newspapers with them. They then spent the next two hours approaching people on the streets and trying to sell them copies of their paper. Julian tried to persuade Siobhan to join in, but she declined. Instead she loitered to one side as Julian stood in the middle of the pavement peddling his armful of journals to passers-by. "Copy of the *Socialist Times*?... Would you like a copy of the *Socialist Times*?... Can I interest you in a copy of the *Socialist Times*?" Julian's comrades were positioned at strategic locations at different junctions around the district in both directions on both sides of the road. After half an hour or so they moved into a nearby pedestrianized shopping street and began again. "Copy of the *Socialist Times*?... Copy of the *Socialist Times*?..." People passing by mostly ignored Julian, a few of them chuckled and shook their head as they walked on by. One elderly man yelled: "No way!... And fuck off! Commie bastard!" as he strode away.

"Fuck off yourself, you fascist asshole!" Julian roared back at him. After a few more inaudible ripostes the old man was out of earshot. Eventually Julian managed to sell two copies; both were to people who recognized him and he had long friendly conversations with them. At about two PM he got a roamphone call from his comrades in the neighbouring plaza and they mutually agreed to call it a day. They went to a bar and had a few drinks. Siobhan sat quietly at the end of the table nursing a beer while Julian and the other WRSL members debated long and detailed conundra from the incomprehensible firmament of Marxist politics that was way out of Siobhan's reach. "Proletarian bonapartism", "petty-bourgeois" and "lumpen-anarcho-syndicalist" were some of the grotesque phrases that were tossed around the table. That evening Julian and Siobhan went to watch a film at the cinema and had a meal afterwards in a restaurant. To begin with Siobhan was hopeful that at last they would have some quality time alone together, but she ended up disappointed. Their conversation was forced and edgy. Julian was in an unforthcoming and morose mood. He seemed wistful and lonely. She got the impression that he didn't feel at home without his WRSL comrades. He had a copy of the *Socialist Times* with him and even in the middle of the movie and while sitting at the table in the restaurant he occasionally removed the rolled-up newspaper from the inside pocket of his jacket and flicked through it. He looked lost and emotionally destitute at having to endure just a single evening away from his political activities and those he shared them with. She looked at him sadly as he pored over the pages, at one point rustling loudly and annoying the rest of the cinema audience.

The following day she had to go back to Nevada and to work. Her parting with Julian at the station was far more melancholy than usual. She felt unfulfilled by their time together. Julian drove her to Durham station. "So, Siobhan." Julian said in a more cheerful tone than the one he'd employed for most of the evening before. "What do you think about what you've seen this weekend?"

"Dunno." she muttered.

"'Dunno'? Surely you noticed what you were being propositioned with."

Siobhan was taken aback. "What are you talking about? I wasn't propositioned with anything." *Even by you* she felt like adding with a stab of bitterness.

Julian chuckled. "Siobhan, you're what is commonly known as a 'contact.' We've been trying to recruit you to the party."

"Well... I had no idea. You can't have been doing a very good job."

"What? Don't you remember what we were talking to you about yesterday?"

"I'm afraid it went over my head a bit."

Julian sighed. "How about the books; you understood those... We were trying to explain to you why you should join us in our struggle; the workers' struggle for the revolution. It's the path to freedom for the whole world... You must understand that the workers' revolution is the only key to freeing the world. There is no reform, no new laws and no new social security benefits that can change a damn thing in the long term. The only solution is social and economic revolution. Capitalism has become the central problem of civilization; it is the root cause of all the problems you hear about in this world. It has got to go! The workers of the world have to rise up and seize the means of production for themselves. This is why you *must* join the party. You have to."

"No, I don't have to if I don't want to." She replied defiantly. She was still frustrated by the lack of attention he had paid her.

"But you *have* to want to!" persisted her boyfriend. "This is the future; this is human destiny." He handed Siobhan a sheaf of pamphlets, leaflets and several larger books wrapped around with several elastic bands. There was also some notepaper with a list of meshboard addresses written on it in his handwriting, which he'd obviously prepared earlier. "You've already taken the first step. This is the second. Please, just study these and let me know what you think."

....

She read some of this second batch of literature from Julian on the plane home. She searched for a couple of the meshboards on her matchbook and scrolled through the pages. She learned about the Bolshevik revolution in Russia. Forty-three years ago the first and most successful attempt at a workers' state was wheeled out. This was followed by the Cold War after the end of World War II and then the collapse of that regime. Much of this literature

182

was very compelling. It was an inclusive explanation for the world as she saw it, a world with many hardships and injustices; and it presented a persuasive and confident solution to that pathology. Its telos was a world set free of cruelty and oppression. There was one major defect in the narrative though; at no point did the Marxist perspective make any reference at all to the Disclosure of the extraterrestrials or Saucer Day. It addressed the period following Mars Day, late 1947, as "an anti-imperialistic lack of confidence". The social collapse following Saucer Day was called "a return to a pre-capitalist social state over much of Europe, its colonies and the Third World." It baffled her how a history of all of human progress could be analyzed in such minute detail and with a level of unwavering conviction, and yet completely ignore the most earthshaking events of the last twenty years. It didn't dismiss them or try to belittle them; it simply omitted them. She closed her matchbook in confusion.

When she got off the plane she switched on her roam and there was no message from him at all. The usual: "*Thanks for a wonderful time. Love you. J xxx.*", or words to that effect, was absent. She drove home and went to bed. Her parents were already retiring for the night when she arrived and she never got to speak to her father because he was already asleep. Her mother poked her head out of the bathroom and kissed her goodnight. "Don't disturb your dad, Siobhan. He's not been feeling very well today."

Siobhan got into bed and cried as quietly as she could, burying her face in the pillow.

....

The following Wednesday Siobhan drove to Las Vegas as usual after doing the mid-afternoon headlines. The sky over the desert was a beautiful, pure ultramarine. Not a single cloud spoiled its face. The sun behind her was a magnesium sting that hit her eyes through the rear-view mirror occasionally. She was just approaching Halloran Springs, California when she noticed something strange, a white line was scrawled across the sky on the horizon. She slowed the car and studied it. It was rising at an angle of about thirty degrees to her right from the distant mountains of the

Mojave National Park. She pulled over onto the hard shoulder and from there to the sandy verge. She thought at first she was imagining it, but after watching for another few minutes realized that she wasn't; the white line was growing. After a while she could follow its expansion as it happened, not in stages like the growing of a plant. Another white line appeared soon after, this time emerging behind her from the direction of Los Angeles. She couldn't see it very clearly at first because of the glare of the sun but she could tell it was rising straight upwards. It appeared to be tapering downwards until she realized that it was a trick of perspective. The white line was actually growing horizontally across the sky and was moving towards her zenith. "It must be an MFO." she said aloud. She recalled the "skywatchers" she had met in Pennsylvania a few years ago. When the front of the white line got closer she could see that it was sprouting from the rear of a structured MFO as it moved along. She squinted to make out the craft. It was vaguely cruciform and very small. Then in a flip of perception she realized that the MFO was actually a completely normal manmade aircraft at a very high altitude. It was no different to the jet airliners she herself used regularly and had been a common sight in the skies for over a decade. She had never noticed them before out here in the desert though. This was obviously because there was no airport nearby and by the time they were flying over this part of the world, the aircraft had reached cruising altitude which was so high they were almost too small to see from ground level. Also they had never before exhibited the strange property of leaving behind them a thick white plume of smoke or vapour. As she watched, another aircraft appeared on the horizon doing the exact same thing; then another and another. After a few more minutes Siobhan had counted a dozen high altitude aircraft fly over the sky above her depositing the same unusual trail. Within twenty minutes the unblemished blue sky was covered by a lattice of these peculiar white lines. The miasma dispersed slowly, merging and overlapping to create a translucent haze across the sky. The sun was filtered perceptibly by it and dimmed. The desert heat was tempered a few degrees. She had a vague recall of one of the conference days in Dubai, but the thought was instinctive and slipped through her mental fingers. She shrugged; it must be some new kind of jet engine, she rationalized and got back into the car. She still felt a nameless unease as she drove on along the highway beneath this spider web of jet trails.

She had been thinking about the books she had been reading, churning and blending the ideas over and over in her head. She had enough introspective power to realize that her concerns over her relationship with Julian were influencing her assessment. It turned out that she was not the only person in his inner circle he had become distant from. The day after she had returned from New Hampshire she had an E-gram from Tanya Spencer, Julian's mother. *"Hello, Siobhan. Hope all is well with you. Do you mind asking Julian to get in touch? I've not heard from him for several weeks and I'm worried about him. Thank you. Tanya."* Siobhan felt a paradoxical mixture of increased dread and relief. Dread that this troubled period of Julian's life was so bad that it had led him to isolate his own parents. Relief because it was not just her that he was rejecting. Did this make the cooling of his ardour for her a symptom of something separate?

As Siobhan neared Las Vegas she decided on the spur of the moment to drop in to Area 51. She turned off onto the highway to Pahrump and accessed the formerly secret military base at its western entrance where there was a proper guardhouse. To her surprise it was manned and the barrier was down. She pulled up and wound down the window. Two men were inside the shack and one came out and approached her. He was dressed in military fatigues and a beret yet his uniform bore no regimental badges. Instead he wore an armband with the insignia of the FDRA. There was a sidearm at his waist. "Good afternoon, miss." he said with a smile. "Can I have your name please?"

"Siobhan Quilley, CBS News."

"Do you have a press card?"

She showed it to him. He studied it for a moment then handed it back and gestured to his colleague. The bar came up. "Can I ask who you guys are?"

"FDRA security, miss."

"I thought Area 51 was open to the public now."

"The director had to restrict access again because we've had too many people driving up to explore. It interferes with the scientific mission."

"OK." She nodded uneasily and drove on. After another half an hour's drive along the tarmac road she came across the facility, curving onto the Papoose Lake section. The "S4" underground complex was bored out beneath the typical Nevadan dry lake bed, a wide flat-bottomed valley with steep sides covered in creosote bushes, yucca plants and other succulents scattering away into the distance, evenly spaced. There was a row of oblong orifices in the sloping sides of the valley just above the bottom. Their camouflaged sliding doors were all wide open and she could see the alien reproduction vehicles parked inside them, silvery smooth saucers that reflected the sunlight in dazzling brightness. She entered the underground base through the sliding door in the hut-like extension near the hangars and walked into the storage area where the fragments of the Roswell flying saucer were stored.

The Perspex containers they had been in were all open and some of the debris was lying on a workbench in the middle of the chamber. Two FDRA technicians worked quietly on one end of the bench; they recognized Siobhan and gave her a cursory greeting. The fragments all looked metallic; some were thin sheets like aluminium foil. Many looked smooth and shiny; others crumpled, or even compacted, like the foil balls that Siobhan used to make as a child. There were also struts of different lengths and thicknesses. Some were square or rectangular in cross section like wood sawn by a carpenter; others were just like conventional I-beams. There was one large circular object about four feet across that looked like a tractor wheel without the tyre. It sat on top of a rubber sheet in the corner. She picked up one of the I-beams and once again marvelled at how light it was, no heavier than polystyrene; yet its surface was cold and smooth like steel. Along the metallic surface inside the two horizontal sections were markings, pictograms or motifs of some kind. It reminded her of

Egyptian hieroglyphics. She picked up one of the smooth pieces of foil and folded in half, folded it again quarter ways, then eighths and again into sixteenths, so that the sheet was crushed into a little package. The pressed foil immediately began to open like a flower. It unfolded until it was once again a single sheet; and the single sheet stretched taut until all the creases were gone and it was as smooth as it had been in initially. The main section of the crashed flying saucer had been placed on top of a collection of forklift pallets. It was a burnished silver-coloured object about twenty feet across, shaped like an Olympic discus and was featureless except for some darker oblong markings near the top where its regular discus shape was broken into a squat turret with a flat roof about nine feet above the base. She ran her fingers over its hull. It felt like metal, very smooth, polished and cold. There was a gaping cavity in the far side of the disk a good eight feet across and mostly on the lower half of the object, but it included some of its rim. It didn't look like a door; there was no mechanism visible, and it was very big and slightly irregular. The sides of the hole were smooth, as if it had been cut open with an oxy-acetylene torch or a power saw. If this had been a normal aircraft involved in a crash, there would have been loose ragged edges to the hole, snapped struts sticking out, ripped flaps of aluminium skin. The cavity opened onto a cylindrical cabin that was made of a very different substance to the outside. It was as black as tar and appeared to be a kind of plastic or wax. The light from the portable lantern within was swallowed up by the gloom of the bulkheads. The only features inside the cabin were four structures that looked a bit like small bathtubs about four feet long. These were built into the deck without any visible seams, welds or rivets. They were made of the same the material as the rest of the compartment. Siobhan laid her hand on the side of the nearest bathtub. It had a slippery and greasy consistency. There was something strange about the acoustics of the cabin. Noises didn't sound as they normally would in a compartment that size and of that material. She walked to a second door at the far end of the chamber, pressed a button and it slid open. In the next space were

187

four transparent caskets. Icicles on the inside surface indicated that the interiors were very cold. She looked inside and saw the same strange cadavers that had become so well-known since the news reports had emerged after the invasion of Area 51. The enormous heads, the large eyes and the featureless mouth and scalp. Four fingers on the hands with flat flared tips like suction cups. Their skin was grey, like milky coffee. From a distance they appeared smooth, but when she leaned in close she could see scales or a mesh-like texture to them. The bodies had no external features at all; no nipples or navel, no genitals or hair. Each one was three-foot-six in height, slightly built with skinny limbs and it also was proportionally smaller than normal. Its child-size feet had no toes; the foot just tapered to a rounded-off end without nails. The most remarkable features were its eyes. They were huge, oval-shaped and deep black, without pupils, iris or whites; or else they were just all pupil. Their corneas reflected the light like black billiard balls. Siobhan remembered one of the most distressing incidents in her relationship with Julian, when she had tried to raise this subject with him while they were sitting in his car at the housing project in Minnesota: *"Lies! Bullshit science fiction stories! A bourgeois utopian smokescreen to distract the proletariat from genuine progressive activism! Fascist anti-Semitic crap!"* Why did he respond like that? All she was doing was bringing up a matter that was so obviously real. She was tempted to suggest that he visit Area 51, but she knew she could never dare broach the issue with him ever again. How on earth could he deny that all this was real? Why had the Marxists of the present day rewritten the entire history of the last decade and a half completely passing over this most pivotal factor? It was like defining Christmas, but leaving out Jesus and Santa Claus. It was as if they were living in a parallel universe where this all just never happened. The problem was, Julian had moved over there with them while she had not and could not. She closed her eyes and sighed.

"Siobhan!"

She looked up and saw a smiling face moving towards her. Two brown eyes, magnified by spectacles, gleaming with intelligence and sensitivity. "Jenny!" She embraced her friend.

"Siobhan! I've not seen you since... Dubai was it?"

"Yes. How are you, Jenny?"

"Better for seeing you! I just got a call from Steve and he told me you were here, so I hot-tailed straight over from the main base." Dr Jenny Bulstrode gave her a tour of the S4 laboratory colouring in the facility with her expertise. "Just look at this, Siobhan." She leaned into the hole in the flying saucer. "This cabin is a regular cuboid in shape. It is ten-foot three inches across by six-five high by seven-one wide... Weird!"

"Why's that weird?"

"It's too big to fit inside the exterior."

"But..." She paused for a moment to contemplate the implications. "Are you saying the inside of this flying saucer is bigger than the outside?"

"Yes." she replied deadpan.

"But... that can't be true!"

"It is true. We've measured it precisely. Do you want to see our calculations? Would you like to measure it yourself?"

"No, I meant... That's impossible!"

Jenny stood up and faced her. She shrugged. "Discuss."

After the tour they both went to the cafeteria and had a cup of coffee. "What's with the extra security?" Siobhan described the way she had been vetted before entering the base.

"The new FDRA director has deployed the agency's paramilitary wing." Dr Bulstrode chuckled bitterly. "He thinks the science project here will be jeopardized by public attention."

"Who's running the FDRA these days?"

"John Crawley; Dealey's own former deputy. We've nicknamed him 'Creepy'."

"I thought there was some plan afoot to turn this place into some kind of museum."

She shook her head and sighed. "Maybe one day, but not for a long time yet."

Siobhan decided to drive out to the eastern border and see what it was like. As she headed away from the base along the Groom Lake Road towards public land she thought about Dr Jenny Bulstrode and how she fitted into Julian's books. Dr Bulstrode was the most ingenious person Siobhan had ever known. She had a far better mind than anybody else Siobhan had ever heard of. She worked harder than any of the other FDRA scientists, even her boss Prof. Pickup. What would Dr Bulstrode's life be like in a communist society? There was a catchphrase in the books that had stuck out in Siobhan's mind: *From each according to his ability, to each according to his need.* This was a slogan Karl Marx had coined in his early writings. It meant that Dr Bulstrode's prodigal abilities would be used for only one purpose, to serve all the people who needed them. This meant she could never be properly rewarded for her exceptional uniqueness. Her rewards would be the same as everybody else's; depending on how much she needed, not how much her abilities produced. Then what would be the incentive for her being so exceptional? There would be none, not unless she was some kind of masochistic milquetoast. It would be a far more sensible simply to keep her head down and pretend to be as mediocre as possible; making sure that her skill and stamina contribution did not exceed the standard dividend. In fact under communism no institution could possibly tolerate innovation of any kind because the people leading the innovation would be immediately sacrificed to the mob as soon as they had achieved it. Indeed it would be a wise strategy to be as idle and incompetent a member of the team as you could get away with. That way your profit margin within the system would be maximized. Another catchphrase came to mind, although she couldn't remember where she had picked it up. It described the situation perfectly: *tragedy of the commons.* She grinned to herself as she drove, pleased that she had formulated a counter-position to Julian's single-minded tirades. If he refused to entertain the idea of MFO's then maybe he would listen to this rebuttal instead. It might make him think twice about his zealous commitment to the

Marxist cause, or at least broaden his mind enough to prevent him being completely absorbed.

The road climbed up into the mountainous ridge between Area 51 and the outside world. She was travelling back along the route she had taken during the invasion in 1958. She passed the guardhouse and began to descend the far side of the ridge. The Groom Lake Road stretched out ahead of her in a straight line and in the distance she saw the darker line of Highway Three-Seven-Five. The backs of the two warning signs appeared on the verges ahead. Then she slowed as she saw another vehicle parked on the loop of road overlooking the border. It was a pickup truck exactly like those used by the security guards of Florenti Inc when Area 51 had been an active secret base before Saucer Day. Inside she saw the figures of a driver and passenger. She turned off the Groom Lake Road and ground up the hill to where it was parked. She stopped her car right behind it and got out. The driver lowered his window as she approached. "Can we help you, miss?" he said with an easy-going smile.

"What are you doing here?" she asked.

"Working." He chuckled. "We're FDRA security."

"I see." She paused. "What is the FDRA's security policy at Area 51 these days?"

"Hey, miss. We only know how to stop people driving up here to the base. You need to call our head office in Washington for a statement on policy."

"So... if you saw somebody driving along this road towards Area 51, what would you do?"

"Head 'em off and arrest them. We'd detain them while we called the Lincoln County sheriff to come and take 'em away. There's a six hundred buck fine for a first offence, six thousand for subsequent infringements."

"Mind you." added the second security guard in the passenger seat. "By law we can shoot them." He patted his holster. "We are authorized to use deadly force."

"Really? How come?"

"An FDRA directive, approved by the president."

Siobhan drove away and parked her car a few hundred yards away down the hill where the border warning signs were. She got out and looked around her, feeling anxious and uncertain. He laid her hand on one of the signs. "Museum pieces?" she quoted aloud. Low cloud had covered the sky and the wind had got up. It was cold and she buttoned her cardigan to her throat. She heard the noise of a speeding engine and looked behind her to see a car rushing towards her from the direction of the base. Its tyres rubbed grit as it tore to a halt beside her. Dr Jenny Bulstrode jumped out. She was breathing hard and her face was pale. "Siobhan! Have you still got your roam off? I've been trying to call you for half an hour!"

"What's the matter, Jenny?"

"I've had a call from your mom. You need to get home now!"

"What's wrong?"

"It's your dad. He's had a stroke."

Chapter 11

Siobhan walked into the Sunrise Hospital in Las Vegas feeling as if she was a puppet and another version of herself beyond her was controlling her movements. Her thoughts were unbelievably nonchalant as she drove from Area 51. It was dusk as she entered the hospital carpark and found a space. She even looked up and admired the crimson glow of the setting sun through the foggy mesh of the new aircraft trails. The corridors of the hospital were waxy and smelled of hypochlorite. She followed the signs towards the neurology centre. She stopped and asked directions from a member of staff, speaking calmly. There was no rush. She reported to reception and was led to a comfortable lounge with a vase of flowers on the table and pictures of desert and mountain scenes on the wall, in a inexplicable attempt to make the people inside feel cheerful when nobody who ever entered its door could ever be so. Her mother and brother were sitting on the settee. As Siobhan walked in they jumped to their feet and hugged her. Gina's cheeks were bright red. She was trying not to cry for Brendan's sake. Brendan himself was outwardly quiet and measured, staring at the floor. He had a plastic toy soldier with him which he clutched like a teddy bear.

They sat together on the settee and waited. Siobhan lay with her head back and her eyes closed, keeping her thoughts as neutral as possible. The night time noises of the hospital sometimes penetrated the room, making her alert to her surroundings. A call on the tannoy, nurses chatting, the rattling of a passing trolley. The moment the doorknob turned she jerked upright along with her family. A doctor walked in wearing surgical scrubs; he was a dark-skinned man who also sported a turban on his head. "Mrs Quilley?" he asked. Parts of his scrubs were stained dark by sweat.

"Yes?" replied Gina.

"I am Dr Singh, chief neurosurgical resident. I've just finished operating on your husband." He had a strong Indian accent.

"And?"

"Mr Quilley has suffered a haemorrhagic stroke to his right cerebral cortex. In other words he has been bleeding inside his brain." He held up a rectangular sheet of transparent plastic with a large egg-shaped blob on it. This turned out to be an X-ray scan of Clane Quilley's head. He pointed to it. "You see here; the haematoma, the spilled blood, is in the parietal and temporal lobes. Luckily it is in a location which was operable and so we have inserted a drainage catheter which is drawing the blood out of the space. This will hopefully restore circulation, lower intracranial pressure and reduce cellular damage."

"Is he going to get better?"

The doctor paused. "We can't be sure at this point."

Gina let out a sob.

"Is he going to die?" asked Siobhan.

"We have cause to be hopeful." the doctor pacified. "It is true that around ten percent of patients who suffer a stroke like this die within a year, but we have been able to treat Mr Quilley's injury very well, as well as possible in fact. Eighteen percent make a full recovery within a year too. Over longer periods that figure rises."

"Can we see him?"

"Of course; as soon as we have him settled into intensive care."

Dr Singh then went away and came back an hour later to escort them to the neurological intensive care unit. A sliding door parted and they entered a huge windowless chamber full of darkness punctuated by the bright coloured lights of monitor screens, spotlights and a gallery of warning displays. There was a large bed every dozen yards surrounded by banks of equipment. "Here." said Dr Singh. They approached a bed on which lay a man Siobhan hardly recognized. He was covered by a sheet up to his naked chest and his arms lay straight on top of the sheet. His skin was perforated by several drip lines and a brown cuff encircled one of his upper arms. There was a humming sound and it inflated like a lifebelt. "That's a blood pressure gauge." The doctor explained. There was a bottle of pink liquid suspended from the bedstead near the floor. Plastic bags of clear fluid were hung on hooks above the patient's bed connected to his arms by transparent pipes; a nurse was squeezing one of them as Siobhan came closer to the bed. A repetitive penetrating bonging sound broke out from one of the displays, but none of the doctors or nurses appeared alarmed. Clane Quilley's scalp was completely covered by a white bandage. It took Siobhan a long time before she dared look at his face. Her father's eyes were gently closed, as if he were asleep at home in bed. His nose and mouth were covered by a clear plastic mask that was fastened by a green ribbon that encircled his lower head. A green pipe sprouted from the mask and disappeared behind the bed into the incomprehensible scrum of medical paraphernalia. As Siobhan looked at her father's face she felt her eyes fill with tears. There was no emotion; they were numb robotic tears.

Dr Singh put a warm hand on her shoulder. "It would be easier for you to go home now and rest." he said. "We've given Mr Quilley sedatives so he will sleep now for at least twelve hours."

Gina had travelled with her husband in the ambulance to the hospital so she had no car and they had to take a taxi home. Once they were in the house Brendan immediately crashed into bed, youthful exhaustion getting the better of him. Siobhan first noticed the time when she looked at the clock and saw that it was now two-thirty AM. As soon as Gina's son was asleep the dam broke and she collapsed onto the settee, weeping copiously. Siobhan rubbed her shoulders in consolation then made her a cup of tea. When she had recovered, her mother described what had happened. "We were just sitting here calmly, talking as normal... and then he winked his left eye at me. I wondered what he was doing, but then he said 'Gina, I can't open my eye'. Then the left side of his mouth turned downwards, and the rest of his face flopped all lopsided. He slid over in the chair and he was so frightened. 'Gina,' he said. 'Help me! I can't move my arm or leg.' I got him lying flat and called nine-one-one. His right side was alright and he could help get himself into the paramedic's gurney with his right arm and leg. The doc said that meant there was a problem with the right half of his brain. He told me the two sides of your brain control the opposite half of your body. On the way to the hospital he got worse. He started babbling all sorts of nonsense, like he was delirious."

They talked for a while longer and then went to bed. Both had trouble sleeping and Siobhan got up several times. She wandered round the house. It had a different atmosphere now, as if its very bricks and mortar had been shocked by what had happened to the man of the house.

....

When they returned to the hospital the following afternoon a different doctor was on duty, a thin white man with horn-rimmed glasses, and he smiled when he came to the waiting room to meet them. "Mr Quilley has made excellent progress." he said. "He has regained consciousness and is responding well to stimuli; that's a good sign." Clane had been moved to a single room in a different section of the neuroscience area. A lot of the equipment that had been fixed to him the night before had been removed. The room was walled by large windows and as they walked up the corridor towards it they saw a nurse sitting on a chair beside the bed. She was holding a plastic cup with a straw in it up to Clane's mouth and he was drinking. They opened the door and went in, but Clane didn't turn his head. The doctor instructed them in a low voice: "He won't be able to see you until you are in his right visual field. Move to the right hand side of the bed."

Siobhan obeyed. "Hello, dad."

Clane looked up at her and squinted, as if struggling to focus his eyes. His left eyelid was half-closed. "Who are you?" he asked.

"Who am I?... I'm Siobhan."

"No. Siobhan is a little girl."

She turned away from him, hiding her face in her hands as she felt tears rising again.

"He's got a touch of amnesia." said the doctor. "That's very common with stroke patients. Try not to worry too much. There's every chance that his memory will return given time."

"How much time?"

"We don't know; I'm sorry."

....

The next day many members of the Quilley's extended family came to visit Clane. The first to arrive were

Siobhan's grandfather and both her grandmothers; her maternal grandfather had died a few years earlier. Her paternal grandparents went in, spoke briefly to Clane and came out weeping. He was their child in the same way she was his. Being a parent never ended. No matter how old one was and how old one's children were, the relationship remained the same. This thought made her cry again as she remembered how last year she had admonished her father for treating her as if she were younger than she was. Her maternal grandmother was more composed, always having taken a lukewarm overview of her son-in-law. Siobhan's uncles, aunts and cousins turned up, but spent most of their time in the waiting room because the doctor would only allow two visitors at a time by Clane's bed. They were all tensed up from their worry for Clane and this triggered spats over unrelated family conflicts that would probably have otherwise been deferred. In order to escape the burning atmosphere Siobhan and her cousin Jessica went for a walk. Once outside the hospital Siobhan switched on her roam; all portable communications devices were banned inside because the transmissions sometimes interfered with the lifesaving electronics there. It bleeped; she had a text: "*Hi Siobhan. I've just heard about your dad being ill. Hope he's OK and gets well soon. Hope you're OK too. J xxx.*" She gasped. "Julian!"

"Is that *the* Julian?" Jessica leaned over to look at the roam's screen. "Your boyfriend you told us all about?"

"Yes. I've not heard from him for a week. I've been worrying lately because he'd gone cold on me."

"Call him."

"Later." She grinned. She wanted to enjoy the luxury of knowing he had reached out to her with the usual affection, what he had not shown her since their rather edgy parting in New Hampshire.

She met the entire family at teatime in the hospital cafeteria and they ate a meal together. Siobhan left before dessert and headed back to the neurology unit to check up on her father. It was forty-eight hours since he had had his stroke and she had hardly left the hospital site. She had called CBS and they had given her compassionate leave;

another newsreader would sit in for her. Since then every waking hour was spent moving between Clane's bedside, the waiting room and the other parts of the hospital. She even visited the chapel for a few minutes to see if any prayers would come out. None did. She slid some coins into the slot of a dispensing machine and it delivered some coffee in a cardboard cup. She put a plastic lid on it and carried it gingerly to the lift bay. The hospital lifts were very big compared to normal ones because they had to carry beds on wheels and other large vehicles. It went up from the cafeteria on the ground floor to the neurology unit on the fourth. The doors slid apart and Siobhan walked down the corridor towards the stroke ward, still treading carefully to avoid spilling her coffee. She passed through another pair of electric doors and greeted the nurse sitting at the nurses' station who was busy writing in a folder of notes. "Have you got one for me?" the nurse asked in a jocular tone and pointed at Siobhan's coffee beaker.

"Sorry, but I'd much prefer to get you a beer for all the good work you guys do."

She smiled. "Thanks, but not while I'm on duty."

Siobhan went around the corner and saw her father's bed in its glass-walled cubicle. She stopped in her tracks. A man she didn't recognize was in the room with him. He was quite short and wore a brown suit. His hair was smooth and black; and he stood upright beside the bed. As she watched he reached out his hand and ran it affectionately over Clane's bandaged skull as if petting a cat. Clane was fast asleep and didn't stir. The stranger's head was bowed in concern. She opened the door of the cubicle and entered. He turned and looked at her. "Hello, Siobhan." He had a cracked voice and spoke in a tone that suggested he already knew her well. He was old and his face was dry and harshly lined; its creases deepened as he smiled. His features were very like those of a typical Amerindian.

"Er... hello. And you are?"

"An old friend of your father's. When I heard what had happened I decided to come and pay him a visit."

"Well... I'm sure he'll appreciate that, Mr..."

The man turned back and looked down at Clane again. "It's a pity he's not awake so I can speak to him."

"The docs are giving him medication to help him sleep. Even when he's awake he's very confused. He might not even remember you." She put the cup of coffee down on the bedside cabinet.

"He will. You're dad's a strong man and he will get completely better very quickly."

Siobhan was taken aback with the assurance in the man's words. The doctors treating Clane had always been cautiously equivocal over his prognosis, usually replying with statistics and catchphrases like: "the chances are..." or: "it's a distinct possibility..." What the stranger said made her feel inexplicably reassured, even though he was obviously no doctor. "I'll be glad of that." she replied.

The man took a step towards her, staring at her hard with his pair of small, glinting chestnut eyes. "You have a lot of your father in you, Siobhan."

"Most people think I look more like my mom." she tittered.

"On the surface, yes; but your father's heart definitely beats inside you... He's very proud of you, you know."

She nodded, unsure of what to say.

"And he will be even more so in the future." Without another word the man walked over to the door, headed out into the corridor and towards the corner without looking back. After he'd disappeared around it Siobhan hesitated and then followed after him. By the time she'd reached the corner he was nowhere to be seen; he must have already passed through the sliding doors and left the ward. She approached the nurses' station. The nurse she'd spoken to earlier was still there. "Excuse me." Siobhan asked.

The nurse looked up. "Yes?"

"Who was that man who just left?"

"What man?"

"That man who came to see my dad."

"Nobody else has come to see your dad, Miss Quilley."

She frowned. "But... he was here! A little old Indian in a brown suit. He walked past here less than a minute ago."

The nurse shook her head. "I promise you. Nobody has walked past here since you did when you arrived with your coffee. I've been here the whole time."

"Really?"

"Yeah." She spoke without irritation.

Siobhan paused. "OK."

Chapter 12

"MOTHERFUCKERS!" Julian yelled at the top of his voice, his mouth tight with rage and his teeth bared like a dog's.

"Sectarian Stalinist bastards!" the woman standing next to him shrilled. "SOPpy scum!"

There was an older man at the front who was slightly more diplomatic. He pointed his finger and shouted: "You are dividing the proletariat with your reformist policies!..."

On the other side of the road the Socialist Organizers hurled abuse back at them: "Petit-bourgeois trendies!"... "Trotskyite morons!"... "I spent three years in the WRSL so I know what a dirty organization you are!"

The choices of weapon for both lines in the battle were angry words and their stacks of newspapers which they brandished in their arms like spears. The members of the Socialist Organizing Party carried copies of *Direct Action*, a similar tabloid the WRSL's *Socialist Times*, which they were trying to sell to the policemen on the roadblock. The attempted persuasion and coherent insults eventually broke down and the two sides resorted to simply gibbering and grunting at each other like apes at a waterhole: Expletives rose above the clamour: "Fuckin'... Fuckin'... SHIT!... Fuckin'... CUNT!... Fuckin'... Fuckin'..." Eventually a group of police officers left the roadblock to break it up. The protest had begun peacefully enough. The newly-formed umbrella group "Toxic Air- No Thanks!" had organized a simple gathering and demonstration in the centre of Boston, Massachusetts but it had ballooned into a full-size march after hundreds of apolitical locals had joined it along with several leftist factions who hadn't originally been invited. The demonstration was to protest against the city's government following an accident at a chemical plant that had released a cloud of caustic gas upwind of a low income housing project. Five people had died, including two children, and over a hundred were in hospital with burns to their eyes and lungs. The officials at the Mayor's Office were running round in circles trying to find a scapegoat to blame. For many local Bostonians the disaster was culpable negligence. For the WRSL it was an act of carelessness and contempt against the poorest and most vulnerable people in society. The lack of proper health and safety precautions at the factory and the positioning of such a dangerous facility right next to a district of deprived housing was symptomatic of the injustice and oppression the proletariat had to suffer under capitalism. Therefore they were keen to join Toxic Air- No Thanks! Siobhan and Julian had travelled to Boston that morning from Durham, New Hampshire on a packed coach with the entire local chapter of the WRSL. After a two-hour drive they arrived in central Boston and parked by the docks. There was a cheery atmosphere as they unpacked their banners and placards from the coach's luggage locker. Some other WRSL comrades joined them from the Boston chapter. The crowd gathered in a narrow street and began walking along the road, escorted by the police, some of them on horseback. The street was quiet with thin pavements lined by a few warehouses and Irish pubs. As they emerged onto State Street and the cityscape opened out, the mood of the march rose. They lifted their placards and tightened their banners. A man at the front kicked off the chanting and before long all three or four hundred protesters were hollering in unison: "TWO FOUR SIX EIGHT- TOXIC AIR IS WHAT WE HATE!" and lead-chorus shouts like: "What do we want!? CLEAN AIR! When do we want it!? NOW!" "CLEAN AIR!" soon became "SAFE CITIES!" which in turn morphed into "JOBS NOT BOMBS!" and eventually "GOLDWATER OUT!". After five minutes of this canon cycle the chant changed. "WAY-HAY! WOE-HO! ELYCHEM HAS GOT TO GO!" repeated over and over. ElyChem was the conglomerate that owed the chemical plant that caused the fatal disaster. Because it had no variations the demonstrators got bored of it after just one minute and switched to "DEALEY FOR PRESIDENT!... DEALEY FOR PRESIDENT!" in even tetrameter. Another very catchy lead-chorus went: "BARRY BARRY BARRY!... OUT OUT OUT!... BARRY BARRY BARRY!... OUT OUT OUT!... BARRY!... OUT!... BARRY!... OUT!... BARRY BARRY BARRY!... OUT OUT OUT!... Siobhan's spirits lifted along with everybody else's. It was fun to walk down the middle of the road with so many other people. The traffic at junctions was held up for them, making her feel important. The fresh sea air blew in her face and her arms swung free. She had a woolly hat on her head because it was a chilly autumn day. People were exchanging smiles and laughing. Julian had introduced her to everybody and they had accepted her almost instinctively as one of them; very few even mentioned that they recognized her from the television. This was so much more fun than sitting around in a bar discussing Rosa Luxembourg and Harold Laski. For the first time Siobhan understood how these people could become an in-group for Julian and why they had, to an extent she was not yet sure of, replaced his family. She was also elated that her own relationship with him had improved during this visit. The police calmly plodded along at the borders of the mobile crowd. The marchers' collective personality changed as they reached the junction of Court Square. There was a heavy roadblock to keep them away from City Hall, the principle target of their ire. A row of police stood shoulder to shoulder behind a steel fence. They were dressed in riot gear and carried truncheons and shields. The march had been routed along Cambridge Street and across the Charles River Dam, and was scheduled to terminate outside Harvard University where there would be a rally and speakers. However the protesters ground to a halt here and began arguing with the policemen. It was then that the separate argument broke out within the march between the WRSL and their rivals the Socialist Organizing Party. She quickly became separated from Julian as he eagerly jumped into involvement with the dispute; he seemed to forget her totally. A few of the others berated both sides to stop. A quiet old man said to Siobhan in a sad tone: "This happened in the Spanish Civil War." Tension rose as the riot officers stepped over the fence and moved forward to keep the warring cabals apart. This was obviously not a deliberate diversion by the protesters yet some of them suddenly realized that they could take advantage of the situation. They ran to the side of the police line and managed to get past the cordon. They threw the fence segments to one side and started running up Court Square towards City Hall. More officers chased after them, but it was too late. Before she knew it, Siobhan was being carried along by the stampede. She didn't dare not follow it in case she fell over and got trampled. Boston City Hall was a square grey stone second-empire block surrounded by narrow alleys at the back and Siobhan was worried that she would be crushed as the crowd tore along them bellowing and roaring with mass rage. The sound of breaking glass came from ahead. "JULIAN!" she yelled in vain above the din of the mob. The alley eventually opened out into the forecourt of City Hall and she saw many of the people who had been happily trooping along in the good-natured protest march now rushing about outside the ornate facade of City Hall throwing objects at it, stones or bricks. They protesters-turned-rioters had wrapped scarves over their lower faces to hide their features; and two of them had a box of matches and were setting fire to the Stars and Stripes that they had just dragged down from the flagpole on the front of the building. The fragile cotton flag burst into flames and was reduced to ash very quickly. The arsonists then stomped and spat on the charred fragments. Siobhan saw somebody she recognized, a friend of Julian's he had introduced her to on the coach called Mick or Chris or Rob. Most WRSL members seemed to have only single-syllable first names making them hard to remember. She ran up to him. "Where's Julian!?"

"He was right at the front; went way head of me. I think he's inside already." He pointed as the rioters now turned their attention on the interior of City Hall; they were bundling in through the entrance under its neoclassical porch.

"Oh my God! We've got to get him out of there!"

"He isn't coming out of there till the job's done."

There was a wailing of a siren from the main road and a squadron of police poured out of a van. They attacked the rear of the mob with their batons and the rioters outside started throwing their missiles at the police instead.

"Siobhan, we need to get you somewhere safer." advised Mick/Chris/Rob. He led her away up School Street along with the other people who had been part of the original demonstration, but whose nerve had also failed when they saw the violence. All of central Boston was under police lockdown which meant they couldn't get back to Cambridge Street. It was quite a long walk to the next place where they could cross the river Charles. Police were everywhere and watched them carefully. Their clothing gave them away; many protesters wore T-shirts with political slogans on or still carried banners and placards. Siobhan kept trying to call Julian, but his roam was not responding. Eventually Mick/Chris/Rob and his friends came across another group of people from New Hampshire and then, in accordance with WRSL tradition, they went to a pub. Beers lined up on the bar and the nervous energy that had built up during the day was released in a torrent of alcohol. They laughed and told jokes, their fear and anger of a couple of hours earlier was transformed into elation. The bar staff tolerated them without complaint; Boston was a major university town and they were obviously accustomed to the excesses of student culture. There was a television above the bar. The sound was turned down, but it showed a news report about the riot in Boston. The incident at City Hall had made the national headlines.

After another hour or two of drinking, a gang of about five men suddenly walked in and gave a great cheer of victory which was immediately echoed by the people already at the table. Siobhan gasped with relief as she recognized one of them. "Julian!" She jumped up and embraced him.

"Siobhan! Are you OK? I was worried about you."

"Yes, I was worried about you too! Why didn't you answer your roam?"

"The police took it off me when they locked me in the cell; I'm sorry."

"What!? You were arrested? Why?"

He didn't have time to answer; one of his comrades drew his attention away. He hardly spoke again to Siobhan for over two hours. He was part of a telephone exchange of information, coming and going from all the other people in the pub. Every so often his roam would ring and he would be in another conversation. For Siobhan it was like being in the bar after the paper sale only worse. An image came up on the TV of a gilt framed oil painting of a man posing in old-fashioned military uniform and Julian raised his fist in the air. "Yes!" A caption under the image said *General Kane Faucheux by Elizabeth Boott 1860*. Later on Siobhan noticed that Mick/Chris/Rob was coming out of the toilets so she went over and stopped him before he returned to the table. She asked him the question she dare not ask Julian. "Why was Julian so happy when the story about that painting came on the TV?"

"Oh, he's the one who burned it." Mick/Chris/Rob replied offhand.

"What?"

"It was hanging on the wall in City Hall. Julian pulled it down and torched it... It's OK, it was a picture of an imperialistic warmonger; and there must be tons of prints of it; postcards, posters, screensavers and whatnot."

"Right." she said breathlessly. She went to the toilet herself and sat for a long time, too shocked to move. Julian had been part of the horde that had sacked City Hall. As part of this vandalism he had taken down and destroyed a beautiful hundred-year-old artwork by one of America's greatest portrait painters. He was proud of his desecration and cheered when it was mentioned on the news.

It was getting dark and raining lightly when they left the pub and walked up the road to Harvard University. The majestic red-brick facade of this most ancient and famous seat of learning in the Americas was illuminated by floodlights. With the closure of Oxbridge and the Sorbonne, Harvard had become the most elite university in the post-Disclosure world. Siobhan looked up at its terracotta gables, shuddering with dread at her narrow escape; at how close she had come to accepting a scholarship here. They went inside and walked across the park-like gardens to a building with a student's common room on its ground floor. Music was playing inside and loud voices laughed. Most of the people in the room were heavily drunk even though it was only seven PM. They lolled about on the sofas or jived to the music on the improvised dancefloor. Julian continued to ignore her and sat at the centre of a circle of admirers, bragging almost as if he'd taken on the American state single-handed. A female student approached Siobhan. "Hi Siobhan, are you feeling left out?" She had a friendly smile.

"You noticed?"

"It's par for the course when you're a woman in this place." She was slim and pretty, but her hair was very short in a way that seemed to be in vogue among the student left. She was also badly dressed with tears in her T-shirt and jeans; another part of standard youth fashion. She had introduced herself to Siobhan at the start of the march, but Siobhan had forgotten her name. Siobhan felt embarrassed about that and rather than asking her for it again, she listened carefully to her conversations with others until somebody called her by name. It was Derry, a girl's name Siobhan had heard a few times in recent years, especially among the young Irish. She and Derry got talking and quickly warmed to each other. Derry was a WRSL member, but not one from Julian's branch. She was a national committee member, part of the party's central management. She also ran the women's section. "We're having a women's meeting tonight if you want to come along."

Siobhan looked over at Julian who was still intoxicated by the excitement of the day, as well as a good few bottles of beer. "Yeah, why not?"

The meeting was to be held in a room above a pub just a short walk from Harvard. Derry explained a bit of the background to the event as they walked along the pavements side-by-side, Siobhan under one half of Derry's umbrella. "You'll hear things and be able to say things you cannot hear or say anywhere else." said Derry. "This is a safe space for women... And we have a special guest tonight." When they reached the pub they walked straight across the bar-room without ordering a drink. Derry did not even look at any of the pub's general patrons. They climbed a narrow flight of stairs and entered a room with a circle of chairs around a bare floor in the centre. It was lit by dim orange lamps hanging from the peak of the sloping attic roof. Rain ran down the windowpanes and the place had a damp atmosphere exacerbated by wet clothes and hair.

There were about two dozen people sitting on the chairs, all of them female. They were not all students; some were mature ladies, middle aged or older. They talked among themselves quietly and in low voices. One of the people was the short-haired girl who had been at the WRSL branch meeting in Durham a few weeks before. She looked at Siobhan and clearly recognized her, but did not greet her. Siobhan was struck by the lack of humour and liveliness within the group. They all had such mournful faces that this could have been a funeral. She had to resist the urge simply to try and cheer them up. Derry and Siobhan took their places just before the chairwoman called the meeting to order. She was a dumpy but attractive woman in her forties with platinum blonde hair and professionally-done makeup. "Welcome, sisters, to this meeting. This is a joint meeting of the WRSL women's section, the Boston Feminist Network and the Harvard Women Students Union. I see several new faces among us..." She went on to explain the background to the event and the structure of the meeting. "And after the break I'll introduce our special surprise guest. So let us begin by sharing our experiences we've had since the last meeting, the experiences of being a woman in this man's world... Tammy, I believe you want to start us off."

One of the older ladies sitting to Siobhan's left, an overweight woman with braided hair and a woollen cardigan, stood up and spoke nervously with her hands clasped in front of her. "Two days ago I got on the bus to go to Beacon Hill and the driver was this mean-looking tough young guy. He sneered at me as I got on and when I gave him a twenty he said: 'You expect me to have change for that, you stupid fat ugly sow?'..." Tammy collapsed back onto her chair, put her hands over her face and began weeping copiously. The women beside her put their hands around her shoulders supportively and the others in the group further away made sympathetic noises like "Ahh." and "There there."

"That's appalling behaviour on his part!" said Siobhan. "He should be fired for that. Report him to the bus company."

"There's no point." Derry replied from beside her.

"But there'll be witnesses..."

"No, Siobhan." she interrupted, gently but firmly. "There really is no point."

Another woman added: "Well, personally I've taken to walking everywhere so I don't have to deal with these men who drive buses."

The chairwoman spoke up: "This brings us to our campaign to encourage more women to become bus drivers. When we have enough in the trade we can call for the banning of male drivers on certain routes." The others in the group all nodded their approval.

"Maybe we can set up an all-woman bus company." said another brightly. "Women only drivers, women only passengers."

Siobhan put her hand in the air. "Wait a minute... Did you say 'banning male bus drivers'? What, all of them? That sounds pretty unfair to me. What if those male bus drivers have done nothing wrong? What if they're always polite and friendly to people like you, ma'am?" She gestured at Tammy. "I've met many really nice male bus drivers on my travels and I'd hate to see anything bad happen to them. It sounds like you're punishing all men for the crimes of just a few, or one even."

The other people in the room turned and looked at her in shock. There was a stunned silence.

The chairwoman took a deep tremulous breath and looked at Siobhan with a controlled frown of disapproval. "I'm astonished to hear you, as a *woman*, say a thing like that. Did Tammy's story mean nothing to you at all?"

"What do you mean?" protested Siobhan. "I was the one who suggested she report him and that I think he deserves to be fired."

The other women fidgeted nervously. One of them addressed the chair. "Jem, I think we should just move on."

"Yes, yes; indeed." the chairwoman immediately concurred with relief. "Who else has an experience they'd like to share?"

Siobhan looked over at Derry, but Derry had her near shoulder turned away. Siobhan noticed a few dark looks thrown at her companion as well as herself, presumably because she was the one who had brought the snake into their garden.

Another member of the circle got to her feet, a skinny academic looking woman with thick spectacles. "Hello everybody. My name is Maxine."

"Hello, Maxine." the circle responded in unison.

"I divorced my husband three years ago. I have the house. I have his car. I have half his savings and he hasn't seen the children once." She spoke triumphantly as if boasting about an achievement. The women all cheered and applauded. Maxine bowed her head in appreciation and smiled.

Siobhan immediately raised her hand. The chairwoman saw her, paused for a moment, giving her a cold glare, and then turned to another woman. "Yes, Larissa?"

The session ended with another regular slot; one of the women read out a list of all the suspected rapes that had happened since the last meeting; although the tone of the meeting made it clear to Siobhan that they meant the word *suspected* in its broadest possible sense. At the break the women didn't go downstairs to the bar to order drinks; they instead made tea and coffee from a self-service refreshments stall. Derry took her cup and walked over to the window keeping her back turned to Siobhan at all times. Siobhan sipped her own coffee and felt her irritation grow. She walked over to the window and addressed her acquaintance in a low voice. "Derry, give me a break. You invited me here remember?"

"And I wish I never had!" Derry hissed back without turning her head. "You've made me look like a fool!... How could you, Siobhan!? How could you? You're a fucking *woman* for Christ's sake!"

"So what if I'm a woman! Am I not allowed to disagree?... I mean, what have we just heard from that Maxine? She takes her kids and keeps them away from their dad. Her children's own father!"

"Fathers are girl-destroyers!"

"What are you talking about?"

Derry sighed deeply and didn't reply.

210

Siobhan continued. "This is after stripping him of everything he's ever owned. You think that's fair?"

"It's justified! He owes it to her. It's reparations."

"*Reparations*? What's that?"

Derry sighed and turned to look at her. "It's what all men owe all women... white men anyway."

"For what?"

"Housewife slavery."

"'Housewife slavery'!?... What does that mean?"

She paused. "Do you ever plan to marry Julian?"

Siobhan nodded. "I hope so."

She shook her head. "Now that's silly, Siobhan."

"Why's it silly?"

She rolled her eyes. "I suppose you think you love him."

"I do." Tears rose in Siobhan's eyes and she blinked them away.

"Then you're brainwashed. You're as downtrodden as all those other subservient wenches on TV... The only reason to marry a man is if you plan to do what Maxine did... You want my advice on what to do with Julian? Use him to have children. Abort the sons and keep the daughters so you can bring them up as part of the new generation that is free from toxic masculinity. After that, wait until the misogynist slime has a tenured position and then divorce him." Her teeth were bared in bitter hate-filled mania as she hissed: "Then... drag him through every alimony court in the land until you've stuffed your purse with every piece of patriarchal booty he has ever plundered!"

Siobhan drew back from her in shock. "Derry, you're a member of the WRSL, just like Julian. I thought you were on his side."

She chuckled sardonically. "So does he!"

Siobhan backed away from her. She stumbled over to her chair and grabbed her raincoat. She headed for the door to the staircase, not looking to see if anybody was watching her leave. She was just about to turn the doorknob when she felt somebody else turning it from the other side. The door opened away from her. She jerked forward as it tugged her hand before she managed to let go. A woman stood before her whom she immediately recognized; in fact Siobhan had interviewed her just a few days before Clane's stroke. "Well well well!" said the woman. "If it isn't young Miss Siobhan Quilley of CBS... Not leaving already are you?"

"I'm afraid I have to." Siobhan manoeuvred herself around the very tall and well-dressed lady, who had a haughty sneer on her lips as she looked down at the reporter.

"What a shame. My husband is in town so do join us for dinner tomorrow evening if you are around."

As Siobhan walked down the stairs and before the door swung shut, she heard the chairwoman announcing the lady's arrival: "Sisters, our special mystery guest has arrived. We are honoured to be joined this evening by Leonora Dealey, the next First Lady of the United States." The circle of women all clapped.

....

Siobhan awoke on a settee in the common room at Harvard where the party had taken place. Watery sunlight filled the room. A frog's chorus of snores filled the air along with the smell of stale Bourbon and body odour. Her mouth was slimy and tasted horrible. She rose to her feet and walked to the kitchenette, tiptoeing around those who had fallen asleep on the floor. She gulped some grapefruit juice and wished she had a toothbrush. When they had left Durham the previous morning there had been no talk of staying overnight in Boston and so she had brought no toiletries. She saw Julian sprawled in an armchair, his head leaning against one of the wings, his arms stretched out. She slowly trod over to him, quietly, not wanting to wake him. She stood as still as a statue, watching as his chest rose and fell under his beer-stained T-shirt. Somebody in another chair stirred, breaking her reverie. Julian inhaled sharply and stirred. Siobhan backed off swiftly and headed for the toilets before he spotted her. Over the next hour everybody woke up groaning in various ways through their hangovers. There was a slow-motion breakfast for the few who had appetites. It was almost midday when they were all ready to walk back to the docks where they had left the coach. It was still raining and the air was as moist as a sponge. Siobhan talked casually to Julian on the walk and managed to sit next to him on the coach. However all the time she was thinking, how could she tell him?

The coach arrived home just after four PM and the group said their goodbyes and disbanded. They were finally alone together when the door shut on his flat in the Durham campus and she decided now was the time. "Jeez, Siobhan; my head is still pounding. I need a bath; mind if I go first?"

"Sure, Jules." She heard the taps running in the bathroom, gave him five minutes to wash then went in.

He had filled the tub completely full and was lying in the steamy water up to his chest. "Ah! That's better." he groaned. "Maybe after the revolution somebody will find an instant cure for a hangover... Then again, some theoreticians claim that post-revolutionary youth won't drink. So we may be the last generation of humans who consume alcohol."

She couldn't just blurt it out, what she had heard last night at the feminist meeting. He would react against it emotionally, and against her personally. Siobhan knew she had to handle Julian carefully, ease him out of his ideology slowly to avoid shock, like a deep sea diver in a decompression chamber. "You know, Julian. I've read all those books you gave me."

He turned his head with a splash to look at her and smiled. "Great. What do you think?"

She voiced the objection she had thought of when she had visited Area 51. She kept her voice calm, reasonable and rational.

Julian rolled his eyes and sighed. "Have you been reading Popper?"

"What's a popper?"

He chuckled. "Karl Popper. That bloody idiot published a book in '46 bringing up the exact argument you just did."

Siobhan cursed inwardly. She had felt so very pleased with herself at Area 51; it had been a real *eureka* moment. Now she discovered that somebody else had thought of the same idea independently fourteen years earlier and that Julian had already heard of it and dismissed it.

"The critique makes a whole array of essentialist assumptions about human culture and psychology that mean nothing. The selfishness versus unselfishness spectrum; the sense of the collective etcetera. What bullshit! How do you know your friend Dr Bulstrode would be disincentivised? You don't know how she would think in a situation in which the social contract was altered at the most fundamental level. Did you not read the chapter in the Isaac Deutscher book about society and revolution?"

"I did, but..."

"Deutscher is probably influenced by the Frankfurt School a bit more than I'd like, Gramsci, Marcuse etcetera; but basically he explains clearly how the revolution is not merely an economic one. It involves a transformation of the vary core nature of human beings. Popper has never even considered this." Julian gesticulated as he spoke, splashing the bathwater onto the floor. "The ignorant fucking fool just picks up the people of today's capitalist world and dumps them into a hypothetical socialist model wholesale, without any thought to the processes and influences that those individuals will experience when actually travelling the road from one state to the other. Frantz Fanon makes a similar point..."

He was off again. Siobhan nodded along mindlessly; her plan had totally failed.

Chapter 13

Siobhan pulled up in the carpark of the stroke rehabilitation centre. It was a much smaller place than the Las Vegas hospital and had a more relaxed atmosphere. It consisted of a quartet of two storey buildings with large windows embedded in a large clean garden where people wandered happily on this cool sunny day. She entered through the sliding doors and reported into reception. Clane Quilley had been transferred to the centre in Carson City two weeks ago. It was a long way from his home in Boulder City, but it was necessary for him to go there to receive the care he needed. Siobhan flew on a one hour bunny-hop from McCarran Field and hired a car at the airport. The doctor was a young dark-haired man who greeted Siobhan warmly, remembering her from her last visit. "I'm pleased to say that your father has made considerable progress this past week. His memory is much improved and his general consciousness status is close to normal. He has regained some use of his left arm and leg; these are all positive signs that his brain is recovering."

"Thank you. That's wonderful."

"I should warn you though, he still exhibits unusual behaviour. This is not uncommon for stroke patients. Some days are better than others, but..."

"What do you mean 'unusual behaviour'?"

"Well, sometimes he insists on speaking in a foreign language, one I don't recognize." He knocked on the door of Clane's room and opened it. "Hello, Clane. How are you? You've got a visitor."

Her father's room was spacious and had an atmosphere more like a hotel room than a hospital ward. There was a conventional medical bed, but also an armchair, a low table and a large TV screen on the wall. The windows only opened a short way for safety reasons, but they were as wide as they could go and a fresh breeze filled the chamber. There were pictures on the wall and a vase of flowers on the window sill. Clane sat in the armchair facing the TV. It was switched on, but the sound was down. A wheelchair was parked in a corner because he still could not walk. There was a square patch on his head where his hair had been shaved during the surgery he'd had the previous month. The hair was growing back, but was still visibly much shorter over that spot. His face lit up with a childlike smile when he saw his daughter. He lifted his left hand a few inches to give a feeble wave. "Siobhan! *Lá maith. Conas atá tú inniu. Féach ar seo! Is féidir liom mo lámh a aistriú anois*."

"See what I mean?" said the doctor.

"He's speaking Irish Gaelic." explained Siobhan. "We lived in Ireland for a few years and he learned it. He was passionate about Ireland and really went native."

"Can you speak it?"

She shook her head.

"Well humour him for a while. Sometimes he switches to English when you've listened to him for long enough."

The doctor left and Siobhan sat on the side of the bed opposite her father. "How's things going, dad?"

He shook his head grimly. "*Ba mhaith liom go raibh mé sa bhaile. Molann an dochtúir sin dom*."

"Dad, is there any chance you could speak English?"

"*Labhair Béarla? Cén fáth*?"

"I want to talk to you and I can't understand you. Could you give it as go?... *Can* you speak English at all?"

He sighed. "Alright, Siobhan; but I must tell you I don't like it!"

"It's OK, dad. I won't be here long. I just wanted to see how you are."

"I miss you, your mom and Brendan. Hope I can come home soon... I still can't walk although it feels good to be able to move my hand and foot a bit."

She chuckled. "Me being here is a taste of home and that's the next best thing... and that reminds me, I've got a little present for you." She reached into her handbag and pulled out a can of Guinness. "But don't tell the docs and nurses whatever you do?"

"Guinness?"

"Yeah. It'll probably do more to heal you than all the meds they're giving you."

He recoiled from the can as if it were red hot. "Siobhan, I appreciate the thought, but I couldn't possibly drink that."

"Come on, dad. Since when were you afraid to bend the rules?"

"No, you don't understand... It's disgusting stuff! I can't abide it."

She paused and sat back. "Dad, it's Guinness. Are you saying you... don't like Guinness?"

He nodded nervously.

"But... but you used to drink pints every other night. It's your favourite drink. Surely you remember that; do you?"

He hesitated with a pensive frown. "Er... yes... but..."

"So what are you talking about when you say you don't like it?"

"I... I'm not sure." His face took on a pitifully confused expression.

"It's alright." She put the can back in her handbag.

Her father's attention was turned to the TV. "Look!"

She turned and saw that the TV was playing a news programme.

Clane fumbled with his good hand to press buttons on the remote control and the TV's sound came on.

"*...Dallas animal welfare group. Rescuers were hampered in their effort by the continuing heavy rain...*" The picture showed images of tumbling torrents in a swollen river under a dark grey sky. Texas had experienced record-breaking rainfall over the past forty-eight hours and this had caused flash flooding all over the state. The story was that of a horse which had been in a field when the floods hit and had been swept away in the deluge. It had been washed up against a fallen tree and some people had tried to pull it out of the water; but they had not been successful. Eventually the flood levels rose too high and the horse drowned.

The moment the story ended Clane immediately broke down in tears. He put his good hand to his face and cried like she had never seen him cry before. She put her arm round his shoulders. "Dad! Dad, what's the matter?"

"The horse!" he sobbed. "That poor horse!"

....

Siobhan decided to stay the night in Carson City and checked into a nearby hotel. She had left her father an hour after arriving. There was no point staying because he wouldn't stop crying. His grief for the dead horse in the news story was so intense and prolonged that the doctor had given him a sedative and sent him to bed. Siobhan E-grammed her mother and told her what was happening. She replied in a positive yet concerned tone. She added a postscript to her E-gram: "*By the way, Siobhan. I've met the most wonderful woman at class. Her name is Millicent and she is such a fabulous lady! I hope you'll meet her soon. Mom.*" Siobhan looked up from her screen and wondered why she felt just the tiniest twinge of apprehension. It was the name Millicent that very lightly tapped her alarm bell, but Siobhan wasn't sure why. "Ah well." she sighed aloud and settled down on the bed. There was no point being worried when she didn't know what she was worried about. She had an awful lot else to worry about that she was only too well aware of.

When she went to visit her father the following morning the doctor was very encouraging and, indeed, when she saw Clane he was almost completely normal. He was sitting up in bed eating his breakfast with the help of a nurse. "It's the cutting with a knife that's the problem." he detailed. "Good job I'm right-handed." When the nurse had gone and they were alone Clane said: "Siobhan, I'm so sorry about yesterday. I don't know what came over me. I can't help it, you know? It's the stroke."

"It's alright, dad; I know. I'm just glad you're over it now."

He lowered his voice. "Do you still have that can of Guinness?"

"I'm afraid I returned it to the liquor store, but I can always get another." They both laughed.

They talked for a while about the family and Clane asked a few questions about who had come to visit him. "It wasn't just the family who visited you." said Siobhan. "A strange old man turned up as well; I think he was an Indian or something."

She had spoken indifferently, simply talking as the memory came into her head. Therefore she was bewildered when her father gasped and said "What!?"

218

"A... a man came to visit you while you were asleep."

"What did he look like!?" Clane barked. His eyes widened.

"Quite old. Short; about five-five. Black hair, Indian-like face. Craggy skin."

"What was his name?"

"He didn't give one. He said he was an old friend of yours."

Clane gaped into space for a moment then a smile bloomed across his visage. "Ha ha ha!" he guffawed and burst out laughing.

"Are you OK, Dad?" Siobhan assumed this was another seizure like the one he had yesterday where he cried over the dead horse on TV.

"He's back!... My God, he's come back!" Clane's face was beaming with joy.

"Who has?"

He looked at her. "Siobhan dearest, he *is* an old friend, a very good old friend. I thought I'd never see him again... but now I will."

Chapter 14

Siobhan looked around for a good place to film. "Over here." She pointed to a street corner opposite the gates where there was a slipstream in the flow of crowds going in caused by a pair of lamp posts and a paper stall. It had stopped raining and just a few misty drops drifted down from the black sky through the beams of the lights. Her two-man notepad set up the camera and sound recorder. She adjusted her makeup and then the camera operator counted her in. "Good evening from Chicago. This is Siobhan Quilley reporting live for CBS News at the Union Stock Yards, venue for tonight's campaign rally. Henry A Dealey is the most successful presidential candidate ever to run on the impendent ticket. If successful he will be the first candidate ever who has never run for political office before. The former FDRA director has defied the pollsters again and again as his campaign has gone from success to success. There is a momentum behind his drive that the other candidates are said to lack. He promises social justice, an end to inequality for Negroes, women and other minority groups. It is now just two weeks until the general election, a flat out battle between Dealey, Kennedy and Rockefeller. None of them have anything left to lose. We're on the final strait. This is Siobhan Quilley, CBS News, Chicago." She held her smile.

"And... cut."

A tidal wave of people squeezed in beneath the decorated main gates which were surmounted by towers with spires like a fairytale castle. As soon as they had uploaded their report to the CBS studio Siobhan and her colleagues dived into the human river flowing into the venue. Julian came and found her; he had travelled with the WRSL by train. It had taken them all night and all of today. He hugged her warmly. "We're going to see Dealey speak! It's wonderful!" He was almost dancing with exuberance. "He's our hero, Siobhan! He is the future. Whether he knows it or not, or intends it or not, he is the spark that will light the fire of revolution!" After a few more minutes he bounded off like an excited puppy to talk to one of his fellow party members. From the start it was obvious that this was set to be a highly unusual hustings. Siobhan had reported on three of Dealey's public campaign events for CBS News and they were all fairly similar and had all the standard American political publicity tropes, but not this one. There were no flags; none were mounted on poles or as wall-hangings and nobody was carrying any, nor wearing any hats, T-shirts or other articles of clothing based on it. There was not a star or stripe to be seen anywhere. Siobhan then did see some groups of people carrying flags, but they were not Old Glory. Some were bright red with the hammer and sickle Soviet motif indicating that the people carrying them were communists. Others were ones she didn't recognize. Most were black bisected diagonally with another colour; red, green or pink. Some flags were just pure black sheets, as if cut from coal-sacks. She took photographs with her roam and did a Mesh search for them. The results identified the black-and-red flags as anarcho-syndicalist; the black-and-green ones as anarcho-primitivist and the black-and-pink ones as anarcho-feminist. She had no idea what any of these things were. There were long Meshpedia articles to explain, but she had no time to read them here. There were a few other flags she did identify as anachronisms from the republican side of the Spanish Civil War. The attendees were about half black and some of the black people wore sunglasses, berets and other vestments that identified them as members of one or another of the various "black power" organizations that had risen as part of the general civil rights movement and had expanded considerably by feeding off the Dealey presidential run. They looked angry and intimidating. Guns were not allowed in the Union Stock Yards, but these men looked as if they ought to be armed. The white people were similar in their clothing and behaviour to those who had been at the Boston demonstration; indeed Siobhan saw a few she recognized from that event. Some were carrying banners with slogans like "DEALEY FOR PRESIDENT!" and "DEALEY TODAY- SOCIALISM TOMORROW!" There was a separate group of about a hundred and fifty people, about ninety percent black, who were walking into the venue from a different direction. They carried no flags or other insignia of any kind. They were also far more smartly dressed. Siobhan recognized the man at the front as Dr Martin Luther King, the Alabama congressman she had met in Dubai.

The crowd diffused into the auditorium for the hustings which was the social hall. The facilities were primitive compared to the usual venues for Dealey's events; which were theatres or sports arenas. Everybody sat on folding wooden chairs facing a plain matchboard stage. The floor was made of naked planks, the lighting was just a row of bare bulbs and there were no curtains on the windows. There was still no sign of any American flags or other emblems of patriotism. There was a large banner hanging over the stage that simply read: *Dealey for President*. With the exception of Julian and his comrades, the audience seemed to lack the enthusiasm Siobhan would have expected at this opportunity to meet their chosen candidate face-to-face. They talked in low voices only to their immediate neighbours. The mood was sombre and reminded Siobhan of the feminist meeting in Boston. She took her place in the press gallery at the back of the room where a dozen or so other reporters were watching with TV cameras and telephoto lenses.

Henry Dealey came onto the stage without any preamble or introduction. He simply walked out of a door at the back of the stage accompanied by his wife Leonora and his running mate, a large Latino called Carlos Maboosa. A fourth person came out a few steps behind them; a short woman holding a tray. She stood to one side by the door. There was nobody else on the stage other than the four of them. The presidential candidate was dressed almost as casually as his audience. This was highly irregular because at his other rallies and debates he always wore a conventional suit, as did Kennedy and Rockefeller. Tonight he had on a loose pair of slacks and a jacket of a different colour under which was a blue cotton shirt with no tie that was unbuttoned to his upper chest. He also had a five o'clock shadow on his chin indicating that he had neglected to shave. The crowd applauded as he walked up to the podium, some were rushing back to their seats from the toilets and refreshment counter because there had been no warning that the proceedings were about to start. The candidate stood there patiently with a smile on his face and waited for everybody to take their places. The noise died down into the silent drum roll of anticipation. "Comrades!" began Dealey.

"Did he say 'comrades'?" asked Siobhan's soundman with a frown.

Siobhan nodded.

"Comrades!" Dealey repeated. "Friends!... Brothers!... Sisters!" He gave a very long pause. Then he shouted at the top of his voice: "White people are evil!"

There was a roar of approval from the crowd.

"Men are evil!"

Another vocal upvote.

"Hets are evil!"

Here Dealey was using a neologism. *Het* was short for "heterosexual". It had fallen into common speech in the mid 1950's to designate people in response to the increased colloquial use of the word *gay* to mean a homosexual man or as an adjective to relate to homosexuality. The word *lez* was its equivalent for women.

"We are all rapists!... Racists!... Misogynists!... Homophobes!... Slave owners!... Conquerors!... Murderers!... Oppressors!" He stood back from the podium and took a deep breath with a pensive and sensitive expression. "White het males are the cancer of the earth! Destroy white het males! Live in paradise!... Tonight I came to tell all of you, comrades, brothers and sisters; that a Dealey presidency means that the age of the white het male is coming to an end!" He ended the sentence with a furious roar.

Siobhan put her fingers in her ears to stop them ringing from the noise of the audience's standing ovation that lasted well over a minute.

"My white skin offends me! I hate it!" yelled Dealey. "Yet swear I will make amends for it, or at least make amends as much as any white het male can! Reparations are coming!"

That word again, thought Siobhan.

After another round of raging applause Dealey spoke in a quieter voice. "I want all the white het males in the audience to join me on stage... Come on." he beckoned.

There was a moment's hesitation, then one man stood up. He was followed by another, then a group of three did.

"What's this all about?" asked the soundman.

"Dunno." whispered Siobhan. She spotted Julian's familiar mop of hair rise over the rest of the audience as he also stood up.

"Line up here along the front, please." ordered Dealey. After they had done this, about thirty white men were standing in an even line facing the audience. "Now!... What would you all like to say to these white het men you see before you?"

The voices of the audience together sounded inhuman. It somewhat resembled the baying of angry dogs. Siobhan could only see their backs from her vantage point but heads were bobbing up and down as people jumped in the air. Fists waved wildly.

"We hear you and understand!" replied Dealey. "We cannot redeem ourselves and we know you can never forgive us, but let us make a gesture of shame! Let us prostrate ourselves now! We place ourselves at your mercy!... Bring forth the instruments of penitence!"

The short woman with the tray standing at the door walked up to the line of white man and picked up an object from her tray. It looked like a fountain pen, but Siobhan couldn't be sure from her distance. The woman with the tray handed it to the first man in the line, who happened to be Julian. She then moved to the next man and handed him a similar object; then she moved on to the next man. Eventually she had given one of the objects to every man in the line. Then she approached Dealey at the podium and gave him one.

Siobhan and the soundman exchanged another worried and confused scowl.

When Dealey spoke next his voice trembled with passion. "Comrades! Brothers! Sisters!... This is what we think of our toxic masculinity! Our hetero-normative sickness!... But most of all, our white skin!... This is what we think of our white skin!" Dealey shrugged off his jacket. His shirtsleeves were unbuttoned; clearly he had planned this. He rolled up his right sleeve to his bicep and raised the object the woman with the tray had given him and drew it across his pale forearm. A red line appeared; blood.

Siobhan then realized that the objects were not fountain pens; they were knives. She gasped.

"Come on!" bellowed Dealey manically at the line of white men. His face was blazing red. "Do it! Cut your privilege into pieces! Show your commitment to the cause!"

As with when they first stood up, one started and the others followed one by one. Julian was not the leader, but he was the most eager. He vehemently threw his jacket down onto the floor and jabbed the knife into his arm with more vigour than anybody else.

"Julian! No!" shouted Siobhan, but her voice was inaudible over the din of the shrieking mob, even to herself.

Dealey was frenzied. He was like some kind of Baptist minister at worship. He thrust his arm in the air so the cut was plainly visible. "Come on!... Cut! Cut! Cut!... Slash! Slice! Tear apart your filthy white skin!"

The others were now holding their own arms up, all with thin red lines of blood. However Julian was still cutting. He was working the knife back and forth as if chopping a beefsteak. The red line on his arm became a gash. Blood began running down his arm to his wrist.

"Oh my God, no!... Julian, STOP!" screamed Siobhan. She got down from her chair and ran down the stairs of the press gallery to the aisle. She ran down to the stage with difficultly because some of the audience were writhing on the floor with ecstasy. By the time she reached the stage the entire right half of Julian's shirt was drenched in his blood and it was dripping down his trousers onto his shoes. She leaped up the steps onto the stage and seized his left elbow to pull the knife back. "Julian, STOP!... STOP!" she yelled in his ear. He turned to look at her. His expression began as embarrassment and annoyance, but then changed to confusion. His cheeks were very pale. Then his eyelids drooped and his body flopped as if it had been transformed instantly into a woollen doll. She grabbed his soggy form to prevent his head hitting the floor too hard. As soon as he was on the ground she wrenched the knife from his grip and threw it against the wall. Then she seized his jacket and wrapped it around his right arm. The bloody immediately soaked through to her hands. "Jesus Christ! Holy hell!" she shrilled. "Will somebody call a fucking paramedic!"

Dealey approached with a concerned look on his face. "An ambulance is on the way, Miss Quilley." he said.

"Are you happy now, you fuckin' irresponsible creep!?" she screamed at him. "GET OUT OF MY SIGHT!"

Dealey's wife took his arm. "Come on, darling." she said gently and led the presidential candidate away.

Julian was semiconscious by the time the ambulance arrived and he managed to step onto the paramedic's trolley himself. They had placed a pressure dressing on the wound for the journey to hospital. She walked beside the trolley as the paramedics wheeled it out to the ambulance. Her clothes, hair and skin were soaked with Julian's blood. She could smell it; she could feel it congealing on her blouse, making the material stiff. It had got into her tights and was squishing in her shoes. Siobhan didn't notice any of the onlookers around her and only much later wondered, did they feel proud or guilty? Outside it was still raining lightly. As they came out under the streetlights one man caught her eye, the dapper, suited figure of Martin Luther King. Siobhan left the side of the trolley and ran over to him. "Dr King!... Dr King, please! You know this is wrong! You *know* it! Speak out! Tell the world! Denounce Dealey!"

The congressman looked at her, and then his sad brown eyes moved to the trolley with Julian lying on it wrapped in a blanket. He turned and walked away.

"Dr King!... Dr King! Please! Do what is right! *Say* what is right! Tell everybody the truth! You know this is wrong! You know Dealey is bad! Don't let him become president! Help us stop him!... PLEASE!"

....

"It was magnificent!" bubbled Julian. He was holding the bedside phone in his one working hand. "The joy of the revolution was there! I felt it. It flowed through me. It was like Orwell's description of Barcelona in late '36. One of those rare glimpses of the glorious future; the potential! It was a taste of life in a workers state; what it could be, what it would be... what it *will* be!" He rambled on for fifteen more minutes. Julian's ability to speak was phenomenal. His mouth was a cornucopia of speech. Siobhan wondered if he would sit and talk forever if ever given the chance. Eventually his interview was finished and he put the phone down. "That was great, Siobhan. I was just live on *Proletarian Radio*, one of the biggest socialist meshcasts in the world."

Siobhan shrugged. Once again she chose her words carefully. "I'm glad you're happy, Jules... But you'd like to be *alive* to see the socialist state wouldn't you? You don't want to die before it comes."

He paused. "Ideally not, of course."

"What do you mean 'ideally not'?"

"The revolution will costs lives. There's no way to achieve it without risking a large number of lives; that's an unavoidable fact."

"I don't want yours to be one of them."

"If mine is not one of them than somebody else's will be."

She paused. "You could have died last night, Jules. You lost two pints of blood. How is you dropping dead on Henry Dealey's campaign trail helping the revolution?" Julian had been sent to the operating theatres as soon as he'd arrived in Mount Sinai Hospital in Chicago. He had severed a major artery in his right forearm that could easily have resulted in death by exsanguination. He had also damaged some of his nerves and his ring and little fingers were partly paralyzed, possibly for the rest of his life. He was now lying in a bed on the trauma ward with his right arm suspended in a sling and a plastic pouch of transfusion blood connected to a drip in his other arm.

"Siobhan... I will do anything to further the revolution. If I thought fucking a chicken would help the revolution I'd be on the way to the closest farm right now with a key to the coop. If it costs my life, for whatever reason, then so be it. That is the ultimate revolutionary sacrifice and sometimes it must be made. If you're not willing to make it then you're not a true revolutionary. You're nothing but a fake! A trendy-leftie! A charlatan!... It could be that the knowledge that I helped make a better world for future generations to enjoy, instead of myself, has to be enough. Unlike the religious fanatic I don't have an afterlife to look forward to once I'm dead. That just makes my martyrdom even sweeter!"

Siobhan had come prepared with a mental bandolier of possible diplomatic plots and astute axioms to level at him, as she had attempted once before; but she was feeling less confident this time. "Jules... those books you gave me. They say nothing about the kind of thing that happened last night."

"That's because those are old books that are useful for tools of basic education but dated when it comes to modern perspectives. Marx and Engels never intended their insights to be indelible stone tablets. Their philosophy is a living thing! It evolves and adapts."

"Those books say that the revolution is one of class struggle. I didn't see any class struggle last night, Jules. I witnessed some kind of blood-letting ritual like something the Incas used to do."

He frowned with irritation. "Don't display your ignorance, Siobhan. Things have changed. The working class had their chance. Fifty years ago they could have done it." His face took on a bitter expression. "They had the world in their hands and they let it fall though their fingers. They preferred to fight their fellow workers! They fought them and killed them in a war beyond any kind of human carnage ever imagined before in our worst nightmares!... They'd butchered Twenty million of each other by 1918!... They abandoned their Russian comrades to isolation and destruction!... And now what do they do? Read *USA Daily* and vote Republican! There is no going back from that. It's over for the white proletariat, Siobhan. An entire new class must be the engine of the revolution; the class struggle is now one of social justice for oppressed minorities!"

Siobhan was dumbfounded; all her rehearsed lines fell into the fire. It was not a conscious decision to go for broke.

"Julian... Please! You have to get out of this. It's a hate cult!"

"What?" He gazed at her with genuine perplexity.

"What have these people ever offered you apart from hate? They've made you hate your parents! Does that really make you happier?... I went to a women's meeting in Boston. I heard them say things they would never say to your face! Do you know what they really think of you? Those women have been taught to hate you! The Negroes have been taught to hate you!... And last night I saw you being taught to hate yourself! You hated yourself to the point where you almost killed yourself!" She seized his undamaged hand. "Julian!... Come away with me! Leave all this behind! It's all bullshit! Hateful destructive bullshit!... Can't you see it!?"

He lay there completely silent, starting into her eyes; a neutral expression on his face. He was lost for words; such a rare occasion that it took on an existential weight of its own and bowled them both over with its import. He blinked first. He looked down and said in a completely different tone of voice, a quieter and weakened voice: "Siobhan... I need to be alone. I need to think."

She felt an overwhelming bloom of affection for him. "Of course, my love. I'll go for a walk and you can text me when you're ready to talk."

Siobhan left the hospital and went for a walk in Douglas Park. She strolled around the pond watching ducks paddling. The rain had stopped and the sun was shining. About an hour later he texted her: "*You can come back now and we'll talk. J.*" There was no row of X's at the end, but he often left those out anyway now. When she entered Julian's room she pulled up in the doorway. Five other people were by his bedside, all WRSL members whom she had met before. One of them was Derry. "Julian?"

He looked at her with a hurt expression, as if he had just found out she had been cheating on him with his brother. "It's strange how the forces of reaction can infect our lives."

"What?"

"Maybe it was my fault, allowing myself to be duped. You do work for the bourgeois media after all; that ought to have been more than a clue for me."

Derry and the others glared at her defensively, standing up and lining themselves along the side of Julian's bed like a guard phalanx.

The memory of the first time she and Julian met flicked through Siobhan's head. She saw him sitting under a tree at Schuylkill reading a book. "Jules, I... I love you."

"And you show your love for me my trying to undermine my life's work?... Honestly!" His voice rose in anger. "What did you think I was going to do, Siobhan? Marry you? Buy a nice detached house in Chevvy Chase and have lots of white babies?... Did you really think *I* would give *you* white children!? That I would take part in creating a new generation of privileged oppressors?"

Siobhan opened her mouth to reply but no sound came out.

"And now you goad me to abandon the socialist cause. What was it you said?" He imitated her voice: "'It's bullshit! Hateful destructive bullshit!'. You actually believed I would commit a betrayal like that?... No!" He took a deep breath and then said in a calmer voice: "I want you to leave now, Siobhan. And I never want to see you again."

Siobhan looked at his steely gaze and the hostile protective sneers of the others. Her vision swam and her head was spinning. She turned around and walked out of the doorway, methodically putting one foot in front of the other. She walked down the hospital corridor, her face trembling. The world looked distant and ethereal, like a picture on a TV screen. There was no future, no past; just the piercing and delirious present.

Chapter 15

Siobhan had never felt such an urge to flee as she did at that moment. She was sitting in the makeup room at CBS Broadcast Center in New York City staring at her own reflection in the illuminated mirror. She made small talk with Valerie, the maternal old makeup lady, who was applying spray to her hair. She had hardly slept the night before and it would be at least three AM before she got to bed tonight, depending on the results. If it hadn't been for Walter Cronkite she would have backed out, even if it cost her her job. Sometimes she doubted if she could have lived through the previous week without him. She couldn't to speak to her father at all now, so the old presenter had become something of a stepfather to her. Clane Quilley had suffered a second brain haemorrhage the previous Friday week, the day after she returned from Chicago. She raced to the acute neurological unit in Carson City and again waited patiently for him to come to after the anaesthetic. He recognized her this time, but his first words to her were: "So there you are, Siobhan. Listen! Have you got the car ready? Park it round the back. These people have kidnapped me and I need you to bust me out." His boss offered her some more time off, but Siobhan felt just as uncomfortable sitting alone at home so she declined. Now she wished she had said "yes". She had told Cronkite everything; her father's illness, Julian. She had cried down the phone to him for an hour at one point. Tonight she would be on air with him again, and this was the one comfort. Her mother was very engrossed with her social life at her evening classes and paid her little attention. She focused her caring instincts on Brendan as she always had since he was born. Even before then, Siobhan realized that she and her mother had always had a fraught relationship. This was why she felt no jealousy about Brendan and never had. There was a knock at the door and the director stuck his head in. "Ten minutes, Siobhan."

"Sure, Bill. I'm almost ready." she replied. She looked down at her roam and saw she had a text from Martin Luther King. "*Pray hard tonight for JFK, Miss Q. I just hope I wasn't too late*." She texted him back: "*Thanks, Dr K. I hope so too.*"

As she entered the studio Cronkite was already sitting at his desk. He gave her a supportive smile. She took her place in her chair and settled her posture. She attached her microphone to her jacket and poked her earpiece in; she heard the director's voice from the gallery: "Testing Siobhan. Testing Siobhan."

"Loud and clear, Bill." she replied. "Am I coming through?" They did a few more sound and screen tests then the commercial warning came through and they battened down for the air. The teleprompter switched on and displayed her opening lines.

"Five... four... three..."

The light came on. "Good afternoon, this is CBS News, going live on the CBS national network and online at wmn.cbs.tv.us. I'm Siobhan Quilley and welcome to our live non-stop coverage of the forty-fifth quadrennial presidential election. It is Tuesday the eighth of November 1960, the date on which the American people choose their next president, the man who will lead the nation into the 1960's and the future. Three men are battling it out; Senator John F Kennedy, Henry A Dealey and New York Governor Nelson Rockefeller. With three candidates, and with the opinion polls indicating; this could be, for the first time ever, a plurality result. Will history be made this evening? We shall see." She smiled and looked at her fellow anchor.

"I'm Walter Cronkite and I will be bringing you complete and uninterrupted coverage of the results when they happen and as they happen. It is six PM and polls have already closed in three states..."

Her broadcasting alter-ego appeared within minutes into the programme and Siobhan was very grateful to step aside and let "TV Siobhan" take over. TV Siobhan was her best friend at that point, coming along to help right when she needed her the most. She took over her brain, her body and her speech. TV Siobhan convened with on-scene reporters at the three campaign headquarters, then interviewed the former President Dewey, an ex-secretary of state, the political editor of *The Washington Post* and many others.

"It looks as though Indiana has declared for Kennedy. This is an important swing state and is worth eleven Electoral College votes. This also goes against the polls which had given the state to Rockefeller..." At one point she had to talk to Martin Luther King live on the air and this was where the ordinary Siobhan truly enjoyed what TV Siobhan was doing. "Dr King, you have caused a major upset among the Negro electorate sector because of your somewhat eleventh hour change of mind. Formerly a staunch advocate for Dealey you are now placing your support for JFK. Can you explain why?"

"I, as a black man and an American, love this country and all her peoples." replied King in his usual poetic style. "In my quest for justice and liberation for Negroes across the land I have made a terrible mistake. I believed the rhetoric of a man who believes you can heal an injustice by trying to cancel it out with another injustice. You cannot! All you get is a double-dose of injustice."

"Are you saying that the Dealey movement is opposed to civil rights even though it supported by so many in the Negro community?"

He nodded. "Correct. Civil rights cannot be achieved the way these people think it can. They truly believe that if only we abuse white people enough, abuse men enough, abuse heterosexuals enough, this will eventually result in some kind of equilibrium. This is a dangerous falsehood."

"Dr King, the last fortnight has seen unprecedented levels of street violence across the country. Riots on the streets by mainly young Negroes. The membership of the Ku Klux Klan has allegedly doubled since June. Are we looking at an upcoming racial war in America?"

"I believe this is what Henry A Dealey wants. He has sucked on the bones of resentment and fuelled the misplaced, unjust and futile quest for indiscriminate revenge." King went on to explain how his swapping benches had divided black America. There were those calling him an "Uncle Tom" and a "coconut". Others understood where he was coming from and also changed their allegiances to Kennedy.

As soon as the studio cut to a location shot Siobhan heard the director's voice in her earpiece: "Siobhan, could you say 'African American' instead of 'Negro' in future?"

"Why's that, Bill? I've never heard of that word before."

"New regulations."

"But Dr King is black and he never says it."

Bill paused and then responded sharply: "Dr King does not work for CBS."

She nodded, still confused. "OK, Bill; 'African American' it is."

The night wore on. TV Siobhan had an additional benefit in which she prevented the ordinary Siobhan from experiencing drowsiness. By ten PM she was on a roll; she had forgotten her troubles and she could have gone on until the next evening. The results came in state by state. Because of the need to concentrate on her work she was unable to assimilate them as easily as somebody watching the broadcast would. By midnight it was clear that Kennedy had suffered major losses; a few to Rockefeller, but mostly to Dealey. Rockefeller lost Florida to Dealey, a traditional fence-sitter and Kennedy picked up Missouri from the GOP. Dealey also won California away from the Democrats, which is usually declared a decider with its fifty-five votes. At one AM Siobhan announced that a plurality was now off the agenda and it was a head to head battle between Rockefeller and Dealey. It was like watching a game of chess in slow motion in which the fifty states of the Union were the squares. In the end Dealey achieved two hundred and seventy-one Electoral College votes, a majority of just two. Kennedy won seventy-seven and Rockefeller and a hundred and ninety. "So there you have it." said Siobhan. "Henry A Dealey is the next President of the United States. The first independent candidate since George Washington to win his way to the White House." There were jubilant scenes at Dealey's campaign headquarters in New York. In the other two, people were hanging their heads. Some were in tears. There were a few more interviews and commentaries and then the programme ended at six minutes past three in the morning.

Siobhan went to her dressing room and collapsed onto the settee. She switched on her roam. There was a text waiting and it arrived with a beep that made her jump in her half-asleep state: "*Told you so. JFK.*" She dropped the phone onto the floor and fell asleep.

....

The staff all left her in peace to sleep. The cleaning lady didn't even come in. She awoke just after nine AM and went out for a walk to see how the city was taking the news. She walked along 57th Street towards the Midtown area. Newsagents were displaying the papers with their headlines: *DEALEY WINS!* and variations thereof. The print media didn't want to be upstaged by their televisual rivals and had worked through the early hours to rush their newspapers off the press. The issues were extra thick, no doubt packed with commentary by everybody who could commentate. She was stopped every few minutes by passers-by who recognized her. She tried her best to tolerate these constant interruptions. The people who approached her were almost always kind and appreciative and said things like: "Hi Siobhan. I'm your biggest fan! You're the best anchor CBS has and I love watching your shows." She even signed autographs when people held out notebooks and pens. It was difficult when all she wanted to do was walk down the street in peace, but didn't want to be evasive towards people who liked and admired her. They might be strangers to her, but she was not to them.

She caught the Subway at 7th Avenue and alighted near her old home in Brooklyn. She wandered slowly along the wide square streets with apartment blocks set back behind large yards and lawns. She looked up at the windows of her old home. The current residents had put in new double-glazed windows. After a few minutes of musing she walked to Prospect Park and caught the Subway back to Manhattan. She knew she would be expected to work again this afternoon. The train was quite full and there were no free double seats so she sat down next to a small old man reading a newspaper. She thought about her old home that she'd just seen. She recalled her teenage years, her school, her friends, what her parents had been like in those days.

The train trundled along, rocketing down the tunnel, rattling noisily, screeching to a halt in stations, accelerating out of them with the hum of its electric motors. "Did you enjoy your trip down Memory Lane, Siobhan?"

She jumped in shock. The old man with the paper next to her had spoken. She looked at him and he looked back at her with a mischievous smile. It was the same man who had come to visit her father in hospital, about whom Clane had been so overjoyed to hear about. She had been sitting next to him in silence for a good ten minutes and he had ignored her. She did not initially recognize him because he was dressed differently. He had on a business suit with shiny shoes. An umbrella rested against the seat beside him at a forty-five degree angle with its tip on the floor, and he had a briefcase on his lap. "Oh, hello." she said. "It's... erm..."

"Your father likes to call me 'Flying Buffalo'."

"Is that your name?"

"Yes."

She tittered. "That figures then. Pretty amazing coincidence meeting you here again."

"Is it?" He raised an eyebrow.

She shrugged, unsure of his meaning. "I'm afraid my dad's had another stroke."

"I know. I went to visit him yesterday. He was unconscious, but he will know that I have been there."

"Thank you for doing that. He was very happy when I told him you had been to see him in Las Vegas... You must have flown to New York last night then."

"Kind of."

"Did you watch my election programme on CBS?"

"Yes, I watched all of your show; it was very interesting. You did a very good job considering the strain you were under."

Siobhan felt unnerved by his perception. She also remembered the first words he had said to her a moment ago. "Mr Buffalo, how did you know that?"

He sighed. "It's a bit hard to explain."

"You asked me if I'd enjoyed my 'trip down Memory Lane'. Were you following me back there in Brooklyn?"

He shook his head. "Siobhan, I experience certain insights by means I can't reveal to you right now. I know about your break-up with Julian."

"What? You know Julian?"

"Yes, although he doesn't really know me terribly well... You need to understand him better, Siobhan."

"Why? He never wants to see me again."

"Your paths may cross again in the future. He might have changed by then... Julian is a familiar type. You see, we live in a world where there is injustice, inequality and deprivation around every corner. Are there worse things than being born into that deprivation? Perhaps being born into a privileged position in such a world and not being the kind of person who can simply say: 'To hell with it! I'm alright, Jack.' and enjoy the fruits of their good fortune. Julian is one of those who can't do that. His empathy will not allow him to. Believe it or not, it is his innate virtue that has led him to behave in such a destructive manner... Marxism is an enticing lure for people like Julian. It delivers a simple explanation for the unbearably inhuman horrors of the modern world, and also an apparently straightforward solution."

She chuckled. "Well I read his books on Marx and they sounded far from simple, but I dislike the same problems he does. I want to find a solution too. I think I might have, but he doesn't want to know. He refuses to look at it."

Flying Buffalo looked at her intensely, but still with a cheerful grin. "Then you will have to show him."

"How?"

The old Indian paused. "What is the one major factor missing from all the news stories coming out of the presidential election?"

"Disclosure?" It was such an obvious answer she wondered if it could be right.

"Correct... Disclosure. It has hardly been mentioned by any of the candidates since the Dubai summit, even Kennedy. Dealey has actively suppressed any conversation of the issue. Yet it is only just over three years since Saucer Day. As a result back then your father was the most famous man in the world, yet now he is a B-list celebrity at best.

The amazing revelations provided by him have been all but forgotten. The hidden information at Area 51 remains hidden; not by forced suppression, but by the indifference of the general public. The truth is now out there for them to see, but they refuse to look at it. Julian is not unusual in that respect. Why is that?"

"I don't know... And anyway, the forced suppression might be returning." She described her last trip to Area 51 including the new FDRA security measures.

"The FDRA is nothing more than a front for Dealey's personal power agenda." said Flying Buffalo. "Think for a moment. Imagine, if you will, a world in which Disclosure never happened. A parallel universe in which there was an immediate and successful cover-up of the Roswell Incident; the government stuck to their original plan, to release a fake news story about it being a weather balloon. As a result, there was no false Martian invasion, no Saucer Day, nothing. What would that world be like?"

She thought hard. "That's all academic, Mr Buffalo; because there is no such world. We can imagine it all we like, but it's not real."

"No, no! You should talk a bit more to your science correspondent. The current work of one Dr Everett is particularly interesting. It is perfectly feasible that such a place that I have just described exists. So, I repeat my question: What would it be like?"

"Well... We would still regard MFO's are a bit kooky; the people who believe in them as nuts. Things would go on pretty much as they did before Disclosure in our world."

"That's a good answer, Siobhan. That is indeed what would happen. The Cold War would definitely have endured for many more years; it would almost certainly still be in progress by 1960. It would most likely have been more evenly balanced, with less territory falling to the socialist bloc. We would probably see a retardation of technological development. It's quite possible that the early 1960's of that world would have the technology of say, the late 1940's of our world. There would be no modern electronics in common use, few jet aircraft; only rudimentary television."

"Why is that?"

"Because the forces holding back such development would have been more successful."

"What forces?"

He replied quickly and irritably with a raised voice that made her jump. "The forces that are well on the way reasserting their control of the world when you people were on the brink of final victory over them!... In ten years time, if they have their way, you will look back and try to remember Disclosure and you will wonder if it had all been just a dream."

"But it was not a dream!" she protested. "It is real. We all saw it."

"Define 'real'. For most people 'real' is what their TV tells them, what their political figures tell them, what their peers tell them. He who controls that flow of information controls what is, for all practical purposes, reality... Have you ever read a book by one Mr Orwell called *Nineteen Eighty-Four*?"

"No."

"Read it." He opened his briefcase, reached in and brought out a paperback book. He handed it to her.

"Thanks." Siobhan looked at the book. It was of an average trim size and thickness. It was brand new and shiny. The cover image had a picture of a severe face with staring eyes and the words: *Nineteen Eighty-Four by George Orwell*. She had heard of Orwell because Julian used to talk about him a lot.

"Your Mr Orwell died a decade ago. He had some deeply perspective insights. It's a great shame he didn't live to the present day. The world needs people like him... It also needs people like you and your father."

"Me?"

"Yes."

She paused. "You told me my dad would get better, but that was before his second stroke. Will he still get better?"

"Yes."

She felt tearful again. "Thank you."

He smiled at her affectionately. "You're an amazing family, you Quilleys. What would the world do without you?... But, as is always the case, it is the best people who get the toughest jobs. I'm afraid you're one of them, Siobhan." He pointed at her.

"What job?"

"What you must do will become clear to you as your tasks come into your life. The first one will be detailed in the text message you are about to receive."

The moment he finished speaking her roam bleeped. She looked at it: "*Siobhan, need you to interview Dealey at his campaign HQ now. Get there and meet with location team. Bill.*" "Shit!... CBS want me to go and interview Dealey."

"Is that a problem?"

"Yes. I can't stand the prick! Two weeks ago he almost got Julian killed."

"What questions do you plan on asking him?"

"Well, the ones chosen by my director for the script of course."

He paused and then said in a low voice: "Siobhan, ask him different ones."

"What? I can't do that?"

"Yes you can. You are the interviewer. You can ask him anything you like."

"But if I deviate from the script Bill will ass-rape me! I'll be busted down to local traffic updates before you can say 'three mile tailback'."

"You can do what is right or you can do what is safe. The two are not always the same... Ah, this is my station." The train slowed and lights filled the windows. He stood up and walked towards to door. "Good luck, Siobhan." he said.

"Mr Buffalo, wait!"

The doors opened and Flying Buffalo decamped with a number of other passengers. She watched him walking down the platform towards the exit until the train moved again and her view was obscured by it entering the tunnel.

....

The Dealey campaign headquarters was at a large Savoy hotel on Lexington Avenue on the Upper East Side. He had hired the entire hotel for the previous month. Siobhan felt physically sick as Valerie attended to her face and costume in the small anteroom that had been designated the CBS hub. She placed the bud in her ear and heard her director coughing. "Bill? Are you here?" she asked, feeling a sense of dread.

"No, I'm in the gallery at the Center. We've got you on DelveLink."

"OK."

"Now, remember; this is only Dealey's third interview after his victory speech, so make it good!"

"Will do, Bill." She moved through to the suite which was acting as a studio. The lights and cameras were set up and ready to go. The new President-Elect Henry A Dealey sat in a velvet chair with his legs crossed; a self-satisfied expression was ramped over his face. "Miss Quilley." he grinned at her. "We must stop meeting like this."

She ignored him and took her place in a similar seat opposite. The teleprompter was positioned correctly. After the sound and screen tests the first question appeared on it: *What will be your first executive orders?* The countdown began and TV Siobhan made her presence known. The camera light went red. With a bit of encouragement from TV Siobhan, she succeeded in smiling at him. "Good afternoon, Mr President-Elect. Congratulations on being chosen to become the thirty-seventh President of the United States."

He nodded genially. "Thank you."

"It is traditional that following the inauguration ceremony the new president makes a number of executive orders. What will yours be?"

He chuckled. "I'm not at liberty to divulge every detail, but we'll leave it with the fact that some new Treasury directives must be enforced to prevent the national debt increasing as it has due to a result of President Goldwater's ridiculous half-doubling taxation programme. I won't say that I will repeal the programme entirely, only Congress has the authority to decide that; but I can restrain it so that its wanton destruction can be limited for the time being..."

As he continued speaking the second question appeared on the teleprompter: *What is the future for the FDRA?* "Mr President-Elect..." She paused, thinking about Flying Buffalo's words. "Erm..." TV Siobhan was screeching in her ear. "Mr President-Elect, a few people have expressed concern that you have forgotten what the D stands for in FDRA. Would you like to explain your position on the FDRA, the drive for Disclosure and the agency's continuing remit?"

"Siobhan, what are you doing?" Bill barked in her earpiece.

Dealey leaned back slightly; his media poise wavered. "I'm not sure what you mean. My policy towards the FDRA as president will be pretty much the same as it was when I was agency director. My successor John Crawley and his deputy Jeffrey Calicos are doing a splendid job and I am very pleased with their performance; I plan to retain them in the directorship for the foreseeable future of my administration."

"Siobhan, What the fuck are you doing!? Get your eyes on the TP! Can you hear me, goddamnit!?" Bill was sounding very worried now; a bolus of terror in her left ear.

"Be that as it may, Mr President-Elect, but the regime of Mr Crawley has made it more and more difficult for independent scientists and researchers to gain access to the formerly secret vaults at Area 51."

"Holy shit!" yelled Bill. "Siobhan! You're screwing up! Look at the TP now!"

Dealey lowered his brow. "I can assure you, Miss Quilley," he answered coolly, "that my administration will ensure the best possible outcome from any scientific endeavours at the site you mentioned. This was my policy as director under President Goldwater's administration and so it will continue with me in the Oval Office."

Siobhan noticed how Dealey would not use the proper name of Area 51. "I wonder if we could talk about who funded your campaign."

"Right, that's it!" said Bill "Siobhan, wrap up! Wrap up now! We go commercial in ten!"

"But for the time being, thank you very much, Mr President-Elect. We're going to have to take a quick break now." She smiled at the camera. "This is Siobhan Quilley, for CBS News with President-Elect Henry A Dealey. We'll be right back."

Chapter 16

She read *Nineteen Eighty-Four* by George Orwell on the night flight to Las Vegas. In between periods of sleep she got about halfway through it. It was a remarkable book. Orwell's thesis was that the ultimate battleground in any conflict was the human mind. She understood why Flying Buffalo believed this book was an allegory of their times. She wondered about the strange man himself. How was it they ended up meeting like that by chance? How did he know so much about her? He even guessed when she would receive a text message. After the end of the interview Dealey had walked out of the room without a word. She had dreaded the reprimand from Bill that she was sure was coming, but he had not said a word. He had merely replaced her for the rest of the shows that day. She would not be dismissed, of this she was certain. Her earlier fears were self-reassured after she thought more about her position. She was far too valuable an asset to CBS. It wasn't only herself noticing the fans who came up to her in the street; they wrote in to the studio as well to gift their praise for Siobhan Quilley, newsreader. She would have to do something far worse than that for them to let her go. She had over a year left on her contract so with any luck today's little *faux pas* would not affect it. If it was not renewed, one of the other networks would be only too happy to snap her up. She had an E-gram from Cronkite. He said nothing direct, after all he was not her official boss and had not seen the script himself; but he guessed something was amiss and subtly probed her for information. He didn't seem to mind; if anything he was amused at the prospect. Siobhan was glad; she would have been far more upset about Cronkite's disapproval than Bill's because Cronkite was somebody she admired and wanted to impress.

The plane landed at six AM. She picked up her car from the long-stay carpark and drove home. Her mother was in her dressing gown with moisturizing cream all over her face and a towel wrapped round her hair. She sat at the table eating toast. "Are you going out today, honey?" she asked.

"I was going to take a trip into Vegas later."

243

"Could you be back by four o'clock? Millicent is coming round and I want you to meet her." A rhapsodic smile came over her face as she spoke.

Siobhan felt adrenalin wash through her, a whisper of unease from her subconscious just like she had had in Carson City the previous week. "Mom, who is Millicent?"

Gina Quilley sighed deeply. "She is the most wonderful person I've ever met. She gave a lecture at class last month and we've been in touch ever since." Gina had been attending evening classes for a few months now. She hoped eventually to gain a degree in psychology. The world of her classes was something she generally kept completely separate from the family. She had made a few friends and sometimes had phone-calls from them. Before his stroke, her husband was uninterested, but humourously tolerant of her studies. "Millicent is so wise and knowledgeable, Siobhan. I know you will just love her as much as I do."

When Siobhan returned from Las Vegas at half past three her mother was frantically making the house. She had the Hoover in one hand and a cloth in the other and she was trying to clean both the kitchen floor and table at the same time. "Mom, what are you doing?"

"Just trying to make the place look nice for Millicent." she panted. Her face was red and perspiration glistened on her forehead.

"The place already looks nice! In fact I've never seen it so spick and span. For God's sake, mom!" Siobhan snatched the cloth from her hands. "This isn't the Queen of England calling you know. Go and clean yourself up. You look like you've been running a marathon."

Gina ran a hand through her sweat-stained hair. "Alright." When she came back from the bathroom Gina continued to potter around the lounge, moving ornaments, straightening picture frames and plumping cushions. Siobhan watched her worriedly. Then her attention was drawn to a screech of tyres on the road outside. It was followed immediately by a loud horn blast. Gina's face lit up. "She's here!" Siobhan ran to the front door. Outside a large white car had just parked diagonally across the street right outside their home. Another car was stationary in the carriageway just beside it. The door of the white car opened and a hunched, misshapen figure emerged. It was an ancient woman with thick white hair. She hobbled towards the pavement with a paradoxical mixture of extreme frailty and omnipotent power. Her movements were jerky and robotic; she planted the tip of her walking stick onto the ground with each step as if she intended to thrust it through the tarmac and implant it in the earth. Her back was stooped over so far that her face was directed almost completely downwards, but her curved osteoporotic spine looked as robust as a tank turret.

The driver of the other car stuck his head out of the window. "Hey, lady! What the hell are you doing parking like that? I can't get past. Move your goddamn car would you?"

"No!" retorted the old woman. "I'm parking it there and that's it!"

The man swore at her and then reversed with another crunch of tyres.

"Hello, Millicent!" beamed Gina.

"Hello, Gina." The old woman smiled back with a totally different expression to the one she'd just had.

"Millicent, this is Siobhan, my daughter. You may recognize her from CBS News."

"Hello, Siobhan." she said in her strong Scottish accent.

Siobhan took her hand and shook it. It was bony with loose dry skin, but Siobhan could feel muscles underneath that were like steel wires.

"Siobhan, could you please go and make Millicent a cup of coffee? Milk, no sugar."

"And half full." added Millicent.

"Sure." Siobhan nodded. She pretended to walk through the kitchen door, but when their backs were turned she jerked into the hallway and tiptoed to Brendan's room. She knocked on his door. "Brendan!" she hissed.

"Go away." her little brother moaned from within.

"Brendan! Open the goddamn door!"

The urgency in his voice made him get off his bed and open his door a crack. "What do you want, Siobhan?"

"Keep your voice down!... Listen! Have you said anything to mom about Boggin?"

"We talked about him a bit."

"Jesus! Dad told you not to!... When?"

"Last week I think."

"Oh shit!... OK, listen; don't tell her anything else about him! Nothing at all! You understand?"

"Why?"

"Just *do* it!... Please!"

"Alright." he said sulkily and shut the door.

Siobhan leaded against the wall and sighed. Then she went to the kitchen to make Dr Millicent Arbroath-Laird her coffee. The moment she saw her she remembered the intimidating old woman at the New Year party at Julian's home and what she had said about Brendan. Luckily the old crone had shown no signs of remembering Siobhan. Siobhan's mind spun as she grappled with whatever hypothetical process had led the elderly psychologist to her door. She made sure the cup was exactly half-full, remembering how excessively Arbroath-Laird has reprimanded Selly the maid for getting it wrong. When she brought it out, Arbroath-Laird was lighting a cigarette. "Millicent." she said. "We don't allow smoking in this house." The old woman snatched the cup without thanking her and looked into it disparagingly. "Well I'm smoking, Siobhan, so there! Now go and fetch me something I can use as an ashtray. If you don't I'll just drop it on the floor." She addressed her without looking at her in the same tone she had used outside when she had parked her car.

Siobhan gaped in shock. She turned to her mother. "Mom..?"

"Just get Millicent a bowl." she answered breathlessly. Her face was tight with fear.

"Mom, what's going on?" Siobhan asked.

"Siobhan!... *Please*!"

"Run along and do as your mother tells you, Siobhan." added Millicent sternly.

Siobhan went to the kitchen; her heart was pounding with fury and confusion. The expression on Gina's face and her tone of voice was of somebody begging. It was as if

246

Arbroath-Laird had just walked into their lounge and pointed a gun at them. By the time Siobhan had given Arbroath-Laird a bowl the guest had already dropped a lump of cigarette ash on the rug. It kept its cylindrical shape as it lay there, looking like a small piece of excrement. It was surrounded by a patch of vitrified nylon indicating that its heat had burnt the rug. The room started to fill with the noxious fumes of Arbroath-Laird's cigarette smoke. Gina and she talked casually as if nothing was amiss. Siobhan went to the kitchen and opened a window, trying not to cough. She thought of her father. "Oh, dad." She felt herself begin to cry. At that moment she would have given anything for her father to have been there. "What's going on?"

Chapter 17

"Mr President-Elect, please raise your right hand and repeat after me." said the Chief Justice of the United States.

Henry A Dealey was standing at the focus of the parapet at the western front of the US Capitol. He had his left hand placed on top of George Washington's Masonic bible. There was revered silence from the dignitaries that clustered around him and from the half a million people packed into The National Mall.

"Only a lightning bolt can stop him now." Siobhan muttered ruefully to her cameraman in the press pen.

He giggled in reply.

The weather was icy and clammy and Siobhan shivered inside her standard issue CBS location parka.

"Repeat after me." said the Chief Justice. "I, Henry Austin Dealey, do solemnly swear."

"I, Henry Austin Dealey, do solemnly swear." replied Dealey with the same reverence.

"That I will faithfully execute."

"That I will faithfully execute."

"The office of President of the United States."

"The office of President of the United States."

"And will, to the best of my ability."

"And will, to the best of my ability."

"Preserve, protect and defend."

"Preserve, protect and defend"

"The constitution of the United States."

"The constitution of the United States."

"So help me God."

"So help me God."

"Congratulations, Mr President!" He reached forward and shook Dealey's hand. The band of the US Marine Corps struck up with *Hail to the Chief* for the first time in Dealey's presence. The crowd in the Mall cheered. The echoing booms of an artillery salute reverberated off the white walls; the huge Stars and Stripes flags draped over them barely deadened the sound. Dealey shook the hands of everybody around him and hugged Barry Goldwater fervently. The Chief Justice then spoke into the microphone on the speech podium. "Ladies and gentleman, it is my honour and pleasure to introduce to you the thirty-seventh President of the United States, Henry Austin Dealey."

Dealey shook his hand again and then addressed the mic. "Mr Chief Justice, President Goldwater, President Martin, President Dewey, my fellow Americans... thank you!" His characteristic smug sneer, his face's neutral expression, had returned. "We stand on the brink of a new era. The uncertainty, confusion, fear and despair of the past decade has evaporated like dew in the light of the dawn. For today is indeed a new dawn. As your president, I will bring the light to all of you; man and woman, black and white, rich and poor... or should I say, poor no longer. I promise you that the time is coming within weeks that you can count on your hands that the reconstruction programme will be, totally, utterly and officially... complete!" The crowd applauded. "The days of darkness will soon be distant memories. America now enjoys an opportunity unique among nations of the world, past and present. We have come out of the dark days of the war and its aftermath as the world's sole superpower. With our allies in the Middle East and the League of the World we can form a new alliance, an alliance of civilization." More applause. "It is my intention to implement the Dubai Treaty as the highest priority of my foreign policy. Here at home its goals have been virtually achieved already..." His inaugural speech lasted another fifteen minutes then all the delegation went into the Capitol for the special inaugural luncheon and Siobhan's team could take a break.

Covering the inauguration for CBS was a far easier job than she had originally imagined. She only needed to do any commentary on camera at the beginning and end of the event. The majority of work was done by the gallery mixing and editing the feeds from the set cameras in the Capitol. After the luncheon President Dealey went to a desk and signed a number of executive orders with Leonora and their children at his side. Siobhan watched the feeds as a viewer, like any other, knowing this was a new beginning, but the beginning of what? The end?

All that evening and all that night the streets of Washington DC were riven by unrest. It started by a demonstration by thousands of members of the Ku Klux Klan. This was set upon by a counter protest of black and leftist organizations. The police spent hours keeping the warring sides apart. The scene was matched by similar insurrections in New York, Los Angeles, Houston and many other cities. Statues of American heroes were vandalized and official buildings were set on fire. In Downtown DC there was a ritual burning of an effigy of Martin Luther King, but this was not carried out by the Klan; it was the work of one of the black power organizations affiliated to Dealey's campaign. At eight AM, just after dawn the next day, Siobhan was riding along Massachusetts Avenue in a CBS van; the driver was skirting round burnt-out cars, the remains of police roadblocks and overturned dustbins. She saw an impromptu street rally in progress. A makeshift podium had been erected out of a dumpster and on top of it a firebrand was raring up the crowd, yelling and waving his hands in the air. Siobhan gasped and couldn't stop herself staring. It was Julian. He never saw her and the van just drove past.

....

The following day she left Washington DC and flew to Carson City to visit her father. As soon as the plane had taken off she opened up her matchbook and called up the Meshpedia page for Dealey. "*Henry Austin Dealey (born March 2nd 1907) is 37th and current President of the United States.*" Siobhan marvelled at how quickly the board updated their pages. "*Before entering politics he was a civil servant.*" She snorted and muttered aloud: "Well that covers a multitude of sins." The page then described his background. She skimmed the paragraph: "*Dealey was born in Youngstown, Ohio to David and Jane Dealey... graduated from the University of Florida in 1928 with a degree in politics and economics... first job as a secretary for the Ohio House of Representatives...*" Siobhan chuckled. She had an image in her head of a gawky young man with steel rimmed glasses shuffling huge piles of paperwork late into the night. She read the next paragraph more carefully. "*Federal Government Career. In June 1947 Dealey was appointed to the Department of Agriculture where he worked as a personal assistant to the Secretary, Clinton P Anderson. In 1951 he was given a seat in the Executive Office on the Council of Advisers..."* She sat back for a moment and thought. In those days her father was head of the Department of Extraterrestrial Affairs. He would surely have known Dealey back then because they were rubbing shoulders with each other in the White House; yet Clane Quilley had never mentioned him. She could hardly ask him now, she mused sadly. Dealey's Meshpedia page gave the impression of a hardworking and ambitious man who was intent on gaining high office, but was willing to do so slowly and quietly, climbing the ladder one rung at a time behind the scenes in a low-key way; forgoing the immediate prestige and glamour of, say, a career in the military or being elected to a lower-level political position. It portrayed him as a patient and self-possessed individual; one who was both willing and able to defer gratification. *"In 1957 Dealey joined the NAACP and began writing for its journals..."* It gave a list of numerous articles. At one point he was editor of the magazine *Africa in America*. That was odd. Nothing in his previous life story indicated a conscience over civil rights, yet shortly before his presidential run he suddenly decided Jim Crow laws were appalling and buses should be desegregated? He launched into this new found quest for black emancipation with gusto that many who fought within it their whole lives never showed. The rest of the page charted his post-Disclosure career as head of the FDRA and his presidential campaign, things Siobhan already knew. The last paragraph covered his personal life: *"Dealey has been married twice... first marriage to Anne Clements... divorced in 1930... married Leonora Saltman 1939... three children, Henry jr, Lesley and Jane..."* Dealey's wife's name was coloured, indicating a link to another Meshpedia page. Siobhan hesitated for a moment and then clicked it: *"Leonora McCrae Dealey, née Saltman (born October 9th 1909) is the current First Lady of the United States."* The page detailed her marriage to Dealey in the opening paragraph. "Not very feminist of you, Leonora." Siobhan chuckled to herself. However the career section of her biography described a very different kind of person; a highly independent and self-made woman who was almost as ambitious as her husband. She had not wed at all before marrying Dealey at the age of twenty-nine. That was somewhat unusual at that time, as well as being quite old to start a family. She had managed to bear three children since then, the youngest of which was already nine. *"...after graduating from Berkeley she studied experimental psychology at St Andrews University in Scotland in a select class of seven students under the professorship of Dr Millicent Arbroath-Laird..."* Siobhan yelped and slammed her matchbook shut.

A stewardess came over to her. "Are you alright, ma'am?"

Siobhan blushed. "Yes... Yes, I'm fine thank you. Sorry, I just had a touch of cramp."

"Can I get you anything?"

"No no!... Thank you."

....

Siobhan left her hire car in the carpark and entered the stroke rehabilitation centre where her father had returned a few weeks ago. Clane Quilley was sitting in the lounge in his wheelchair facing the window. Beyond it was the elegant garden in the hospital grounds. Other patients sat around in chairs and on settees, sometimes on their own and sometimes in groups playing cards or watching the television. She approached him, fingering the can of Guinness in her handbag. "Hi, dad. How are you?"

He turned his head. His left eyelid still drooped slightly. "Siobhan" he pointed out of the window. "Look!"

She followed his finger. "What?"

"Birds!... Do you see them?"

She squinted her eyes and studied the garden hard, mostly to humour him. "Er... yeah, dad. There are quite a few birds out there. I'd expect that in a garden."

He suddenly glared at her and said cuttingly: "Haven't you been here rather a long time now, Siobhan?"

"No, dad. I just got here."

"I'd like to be left alone now." he growled and shifted himself in his chair away from her.

She sighed and walked away. The doctor was standing in the lounge doorway. "Don't take it to heart, Miss Quilley. He gets snappy like that with everyone."

"How has he been?"

"He's still making slow but steady progress. His injury is severe and it will take some time to recover."

"Is he likely to have any more haemorrhages?"

He shrugged. "We're doing everything we can to prevent that; controlling his blood pressure, monitoring him every hour."

She nodded.

"You know... It might help if his wife came to see him again."

"Hasn't she been here?"

"No, not for two weeks now."

Siobhan paused. "I see."

....

Siobhan had been visiting her mother as many times as she could endure, just for the sake of Brendan. She used to take him out for some fresh air as often as she could. He had developed a chronic wheezy chest and the school had complained that he reeked of cigarette smoke. Siobhan arrived home at four PM and crossed her fingers. She breathed a sigh of relief when she saw no white hatchback blocking the road. She opened the front door and was hit in the face by the stench of stale cigarettes that was now a permanent part of the house's ambiance. The white wallpaper was stained a dark yellow from constant exposure to tobacco tar. The armchair over by the window was now officially called "Millicent's chair" and Gina had brought a small table and an array of ashtrays. She was in the kitchen and Siobhan stuck her head in. "Hi, mom."

"Hello." replied her mother tonelessly without looking at her. This was the average extent of their conversations these days.

"Is Brendan in? I thought I'd take him to the movie theatre."

Gina sighed. "Do you need to ask me? Check in his room and see for yourself; you're not a helpless baby."

Siobhan walked to her brother's room feeling nothing. She'd given up any sense of sadness at her mother's transformation months ago. "Hi, Bren."

"Hi, Siobhan."

"Want to come out to the movies?"

"Yeah!"

When she arrived at the cinema they were in time for the last matinees which were not very crowded. Siobhan had learned through experience that these were the only ones suitable for Brendan. She also had to choose a seat as far away as possible from other patrons. The reason was his constant coughing. By the time the film finished it was gone seven PM and getting dark outside. When they arrived home Siobhan's heart sank. The white hatchback was parked in its usual place, obstructing the road. "Damn! She's normally gone by now!" she muttered. When she opened the door she heard the crusty Scottish voice of Dr Millicent Arbroath-Laird. Brendan ran into the kitchen. Siobhan wasn't entirely sure how many times the old lady came to see her mother, but she was always there when Siobhan called round so it was likely that it was most, if not all days. Whenever she entered the house while Millicent was there the same thing always happened. Her mother would greet her by curtly asking her to make Millicent a cup of coffee. Sure enough Gina turned to her daughter with her usual passive-aggressive smile. "Joanne, could you please make Millicent a cup of coffee? Milk and no sugar. And please remember, make sure it is half-full only."

Siobhan paused, wondering if she'd misheard. "What did you just call me?"

"I called you Joanne."

"Why?"

"Because that's your name." The two older women exchanged looks. "Millicent and I have decided to change your name to Joanne."

"What!? My name is Siobhan!"

"Not any more it's not!" barked Millicent.

"Wh.. why?"

"Siobhan is a silly name." said Millicent. "It's an Irish name and you are not Irish." She lit another cigarette.

Gina nodded. "That's true. You're not Irish. None of us are."

"But... but we are. I'm descended from Brendan and Colleen Quilley. Mom, you are descended from William and Lillian O'Reilly who were on the same ship over! We're as Irish as shamrocks!"

"Nonsense!" roared Millicent. "You are not the tiniest bit Irish so I don't know why you insist on using such a stupid name. Anyway, your mother gave you that name so she can take it away. From now on you will answer to Joanne... Only Joanne! Understood?"

Siobhan just had a terrible thought. For the last few visits she had noticed something had changed about the facade of the house but she couldn't work out what it was. Now it suddenly struck her. She ran out of the front door and sure enough, the Irish tricolour that her father always had flying on a flagpole above the front door, the same flag he used to hang from the window-ledge of their New York apartment, was gone. The pole was bare. She stormed back into the house. "Mom! You've taken down dad's flag!"

"Yes, Joanne. Millicent and I took down that flag and burnt it. Why would we have an Irish flag on our house when we are not Irish?"

"What!?... Dad is lying in hospital. He almost died! He's hardly able to move and talk... and you took down his flag... and you destroyed it! How could you!?"

"SILENCE!" yelled Millicent. "Do not raise your voice to your mother, Joanne!"

"Joanne, where is Millicent's coffee?" asked Gina.

"She hasn't bothered to make it yet because she's too lazy!" snapped Millicent. "Go and get me my coffee, Joanne! Go and make it NOW!"

Siobhan took a step towards Millicent. "Go fuck yourself, you geriatric school bully!" It was such a relief to say those words. Siobhan felt a blast of euphoria.

Millicent arched herself backwards in her chair as far as her rigid aged spine would allow and let out a gasp of horror.

Gina screamed long and loud as if in physical agony, and then burst into tears.

Siobhan almost danced out of the lounge; she hardly noticed the thick fog of malodourous smoke that filled the house. She was about to go to her room when she heard Brendan's voice from the kitchen. "That's right, Boggin... I'm not sure... Yes, it was a good movie, but the ending sucked..."

Siobhan stopped and went back into the kitchen. Her eight-year-old brother was sitting at the kitchen table with his back to the door, completely alone, talking to the wall. Horror filled her as she realized that his voice was also audible from the lounge. Gina and Millicent came through the door; both were staring intently at Brendan.

"Boggin, don't be stupid... I know you're not stupid, but I mean, like..."

Her mother looked worried in a controlled and tense way, as she had done when Siobhan had first told her about Brendan's imaginary friend. However Millicent's expression was different; it was a look of satisfied greed. Her black beady eyes were wide open between their wrinkled liver-spotted lids and she was almost smiling.

....

Brendan was scared. He insisted on Siobhan accompanying them to the doctors. Gina wasn't happy about that, but eventually capitulated. He held his mother's hand, but kept his eyes on Siobhan. Dr Millicent Arbroath-Laird came with them of course. She already knew a "good paediatric psychiatrist" in the area and made the appointment. She took charge of everything, booking them in at reception, telling them which chair to sit on when they went to the waiting room, speaking to the doctor first alone before his consultation with Brendan and his mother. Siobhan had never felt so helpless and frustrated in her life. She was screaming inside: "STOP!", but there was nothing she could do. Her mother was hardly speaking to her at the best of times; how was she meant to talk her out of this situation? Gina dutifully obeyed every word Millicent uttered. Siobhan sat next to Brendan with their mother on the other side. There were four other families in the waiting room. Four pairs of stoic fearful-looking parents sitting with their children. The younger children were playing happily with the toys supplied from a box in one corner. A door opened at the far end of the room and a bald man in a grey suit came out. "Brendan Quilley please."

All three of them got up. "No, Joanne! You shall stay here." ordered her mother. She pushed Siobhan hard on the shoulder, forcing her back into her seat. Gina and Millicent led Brendan into the doctor's office. As soon as Siobhan was alone in the waiting room one of the other mothers leaned over to her and said: "Don't worry, it'll be alright. Dr Lenninger is very good." The mother smiled sweetly and looked over at a blond boy of about five playing with a train set; presumably her son. "He's one of the world's leading experts in dealing with the...er..." She lowered her voice. "imaginary friend... problem."

Siobhan nodded. She dared not speak because she wasn't sure she would be able to control what she said. She looked at the little blond boy. Every so often he would look up from the train set and speak a few inaudible words to his companion in the thin air in front of him.

After half an hour Gina, Brendan, Dr Lenninger, a nurse and Millicent emerged from the office. "Well thank you very much, doctor." said Millicent. She and Gina walked over to where Siobhan was sitting; the doctor went back into his office. However Brendan was walking in another direction; the nurse had him by the hand and was leading him over to a third door at the far end of the room, a large heavy door that was painted pure black. Just before they passed through it the boy turned and looked at his adult sister. His expression was unreadable. The door shut behind him with an obtrusive thump. "Mom, Millicent, where's Brendan going?"

"We opted for the three-week intravenous treatment." said Gina.

"What do you mean?"

"Dr Lenninger proscribed Taniflen." said Millicent. "It's a highly effective paediatric antipsychotic. There are two treatment options; a three month oral course, that's pills; or three weeks of intravenous injections. The latter unfortunately can only be done under in-patient conditions.

Therefore Brendan is going to a psychiatric institution for the three-week intravenous Taniflen."

"No!" croaked Siobhan.

Millicent frowned. "What do you mean 'no', Joanne? Do you care about your brother's mental health or not?"

Siobhan's mother was staring at her daughter with an expression on her face of utter contempt.

....

Siobhan went back to see her father the following day. He was fast asleep. The doctor had given him some sedatives. Siobhan took a seat by his bedside and watched as he breathed peacefully through his nose. His eyelids flickered as he dreamed. "Hi, dad." she began. "I know you can't hear me right now, and you probably wouldn't understand me if you could. But you *must* get better soon... Please! We need you!" Tears rolled down her cheeks. "Please, dad. Get better and come home."

....

When she left her father and went back to her car she felt the sudden urge to talk to Flying Buffalo, the man she met on the New York Subway; but she had no way of reaching him. She sat in the driving seat and switched on her roam. The text tone beeped and she saw she had one from Dr Jenny Bulstrode; it had been sent only half an hour earlier while her roam was off. She opened it immediately, curious because she hardly ever received texts from her. "*Siobhan. Been fired. Jenny.*"

Siobhan gasped. She tried to call, but Dr Bulstrode's roam was switched off. She texted her back: "*Heading for A51. Where are you?*" Siobhan got a reply while she was driving down Highway 95 over the speed limit. Dr Bulstrode was at a hotel in Las Vegas. She was in the bar working her way through a bottle of Soave. This is itself was alarming because she very rarely drank; even at the after-conference party in Dubai she had hardly touched a drop. Her cheeks were flushed from the wine and her eyes bloodshot from crying. When she saw Siobhan she burst into tears again. "I've been fired!" she repeated. "Just like that."

"Who by? Pickup?"

"No, the president."

"Dealey!"

"It's only his third day in office and he finds the time to kick me out of my job."

"Why?"

"They don't need a reason, but they've given me one anyway. They're closing down the research project on the spinning disk. It's budget's been cancelled; all the staff have been kicked out... Me!" She pointed at herself. "Dealey wants the Area 51 scientific mission to pour all its effort into the Digby Carrousel, something I will have nothing to do with."

"I guess Pickup is still on board then."

"Of course!" She chuckled bitterly. "He's a big Digby man. He knows good politics even if he's blind to good science." She downed half her glass of wine.

"What are you going to do now?"

"I've called John Kennedy and he's invited me to Boston to talk to him. I'm getting a flight tomorrow."

"JFK? Why is he involved?"

"You remember how he backed us in Dubai? I think he might have something up his sleeve."

Siobhan paused. "I'd like to come with you."

Dr Bulstrode's face lit up. "I'd like that too, Siobhan."

"Wait a sec!" She checked her roam. "Damnit!... Sorry, no I can't. I've got to work tomorrow in LA."

"That's OK. We can catch up next time you're free. I'll let you know what Kennedy says."

Chapter 18

"Five... four... three..."

"Good afternoon, this is CBS News, going live on the CBS national network and online at wmn.cbs.tv.us. I'm Siobhan Quilley and here are the latest headlines for Friday July fourteenth 1961. President Dealey announced this morning that the US domestic side of Article One of the Treaty of Dubai for Global Disclosure and Reconstruction has now been officially achieved in line with his hundred-day plan. He is now redoubling efforts in order to ensure the opening of 'Digby Town', the three thousand acre site in North Carolina which is home to the project's manufacturing plants. It is said to be the product of a unique new public-private partnership system in which the FDRA joins forces with the corporations Westinghouse, General Electric, Grumman, Lockheed Martin and several others to create the first mass-produced and commercially available 'new tech'. This consortium will be the world's first production system for free energy technology, machines that require no fuel and so will produce infinite energy. The president also reaffirmed America's commitment to the upcoming League of the World expedition to Europe for the reconstruction effort on the continent under Article Four of the Dubai Treaty... The California Coastal Erosion Prevention Scheme delivered its report to Congress today with a recommendation that urgent measures be taken to save over twenty square miles of land being swallowed up by the Pacific Ocean by the year 2000. Increases in wind-speed, changes in ocean current patterns and more frequent storms due to climate change will accelerate the process exponentially above all previous estimates. The manager of the scheme recommended a multi-billion dollar coastal defence strategy that includes the construction of million-ton concrete breakwaters... In Canada today the Wilbert Smith National Laboratory is preparing for the first operational tests of its SQEC, the Superpositioning Quantum Electron Collider, the largest single machine every built. It is constructed in a circular tunnel that is twenty-seven miles in circumference and runs beneath the US-Canadian border at Abbotsford, British Columbia. It is a completely new design of particle accelerator that has never been built before. The director of the project, Prof. Bertrand Lampson, declared that this is 'the most exciting day of my life. The ultimate secrets of the universe are finally within reach'. There will be a full report on the SQEC in a few weeks on CBS News... Latest figures from the New York Stock Exchange. The dollar remains strong against all the world's currencies at four-seventy-six Emirati Dirham and ninety-one Irish pence. The Saudi Riyal is currently selling at one dollar and one cent. The price of gold is down to twenty-three dollars and eighty-five cents per ounce... And now it's time for the news, travel and weather where you live."

....

"It's ready." Dr Jenny Bulstrode has the playful, childlike grin of a true adventurous scientist. Siobhan and John F Kennedy followed her through to the garage. The building they were in was a rented unit on an industrial estate in New Jersey. Prototype E was propped up on a forklift pallet at the end of the room with the adjoining door to the workshop. The six-foot wide metallic ring was wrapped in a web of wires, pipes and conduits. There was a double row of folding camping chairs arranged in a loose double arc in the middle of the garage. "OK, let them in."

Kennedy opened the sliding door; sunlight poured in onto the dusty concrete floor. A cluster of a dozen people were waiting outside. "Come on in, ladies and gentlemen." he said. "Take a seat. Dr Bulstrode is ready to begin the press conference."

Dr Bulstrode was wearing her usual lab-coat. It was covered in grease and oil stains. Her hair was tied back with an elastic band. "Hi there. Thanks for coming." she said.

The people in the seats smiled. Some were taking photographs and filming the scene. Siobhan had wanted to cover this story for CBS, but hadn't been allowed to.

"Welcome to Spinning Disk Incorporated. I'm going to demonstrate for you the effects that can be generated by one of the two systems we have been developing here." She picked up a remote control device, similar to one used to operate a model aircraft. She pressed a button. A faint humming sound emerged from Prototype E. Slowly it got louder. "Bear with me; the torus takes a while to build up to generation levels." The humming buzzing noise increased until the machine sounded like a bees nest. Dr Bulstrode pressed another button and the machine lifted into the air. The chunky doughnut-shaped steel hull rose to chest height and stopped dead, as still as if it were laid on an invisible shelf.

The small audience remained cool, but looked impressed.

"The machine achieves lift and propulsion by generating its own gravitational field. Inside the torus is high pressure mercury vapour rotating at very high speed. This apparatus can remain stationary in the air indefinitely. Alternatively it can move in any direction and reach speeds limited only by the durability of the airframe. It requires no fuel; its energy is produced internally by its own function. Its practical applications are many and revolutionary. It can be the basis of an aircraft or spacecraft far superior to any other ever conceived. It can generate electricity cleanly, safely, for no cost and in infinite amounts. That means an end to poverty, to environmental destruction, to famine... There is no patent on any of this new tech. What you see before you was not salvaged from an MFO crash nor was it appropriated from the FDRA scientific mission at Area 51. It was built right here, in the workshop behind me by Spinning Disk Incorporated. I know that you have heard every boast I have just made from the government and its associates regarding the Digby Carrousel. Although what they said it literally true, the fact of the matter is the achievements we have made here outstrip the usefulness of the Digby system on all factors. This is why we have decided to go into business. We formed Spinning Disk back in February to produce this new tech commercially and compete with the Digby consortium directly on the open market."

One of the reporters raised his hand. "Isn't this something of a David and Goliath story?"

Dr Bulstrode laughed. "You might say so. But isn't that the nature of the American Dream? We have an idea which we believe is superior to the one given by our rival. Sure, the consortium is way bigger; it has the investment, the state sanction, the existing capital, but their product is inferior to ours." She smiled. "And remember... in the story David won."

"And they're not entirely without state sanction." added Kennedy. "I am personally willing to lobby for Spinning Disk in the US Senate." There were a few more questions and answers. The journalists were interested and promised to write encouraging stories.

After the press conference Siobhan said to Dr Bulstrode: "Can you get a working vehicle ready in time?"

"When is the opening day of Digby Town?"

"September fourth."

"That's only six weeks, but I can do it... And you will definitely be covering it."

"Yes, the programme has been planned and I've been assigned."

"Great!" The two women smiled at each other mischievously.

....

Siobhan flew to North Carolina feeling a frisson of excitement. It was like being a child preparing a prank. She forced herself to talk normally to her CBS colleagues on the plane, but it was an effort. Those who knew her well may have suspected something. The flight from New York was only a few hours then the aircraft descended into Raleigh Municipal Field at eleven AM. She checked her roam and sent the text she had prearranged. A fleet of buses were waiting outside the terminal building to drive the CBS team to the ugly complex of boxlike factories and warehouses that was collectively known as "Digby Town". There was a huge crowd packed into the courtyard by the gate, including officials from the government and the corporations involved in the project. American flags were draped everywhere, making Siobhan think of the Inauguration Day ceremony in Washington DC back in January. There were other banners too displaying the symbol of the Digby Carrousel, a double circle with five straight lines between the centre and edge. She was directed to a press tent where she and all the other media representatives were given a briefing by the Digby consortium public relations officer.

She was given a programme giving a list of the day's proceedings. She studied the timeline carefully then went to the toilet to send a discreet text: "*President scheduled to speak starting 12.40.*" After that she and her location team went to the press corps area to arrange the best camera angles. Siobhan's amused anticipation increased when she saw that Prof. Angus Pickup was present, sitting in the VIP seats near the podium. The red ribbon was stretched taught across the gateway. A band played a quick march and the Mayor of Raleigh made a speech, then the Mayor of Durham did the same. The Governor of North Carolina spoke for over half an hour saying how proud he was; and then it was time for the highlight of the opening ceremony. The master of ceremonies approached the microphone: "Ladies and gentlemen, people of the world... the President of the United States!" Everybody jumped to their feet and gave a standing ovation. The band played a fanfare as Henry A Dealey walked up onto the stage and approached the podium. Siobhan sent a text: "*POTUS on stage now.*"

The reply was immediate: "*OK. On my way.*"

"Ladies and gentlemen, my fellow Americans, people of the world." began Dealey. "In 1915 a humble farmer's wife from Canada with an amateur passion for science made a discovery that would change the world. Jemima Digby found out that by placing a piece of purified mantalite close to the twenty-fourth isotope of magnesium, known as bersillium, they repelled each other in a similar effect to the magnetic homopole reaction. At first Mrs Digby incorrectly thought that was what this was... but then she realized it must be something very different. She was astonished to discover that the force that emanated from the two minerals was not magnetic; it was a completely different kind of force. The combination of these two substances had tapped the infinite energy spring of the zero point field..."

Siobhan leaned over and whispered to her cameraman: "Duane, switch on and start rolling."

"Why, Siobhan? We're on air with the house feed at the moment."

"Just do it." She winked at him.

A car drove up the aisle between the rows of seats accompanied by another fanfare from the band. "Ladies and gentlemen." said the president enthusiastically. "What you are looking at now is the first car ever built with a Digby Carrousel engine!" There was delighted applause from the audience as they watched the car trundle up towards the stage. "This car will drive for thousands of miles without stopping once. Its range is limited only by its need for lubrication oil, for maintenance and the endurance of the driver. Think about the rising price of gasoline and contemplate how much money you will be saving by purchasing one of these cars."

In Siobhan's eyes the vehicle looked ungainly and primitive. It was larger than an average car and its front section looked swollen in comparison to the rest of the frame. There was a large bulge in the middle of the bonnet that must have obstructed the driver's view. Yet the way the crowd were clapping one would imagine it was the fastest racing car. She noticed a row of people in the VIP slot who were dressed in traditional Arabian gowns and headscarves. Two were people she recognized; King Abdulaziz al Saud and Sheikh Zayed bin Khalifa Al Nahyan of the United Gulf Emirates. They greeted the new car as enthusiastically as everybody else; which was odd when Siobhan thought about it. Surely the advent of cars that needed no petrol would spell and end to the primary industry of their nations.

"Ladies and gentlemen." continued the president. "Motoring is just one of the many applications for the Digby Carrousel. The machine can be altered to fit inside a ship's hull, an aircraft, a power plant, a railway locomotive. Already desalination centres powered by the Digby Carrousel are relieving the Abyssinian famine by irrigating the drought-stricken land with purified seawater. Understand this, we are looking at an end to poverty and environmental destruction forever. A new era of plenty and happiness for all humanity is about to dawn. In a moment I will invite all of you to visit our Digby centre's fantastic showrooms and view our entire range of coupes, sedans, station wagons and RV's..."

A text arrived: "*1 minute.*" Siobhan looked up and studied the blue sky. There were a few large clouds, but it was a typical fine and warm Southern day at the end of summer. There were none of the new thick aircraft trails that were becoming more and more common. She spotted a black speck in the distance to the north. As she watched it grew larger. "Hey, Duane." She nudged the cameraman. "What's that?"

He looked. "It's an MFO!" He pointed the camera at it.

The object grew bigger as it approached at high speed. Soon its disk shape was discernable. There was a commotion in the crowd as other people spotted it. Fingers pointed into the sky. Dealey saw it a few seconds behind everybody else. "...feel free to take one of them for a test-drive... What's that?"

"Duane, train on me!" ordered Siobhan. As soon as she was in frame she began speaking, feigning alarm and confusion in her poise. "This is Siobhan Quilley for CBS News here at the opening ceremony of Digby Town and a mysterious flying object is approaching the venue. This is a CBS exclusive here in Raleigh, North Carolina, at the Digby Carrousel manufacturing super-plant. We have an MFO situation here!..." She continued talking to the camera. She couldn't be sure that she was live on air, but she was fairly certain that by now the gallery would have got wind of what was going on and cut to her personal feed. Either way, everything she was saying would be recorded and almost certainly broadcast as a report. The metallic saucer-shaped vehicle looked far more elegant in the air than it did when she'd last seen it propped up on a ramp in the workshop. It flew in over the crowd, descending rapidly. The audience were now hollering and some had left their seats and were running away. The US Secret Service guards were well-trained. Within moments five of them had leapt onto the stage and bundled on top of the president. Three of them dragged him away while two more trained their pistols on the approaching disk. Within five seconds Dealey was out of sight. The disk was eleven and a half feet wide and had a dome-shaped top surmounting the steel lifebelt of its engine. It had been adapted from Prototype B since the press conference. It circled over the ceremonial space at about fifty feet. Its engine hummed like a storm of wasps. Two of the windows in the dome opened and human hands appeared sticking out of them. They were both holding some oblong white objects. They let these go and they fell down towards the crowd. As they fell they separated into fragments that rippled and wheeled like snowflakes. Siobhan caught one of them. It was a postcard-sized piece of paper. She held it up to the camera. "My goodness!... This is one of the pieces of paper the MFO has just dropped. It has something written on it. I'll read it out to you: 'Why waste your time with the Digby Carrousel when you can get something better? Go to wmn.spinningdiskinc.co.us for details or give us a call on 908-527-6161 Spinning Disk Incorporated'. I don't know exactly what this means, but we clearly have a very bizarre situation at the moment. This is Siobhan Quilley for CBS News bringing you this exclusive live report. I repeat, an MFO had invaded the opening ceremony of Digby Town. The president is being evacuated as we speak. We believe he is safe. I repeat, the president has not been harmed. The MFO has dropped sheets of paper with a printed message on them in plain English..." The disk descended onto the stage and came to rest. The humming decreased as its engine powered down. Some of the crowd who had bolted when the craft first appeared were now returning in knots and bunches; their curiosity had overcome their fear. Siobhan ran towards the stage with the cameraman behind her. "The MFO has landed!" She continued to address the newsroom as she ran. "It has come down on the stage. We are going to get as close to the object as we dare... My goodness! A door is opening on the side of the vehicle... No! Two doors!... There is somebody inside getting out. We don't know who or what these beings are... My God! It's Jack Kennedy! Ladies and gentlemen the senator and former presidential candidate John F Kennedy has just emerged from the MFO! Somebody else is getting out of the craft on the other side... It's a woman. I don't believe it! It is none other than Dr Jenny Bulstrode, the heroine of Saucer Day! Let's go and talk to them..."

Chapter 19

"Siobhan, are you sure you knew nothing about this beforehand?" Bill was no fool, but he also could prove nothing. "Not a thing, Bill. I swear." she lied.

"Alright." Bill wore a knowing grin on the Mootster videophone app and his voice was calm. "I'm not complaining, Siobhan. In fact, did you know our viewing figures broke new records yesterday?"

"No, but that's excellent news."

"And it's mostly down to you."

She smiled modestly. "Cool." She had watched reruns of her impromptu report over and over again, along with her on the scene interview with Kennedy and Jenny, with enormous relish.

He paused. "OK, now make a note about the Digby doc. We start shooting next Tuesday."

"I'm ready."

"We'll need you to test drive one of the Digby cars somewhere out west. It'll be a long journey. Because of this I've had an idea. You remember I was planning on sending you to Canada to do a location on that big atom-smasher thing?"

"Yes."

"Well why not combine the two? Drive there in the Digby car with the doc crew; then meet the news crew at the laboratory for the location shoot. Then we've killed two birds with one stone."

"Makes sense."

"Right, talk to you next week."

"OK, Bill. 'Bye." She waved at his image on the matchbook screen and then ended the call. She was sitting by the window of her bedroom in what was feeling less and less like her own home every day. The window was wide open even though it was a chilly early morning. It was the only way she could breathe comfortably. She left her room and knocked on Brendan's door across the corridor, and entered when he called. "Hi, Bren. How are you?"

Her younger brother rolled over in his bed. "Not bad." the act of talking started another coughing fit. "I wish this cough would go away."

"It will do... very soon."

He paused. "Siobhan... I still haven't seen Boggin. I've not seen him since I got back from the hospital. I miss him. Where is he?"

"I don't know." She blinked back tears of anguish and rage. "I have to go out now, Bren. I've got a nice surprise for you later."

"OK." He rolled back onto his side.

As Siobhan walked down the corridor she heard her mother's voice. "Joanne seems to think she can just swan in and swan out as she pleases. She does not like responsibility and she never has."

"Well I feel sorry for you." replied Millicent.

Siobhan stopped outside the door to the lounge which was wide open as it always was when Millicent was in the house; which was about seven hours of most days. Siobhan continued to cry. Her mother and Millicent were having another deep personal conversation, like they did all the time. These often involved criticisms of "Joanne". Even though these were ostensibly private discussions just between them, the two women always spoke in loud voices that were clearly intended to be heard all over the house. Siobhan stood there for a few moments, savouring her anger for the first time. For a change, her ire had a sugar-coating of delightful anticipation. She had considered walking in and simply telling Gina and Millicent what was about to happen, but she stopped herself, deciding it would be far more satisfying for them to find out the bad news for themselves. Siobhan walked across the lounge towards the front door, turning her face away from Gina and Millicent so they couldn't see her tears.

"Where are you going, Joanne?" demanded her mother.

"Out." She slammed the door behind her. She wiped her eyes with a tissue then added in a quiet voice that nobody else could hear: "And, mom, you have just called me 'Joanne' for the last time."

She drove straight up the Ninety-Five to Carson City and arrived there at midday. The doctor met her at reception and took her to his office for a private conversation. "Miss Quilley, we are discharging your father at a much later point in his rehabilitation than we would normally. In most cases we would have offered him a trial period of home recovery several months ago."

"Why's that?"

He paused. "It has not escaped our attention that... his wife, your mother, has not paid him any visits. Am I right in thinking this is an indicator that all is not well at home?"

She nodded. "You could say that."

"It is essential that your father avoids stress as much as possible. I'm well aware that it is too much to ask that he eliminate all stress from his home life. That is impossible of course; however, we felt it necessary to stabilize his condition as much as we could here at the centre before allowing him to return to the normal world. We cannot keep him here forever; we've kept him for as long as we can. He badly wants to return home and probably already suspects all is not well in his relationship with his wife. It's vital that he continues to take his medication; to maintain his blood pressure at a low level."

"I'll see to it that he does."

The doctor smiled. "Thank you. We will be contacting the medical social workers and occupational therapists in your area to keep a good eye on him as well."

Clane Quilley was dressed in a suit and was smiling from ear to ear. "Hey, Siobhan! This is it! The day I go home." He could walk now, but his left leg was still weaker than the right so he limped. He had had regular physiotherapy to prevent his muscles wasting. He still couldn't use his left hand as normal, but he could grip large objects. He talked cheerfully on the drive home about anything he could think of except the family. They stopped for a meal at a roadside cafe and he happily gulped down a Guinness. Siobhan told him nothing. There were no words that could prepare him for the situation he would find. Siobhan was pretty sure that Millicent would still be there when she arrived back in Boulder City and partly hoped that she was; it might be better. She was indeed; her white hatchback car was parked in its usual place, diagonally across the road. "Who the hell parked there?" demanded Clane as Siobhan eased her car in by the curb.

Siobhan didn't reply and just got out onto the street. Clane followed and stared at the house. His face fell at the sight of the bare flagpole. "Siobhan, where's my *Tridhathach*?"

"It's hard to explain, dad. Let's go inside." She opened the front door and ran in ahead of him. "Hi, mom! Hi, Millicent! We're home."

Clane began coughing as he walked in. "Jesus Christ! Where's all this smoke coming from!? I'm going to call the fire department!"

Gina gasped. "Clane!"

Her husband entered the lounge and took in the scene before him. "Gina...?"

"Clane, you're... you're home." she said with a terrified look.

He shrugged. "Apparently... Well, don't all jump for joy at once." He pointed at Millicent. "Who are you?"

Gina recovered herself. "Clane, this is Millicent... She's the best friend I've ever had."

Millicent did not react. She stared straight ahead of her; her sallow creased cheeks were flushed.

"Daddy!" a new voice came from the corridor and Brendan ran up to his father and embraced him.

"Brendan! My beautiful boy!" Clane picked him up. Then he put him down again and stared at him in distress. "Brendan, what's happened to you?... Oh my God! You're sick!"

"I'm fine, daddy." Brendan replied and dissolved into another fit of coughing.

Clane turned around and looked at Gina, then at Millicent. A magnificent frown of anger slowly blossomed on his brow. "What the hell has been going on here!?"

By now Gina had recovered. She stood up and addressed her husband. "Clane, could you please go and make Millicent a cup of coffee. Milk and no sugar, and ensure that the cup is half full only."

Clane paused, then he smiled thinly. "Of course... But first, Millicent; could you put out your cigarette please? We don't allow smoking in this house."

Millicent looked up at him from her chair for the first time and sneered. "Well, I'm smoking, Clane, and that is final. If you don't like it, too bad!" She pulled out another of her foul black-centred cigarettes and lit it. "Now go and get me my coffee!"

Clane bowed his head politely and then went into the kitchen.

Gina snorted. "He's even slower than Joanne."

Siobhan was confused. She wasn't quite sure what was happening; then she heard the sound of a plastic bucket being filled from the kitchen tap. Clane hobbled out of the kitchen into the lounge holding the bucket in his good hand. Then he seized the bottom of it with his left hand, drew it back and then tossed the contents all over Millicent. Gina screamed again as if in physical pain and collapsed to the ground. Millicent groaned. Water covered her body and flowed down onto the floor like a fountain. Her blouse was soaked and it clung to her sagging fleshless bust. Her snowy hair was matted down onto her skull. The cigarette was still gripped between her first and second fingers. It was completely extinguished and it drooped as the paper absorbed the water. "I said, Millicent,..." Clane spoke in a perfectly polite and composed tone. "...that we do not allow smoking in this house."

Dr Millicent Arbroath-Laird grabbed her walking stick and stomped towards the doorway. Water continued to drip from her saturated clothes. As soon as she was outside Clane slammed the door behind her. Gina pushed past him and opened the door. She ran down the pathway weeping hysterically, calling Millicent's name. Millicent ignored her as she got into her car and she trapped Gina's fingers as she shut the door. Gina pulled her hand back with a yelp of pain. Millicent shut the door properly and put the car into reverse. She backed it right across the road, crashing into a motorcycle that was parked there. It fell over and clattered to the ground. "Millicent, don't go! Don't leave me! Please!" Gina threw herself chest-first onto the bonnet of the car.

"Gina! No!" Clane and Siobhan both ran up and dragged Gina off the bonnet just in time before Millicent accelerated. She turned sharply into the carriageway and sped off until her car was out of sight around the corner. Gina turned on her husband in fury. "Damn you, Clane! Damn you! You took her away from me!"

"What are you talking about?" protested her husband.

"And damn you too, Joanne! Damn you to hell!" Gina shrieked at her daughter.

"Who the *feck*... is 'Joanne'!?" yelled Clane.

....

Siobhan looked up at the walls of the factory and almost burst with pride. It was a long clean two-storey modern building on the same industrial estate as the original Spinning Disk Inc. unit, but this one was a dozen times the size. Jenny was busy talking to a group of her new employees; all of them were dressed in boiler suits with the Spinning Disk Inc. logo on the breast. They were all top engineers and construction experts and she had recruited them within the last few days. She saw Siobhan and bounced over to her like an exciting dog. "Siobhan! What does it feel like to be a millionairess?"

"What do you mean?"

"We've been inundated with pre-orders since last week. Over a hundred and fifty thousand people have laid down deposits for their own antigravity disk and we haven't even started building them!"

"But it's your company, Jenny; not mine. That money is all yours."

She laughed. "In case you've forgotten, Siobhan, you own a ten percent share in Flying Disk Inc."

"Yes, but I only paid you two hundred bucks for it."

"It's now worth about twelve hundred thousand bucks. Not a bad return on your investment I'd say."

Siobhan gasped and then laughed. "I've got no idea what I'd even begin spending that much money on!"

"You could always reinvest it."

"Why not?"

"You'll get ten times more if you do!"

"We're going to win this one!"

"We already have, Siobhan. I can't thank you enough for arranging that media spot for us last week."

"You're welcome; I loved it... Did you see Dealey's face afterwards?" President Dealey had called a press conference the day after the foiled opening ceremony at Digby Town and made a big joke out of what had happened. He pretended to find it funny and even thanked the 'pranksters' who had brightened up everybody's day. He explained how the vehicle had been held up by wires. Even in the White House Press Briefing Room the audience had chuckled genially.

Jenny pointed to the building. "This is where we are going to mass-produce our first flying vehicles... But this is just the start! We will expand and adapt until spinning disks and vapourized mercury torus generators are in every home, every vehicle, every power plant every waterworks in the world! This is what is going to save the earth, Siobhan; not some fiddly little flywheel of Fisher-Price blocks."

"Er... while we're on the subject..." Siobhan pointed at the car that had just been delivered.

Jenny raised an eyebrow. "Is that what I think it is?"

The car was built by Ford and had rolled out from the production plant in Digby Town the previous week. Its model was called *Perpetual*. It was a sedan although it looked like a pickup truck accidentally built back to front. It had the CBS logo stencilled on the side and the words: *Powered by a Digby Carrousel*. Jenny went over to it and lifted the bonnet with the mien of an expert. "Hmm... I see they've found a way to set up a power-train." The engine consisted of a large metal cylinder with cables attached to each end. Below that was a gearbox, Jenny explained. "It looks very neat, but it's not." She pointed at the central cylinder. "The Digby mills inside this all have to rotate with perfect timing or the entire drive will seize up. This is a four-mill engine; that means eight sets of counter-rotating flywheels. It will probably need a lot of maintenance; I hope you're not planning to drive too far in this."

"To Seattle actually."

Jenny whistled. "Good luck!... This isn't your own rattletrap is it?"

"No, CBS bought it for the programme I'm making. I've got to pick up my film crew in Chicago."

Jenny chuckled. "I'll race you in Prototype B."
"Ooh! Let me see now!"

....

The sky rolled above her and the road rolled beneath her. She daydreamed as she drove along the I-Eighty towards Cleveland, Ohio. The Digby-powered sedan was not hard to drive. Its basic controls and instruments were the same as an ordinary car except it only had three gears and there was no patrol gauge on the dashboard. Because of the enlarged front section the driver sat in a more centralized position relative to the wheels so Siobhan found herself undershooting corners to begin with until she got used to it. The engine noise was different; it made a musical warbling sound as opposed to the familiar growl of the internal combustion engine. There was no ignition; the mills simply began rotating when she inserted the key under the dashboard and turned it. At the back there was no exhaust pipe or petrol cap. The lack of a petrol tank made for more storage space in the boot. The car produced no emissions at all and Siobhan understood the attraction of the idea when the large cities of the United States were becoming more and more polluted with fumes from road traffic; indeed it was becoming a major health risk for their populations. With vehicles run on Digby Carrousels the atmosphere in the centre of Los Angeles could be as fresh as that deep in the Appalachian Mountains. However the Ford Perpetual had a very heavy feel to it and Siobhan found uphill climbs stretched the engine to its limits. Even with her foot on the floor she often wondered on some gradients if the vehicle would grind to a halt and roll back. This particular car's Digby returned seventy brake horsepower, about the same as a fifteen hundred CC petrol engine; however the car itself was clearly far bigger than most conventional cars with that size engine. On the flat freeway Siobhan found its acceleration annoyingly slow and she could never push the vehicle past sixty miles per hour. This made overtaking out of the question and she was very vulnerable to lorry-bullying. Some of the other drivers noticed this and she got some gestures of ridicule through rear windows. Ideally this car needed a more powerful Digby; but the one it already had was almost too big to fit inside it. How practical was this kind of new tech? She consoled herself with the thought that the Digby's faults helped Jenny and Spinning Disk Inc.

The long drive gave her time to think, especially about recent events. She felt more at peace with her feelings for her mother than at any time since her early childhood. This is not to say that she had stopped hating her mother. Not at all; she hated Gina Quilley more than anybody else in her life. However she was at peace with her hatred. She no longer felt ashamed of it. She now realized that hate is as much a natural human emotion as love. She had learnt to integrate her hate. The problems with her mother dated back a long time before she had fallen under the spell of Dr Millicent Arbroath-Laird. When Siobhan was eleven years old her mother had found herself a boyfriend. She had driven her daughter to a plush beach villa on Long Island and introduced her to her new lover, the businessman Norman Rockliffe. The way she settled Siobhan into her new life with Rockliffe was like a woman who had been widowed starting out again with a second marriage. However all this time her father was very much alive and well. Clane Quilley was in Japan taking part in "Operation Blacklist", the relief effort to clean up the mess made of the country by World War II. He sent the family numerous letters and her mother instructed Siobhan not to say anything about Rockliffe when she replied. She told her eleven-year-old daughter to lie to her father and her own husband. After Clane's return her mother continued her relationship with Rockliffe in secret and insisted her daughter collude with her. Siobhan could bear it no longer; she broke down and told her father everything. As a result Clane was arrested for affray and assault at the Rockliffe mansion and ended up losing his job and having to move thousands of miles away from her for work. Her parents then divorced. Siobhan had never really acknowledged the trauma of this experience. The bitterness generated for her mother had been festering deep inside her for fifteen years. Gina had never apologized for what she had done, even though she and her husband had made up and remarried.

They had been happily married ever since so presumably they had straightened out the feelings that lay between them; however Siobhan and her mother had made no such reconciliation. As for her father, Siobhan had never felt such love for him as she did now. It was like being a small child again and gazing into his eyes with adoration, running her little hands though his curly ginger hair, as it was when he was a younger man. Another emotion she had not integrated until now was the terror she felt when he had his stroke, the possibility that she might lose him forever. There were still a lot of questions that needed answering about how Dr Millicent Arbroath-Laird ended up taking over her family and Siobhan intended to address those very soon; but all that mattered now was that it was over. Her brave, noble and chivalrous father had removed Millicent's toxic presence from their house, immediately, completely and decisively; like a knight on horseback slaying a dragon. He had delivered her and Brendan from evil. He was her eternal hero. The remaining problem was that removing the evil from the house was one thing; removing it from Gina's mind was another. The night after Millicent left, Clane and Gina had had a blazing row. Gina had berated her husband for ruining her life. She wept and wailed all evening. Clane had insisted that she buy him a new Irish tricolour to replace the one she and Millicent had struck from the pole and destroyed; she refused, and she continued to call her daughter "Joanne". "Her feckin' name is *Siobhan*, woman! What is wrong with you!?" Eventually Siobhan brought him a new flag online and the day it arrived she and her father solemnly hoisted it back up the flagpole at the front of their house. Some of the neighbours came out to watch and a few even applauded. Siobhan realized that Millicent had not made herself popular with them either due to her bad car parking and other forms of her antisocial manner, and they were also pleased to see the back of her. Gina sat in the kitchen with her arms folded while the flag was being raised. Siobhan and her father had discussed alerting a psychiatrist. The good news was that Brendan's bad chest improved quickly and significantly now that the house was free of cigarette smoke. However he was still not the same boy he used to be before his mental treatment and both his sister and father were worried about him.

She reached Chicago at eleven PM after driving the whole day. She checked into her hotel and made contact with the film crew. They had arrived much earlier and were having a nightcap in the bar. The following morning they all got into the Digby car and headed off on the I-ninety for the long drive to the west coast. Along the way they shot footage in accordance with the mandate of the CBS programme plan for the documentary on the Digby Carrousel. Siobhan was honest as she spoke on camera, giving all the reasons why she thought the Digby was inadequate as an effective alternative to fossil fuels. As she walked she wondered if it was worth it. How many of her pronouncements would end up on the cutting-room floor... or rather how few would not? She knew that on a two-day shoot they would film around twelve hours of footage, yet the documentary was scheduled for an eighty-minute slot. What's more this expedition was just a small part of the whole production and they were contributing a maximum of ten to fifteen minutes of the entire film. They could edit her to make her say appear to say anything. She enjoyed the journey though; the unit were two men and a woman whom she instantly got on with. The highway displayed the exquisite natural beauty of the United States like an art gallery. They stopped for the night in a remote motel on the Great Plains in Wyoming at a small town called Buffalo. The crew made cowboy-and-Indian jokes as they went to their rooms and to bed. In the morning the car wouldn't start. Siobhan pushed the key into the engine lock; the mills turned over a few times and then made a hissing sound and stopped. "Oh dear." said the unit director. "What now?"

There was a garage in Buffalo, but the old man running it appeared baffled by anything more modern than wood gas tractors. Nobody in the team knew anything about car mechanics, let alone the intricacies of this new type of engine. They decided to call the CBS office at Broadcast Center in New York and seek advice. There was no roam signal anywhere in the vicinity so they had to take it in turns to use the motel's ancient payphone. CBS told them to "stay put for a couple of days" until the next bus left the town. Siobhan had an idea that was so aptly amusing that it made her laugh out loud. She insisted the cameraman film her as she made a call. "Hello, Jenny. It's Siobhan. I wonder if you could help us out by giving us a lift... Yes we're filming a documentary for CBS about the Digby Carrousel, but our brand new Digby-powered Ford Perpetual car just has broken down in wide open Wyoming... Yes, could you take us to Seattle in Prototype B?" Dr Jenny Bulstrode was laughing so much on the other end of the phone that she could hardly affirm.

"How long do we have to wait for her?" asked the sound recordist.

"Not long." responded Siobhan with a sly smile. Twenty minutes later the disk-shaped vehicle appeared in the sky to the east. The unit watched with fascination as it buzzed down and landed in the carpark. The gloating face of Jenny appeared at the window. "Morning, guys! Heard you had a motor breakdown. Wanna lift?"

The members of the film crew at first refused to believe she had flown all the way from New Jersey in just twenty minutes; however they all agreed to let Jenny ferry them to Seattle. The vehicle was just a two-seater so Jenny had to take them one at a time, but the round trip to Seattle was only about fifteen minutes so within an hour they were all there. Siobhan was the last to travel. The interior of Prototype B was cramped, but the low seats were comfortable like a sports car. There were broad windows to give a good view outside. Siobhan gripped the arms of her seat as the vehicle rose into the air like a rocket. Within seconds Buffalo was far below and she felt exposed as if she were in a balloon gondola. "It's OK. You're perfectly safe." soothed Jenny. The craft sped through the sky, and the clouds and land below scrolled past like a time-lapse film of an aeroplane flight. The feeling was precarious, as if they were riding along a tightrope, but it was also exhilarating. Jenny operated the craft using a computer panel and a pair of joysticks on the arms of her seat.

"That doesn't look too difficult." noted Siobhan.

"It's not. Do you want to learn how to fly one of these? I'll teach you sometime."

"Neat. How fast are we going?"

"About forty thousand miles per hour."

The magnificent snowy peaks of the Rocky Mountains passed below them and a few minutes later the land settled again and she saw the sea. The coast was cut by numerous inlets and bays and in their direction of travel was a skyline of tall buildings. The disk dropped like a stone, yet she still felt no inertia; looking out of the windows was like watching a three-D movie on a screen. The vehicle came to rest in a park next to a busy road and her colleagues were sitting on a bench waiting for her.

....

They couldn't stay in downtown Seattle for long because another riot had broken out. The city was well-renowned for its uprisings and this was one of the worst. They didn't stay around to find out who was battling it out this time. It might have been one of the black groups versus the white advocacy groups, or the Marxists versus the fascists, or the feminists versus the men's rights movement; most likely it was a combination of all of them. This was the norm for American urban life at that time. Siobhan and her colleagues caught a taxi to another part of town where they did a bit more filming before heading for the airport. There she bade the filming unit goodbye as they caught their plane home. She hired a car to drive to Canada and thankfully it was a good old fashioned conventional petrol-and-pistons one. Dr Jenny Bulstrode went ahead in Prototype B; she was also curious to see the Abbotsford laboratories. It was only a two hour drive to the border which Siobhan crossed without any trouble at Sumas. As soon as she'd driven away from the customs booth she was faced with a long straight road that led between a series of large buildings on both sides of the road; they were sealed off behind a high barbed wire fence. The buildings were square white structures. Many were windowless or had few and small windows. Siobhan spotted a large white dome that looked like a radome of the kind that can be seen at signals intelligence bases. There was a turnoff onto a drive leading to the entrance gate where there was tight security and private guards manned an armoured barrier. There was a decorative sign surrounded by a small garden with an official Canadian bilingual message: *Welcome to the Canadian Organization for Nuclear Research at the Wilbert Smith National Laboratory- Bienvenue au Conseil Canadien pour la Recherche Nucléaire au Laboratoire National de Wilbert Smith.* She had to go through a thorough security vetting in the reception area of CCRN, a far more intrusive one than she had from Canadian customs at the border. Then she was allowed into the facility and taken to a comfortable sitting room to wait for her appointment. The CBS News film crew she'd be working with on this project were already there and they greeted each other warmly as they all knew each other. Jenny was there as well. Prof. Bertrand Lampson arrived half an hour later. Siobhan was astonished at his appearance. When she had first heard his name she had an image in her head of an old man with half-moon glasses and a scruffy grey beard wearing a waistcoat with a pocket watch under his lab coat. Prof. Bertrand Lampson was instead a tall and lithe young man about her own age with long, flowing silky black hair which he tossed around as he walked. He strutted cheerfully up to them with his arms swinging. He was dressed very informally too with a dark summer blazer and a black T-shirt underneath. "Hello, how do you do?" He shook all their hands and smiled with the cleanest whitest teeth Siobhan had ever seen. They were like polished pearls and they reflected the sunlight with an almost dazzling intensity. "I'm Prof. Bertrand Lampson of CCRN and I'm one of the experimental managers for the SQEC." He pronounced it "Ess-queck." His accent was English and was reminiscent of Yorkshire or somewhere in the North Country; although she couldn't place it exactly having never been to England. Prof. Lampson led them out of the room along a wide clean corridor that smelled of ozone. After she had examined him again Siobhan realized that her initial impressions of Lampson were wrong. He was much older than she had initially thought, in his mid-forties at least; but he had that eternally youthful boyish physiognomy that some men are lucky enough to enjoy. He was also much less good-looking at a second glance than he was at the first. His handsomeness was there, but it was a very androgynous kind of handsomeness. His skin was fresh but pasty and sun-starved. His smooth cheeks were not only clean-shaven; they looked as if he had never shaved. His voice was also very high-pitched for a male, an effeminate nasal contralto whine. Then something else happened that lowered him even further in her esteem. Just before they entered the lecture theatre he had taken them too he turned to Jenny and said: "Well, if it isn't Dr Jenny Bulstrode of Martian Central. Still waiting for the ZPF to knock on your front door and say hello?" His tone of voice and facial expression were mocking. He then swung around and minced into the next room without waiting for a reply, running a hand through his immaculate black hair.

Jenny frowned at the back of his head. "Arrogant son of a bitch!" she whispered.

"What's the ZPF?" asked Siobhan.

"Zero point field, the theorized source of the new tech energy."

There were about two dozen people in the lecture theatre so this wasn't a visit exclusively organized for CBS. Prof. Lampson took his place on the stage and basked in the attention of the audience, a situation in which he looked very much at home. "SQEC, the Superpositioning Quantum Electron Collider." He uttered the words with relish. A display screen behind him lit up and computer generated diagrams appeared. "The biggest and most expensive machine ever built. It stretches in an underground tube the size of a railway tunnel all the way from here at the WSNL to Maple Falls, Washington State and north to the Fraser River. The particles in the accelerator cross the US Canadian border fifteen thousand times every second... and they don't even stop to have their passports checked!" He paused for effect and the audience laughed politely. Siobhan guessed it was a joke he had told many times before. The video showed an image of a circular structure hundreds of feet below the ground. "We take the superpositioned electrons and drive them to enormous energies just a few minuscule points short of the speed of light, and then we crash them together head on!" He drove his skinny fist into his opposite palm to illustrate. "It has taken ten years to build and cost four billion US dollars... and we started testing it in July. If all goes well we hope to begin the first collisions at the SQEC by next October. The results of our experiments will tell us at a very fundamental level how the universe works. We will learn this in a way no other particle accelerator laboratory can possibly teach us." He talked on for another twenty minutes giving details of the SQEC's history and function. When the slide show stopped so did he. "Right, any questions?"

A chubby old man on the front row raised his hand immediately.

Lampson pointed at him. "Yup, Wesley."

"Prof. Lampson, what you are doing here at the CCRN is reckless and irresponsible, and it could threaten the very planet we live on!"

"Ooh!" Lampson tittered and recoiled comically with his typically effete poise.

"The particle collisions you will be generating will almost certainly produce micro-black holes and strangelets that could start a chain reaction that could turn all matter on earth into a strange star or else engulf the planet into the black hole! Bert, you might end up with the blood of all mankind on your hands!" He turned to address the audience. "I am Prof. Wesley Harrison. I am formerly the head of physics and cosmology at UBC Vancouver. They used to call me 'the Particle Hunter' and I won a Nobel Prize in 1938..."

"You're a nobber, Wesley! A total nobber! You always were."

"I taught you all you know, you clueless little faggot!" Harrison yelled.

Lampson pressed an intercom button. "Security!"

As he was dragged out of the room by a pair of uniformed heavies Harrison continued to beseech the audience: "Don't let them do this! They're going to destroy the planet!... Find out more at wmn.ccrndanger.co.ca!"

Siobhan scribbled down the meshpage address on her roam. She also did a quick Mesh search for "nobber":

"Nobber. noun. colloq. chiefly Brit: a person who has said or done something foolish. orig: Manchester and/or Lancashire late 19th c."

Lampson continued. "Just to reassure anybody who was alarmed by what that strange old idiot... who also somehow happens to be my former tutor, just said; there is virtually zero chance of anything like the scenario he talked about happening. All micro-black holes are annihilated within a tiny fraction of a second after being produced by a special kind of quantum radiation..." After the Q and A session he led the visitors down a stairwell to a huge chamber crammed with machinery. They all had to put hard hats on like the kind builders wear. The massive underground space was dominated by a gargantuan hexagonal structure that reminded Siobhan of some of the places in Area 51. Lampson explained what it was for a few minutes and answered people's questions. It was one of the experimental machines that analyzed the data from the planned particle collisions in the accelerator.

....

Siobhan, her colleagues from CBS News and Jenny ate dinner at their hotel in Vancouver. The ambiance at the table was cheery, but Siobhan couldn't join in. She had been deeply disturbed by what she had heard at the CCRN and had spent several hours on her matchbook after filming had stopped, looking up the details of what Prof. Harrison had said. She got up to go to the toilet and walked past a table where a small old man was sitting eating a bowl of some pasta dish. She had already walked past him before his presence registered and she did a double-take. "My God!"

Flying Buffalo looked up at her. "Hello, Siobhan."

"Mr Buffalo, what on earth are you doing here?"

He shrugged. "Eating a meal."

"No... I mean... how did you get here?"

He chuckled. "What an odd question. This is the Vancouver Granville restaurant, not the moon. Why shouldn't I come here for dinner if I like?"

"Because I'm here too and so it's another weird coincidence... Are you following me around? You must be!"

He rolled his eyes. "Sit down, Siobhan." He gestured to the chair opposite. She sat down at the table looking at him. "Waiter, another glass please." When the waiter had put another glass on the table Flying Buffalo filled it with white wine from the bottle beside him. "Now, Siobhan." he continued. "Why do you believe me meeting you here like this is not a coincidence?"

"Because it's too unlikely to happen by chance."

"Well then what *is* likely enough to happen by chance?"

She stuttered, unsure of what he meant. "Well... er... something more likely than this."

"So how do you separate one from the other? Where's the cut off point?"

"Pardon?"

"Above what statistical ceiling would you declare something to be a coincidence and below which you would not; and why?"

She pondered for a few moments but drew a blank. "No idea, Mr Buffalo."

He chortled triumphantly.

There was a long silence then she said: "Dad's better."

"I know, and I'm very happy about that."

"You said he would get better. You were right."

He nodded and swallowed another spoonful of Macaroni cheese and said nothing.

"Things were... pretty awful at home before he came back."

"You're not out of the woods yet in that department; you know that don't you?"

She nodded. "Mom is... not who she used to be, even though Millicent is gone."

"You do realize that it wasn't just bad luck that brought Millicent Arbroath-Laird into your home."

She sighed. "I wasn't sure."

"You can be sure, and you need to talk to your dad about it." He took a sip of wine.

"Did my dad not tell you?" She paused. "Mr Buffalo... how do you know so much about us?"

He looked hard at her and gave a slight frown. "You know, Siobhan. I'm disappointed in you."

"Why?"

"You're a very intelligent young lady. You have an excellent brain in your head, but sometimes you just don't use it."

"What do you mean?" she retorted.

"I really enjoyed that stunt you and Dr Bulstrode pulled at the opening pageant of Digby Town, but at the same time you have missed something very important and extremely obvious about that event. Something I assumed you would easily spot."

"What."

"Somebody needs to speak to you... and you need to speak to somebody."

"Who? Where can I find them?"

"You don't need to. They will find you... Now, if you'll excuse me, I must go." He drained his wineglass and got up. He walked away without saying goodbye and pressed a button for the lift. He stood by the lift door waiting with his back to the room.

"Mr Buffalo, wait a moment!" Siobhan got up and ran after him. He ignored her. The lift arrived and the doors opened. He walked inside and turned round to push the buttons on the floor selector; as he did so he looked at Siobhan and their eyes met. He gave her his crafty, knowing smile which he maintained as the lift doors slid shut, hiding him. "Wait!... Elevator!" yelled, Siobhan. A passer-by slammed the tip of their unbrella down on the call button just as the doors finished closing. They were just in time; the doors opened. "One second, Mr B..." She walked into the lift car to talk to him. It was completely empty. She was so startled that she yelled out loud.

....

She retired to her room early that night and lay still in bed staring at the ceiling. The lights of the city streets outside the hotel window comforted her slightly, but she was still worried something might come for her, something malevolent. She had never really believed in the supernatural. Sure, she knew there were extraterrestrials, but she didn't think that counted as supernatural. If there were friendly ghosts like Flying Buffalo then there might be hostile ones too. The plots of all the horror movies she'd seen over the years ran though her head in an end-to-end double bill. She rolled onto her side. There was no alternative but to try and distract herself with other thoughts. To begin with, she replayed her conversation with Flying Buffalo and contemplated what he meant by: "You have missed something very important and extremely obvious about that event..." What could it be? As she listed the various possibilities she felt her mind clouding over. She was finally drifting off to sleep. "The Digby Town opening ceremony..." she mused groggily. "Digby Town is now open. It was a happy day... Everybody was there to see it. Good old Digby Town. How proud this must make..." Then it struck her. She grabbed hold of the revelation and grasped it like a mental meat hook to prevent it being washed away in the rapids of approaching sleep. She forced herself up from the halfway house between waking and slumber. She sat up. "Of course!" she exclaimed aloud. "He's right, it *is* obvious!... She wasn't there! Everybody was there except *her*!"

Chapter 20

"I appreciate your help." Siobhan said to the research editor who was sitting across the desk from her.

"That's alright, Miss Quilley. We're glad to help CBS; you do a great job."

She smiled and nodded. She was sitting in the offices of a local news agency in Vancouver. She had made an appointment as soon as she could the following morning.

"What was the name of the person you're looking for again?"

"Jemima Digby."

After she left the news agency she met up with Dr Jenny Bulstrode and they flew in Prototype B to the address given to her by the researcher. It took them about half an hour this time because the address was in New Brunswick, on the coast of the other shining sea. Jenny took the craft to an altitude above which conventional aircraft operate to eliminate the risk of collision. They landed in the middle of a park near the dockland area of the city of Saint John just five minutes walk from their destination. It was now early afternoon because they had crossed four time zones on their brief flight. Siobhan felt a disconcerting sense of time travel. She and Jenny walked along the straight roads of the city between cute turn-of-the-century red brick houses. It was a cloudy day and the sea breeze blew in from the Bay of Fundy. Siobhan followed the print-out map the researcher in Vancouver had given her until they arrived at a boxy prefabricated row of two-storey flats. There was a large lobby area with pigeonholes for post. The only people they saw were elderly indicating that this was sheltered accommodation. The concierge let them in and gave them directions so they climbed a flight of outside steps and walked along a terrace until they came to the right flat. The door was opened by a short old woman with patchy hair hanging down the sides of her head that was mostly white, but a few streaks of peroxide blonde in it indicated that she had dyed it a long time ago. Her chin protruded and several yellowed lower teeth stuck up in front her thin upper lip. "Who are you? What do you want?" she asked gruffly.

"Mrs Digby? I'm Siobhan Quilley of CBS in the United States and this is Dr Jenny Bulstrode formerly of the US Federal Disclosure and Reconstruction Agency. We were wondering if you could spare a few minutes to talk to us."

Her bare eyebrows rose high above her watery blue eyes. "Now you'd like to talk to me? *Now*!?"

"If you please."

"And what if I choose to ignore you the way you have ignored me?"

Siobhan paused. "I would ask you not to." she smiled politely.

The old lady grumbled. "Alright, come on in." she pushed her door wide.

Jemima Digby became more amenable once they were inside. Her flat consisted of just two rooms, not including a small toilet-cum-bathroom. "I've been living here fifteen years, since my husband died." she explained. She spoke with the strange accent that many people on the remote eastern coast of Canada do; an indefinable mixture of Canadian, Scottish and rural English. Her walls were covered with pictures; most of them framed monochrome photographs of people, presumably her family. Ornaments of many kinds covered the horizontal spaces in the lounge; model ships, chinaware and brass casts. She made them a pot of tea in a dirty kitchen that smelled strongly of disinfectant. "You're not the first people from the FDRA to come here and see me, you know." she said as she handed out cups to them like a croupier dealing cards. "Nor the first reporter. I've had a few of you fourth estaters here, asking me questions and then ignoring me when I give you the answers you don't want... Milk or sugar?"

"I'm no longer with the FDRA, Mrs Digby." said Jenny. "I was fired in January."

"Oh!" She looked at them with renewed interest as she put the teapot down on the table.

"I wasn't even sure if you were still alive, Mrs Digby." said Siobhan. "Then I remembered last year that Prof. Pickup at the FDRA told me you had been informed about what happened to your discovery."

"Oh aye. They came and told me." She became sarcastic. "They announced: 'By the way. We're developing the machine you invented. You don't mind do you?'... Let that brew a minute." She pointed at the teapot.

"You mean they can do that without your permission?" asked Siobhan.

"Yes, that they can. I tried to stop them, but they still had the original papers Freddy and I signed in '21. I didn't have a leg to stand on."

Jenny shook her head in disgust. "Damn them! They're willing to enforce contracts based on pre-Disclosure legislation. That violates FDRA policy on truth and reconciliation."

Siobhan added: "I thought it odd that you were not invited to the opening of Digby Town seeing as you invented the entire thing. I assumed you'd be the guest of honour."

"Oh, but I was invited." She poured out the tea.

"Were you?"

"Yes, but I refused to attend."

"Why?"

"They gave me a script to read out. They told me that if I said anything else I'd be breaking my confidentiality agreement."

Siobhan and Jenny growled sympathetically as they sipped their tea. "How could they treat you like that!?" spat Jenny. "There would *be* no Digby Carrousel if it wasn't for you. You deserve to have all the rights returned to you and a patent issued immediately with your name on it. You should be paid a royalty on every single Digby engine that rolls off the line."

"No, no; that's not the point." said Jemima Digby.

"It is the complete point!" insisted Jenny. "You are an engineer and an inventor! This machine is *your* creation. It is a machine that can change the world. You should make the decisions about its development and application."

"Yes, but you see, I don't want them to develop it at all."

Jenny paused. "What do you mean you don't want them to develop it at all?"

"I don't want anybody to use my Carrousel."

"Why not?"

"Because it doesn't work."

There was a long silence and the old lady chuckled at the expression on their faces. Her bare gums were pink between her remaining teeth. "Let me show you something." She went into the lounge for a minute and came back with a photograph album. She opened it on the table and pointed to a series of aged black-and-white prints held in place by white corner pockets. "This is our old farm at Amherst... That's Maximus, our prize bull... This is my husband Freddy. We got married in '98 in Halifax; the best wedding the city had ever seen. Look at my dress! Freddy looked so handsome on the day... Here's my sons, John and Leslie, working on the harvest... This is my daughter Julie. She's a school principal now; got four kids of her own... This is Bessie, our first tractor... We had to scrap her in the end; very sad... But then we got this one." She indicated a print of an old fashioned tractor parked on a muddy lane between a pair of fields. It looked like an ordinary farm vehicle of the era except that it had a large circular box attached to the near side of its engine. "This is the photo we took just after we fitted it with the Carrousel, see?... I invented the thing by accident. You see, I used to collect strange minerals and do experiments on them; add salt to them, add sugar, mix them together, burn them, melt them. Stuff like that; it was a hobby of mine. I used to buy specimens by mail order or pick them up from prospectors and panners. At one point I ordered a sheet of mantalite, a ferrous compound, and also some bersillium, a magnesium isotope that had just been discovered. I left the two samples on a table one evening and went to bed. In the morning I came downstairs and saw that the two pieces had moved. They were about a foot apart from where I had originally placed them almost touching. I asked Freddy and the kids if they'd fiddled with them and they said 'no'. So I pushed the two bits back together to see what would happen and, lo and behold, I came back a few hours later and they'd done it again. I thought they might simply be magnetic and of poles alike, but I ruled that out quickly. Only the mantalite can have any possible magnetic field and that is miniscule, a microgauss if that. So after a few more tests I decided to heat up the mantalite and smelt it to remove any impurities. What do you know, the effect strengthened to the point where I could hardly keep it together with the bersillium by shoving with all my might. I realized this was a completely new kind of force, maybe something related to gravity. That's when I had the idea of using them to move a counter-rotating pair of wheels. I ordered more of the mineral and forged them into vanes which I arranged on the spokes of two wheels. At first it didn't occur to me that I could make it into any kind of engine; I just thought it might make a nice decoration for the garden or whatnot. It was Freddy who suggested that we might be able to scale up the design and set it on a driveshaft..."

"And you did?" asked Jenny rhetorically.

"Yes." the old lady pointed at the photograph of the tractor. "It took a lot of adapting and experimenting. I must have made a dozen wheels and spent thirty or forty dollars on mineral orders. Gradually we became pretty famous. The newspapers did a story on us; journos came from all over the place to get interviews. What's more some other farmers approached us asking us to modify their tractors. Then we had people from the towns wanting their cars done. We even had the Halifax Bus Company trying to sign us up. Freddy and I sat down and discussed the possibility of going into business. We knew the first step was to register for a patent, but when we sent off our application forms we received a letter from some folks from the States asking us for a meeting; important folks, industrialists. We agreed, assuming they wanted to hire us to work on some machinery of theirs. We met them at this grand old room in this big office in Montreal. There were a dozen of them sitting round this conference table; guys in plush suits. They told us they didn't want to hire us; they wanted to *buy* our patent."

"How much did they offer?" asked Siobhan.

"One and a half million dollars US. That's a lot of money today; think how much it was back then."

"It was peanuts." muttered Jenny angrily.

"Did they tell you who they were?" asked Siobhan.

"No. They said they were lawyers; representatives of several major US-based companies in the manufacturing and electrical industries. They never once named them... The thing is, Freddy and I were in pretty awful financial straits back then. There was a heavy mortgage on the farmhouse, we'd had a run of bad harvests. Every year the farm yielded less and less. Our debts were getting worse and worse... This was a magic wand that would wave all that worry away. We didn't hesitate to agree. We had a second meeting and we brought our own lawyer. We had a ton of paperwork to sign. This was not just development rights, you understand; we were selling the entire invention for their exclusive use. We closed the deal and the money was in our bank. Then these folk took us back to the farm in their cars and they watched as Freddy took the Carrousel off the tractor. I handed over all the other Carrousels I had made. The guys in suits put them in the trunks of their cars, said: 'thank you very much' and drove away. We never saw them again."

Jenny ground her teeth and shook her head. "My God, they really screwed you didn't they?"

Mrs Digby sniggered knowingly. "You think so? No... It was Freddy and I who had the last laugh."

"How come?"

She poured out some more tea into her cup. "Even though we could no longer use our Carrousel or sell it to anybody there was no law stopping me carrying on playing around with it privately at home. I built a number of other Carrousels and after a while I noticed something. The effect started dropping off."

"What do you mean?"

She picked up a pair of teaspoons and held them together to illustrate. "You take fresh specimens of bersillium and mantalite and you get a really forceful repulsive effect; like I said, I originally mistook it for something magnetic. These were the specimens I processed for the Carrousel. However, before long I noticed that my Carrousels were losing power. They were spinning slower and slower. This was because the repulsion gradually became weaker over time. It happened very gradually; in fact it took over four months of continuous interaction before it became noticeable."

"Why is that?" asked Jenny.

She shrugged. "Don't know. We can't possibly know until we solve the mystery of the effect to begin with. Freddy and I purchased more mineral and replaced the vanes to restore the Carrousels' function, but eventually the same thing happened again."

"So in order for the Digby Carrousel to work, it needs its active ingredient regularly replaced?" asked Siobhan rhetorically.

Jenny added with a sardonic half-smile: "Perhaps 'refuelled' would be a better word."

"Correct." said Jemima Digby. "See what I mean about Freddy and I having the last laugh? Those lawyers had paid us a million and half bucks for a machine that didn't work. It's not free energy if it needs refuelling, no matter what that energy source is. It was too late for them; the contracts were signed and the money was ours."

"That depends. How often do you need to refuel the system?"

"I estimated that the five-foot test Carrousels I made would need about five ounces of both ingredients every twelve months. The stronger four-foot one with the thicker vanes that Freddy designed for the tractor would need a lot more. Two or three pounds per year."

Siobhan laughed. "If I were playing the stock market I'd buy mantalite and bersillium commodities now."

"It's not that simple." said Mrs Digby. "You need a regular supply of those commodities to make the industry viable."

"Are they very rare?"

"Not the bersillium. That can be quite easily synthesized from regular magnesium. The problem is the mantalite; it occurs naturally and has to be mined. Bersillium without mantalite is useless. However there are not many mantalite deposits that we know of. There is a single quarry in Mexico, which is where Digby Town is getting its current supply from; however that is going to peak within three years at the current demand alone, not to mention the demand the consortium is forecasting. Even at the moment that quarry is only breaking even because of a massive state subsidy."

"Of course." said Siobhan. "The US Government is hyping up the Digby like it's a goose that lays golden eggs."

"But it's just a bubble." said the inventor. "The industry itself is completely and utterly unsustainable."

"Is that the only mantalite source we know of?"

"The only known deposit big enough to be worth mining in all the Americas."

"What about further afield?"

"Some lodes were discovered in England in the 1880's; but even if we could mine those by solving all the current political problems in England, how long would they last if the industry has its way? It's not just the mining of the mineral it's the refining process. It is a complicated and expensive job to prepare a piece of crude mantalite ore for use in a Digby Carrousel. You realize that the world's energy strategy at the moment is eventually to replace totally the entire energy infrastructure of the world with the Digby. All oil, all coal, all hydroelectric power, all nuclear power, gone! Nothing left at all except my Carrousel."

"I know; that's what they decided on in Dubai." said Siobhan.

"It's insanity!" Mrs Digby shook her head. "It is social, political and economic suicide!... I read the original reports from the British geologists and I worked out that if we go full Digby then the entire world will pass peak mantalite within eighteen months. We'll be left with a planet run on machines that involved an extraordinary amount of time, effort and money to create... that simply have no fuel supply. It's like spending all your dough on the best portable electronic computer in the world for a trip into the deepest jungle and then arriving to find you forgot to pack the batteries... This is why I don't want people to use my Carrousel. This is why I am having nothing to do with Digby Town."

Siobhan sighed. "In Abyssinia right now the farms are being irrigated with water from Digby-powered desalination plants. The population depends on them. My father organized the whole project."

"Those people will all be dead from starvation within five years." the old lady answered dispassionately.

There was a long silence. Jenny and Siobhan looked at each other. Siobhan spoke first. "We need to talk to Jack."

....

Siobhan and Jenny thanked Jemima Digby and then left her to fly southwest to Washington DC. Senator John F Kennedy was in a meeting so the two women waited patiently outside his office for him to return. When he did he listened to them grimly. "It's all falling into place. This is all part of the plan. What will happen when Mrs Digby's machine is in everybody's house, everybody's car, every town's power plant and every ship's engine-room... and then one day we all wake up one morning and they suddenly stop working?"

"Chaos." said Siobhan quietly. She felt her lip trembling.

Kennedy nodded. "*More* chaos. And what does chaos make?"

"Order." Siobhan answered immediately without understanding what she had just said.

"A new world order; Dealey's order. That's why Dealey likes chaos. There will be no alternative but to go back to fossil fuels. That's what everybody will demand in the throes of their panic. All new tech will be tainted forever. We'll go back to the pre-Disclosure age and wonder if it even happened at all."

"Down the Memory Hole." said Siobhan. She had read the book Flying Buffalo had given her, *Nineteen Eighty-Four* by George Orwell, several times now. "Oceania has always been at war with Eastasia."

"What about our spinning disks?" asked Jenny.

"Have you seen what the newspapers are writing about you, Jenny?"

"Of course. The same thing Pickup and Dealey have always said about me. We're still getting fifty new orders a day though."

The three of them looked hard at each other. "Jenny." said Kennedy. "It may be worth employing a few extra security guards for the factory."

She nodded gravely.

"What can we do?" asked Siobhan.

"I think we have grounds to impeach Dealey... We have to try at least. We must be careful how we do it. I can't be involved directly because he beat me in the presidential election and it will just look like sour grapes... I'll get to work on that."

"I'll help in any way I can."

....

After their meeting with Jack Kennedy, Siobhan and Jenny drank some coffee in the public cafeteria at the Capitol and Siobhan switched on her roam. The text alert flicked onto the screen and she opened it. There was one from her mother: "*Joanne, if Millicent cannot have this household then neither shall you. Mom.*" Siobhan frowned. Jenny noticed her expression. "Anything wrong, Siobhan?"

"I've just had a weird text from my mom." She dialled her father's number. He answered immediately and she told him what had happened.

"I've just had one from her too, Siobhan; saying the same thing. I'm going to go home and check everything's alright."

"Where are you now?"

"The pub. I'll call you when I get there," He ended the call.

She sat back. A dark chill flooded through her.

Jenny looked concerned. "Is everything alright, Siobhan?"

"Jenny could you take me home please?... Right now."

"Of course."

As they walked to where they had parked Prototype B. Siobhan felt her pace pick up. She felt the urge to run. The aircraft was where they had left it, sitting on the grass by the Taft Memorial with a few curious members of the public examining it. They jumped into their seats and shut the doors. Jenny switched on the engine and within a few seconds the US Capitol had disappeared below them. The thick jet trails that Siobhan had first noticed the previous year were very heavy this day and their view of the land was completely cut off as they ascended above the airways. "Jenny, can you make this thing go any faster?" asked Siobhan in a more tetchy voice than she intended.

"Take the bus if you prefer!" she snapped back.

"I'm sorry, Jenny. I'm just worried. Something's happened; I can feel it."

"It's OK. I'll go to about eighty thousand feet; we should be safe to add a thousand knots or so there."

Siobhan gripped the arms of her seat as Prototype B descended towards southern Nevada, but this time it was not due to vertigo. They came through the cloud layers and she saw the blue thread of the river Colorado. Boulder City was a small grey patch of low-level urban covering a short distance from the jagged metropolis of Las Vegas. As they came low enough to see the street layout she tried to tally the view with her memory of her hometown from the familiar ground level perspective. She noticed there was a wisp of smoke rising from one spot. She looked at it and desperately tried to calculate how this spot was not her own home, yet seconds later she realized that it was. Tears of dread escaped her eyes as the craft landed in the middle of the street in front of a fire engine. A pair of firemen were grasping a hosepipe which released an arcing jet of water into the air to land on top of the burning house; her house. Several more firemen were hacking at the front door with axes. A huge cloud of brown smoke was pouring out of the windows and flames flickered behind it. As soon as she got out of the vehicle her father ran over. "Siobhan!" He was also in tears and his skin and clothes were stained by soot. "I tried to get her out, but I couldn't!"

"What's going on!?"

"Your mom's in there! She's gone nuts! She's set fire to the house!"

"Where's Brendan!?"

"At school!"

There was a loud boom and the sound of shattering glass from the house and a huge ball of orange fire burst from the lounge window. The firemen reeled back and threw themselves down onto the lawn. A few blades of grass in the garden were burning. A woman's scream from the building rose above all other sounds and a crawling human figure appeared on the roof. It was Gina Quilley. "Get her out with your ladder!" Clane yelled at the nearest fireman.

"We can't!" he retorted.

"Siobhan!" shouted Jenny. "Get in!" The buzzing sound of Prototype B rose as she activated the engine. Siobhan understood immediately; she ran over and leapt into her seat. She left the door open as Jenny directed the aircraft into the air. Siobhan held her breath as the vehicle flew through the plume of smoke rising from the front windows of the house. Gina was on her hands and knees with her feet in the gutter. She had climbed onto the roof by opening the skylight in Brendan's room. She was gasping and spluttering like somebody drowning. She fell flat onto her chest and lay still. Jenny brought the flying disk down to hover just above the roof as Siobhan leaned out of the door on her side. As soon as her mother was within reach Siobhan seized the shoulders of her blouse and pulled. Gina was heavy; the material began tearing beneath Siobhan's fingernails. Siobhan could hold her breath no longer and took in a lungful of air and smoke. Her diaphragm convulsed and she almost lost her grip as she coughed. As soon as she could, Jenny leaned over to help and together they lifted Gina into Prototype B. The vehicle only had two seats and so they had to drape her body over their laps. As soon as her centre of gravity was inside the machine, Jenny returned her hands to the controls and the craft lifted off the roof with Gina's legs still dangling out dangerously. Siobhan held onto the waist of her mother's skirt with all her strength. Jenny lowered the vehicle down onto the road as quickly as she could. An ambulance had turned up and the paramedics lifted Gina onto a patient trolley and began attending to her; putting an oxygen mask over her face and listening to her chest with a stethoscope. Clane was weeping loudly and embraced Jenny. "Thank you!... Thank you!"

....

There was a red tape stretched in a big square around the house with the words *FIRE DEPARTMENT- DANGER* printed on it. Clane and Siobhan pushed the tape down and kicked their legs over it. Clane pushed against the scorched front door. It grated on its warped hinges and he had to shove it hard to get it open. The interior of the house was completely covered in black soot. The stench of burnt timber filled the air. There were a few seared metal springs lying in a pile on the floor of what had been their lounge; all that was left of the furniture. There was a pool of water on the floor. At first Siobhan thought it was residue from the firemen's hosepipe even a whole a week after the fire, but then she looked up and saw the holes in the roof, and she remembered there had been some rain the night before. "Definitely time to call in the builders." Clane spoke with a rueful half smile. There were three petrol cans lying in the middle of the kitchen floor, roughened and thinned by the heat. Clane kicked one of them. "Well that's how she started the fire." he said.

"Do you really think we can fix this, dad?" asked Siobhan.

He snorted. "We'll just have to wait and see what the surveyors say."

They were silent for a few minutes. "We should go and see mom." said Siobhan.

"Yeah." They drove to the Southern Nevada Behavioural Health Centre in Las Vegas. The doctor was a kindly old man in a tight-fitting white coat. He took them to a room with a TV screen on a table and he switched it on. The screen lit up with the fisheye view of the interior of a padded cell. An adult feminine figure lay on the floor rolling around like a child. Her arms were immobilized by a strait jacket. Despite her unusual attire the individual was easily recognizable as Gina Quilley. Her brown hair was ragged and unkempt. It lay splayed beside her head on the cushioned floor. The speakers of the TV provided a sound link from the room. Siobhan clearly heard her mother's voice weeping and moaning. "Millicent." she sobbed. "MILLICENT!"

"We're continuing with the Olanzapine for now." said the doctor. "If she doesn't respond within another three days we'll try a different regime. Our nursing staff are taking good care of her. We're keeping her clean, giving her nutrients, making sure she doesn't become dehydrated.

"Thank you." Clane said quietly as looked at his wife on the TV screen. His face was flushed and subdued.

As Siobhan looked at her mother kicking her legs and flailing with her head she felt all the hatred she had previously felt for her melt away. All that was left was pity. "Thanks, Doctor. I appreciate what you're doing for her. I hope she gets better soon."

When they were back in the car and driving they were silent for a long time. Then Siobhan said to her father: "We shouldn't let Brendan see mom like that."

Clane nodded. "I agree."

After another hesitation Siobhan said: "There's something you should know about Millicent. I met her once before; I mean before she got involved in our lives. She was at Julian's house in Minnesota when I first went there. She is the founder of something called Brentwood Institute of Human Relations."

"What's that? He frowned in confusion.

"Some kind of psychological strategy organization. They work for corporations, governments, things like that."

"Doing what?"

"I don't know. They don't explain it terribly well themselves. Anyway, Dr Millicent Arbroath-Laird is one of their head honchos. What's more she taught Julian's mom at university in Scotland and... Leonora Dealey."

"The Wicked Witch of the White House? Really?"

"Did she come into our family for a specific reason?"

"What reason?"

"To break us apart. To make mom hate me, to make me hate mom; or both perhaps."

"Why would she do that?"

"I don't know."

They returned to the hotel they had been staying in since the fire, paid for by their insurance. Siobhan went to her room and opened her matchbook to do some more research. There was some kind of connection between President Dealey and their family; but what was it?"

Chapter 21

"Five... four... three..."

"Good afternoon, this is CBS News, going live on the CBS national network and online at wmn.cbs.tv.us. I'm Siobhan Quilley and here are the latest headlines for Monday January twenty-second 1962. Three people have been shot and killed in overnight scuffles between rival protesters in the ongoing dispute at the George Washington University in Washington DC. The pressure group 'Decolonize GWU' are demanding that the university change its name to the 'North American People's University' and remove all statues and other images of George Washington from the campus. Approximately forty other people have been injured and are being treated in hospital... Dr Jennifer Bulstrode, the CEO of Spinning Disk Incorporated, has been released from FBI custody with charges pending after an investigation by the FDRA into alleged gross breaches of Federal and state regulations relating to health and safety, employment rights and environmental protection committed by her company during 1961. The local authorities have evacuated over three hundred homes in the vicinity of the Spinning Disk plant in Garwood, New Jersey and the plant has been impounded. Over four hundred product recall orders have been issued by the FDRA for aircraft manufactured by the company... The Fifth Fleet of the US Navy departed their home base at Norfolk, Virginia for the voyage to northwest Europe as part of the League of the World commitment to redevelop the region under Article Four of Treaty of Dubai for Global Disclosure and Reconstruction. The aircraft carrier USS *Forrestal* and its supporting vessels will be taking part of Exercise New Light in the eastern Atlantic Ocean before active operations on the continent and the surrounding waters... A dog called Kelsey became a have-a-go canine hero today when she chased away a group of four men who were trying to snatch the purse and shopping bag of her owner, seventy-four year old Mrs Victoria Pearce of Lawrence, Kansas. The chief of police for the area has declared that Kelsey showed 'extreme loyalty and courage' in defending her owner. The attackers left with nothing and were later arrested and charged with assault and attempted robbery... Latest figures from the New York Stock Exchange. The dollar is currently selling at four-fifty-five Emirati Dirham and eighty-six Irish pence. The Saudi Riyal is currently at an equal level; it is worth one dollar exactly. The price of gold rose overnight to twenty-four dollars and twelve cents per ounce... And now it's time for the news, travel and weather where you live."

....

Siobhan eased back on the throttle of her Quicksilver 7 flying disk. This was a four-seater adaptation of Prototype B that had been designed for mass-production. Over fifty models had come off the line before the attacks by the FDRA began. Flying the antigravity vehicle was easier than driving a car and Jenny had taught her how to do it, which only took a few hours. The craft descended to two hundred feet and she circled over the rooftops of Spinning Disk Inc. A steel fence had been erected around the factory and armed FDRA guards strutted up and down in the forecourt. She lowered the craft until it was hovering just above the seven-foot fence. The guards ran over to her. She opened a window. "Hey! Where's Dr Bulstrode? What have you done with her?"

"She's at headquarters." answered one of the guards. "By the way, ma'am. There is a product recall order on your vehicle. Please land immediately and step out!"

Siobhan laughed. "Come and take it!" She slammed the window shut and pulled up on the vertical power lever. The Quicksilver soared away above the factory like an eagle. She never even heard the guard's retort. Three minutes later she landed in an alleyway at the back of a hotel in Washington DC a few blocks away from the headquarters of the Federal Disclosure and Reconstruction Agency. She didn't want her disk being confiscated and therefore wanted to hide it as well as she could. She peeled out of the alley onto Virginia Avenue trying to act as normally as possible. She wrapped her scarf around her chin against the cold and avoided the icy patches on the pavement. It was a ten minute walk to the obtrusive post-modern castle-like FDRA building. She reported into reception and demanded to see

Dr Jenny Bulstrode. It took an hour for Jenny's interview to finish. She didn't speak to Siobhan or even meet her gaze until they were outside. At first Siobhan was worried that Jenny had been offended by Siobhan's news broadcast, but in fact Jenny simply wanted desperately to be out of the FDRA building. "What did you tell them?" asked Siobhan.

"Nothing. What's the point? I could easily prove them wrong, but they already know they are wrong; and they don't care. It's true we have mercury on the premises; of course we do, we need it to fill the toruses."

"But we have a hazardous materials license don't we?"

"Damn right! I went through everything by the book when we were setting up the company. We store it correctly, the whole team is trained to handle it and I always make sure they have on protective clothing... The FDRA are lying."

"Are they going to release us from the shutdown order?"

"Yes... but they're going to replace it with a dissolution order."

"What!?"

"They want to ruin us. They want our flying disks off the market."

"Why!?"

She sighed. "You *know* why!"

They walked along in silence for a while. "I called Jack." said Siobhan eventually. "He says our only hope is the impeachment. We kick Dealey's ass, and then we kick the ass of his hired thugs, the FDRA!"

"What can we do?"

"Go home and get your lawyer into the loop. I have to go to Ohio. We may be able to dig up some dirt from Dealey's past that can help us."

Jenny looked tearful. "I'd rather come with you. I can't bear to sit at home alone right now."

Siobhan's heart ached at the sight of her. "Have you got your brief on the roam?... OK, you can do your business on that."

....

A collective love affair with Henry Dealey had blossomed in Youngstown, Ohio. The bustling Midwestern city was festooned with pictures of the current US president. His face was used on advertising posters, humourous caricatures of him in memes, and people wore badges and hats with the images and slogans of their favourite son. The river Mahoning meandered through the heart of the city, still and covered with crackling ice on this cold January day. They parked the flying disk in some bushes by the riverbank. Snow lay piled up at the sides of swept roads and pavements. Siobhan had already done some research on the Mesh. People were filled with pride for what Dealey had achieved. Many locals were interviewed giving anecdotes of the president's childhood and youth in Youngstown. The Youngstown City High School had recently been renamed the Henry A Dealey High School. The clerk at the Mahoning County Records Office recognized Siobhan from the television and greeted her warmly. "I guess CBS want to learn some more about our great new President, Mr Henry Dealey. Well I can tell you, Miss Quilley, he was my best friend at school and we were buddies for many years after that."

"That's nice." She smiled at him. "He must have been very popular around town because everybody seems to have been his friend."

"He was gold nugget of a man." replied the clerk fervently, completely missing Siobhan's low key sarcasm. "One of the best pals a guy could ever want... This way, Miss Quilley."

The reading room had a computer console that contained a huge archive and registry dating back several centuries, most of which was not available on WorldMesh; hence the need for Siobhan to travel here. Jenny had no press pass and so had to wait in a diner while Siobhan went in alone. She used to search function to find references to Dealey's name, however much of the older archive was digitized image scans of paper documents and so had to be looked at individually. Siobhan spent three hours flicking through old newspapers dating back from Dealey's birthday. Then she examined the registrar's records. Every so often she made notes with a pen on a paper pad she had been given by the clerk; she had to leave her roam and matchbook at his desk.

When she had finished she was sleepy and her head ached from eyestrain. She thanked the clerk and then went to the diner to meet Jenny. Jenny was on her third or fourth coffee. As Siobhan walked in she was on the roam to her lawyer. Siobhan ordered another cup for them both and then waited patiently for Jenny to finish the call. "How did you get on, Siobhan?" she asked.

Siobhan shook her head and sighed. "I found lots of new information on Dealey." She showed Jenny her notebook. "But the earliest reference there was for him in the county records was a fifth page newspaper slot in May 1957."

Jenny frowned. "That's not long ago."

"No. Of course it picks up a lot after that; come forward to his FDRA years and his presidential run and the Youngstown rags can't shut up about him... but there's not a word about him beforehand."

"That's odd."

"That's just the start. I went through the registers of births. There was no Henry Austin Dealey born when he is supposed to have been born on March second 1907. In fact there has never been anybody of that name born anywhere in Mahoning County ever. I couldn't even find a family-member with the surname of Dealey who got born, married or died anywhere in the county at any time since the records began in 1797."

She gasped. "That's not possible!"

"I'm only reporting to you what I found." Siobhan gave a nonplussed smile.

"But... he has to be a native born US citizen to be president which means his background must have been checked!"

"Not as thoroughly as I just have."

"He has a birth certificate; it was published in his official nomination papers."

"Not one issued from this registry office."

Jenny hissed. "That birth certificate must be faked."

"According to what I've just seen, the whole published life story of our current president may well be faked."

She laughed. "Then how come everybody round here seems to remember him?"

"Folk mythologies are very easy to construct, especially when there's fame and fortune involved. I know for a fact CBS paid many of the Dealey's 'old friends' you saw on TV partying in the street at the inauguration for their life story with the new president. And did you see the souvenir shop we passed on the way here; all its shelves packed with Dealey merchandise? There is virtually a 'Dealey industry' here that is clearly very important to the local economy."

Jenny paused. "If President Henry Dealey is not who he says he is... then who the hell is he?"

She shrugged. "Search me."

Chapter 22

Siobhan looked down from the window of the aircraft and saw the green fields of Ireland. Her heart filled with intense emotion that had never come to her before from just seeing a piece of land. It was not her first visit to Ireland; in fact she had lived there during her adolescence when her father was on the staff of the US embassy in Dublin. Maybe it was what her father always used to tell her about how no Irishman exists without some of his heart in the Emerald Isle. The plane bumped down on the runway and came to a halt by the terminal. The airport looked exactly the same as it had when she'd first arrived all those years ago as a teenage girl. Things moved very quickly. She and her camera crew were caught in the flow as the troops were quick-marched off the aircraft. A convoy of buses were waiting at the arrivals doorway and they were immediately packed aboard, soldiers with kitbags on their laps. There was going to be no time for sightseeing. The buses set off at speed towards the docks as if there wasn't a moment to spare. It was a typically damp Irish spring day with light drizzle falling from a swollen sky. The horizon of Dublin harbour was blocked off by the rusting square hulks of the car ferries that used to connect Ireland with Great Britain, but hadn't sailed in five years. Between them sat a grey US Navy littoral troop carrier. The buses stopped in a row and a non-commissioned officer hammered on the side of the vehicle: "Out, all of you!" Siobhan and her team followed the soldiers up the gangway into the dark interior of the ship. It was dimly lit by dome-shaped bulbs in small cages built into the bare steel overheads. She sat on a bench next to the men and did a few quick reports for CBS that were uploaded and transmitted by satellite for broadcast. The engines of the ship rumbled and she felt the vessel rock in the waves as it got underway. She fell asleep lying on the bench, still jet-lagged from the flight over from New York. The movement of the ship lulled her into slumber, but every so often she was woken up by a voice or somebody walking past. Halfway through the voyage she was given cold military rations to eat. After six hours of the journey she was feeling slightly queasy with seasickness and so was

relived when the order was called to stand to for landing.
She and her camera crew put on blue flak-jackets and a
helmet with the word *PRESS* stencilled on it. She felt more
at home with her military companions now that she was
dressed more like them. They filed along a corridor and
down some stairs until the came to the landing stage of the
carrier. Its doors were open and four landing craft were
slowly filling with green-clad men with helmets on and
rifles at the ready. Fresh salty air blew across them and
Siobhan breathed it in with relish. She climbed down into
one of the craft and stood shoulder to shoulder with the
soldiers. The men were cheerful. They chatted and laughed.
There was no sense of impending danger. As the landing
craft pulled out of the ship's stage Siobhan stood on tiptoes
to gain her first ever look at Great Britain. The first thing
she saw was a tall steel tower that was reddish-brown from
rust in the overcast-filtered sunlight, rising above the land a
short distance inshore from the mottled beach. It tapered
from bottom to top and had a superstructure at its peak. In
fact it looked the same shape as the top half of the Eiffel
Tower in France and at its foot were a row of shorter
buildings and a promenade as if this had once been a
seaside resort in happier times. There were metal pilings
stretching out into the surf indicating that piers had once
stood there. The landing boat moved quickly and after just a
ten-minute trip, the bottom of the vessel bumped as it ran
aground on the beach. The ramp at the front lowered and
the crowd of soldiers shuffled forward; hoarse orders were
shouted. Siobhan ran down the ramp after the others and
yelled in shock as she plunged knee-deep into the cold surf.
"Keep going!" commanded the man behind him. The water
poured off her trousers as she ran up the beach after the
landing force. They reached a concrete seawall and she
expected them to carry on further because it seemed like
they were trying to get somewhere. Instead the unit she was
with dug in and set up tents on the beach. From the other
side of the wall inland the noises of battle were a constant
background; gunfire, the explosions of ordnance detonating.
The roar of jet aircraft flying overhead ebbed and flowed.
More ships appeared offshore and landing craft relayed

more personnel to the beach. Along with infantry they dropped off tanks and other armoured vehicles. Siobhan did her job as an embedded war correspondent diligently. She interviewed the troops, sent recorded updates to the studio. After Bill had offered her this assignment she had thought about it for a while. She assumed that her father would not want her to do it, but he shrugged and said: "Go for it; should be fun. It'll make a nice change from the studio."

"You don't think it'll be dangerous?"

"Nah way. There's nothing in left in Britain today except a few groups of nomadic people living like the Plains Indians. Most of them died when the country collapsed after Saucer Day. The place needs taking over and rebuilding. Article Four is one part of the Dubai Treaty I support."

As Siobhan observed the activities of the forces she gained a very different impression. It appeared that a full scale invasion was being carried out against a heavily-armed foe. However, she had yet to see anybody injured. Not one wounded solider had been medivacked back to the beachhead. Clearly the battle was going very well for the League of the World. Night fell. She ate a meal of meat and vegetables from an oblong mess tin that reminded her of her first trip to Area 51, when all this began for her in her life; then she slept in a sleeping bag on the sand which was very comfortable and she had a peaceful night despite the noise. She awoke at dawn, staring up at a broken sky with a few fading stars peeking between the fast-moving clouds. The sounds of the battlefield had stopped and there was silence apart from the squealing of seagulls and the rustle of the surf. When it got lighter the press and the troops were served tea in tin cups without milk or sugar. Then the announcement went round that the unit was moving out. She climbed into the back of a lorry and sat on a bench under a tarpaulin, unable to see out except from the gap at the back. As they headed inland in a slow moving convoy she saw that the seaside town they were leaving was burning. The buildings were almost all on fire and smoke filled the air above it. Apart from that she could see little except the front of the lorry behind them. The English countryside was as green and moist as that of Ireland except there were no farmer's fields. What used to be cultivated land had now gone to seed; it was all covered by long grass, bushes and small trees that had sprouted since Saucer Day. The road was of poor quality and had obviously not been maintained for many years. The landscape became more rugged and bare. The road started inclining radically. After two hours of driving the convoy ground to a halt. There had been a few stops due to log-jams, the kind that always happen in long rows of vehicles; however these never lasted longer than a minute. This time the lorry stopped for longer. The driver cut the engine. The soldiers around her did not react; most were taking the opportunity to catch up on their sleep. After ten minutes Siobhan decided to go and take a look. She and her camera crew climbed down from the back of the lorry and walked along the side of the road past all the vehicles to the head of the column. Now she was out of the lorry she had a much better view of the surrounding countryside. The road was a narrow lane cut through a heathery moor. A range of dark mountains covered the horizon. The scene reminded her of the mountains of Ireland where she'd hiked as a teenager. Before she reached the front of the convoy she heard raised voices. When she arrived she saw the source of the argument. She looked over her shoulder to order her notepad to start filming, but they already were.

A posse of rough-looking men stood across the road with weapons of many kinds; a cricket bat, a hockey stick, a gardening spade, a tree branch. They were all dressed in shabby clothes and were thin and looked undernourished. "Leave us alone! We're innocent and you're killing us!" one of them shouted in a northern English accent similar to that of Prof. Bertrand Lampson.

"Stand aside!" commanded the officer on charge of the convoy. "We are proceeding to secure the Nidderdale area; do not interfere with our operation."

"You've been killing us! We're survivors of your attack on Blackpool! There are women and children in our group."

Siobhan looked ahead up the road and saw that there was a huge crowd of people walking away up into the hills. The commander shouted orders and the soldiers began emerging from the lorries and lining up in front of the vehicles facing the armed men. Siobhan's heart missed a beat. When they opened fire she hardly heard it. She felt as if she had entered a virtual world. She swung round to shut the scene out of her senses, but her cameraman grabbed her by the shoulders and forced her back. "No, Siobhan! We must film this! The world needs to see it!" When she looked again the vehicles were all moving. The men all lay at the sides of the road with their inadequate weapons scattered around them, trails of blood leaking from their motionless bodies. The larger crowd of people ahead were all screaming with fear and running. As her own lorry drove past, a sergeant she had been speaking to earlier helped her and her notepad back into the vehicle. He spoke to her with a face twisted by controlled shock. "We're not monsters, Miss Quilley... We don't enjoy this kind of duty. But this is war; if we don't obey our orders *we* will be shot."

....

The taskforce reached its destination and pitched down in a steep valley with a stream running through it. As more men and vehicles arrived the new encampment quickly grew larger. The only sign of previous human habitation was a dry stone wall running alongside a muddy lane. Beyond this was a primeval landscape of coarse grass, rocks and gorse. The crowds of refugees from the coast had moved further inland; Siobhan hoped they were heading for another town. She walked a short distance from the camp, her jacket pulled tight because a light rain was falling and it was windy. It was at least ten degrees colder than it had been on the coast. The lane turned a corner and she saw a hole in the ground that was clearly artificial. The soil had been dug away and the underlying rock exposed. She bent down and picked up one of the rocks. It weighed about three pounds, was slippery from the rain and chilled her hands like ice. It was rough, heavy sandstone; dark grey in colour. However it had veins running through it that were a light blue-green. The shade was unusual and not completely unfamiliar. Siobhan had to ponder for a moment to remember where she'd seen it before. It was the colour of the slats of the Digby Carrousel. "Mantalite!" she exclaimed aloud.

....

It was raining hard as she stood on the flight line. Drops fell through the beams of the base floodlights like insects. The sky beyond was as black as a cave. She moved into the shelter of the aircraft's tail and her notepad followed. The aeroplane's four silent jet exhaust nozzles yawned like pythons on each side of their workplace. The cameraman signalled to her when he was rolling and she began speaking, raising her voice above the wind and roar of distant jet engines. "I am at Clogham Air Base in County Westmeath, Ireland. Behind me is a US Army Air Force Grumman B62 aircraft about to depart for a bombing raid over an undisclosed location in Europe. The League of the World's invasion and occupation of Britain has now entered its second phase after achieving its primary aim of securing the mantalite deposits in the Pennine Mountains of North Yorkshire. Mantalite is a very rare but essential ingredient for the Digby Carrousel, a supposed free energy device that is in reality nothing of the sort. It is not currently known how many British civilians were killed in this operation. The host of the taskforce is now on standby to invade and capture the continental mainland and these air force bombing raids are a prelude to boots on the ground. This is Siobhan Quilley for CBS News Clogham Air Base, Ireland."

"They'll never air that, Siobhan." said Duane the cameraman when he had cut.

"I know, but I'm going to say it anyway." she replied.

The interior of the high-altitude bomber was bare and mechanical compared to an airliner cabin. She was secured into her seat by one of the crew with a helmet on her head with an intercom through which she could speak to people. There was little soundproofing and as soon as the engines spooled up the intercom was the only way they could talk. The aircraft moved with the abruptness of a galloping horse and seemed to ascend almost vertically. Darkness saturated them as the interior lights were switched off. Siobhan had a very limited view out of a single window, but she soon became used to it. The rain stopped and a beautiful star field appeared as they broke through the overcast. A gibbous moon lay close to the horizon. After about two hours there was activity among the crew as they reached their target. Siobhan could see nothing of the night-shaded land below except a few tiny points of light, as if a couple of stars had fallen to the ground. Europe was still in the same state that eastern Pennsylvania had been during her time at Eberly, so she guessed that these were open fires or maybe electric lights from the few people who owned portable generators. There was a series of noises that she felt through the airframe more than heard; the hum of electric motors, bolts clicking. Then the aircraft wobbled as it released its load. Siobhan leaned forward to see the land below behind the aircraft through the window. It took several minutes for the ordnance to fall all the way to the ground because they were at such a high altitude. The land below lit up in a series of orange flashes that flickered as the multiple bombs detonated on contact. They left behind a glowing network of tangerine threads through faceless charcoal black like the embers of a campfire. The aircraft banked hard onto a reciprocal course and headed back to Clogham.

As soon as she was allowed to disembark from the aircraft she addressed the camera with the cooling jet exhausts in the background. The rain had now stopped. She maintained her normal "TV Siobhan" broadcasting manner. "We have just witnessed the LoW military forces committing another war-crime, following last week's assault on the English coastal town of Blackpool. This aircraft behind me has dropped bombs on innocent and defenceless people over former communist Europe. The League of the World is therefore guilty of mass-murder. This is Siobhan Quilley for CBS News Clogham Air Base, Ireland."

As soon as she returned to her hotel room in Dublin she saw that, as she predicted, she had received a number of furious E-grams from Bill, her director. She composed a reply: "*Hi Bill. I'm sorry you didn't find any of the reports I shot suitable for the air. The problem is, I just can't lie anymore. I don't believe this constitutes a breach of my contract; in fact I am working especially closely according to the constitution of CBS. If you disagree then propose a change to the constitution or terminate my contract. Best wishes. Siobhan."* She closed her matchbook and went to bed, falling immediately into the most peaceful and untroubled sleep she had enjoyed in years.

Chapter 23

Siobhan looked up at the ugly red-bricked wall of Broadcast Center. She saw it differently now she was faced with the possibility that it might be for the last time. Bill had sent her the details of her appointment in a single sentence E-gram. There was a subdued atmosphere as she walked into the office and the editorial team deliberately avoided her gaze as she crossed the floor to Bill's office. "Come in, Siobhan." he said gruffly as soon as she knocked. "Sit down." William Blane, the chief director of CBS News, was a fit and handsome middle-aged man, a legend in the company. However his reputation included a bad temper and unfairness which Siobhan agreed with wholeheartedly after working with him for many years. He paused and sighed; he rubbed his forehead awkwardly. "You know, Siobhan, I was delighted when you first joined us here..."

"Cut the crap, Bill!" she interrupted. "Am I fired or not?"

He smiled thinly. "Not."

"I see." Siobhan didn't know whether to feel relieved or disappointed. "I take it this was not the outcome you wanted."

"My recommendation to the board was that you be let go."

"And they decided to keep me on?"

"For now." He sighed again. "Siobhan, why do you have this drive for self-destruction? You can be so good. At your best you are brilliant. The best the network has never had. All you have to do is read the news properly. Tell the truth!"

"I do tell the truth. That's the point. It's written into the CBS constitution that we report the news accurately..."

"Don't lecture me on the constitution, Siobhan!"

"Well somebody needs to!"

His face reddened. "Don't speak to me in that tone, Siobhan!"

"Or what!?... How are you going to stop me!? You can only fire me once you know!"

He hissed between his teeth as he struggled to remain calm. "I'm trying to help you Siobhan... I need you to understand that the truth is not a simple yes-no and black-white thing. A few more years in journalism will teach you that."

"Did the LoW carry out massacres of unarmed European citizens last week... or did it not?"

"The LoW is doing what is necessary to deliver Europe from its post-Disclosure barbarism, a state of existence that has so far killed a hundred and fifty million people, over half the population of the continent. Under LoW occupation we can now rebuild the entire place in the same way we did the devastated regions of the United States. Have you considered that not intervening the way they did might have constituted passive mass-murder through inaction?... No, you choose instead to ignore all the other sides of the debate and try and use the CBS News platform as your personal political soap box!... What do you think you're doing; running for Congress? Did you really think I would okay that bullshit for broadcast? What planet are you living on Siobhan?"

She didn't reply. She had no idea what to say. She stared at her feet, damming up her tears with her eyelids.

Bill continued in a deadpan voice. "There's a policy seminar this afternoon in the Paley Room. I'd like you to attend. CBS is playing host to a very distinguished visiting lecturer who is an expert in the field..."

Siobhan left Bill's office at the end of the meeting and waited for the time of the seminar in the cafeteria. Her colleagues came and went as two hours passed. Normally they would have sat down beside her and talked to her, but today they avoided her as if she were suffering from a contagious disease. She headed for the Paley Room five minutes before the event and took a seat around the shiny conference table. The chair of the seminar was a skinny young woman from administration whom Siobhan knew by sight and not name. Siobhan zenned out and daydreamed as the woman gave an introduction to the seminar calling it "Dialectics in structural organizational studies" and with a flourishing crescendo, her voice trembling with passion, she announced: "...And now let me introduce our guest lecturer. We are very *very* honoured indeed to be joined by Dr

Millicent Arbroath-Laird from the Brentwood Institute of Human Relations."

The entire audience jumped to their feet like Jack-in-the-boxes and applauded wildly, with the exception of Siobhan. She stared in fascinated horror as the familiar deformed tortoise-like monstrosity hobbled out of a side door; her arched back shoved forward like a battering ram, as sturdy as a Galapagos carapace. Siobhan was out of the door before the old lady reached her seat and sat down, enabling her to raise her head and see the audience. Siobhan did not look back to see the others' reaction to her flight. She did not slow her pace until she was out of the door and a safe hundred yards or so down Eleventh Avenue. She walked briskly to where she had parked her car by the docks and went for a random drive. After half an hour of cruising the blocks of Manhattan she found herself at the Battery, a stretch of grassland and ornamental gardens on the southern tip of the island. She stopped the car and looked northwards at the shark tooth skyline of New York City. The domed phallic symbol of Earth Tower rose far above all the other pinnacles, glinting in the watery sunlight.

She could not linger long because another riot broke out. A group of about fifty people dressed from head to toe in black overalls and hoods had been gathering around a nearby bandstand. A contingent of police arrived and immediately the urban ninjas rushed at them, hurling abuse and throwing missiles. It was such a common sight in America today, Siobhan thought. She sadly recalled her memories of Julian as she drove away. She headed through the Lincoln Tunnel into New Jersey and went to Garwood where the headquarters of Spinning Disk Inc was located. The factory was still boarded up. It looked lost and lonely behind the row of chipboard barricades topped by barbed wire rolls. Some local youths had scrawled illegible graffiti on them. A pair of FDRA guards still stood at the chained up gate looking bored. Siobhan tried to call Dr Jenny Bulstrode, but her roamphone was switched off again.

Siobhan drove westwards through the New Jersey metropolitan region until it thinned out to nothing and she was in the green autumnal countryside. When she reached a thickly-wooded area, the beauty and peace of the place brought tears to her eyes. She had to pull over and weep into a tissue for a while. She had the introspection to realize that she was suffering an extreme emotional state; something that had happened to her before. Half an hour later she continued her impromptu journey, but around the next bend she was almost run off the road by a convoy of speeding military vehicles, jeeps and lorries. She braked hard and cursed them, looking over her shoulder as they disappeared behind her. "Goddamn douchers!" She shouted and parked again on the following bend. The road ran along the top of a ridge below which was a meadow and a stream at the bottom. A loose row of standalone trees marked the edge of the waterway. She burst into tears again. Everything in the countryside was so perfect, but human life was a basket of errors. The whole world looked insane to her; other people behaved like lunatics... Or had she misjudged the situation? Was *she* the aberration in a world of normality? Either way, there was no place for her. Did she belong in a mental asylum like her mother?

Siobhan was about to drive on when she saw something in the sky. She thought for a moment that it might be an aircraft, then a kite; then she realized that it was neither. It was a white circle in the sky, standing completely still against the blue welkin. It looked about a quarter of the size of the full moon. She thought it might be some kind of balloon, but the movement of the clouds indicated that it was too windy for a balloon not to be visibly moving. It was at about a thirty-degree elevation and a small cloud passed in front of it, giving the object a minimum range. It also made it clear that it was of some considerable size. She got out of the vehicle and shaded her eyes, squinting to see it in more detail. It was getting larger. By the way it was reflecting the sun she could see that it was spherical in shape; it looked like a golf ball. Soon she could hear a noise coming from it, a whining warbling sound. "What the fuck...!?" she muttered. It was now the apparent size of a basketball and she could see that the white surface of the sphere was faceted, making it again resemble a golf ball. She was terrified and fascinated at the same time. She felt the urge to flee, but her feet were rooted to the spot. The craft was enormous. As it descended to the meadow it cut off the sunlight. Its shadow was colder than normal shade would be. Siobhan started trembling from the chill as well as fear. It stretched from one side of the meadow to the other; its equator towered over her zenith. The whining noise was deafening, but then it died down to a whisper. There was a cracking crunch from the bottom of the slope as the bottom of the craft settled on top of two of the trees, breaking their upper branches. Then it stopped. It stood as dead still in the air as if it had been rooted into the ground with invisible foundations. Siobhan was in a strange state of mind, as if she knew everything that happened was about to happen before it did, like a continuous sense of *déjà vu*. A hole appeared in the surface of the object about twenty feet away and slightly above her so it was on the lower half of the sphere. She found herself walking forward. She climbed over the wooden fence at the side of the road and took a few steps through the long grass of the meadow. What happened next would haunt her for the rest of her life. A figure appeared in the hole; a luminous man... No, it wasn't a man. It was a creature that looked vaguely human; it had two arms and two legs, it had a head. But its head was too large and its body comparatively too small for it to be human. It had two huge bright yellow eyes and its body glowed green as if phosphorescent, casting an unearthly light into the shadow cast by the craft. Like the object it emerged from, it floated in the air, apparently weightless. The creature moved gently and gracefully as if underwater, waving its limbs and rotating its head like a fish in an aquarium. Siobhan was transfixed. As frightening and unearthly as it was, the entity was beautiful. She sensed emotional warmth coming from it. It looked hard at her as if trying to communicate. She heard no words at all, but then a phrase appeared in her head, spoken in a calm and mellow masculine voice as if from an internal loudspeaker: "Look out behind you."

Siobhan turned round slowly as if she were also trapped in an aquatic realm like the creature. A solider was crouched on the grass with his rifle pointed upwards, levelled at the being. The report of gunshots broke the spell. Siobhan ducked as the bullets cracked past her ears. The being fell to the ground at a normal speed, as if whatever power that had been suspending it was switched off instantly. It lay on the ground about a dozen yards ahead. She couldn't see much of it because it was partly hidden by the long grass and before she had the chance to move forward for a closer look, a deafening voice yelled in her ear: "Get out of here! NOW!" A pair of rough hands seized her shoulders like a vice and she was wrenched backwards. She yelped in pain. A gang of soldiers surrounded her, pushing at her, shoving her, terrifying her with their loud voices. She was led to the road and forced into the back of a lorry, one very similar to the ones she had ridden in in Britain the previous week. She was propelled down onto the floor by a punch to her back and found herself lying face down on the oily metal floor. Her arms were wrenched behind her and handcuffs bit into her wrists. The men came and sat on the benches beside her, but she could only see their boots. The vehicle started moving; she could feel its every motion through her cheek pressed to the floor. The lorry drove for an indeterminate amount of time and then the engine stopped and the tailgate opened. A steel toecap kicked her in the side. "On your feet!"

"I can't get up with my hands tied... AHH!" Her wrists were almost broken as a hand grabbed the chain between her handcuffs and dragged her across the floor and out of the lorry. She was frogmarched across to a doorway in a grey breezeblock building and taken to a room with a few chairs and a table. It reminded her of the interrogation room at Bethesda where she'd ended up after coming home from her disappearance at Area 51. Her captors shoved her down onto a chair with her handcuffs still on. Her hands were trapped painfully under her bottom. A military officer dressed in utilities with insignias of high rank came into the room and stared at her with a severe frown, as if he were a school headmaster reprimanding a naughty girl. He sat at the table opposite her. "Tell me, Miss Quilley." he began with no introductions or preamble. "What was it you saw today in Warren County?"

She cleared her throat, but her voice was still hoarse. "I saw a white ball-like thing..."

"No, Miss Quilley." He interrupted gently. "You saw nothing at all."

She shook her head.

"Please make sure you remember that. You saw nothing unusual at all; understood?"

She didn't reply.

"We can make life very difficult for you if you don't cooperate. Not only for you, but for your mom and dad; and for your little brother... If you don't want that to happen, then make sure you don't forget, you saw nothing."

She paused then nodded her head.

The officer left and some more men came into the room. They were far gentler and friendlier than they had been up till then. They removed her handcuffs and escorted her to a place outside the building where her car was parked; somebody must have driven it from where they apprehended her. She looked at her watch; it was less than an hour since she'd first seen the white sphere. She drove out of the gate of the military base and switched on her SatDirect to get her bearings. She had been taken to the Army Chemical and Biological Warfare Centre in Edison, New Jersey, not far from Staten Island. As soon as she'd switched on her roam she had a text from Bill. "*Call me ASAP.*" She did so on the car's roam system. "Siobhan?" His voice was not harsh. "I hear you walked out of the seminar today."

"Seminar?" It took a few moments to recall what she'd been doing before her arrest. "Oh, yes..."

"Well, 'bolted like a rabbit' are the words used to describe it."

"So I did... I..."

"Are you alright? You sound weird?"

"Yes, I'm fine."

He paused. "Good. In that case why weren't you at the programme briefing?"

"Which one?"

"You're doing the Seven tonight with Ray. Remember, Chuck's on vacation and you agreed to cover."

"Did I?"

He sighed impatiently. "Yes... Look, never mind. Just get into makeup on time; can you do that?"

"Yeah... Sure, Bill."

"Good." he hung up.

Siobhan drove across Staten Island and hopped the bridges like stepping stones through Brooklyn and onto Manhattan. She worked the controls of her car like a robot. Her feelings were still semi-detached. She stumbled from the carpark into the makeup room and collapsed into the seat. "Hey, Siobhan." the makeup lady greeted her.

"Hi, Valerie."

"You OK?"

"Yeah." A second person had recognized her subdued manner.

"You heard what's happened, about the chopper crash?"

"What chopper crash?"

"A helicopter came down in New Jersey; in the hills near Easton. It'll probably be your lead story."

Siobhan looked at Valerie in the mirror as the makeup lady brushed her hair. "What happened?"

"It was carrying toxic chemicals of some kind so the military has sealed the whole area off."

Siobhan's head was spinning as she walked down the corridor to the studio. She took her usual place behind the newsreader's desk and scrolled through the briefing document on the desktop console. In the woods of Warren County, exactly at the spot she had been arrested earlier in the day, a helicopter had crashed killing both pilots. It had been carrying a large load of an industrial chemical called polyethylspidroxic acid. This was a highly poisonous substance that caused liver cancer in humans even in very small doses. The governor of New Jersey had declared a state of emergency and the whole area had been designated a no-go zone for ten miles in all directions. The chemical might contaminate the soil so farms would have to be closed. It would be eighty years before people in the area could eat the produce of their garden vegetable patches. Environmental pressure groups were up in arms. President Dealey had ordered an immediate suspension of all helicopter flights carrying the chemical. Siobhan opened a Mesh browser and called up an amateur video sharing board. There had been an immediate public response to the disaster, including street demonstrations across the Hudson in Jersey City. She pressed on one of the video panes and the amateur footage began playing. A local assemblyman or state senator was making a speech at a crossroads on a make-shift podium. His voice played through her earphones: "*We are being bombarded! We are having poison dropped on our heads by incompetent and uncaring corporations. These are chemical weapons in effect, not intent; if you're riddled with cancer and your child is born with three arms it doesn't matter a jot to you what the motive was of the people who caused it.*" A riot was in progress somewhere else and police were breaking it up with teargas. A man was standing in another location holding a placard. He was wearing a suit with a wing-badge on the chest and striped epaulets, a pilot's uniform. "*You people!*" he yelled. "*You fuckin' people! You don't fuckin' know what you're talking about and you're fucking up our businesses!*" His placard read: "*HELICOPTER AIRFREIGHT IS SAFE! THE EASTON CRASH WAS NOT OUR FAULT!*"

"Siobhan!" A loud voice broke her concentration.

She jumped and looked up to see Bill's frowning face. "Yes?"

"You were in a goddamn trance, Siobhan. We hit the air in five; are you going to be in a fit state to present?"

"Yes, Bill. Sorry, I was just cramming the brief."

"Alright." He continued to look at her with concern as he walked back to the gallery.

Siobhan looked across the room. She squinted her eyes against the glare of the lights and took in the round staring black pupils of the camera lenses. She heard voices in her earphones and responded mindlessly as the sound engineer tested her microphone. Behind the cameras the crew were scurrying around in preparation for the upcoming live programme. "OK, we're in commercials. Two minutes." Bill's voice pronounced.

"Standing by!" called out the camera manager.

Words appeared on the teleprompter. Siobhan seethed with inner turmoil. She felt she was being torn in two by explosive forces within her. She thought about her experience that day, but also her mother, father and younger brother. The countdown ran down second-by-second. The red light on the cameras went on.

"Right, we are live in five... four... three..."

"Good afternoon, this is CBS News, going live on the CBS national network and online at wmn.cbs.tv.us." The routine words were out of her mouth before a single neuron of her brain had fired. "I'm Siobhan Quilley and here are the latest headlines for Tuesday tenth of April 1962. A helicopter has crashed in a remote wooded location in Warren County, New Jersery..." She stopped and stared. He was barely visible behind the shine of the arc lights, but there was no mistaking him. He stood against the wall at the back of the studio, looking over the shoulder of the switchboard operator. He was over thirty feet away, but he gazed hard into her eyes with an intensity that would not have increased if their noses had been touching. His expression was neutral, neither laudatory nor reproachful. It was Flying Buffalo.

Bill didn't hesitate for a second; his voice was in her earphones: "Siobhan, what's wrong! Talk! Now!"

Siobhan had only a few seconds. She knew that Bill would immediately cut the broadcast with the emergency breaker the moment he realized something had gone badly wrong. "None of this is true!" she shouted. "There was no helicopter! It was an MFO! They're lying to you..."

The red light on the camera went out. There was a stunned tortuous silence in the studio. The crew gaped at her, eyes wide and mouths open. Bill slowly walked out of the gallery door and stood in front of her. His face was blazing like a red chilli, but there was no anger in his voice when he spoke. "Siobhan, go home."

"Bill, I..."

"Just go home, Siobhan. We'll talk tomorrow."

Nobody looked at her as she got up from the newsreader's desk and walked out of the door. She changed into her own clothes in wardrobe and headed out of the building. A hush had descended on Broadcast Center as if a magical fog had put everybody to sleep.

It was completely dark outside and thin but persistent rain fell from the sky. As she walked along West 57th Street the reality of what she had done rolled over her like a tornado. Her pace increased and she looked over her shoulder to see if she was being followed. She pulled out her roam and dialled her father. It rang for a minute then went to voicemail. She cut the line and tried again. "Pick up, dad!" she hissed, but there was no answer. Car headlights formed illuminated threads in the puddles and their tyres hissed like water on a hob. She looked back again; there was still nobody there. She also looked around for Flying Buffalo. She hadn't seen what had happened to him since she left the studio. "Mr Buffalo!" she called out loud. "Mr Buffalo, are you there?" An old lady walking a dog gave Siobhan a worried look and moved to the edge of the pavement as she passed her by. He was nowhere to be seen. "Mr Buffalo, if you can hear me, please take care of my dad and Brendan! Please! And my mom too. Don't let those bastards hurt them; please!" She reached the junction with 8th Avenue and stopped to check her surroundings again. Her heart missed a beat as she spotted two men on the other side of the road watching her. They were dressed in raincoats and cloth caps; and they stood still, studying her carefully as if waiting to see what she would do. She turned left and strode northwards, quickening her pace. She looked over her shoulder; the two men had crossed the road and were on her track behind her, still staring at her intently. She started running and didn't stop until she'd reached the pedestrian crossing leading to Columbus Circle. The traffic was fast and thick, too much so to jaywalk. She jabbed the button but the lights stubbornly remained *DON'T WALK*. Her two pursuers were also running and approaching fast. The traffic stopped and she was moving again before the lights changed to *WALK*. She pounded across the paved area around the central monument and over the street to the other pavement. The lights were on her side and she didn't have to wait this time. She looked back and saw to her relief that the traffic had begun moving again just in time to trap the two men on the island of Columbus Circle. She made the most of her advantage by increasing her speed and sprinting towards the marble tower of the USS *Maine* Monument, behind which was the unlit coal-sack of Central Park. Once she was in the park she felt safer. There was complete darkness and lots of places to hide; making it much more difficult for her hunters to find her. She bolted deep into the greenery until she felt comfortably concealed and then hid behind a laurel bush. From here she could watch the streets behind her with virtual impunity. The two men crossed over from Columbus Circle and stopped at the park gate. They looked left and right then into the park. They conferred for a few minutes, wondering what to do, then they turned their backs and walked away.

Siobhan smiled with satisfaction. She decided to wait a few minutes before continuing her journey. She was a long way from home. She did not work in New York very often and so had no fixed address in the city. Instead she stayed at the apartment of a friend of hers called Janey, a woman who worked as an administrator at Broadcast Center whom Siobhan had befriended a few years ago. The problem was that Janey lived in Astoria, about four miles away on the other side of the East River. She would have to travel all that way without being detected by the people who had been following her and had quite openly threatened her life a few hours earlier. Siobhan was about to call Janey on her roam and then stopped. Government intelligence agencies were perfectly capable of tracking people using the transmissions of their portable communication devices. She panicked as she envisaged them homing in on her now. She ripped the batteries out of the roam and it went dead then moved to another bush. She felt less worried as five minutes passed. The two men who had been chasing her had not returned, so obviously there was nobody who could tell them where she was. She sat on the damp grass and waited. The soil and vegetation smelled pleasant, and it was not too cold. Rain dripped from the tree branches onto her head. After another five minutes she decided to risk the journey back to Janey's home. She got to her feet and started walking towards a pathway that led to the street. Strong hands slapped over her mouth and grasped both her arms. She tried to scream but her voice was stifled. She felt the hands dragging her sideways. "Be quiet! We're not going to hurt you!" a voice whispered in her ear.

She continued to struggle, making as much noise as she could.

"Keep calm, Siobhan!" The two men who had grabbed her frogmarched her to one of the small lanes that ran through Central Park that had streetlights. A large black van was parked there and another man held open the sliding door at the side. Siobhan was forced inside. The hand from her mouth lifted as her captor used it to grasp her ankles. "AHHHH! Let me go!... HELP!" she screamed.

"Shut up! We're here to help you!" retorted the voice and the hand gagged her again. Once they were all inside the van its engine roared and it moved sharply. "Listen, Siobhan." said the voice. "My name is Terry and I'm not going to hurt you. I've come here to save your life... If I take my hand away from my mouth will you please not scream?"

The voice had a reassuring tone. She nodded. The hand eased. "Who are you?" she demanded as soon as her mouth was free.

"A friend... Please just lie still while we take you to safety. We'll explain everything when we're out of here."

The van drove slowly, stopping and starting many times; presumably as it negotiated the intersections of Manhattan. There were two men in the front seats, one of which was the driver. The man in the back lay beside Siobhan on the floor, but he no longer held onto her. After a while the vehicle sped up, indicating that it had joined a highway. Nobody spoke to her, but slowly her fear eased somewhat. The man's voice and the atmosphere of the situation was not what she would expect from a gang of murderers. She caught the occasional glimpse of the man beside her, Terry, in the flicker of a passing streetlight. He had a handsome face with kind eyes; again, not how she imaged a homicidal maniac would look like. She had lost track of the time but guessed that it was two to three hours that the van cruised along the highway. Then it exited and drove along some smaller roads for forty minutes or so. Eventually it stopped and Terry opened the side door, allowing her to exit. Chilly fresh air filled her lungs. She was surrounded by a group of people who led her towards a building with lighted windows. There was darkness everywhere else, indicating that she was in the countryside. Loose gravel ground under her feet. A house loomed ahead that looked like a farmhouse. She was ushered through a door into a warm interior with bright lights that dazzled her after hours of darkness. There were lots of people in the house, dressed casually or in military utilities. Siobhan felt she was being brought in late to a gathering that had already been in progress for some time. A rustic and traditional farmhouse kitchen lay before her with a big wooden table around which were a number of people. In front of them were matchbooks, folders and papers as if they were all having a meeting. When Siobhan saw the man at the head of the table her jaw dropped. "Jack!"

"Hello, Siobhan." Senator John F Kennedy smiled at her awkwardly and sympathetically.

"What the...!?"

He held up his hands. "Siobhan! Please listen. I have to apologize for the manner in which you were brought here."

"What's going on, Jack!?"

He paused. "An end to evil."

"What do you mean?"

He looked embarrassed. "Won't you sit down? I'll explain."

She hesitated then took a seat at the table beside him, still trying to comprehend seeing him in this odd location. He was dressed as she had never seen him before, in denim and cotton. He had not shaved for several days. "Jack, I have no idea what's going on here, but I'm guessing it's to do with the MFO incident in New Jersey, right?"

"Yes, that event has acted as an opportunity for us to make our move, as has your admirable outburst on the news this evening." He rotated a matchbook towards her and pressed the play button. She saw herself on TV shouting: "*None of this is true! There was no helicopter! It was an*

MFO! They're lying..." The picture cut immediately to an advertisement for car insurance. Jack stared at her with an expression of deep respect and said quietly: "It might have been more strategic to sacrifice you, Siobhan; but we couldn't. Not after that."

She shivered. "Was I about to be killed?"

"Probably."

"So those men who chased me in New York..."

"Were CSA, yes... We don't know if they were the actual assassins, but after witnessing an MFO event together with your refusal to read the CBS script we are pretty sure you would have been listed for disposal. You're too famous and too many people listen to you... Of course it's a gamble because if you were found dead in your apartment from a 'drugs overdose' a lot of folk wouldn't believe it; but they most likely balanced out that risk."

She paused. "The officer at the base said it was not just my own life that was forfeit. They threatened my parents and Brendan."

He said nothing and bowed his head.

"What about them, Jack? Are you going to rescue them too?"

"The best way we can help your mom, dad and brother is to launch our operation."

"What operation?"

"A lot has being going on these last few months, things I've not been able to tell you or Jenny... We're going to take over the country."

"Who's 'we'?"

"Myself and some select members of the armed forces."

"A *coup d'état*?"

"Call it that if you will."

Her instincts riled. "Jack... you *can't*!"

He hardened. "Yes we can, Siobhan! It is written in the Declaration of Independence: *'When a long train of abuses and usurpations, pursuing invariably the same object evinces a design to reduce them under absolute despotism, it is their right, it is their duty, to throw off such government, and to provide new guards for their future security.'*... Does that not describe the current situation in

America? The Dealey regime is *not* a legitimate administration!" He softened back and smiled. "Siobhan, I understand that you're a good ol' rosy-cheeked American girl who has a reflex against this kind of talk. It's natural; you've been brought up that way. So was I and I had that reflex too for many years. Things like that just are not *supposed* to happen in the US of A... But reality has caught up with the American Dream. There is no other way."

"How long have you been plotting this?"

"Since Dubai... Remember me saying how Dealey stole the election? Remember when you and Jenny went to his hometown and it turned out he never lived there... He is not even who he says he is! God knows who he is really; it doesn't matter. What matters is that he has to go. I'm sorry I couldn't let you and Jenny in on my plans. Secrecy was essential and it was also for your own safety."

She looked down at her hands; they were trembling.

"It is now also the only way we can protect your family. In a few hours Dealey and his accomplices will have far more to worry about than carrying out reprisals against your parents and brother."

She looked up at him. "Alright, I'm in. What can I do to help?"

Terry interjected. "First things first, Siobhan. We have to remove your implant."

"My what?"

"Siobhan, roll up your left sleeve." said Kennedy.

She did so, exposing the strange mark that she had first noticed many years ago when she was at Eberly. A strange circular burn or rash with two blotches inside it.

"When did that first appear?" he asked.

"Four years ago, when I got out of Area 51."

Terry and Kennedy exchanged a glance. "You'd better come with me." said Terry gravely.

He led Siobhan up a flight of wooden stairs to the upper floor, which was as pastoral in its furniture and decorations as the ground floor except that one of the bedrooms had been converted into what looked like a doctor's surgery. Inside was an elderly man with a beard and a white coat. Standing next to him was a teenage girl wearing a white dress. Siobhan stopped in her tracks and stared. She had met this girl before. She was clearly older now; she had grown taller and had a full feminine figure, but there was no mistaking the young girl she had encountered during the invasion of Area 51 in 1958, the child with the large blue eyes and bright blonde hair. "Hello, Siobhan." she said in her gentle voice.

"Kerry?"

"It's good to see you again."

"What happened to you? I asked about you in Bethesda and they said you were being kept on a secure ward..."

"I escaped. Then Jack and his team rescued me. I've been looking for you ever since, Siobhan! I've been watching what you do and I admire you so much. I wanted you to join us back then, but Jack said 'not yet'..." She then noticed the doctor gazing at her impatiently. "There's no time now, Siobhan. I'll tell you everything later. We need to remove your implant. I can see it there inside you; it's been there since they let you go. That's why they didn't keep you there."

"Allow me to examine you." said the doctor in a gruff voice. He had a strong German accent. "Please, come with me. Leave your roamphone behind." He took Siobhan into a bathroom next door where an upright tent had been set up, similar to one found at a campsite except this one had a copper mesh attached to its exterior. Inside the tent the doctor switched on a lamp to reveal a workbench with some unusual-looking electronic devices. The doctor picked one up and held it over Siobhan's upper left arm. "Hmm, non-ferrous. Alright." He picked up another different one and did the same. "Aha, we have a strong electromagnetic field here." He used a third tool. "And... yes! See that? An eight hundred megahertz pulse... Let's go!" He took her back to the bedroom and unpacked a case containing objects carefully wrapped in green paper and placed them on a small table. "Lie down on the bed on your right side."

"Will this hurt?" asked Siobhan as she obeyed.

"I will try to minimize any pain you will feel." said the doctor. He laid a sheet of green tissue paper with a square hole cut in it over her arm. Siobhan had her back to him and so couldn't see what he was doing. "You will now feel a pinprick as I inject some local anaesthetic. This will reduce any discomfort the rest of the procedure will generate."

Siobhan winced as she felt the hypodermic needle penetrate her skin. Within a few minutes the area started tingling and then went completely numb.

"It's right at the centre of the mark." Kerry said.

"Yes, I can't feel it so it must be quite deep." said the doctor. "Ah, there it is." Far sooner than Siobhan expected the doctor said: "Right, we are finished, Siobhan. I am just going to put a dressing on the site." He removed the green tissue paper and slapped a large sticking plaster on her arm. Siobhan sat up. Her upper arm was still completely numb. "All done?" she asked.

"The local anaesthetic will wear off in a few hours." said the doctor. "The incision will be sore after that, but we can give you painkillers to ease it. Also you need to rest the arm for a few days."

Siobhan looked down at the table. There was a plastic dish with a wad of cotton wool soaked in blood. Lying in the middle of it was what looked like a metal splinter about a quarter of an inch long. "What on earth is that?"

"Your implant." said the doctor. "This was placed inside your body when you were held captive at Area 51."

"Why?"

He shrugged and smiled thinly. "We don't know. These objects are an enigma. I have treated hundreds of patients who have them. They are made of solid metal with a sheath of an unidentified substance, yet they exhibit the capabilities of electronics. They also do not cause an immune response. If you are stung by a bee, your skin around the sting swells up as your immune system reacts to the presence of a foreign object in your body. It doesn't with these; in fact blood vessels and nerves grow around the object as if it is just another natural part of your physiology... Do you mind if I keep this for research purposes?"

She nodded. "Sure... But I don't understand..."

"Siobhan." He held up his hands. "There is no time to discuss this. We can talk about it later. We are planning to move now."

....

The safe house Siobhan had been taken to was in a small village called North Branch in upstate New York. The forty or fifty people who were in the house all left at the same time in a convoy of vehicles. Siobhan rode in the same van that had taken her from New York City. She looked at her watch; it was almost midnight. She remembered that Bill had told her that he would speak to her tomorrow just before sending her out of the studio and she wondered if she would be able to do so. As soon as this thought passed through her head she realized how foolish it was. She had not yet grasped how much her life had changed as a result of the day almost gone. Everything she had assumed, all of her daily routine; her job, her home, even her country, had now transformed forever. Maybe even her family. She shivered as she thought of her parents and Brendan again. "God, keep them safe!" she muttered.

They drove down the highway; other vehicles passed them in total ignorance that they were sharing the road with the forces of national revolution. They arrived at Stewart Army Air Force Base at one thirty AM where the guards at the gate let them through to a whole squadron of waiting aircraft. They did not stop them to ask questions and acted as if they were expecting them. Siobhan was impressed. It seemed that at least some of the US military was on the side of Kennedy's insurrection. What about those that were not? Would all this end in a second civil war, just a single century after the last one killed a million Americans? The aircraft was a large transporter without the frills of a civilian airliner. It reminded her of the bomber she had ridden aboard in Ireland the previous week. Soon after takeoff her ears adjusted to the noise and the gentle movement of the air pockets lulled her to sleep. It was still very dark when they landed six hours later, although the eastern horizon was glowing. There was enough light for Siobhan to recognize the landscape. Together with the warmer air and familiar subtle scent of aloe vera and agaves she knew she was in Nevada. She could see the lights of Las Vegas in the background and realized she was at Nellis Field. More vehicles were parked waiting to take the task force forward, including a reassuringly large column of tanks. They headed north towards Highway Three-Seven-Five; it reminded Siobhan of history repeating itself. She had done this in 1958 during the invasion. However this time the atmosphere was more sombre and tense. The base camp was far further away from Area 51 for safety reasons and when they arrived the sound of ordnance detonating was clearly audible over the mountains to the north. John F Kennedy called Siobhan to a tent that had been set up as a TV studio with a camera and green screen behind a desk. "I'd like to offer you a new job." said the senator. "Can you make news reports on our operation for the alternative media?"

"I guess so, but which news channel is this?"

"One we have set up on WorldMesh video sharing boards. No mainstream TV channel will cover this; all the major networks are loyal to Dealey... as you know."

She nodded. So she became a reporter again for "New American News". She spent a few hours in the tent in front of the cameras reading reports. However the director also asked her to provide some personal commentary. "...Air-strikes against FDRA positions at Area 51 have been highly successful and ground forces will be moving in on the secret base very soon. Once it looked as though the facility had given up its covert agenda forever, but a new hidden world has emerged that is even worse than the original." She felt tearful as she thought of her family. They were just a few miles away in Boulder City, but she couldn't reach them. There was no reference at all on the mainstream media to what was going on; CBS and the other networks were just broadcasting the usual trivia. However, many amateur WorldMesh content creators had posted photographs and video clips showing unusual military activity in their local areas. Multiple fast jets flying overhead, relatives who were military personnel called up for emergency duty, bases on high alert. The Dealey regime's immune system was responding and the American public sensed it subconsciously. Siobhan stared hard into the camera lens. "People often ask me, what is the greatest achievement of the human race? Discovering how to use fire? Inventing the wheel? Building the Pyramids?... I tell you now, if humanity can drag itself out of the black pit that it has sunk into, all other accomplishments will pale by comparison. It will definitely be the very greatest thing mankind has ever done."

Chapter 24

The sun was setting over the mountains and the desert glowed orange. Siobhan stood at the edge of the temporary headquarters block at the side of Highway Three-Seven-Five. The evening chill had set in and she was wrapped in an insulated army jacket. The air-strikes had ceased in order to allow the ground forces to assault the base. Kennedy came and stood next to her. "You did a good job today, Siobhan. Our uploads have had almost a million views already."

She nodded.

"I think you're ready for a new challenge. Would you like to accompany the forces into Area 51 as an embedded reporter?"

She both laughed and cried to herself as she imagined the shock-horror on her father's face if he had been there. "*No feckin' way!*" Clane Quilley would have said. She grinned at him. "Yes, Jack. Sure."

She was allowed a few hours to sleep before the host got underway. She woke on her folding cot in her tent and changed into heavy military clothes with a flak jacket. She put on her blue helmet with the word PRESS stencilled on the front. There was no mirror to admire herself in as there had been in Ireland. Kennedy came in. "Siobhan, it's time."

"Alright..." She thought of her father again. "Jack, could I have a gun?"

Kennedy raised his eyebrows. "Well... Siobhan, you're press and weapons are for the soldiers only for obvious reasons."

"Come on, Jack. Can't you spare me a weapon; just a small revolver or something?"

He paused. "Have you used a gun before?"

"Sure. My dad made sure I was trained after Disclosure."

"Very well." He left the tent and came back a few minutes later with a Browning 1911 automatic pistol and an M-Sixteen assault rifle, along with a dozen clips of ammunition for both.

"Holy shit, Jack! I only want to protect myself; I'm not planning on storming S4 single-handed!"

"It's what your dad would want." he replied. He showed her how to load and unload the magazines and chamber rounds; as a revolver-shooter only, this aspect of weaponry was new to her. He also gave her a few tips on handling the rifle and helped her strap on the holsters and bandoliers. "OK, you're ready... My God, you look scary!" They both laughed nervously.

....

Siobhan's first trip into Area 51 had been in daylight, riding in a minibus with big windows. This time she was crouched in the back of a windowless steel box in pitch darkness alongside nineteen men in full battle gear. The way the armoured personnel carrier jolted around as it drove made it obvious they were travelling across rough virgin ground instead of the sedate cruise along the Groom Lake Road. It was three AM, the witching hour, and loud bangs outside the vehicle indicated that fighting was going on around them. Just before they departed, they heard from an intelligence source that Dealey loyalists were planning an air-strike against the ground troops and Kennedy ordered his own aerial units scrambled to intercept them. He also took Siobhan to one side and warned her, offering her the option to change her mind and back out. She had said "no" instinctively and wondered why from the moment after she said it. Now it was too late. She gritted her teeth and prayed that their own vehicle would not be attacked. She calculated that they were about halfway from Highway Three-Seven-Five to the secret base. The noise around them had faded into the distance to her relief, indicating that the attack had been driven off. Then the APC stopped for some reason. The rear ramp descended and light flooded in. She realized that she had badly underestimated their progress and they were actually at the surface buildings of Area 51. She and the soldiers had to hide behind the vehicle and she heard multiple shots. The officer commanding the squad explained to her that the base's resident FDRA guards had been reinforced by US Marine Corps units who were still with Dealey. Siobhan had a camera on her helmet that captured his words and broadcast them on a livestream to the WorldMesh video boards: "This is difficult for us, firing on American forces." he said. Siobhan remembered the sergeant she had spoke to in England the previous week who said something similar about shooting the local protesters. She wondered when Americans soldiers ever got to fight a war they actually wanted to. The men every so often peeked out, fired off a few volleys and then ducked back. The sun had risen and it had been quiet for more than an hour when the order was given to advance. There were dead bodies lying on the concrete apron beside the hangar entrances, both military and FDRA. Rows of prisoners were lined up, disarmed with their hands on their heads. She followed the line of troops inside and they descended through the giant blast doors into the underground section of the base. The live Mesh stream was cut off as she entered the subterranean world, but her camera would record everything and upload it after her signal returned. It took a long time to make their way down through the office blocks and laboratories, past the nursery area to the transport tube hub. Each floor had to be searched and cleared. The interior of the base was mostly guarded by the resident FDRA who were a lot softer than the military; they almost always surrendered on the spot. There were a few skirmishes and some wounded men and a few bodies were carried past Siobhan's position, but within another three hours the entire known base was in Kennedy's hands. Siobhan trembled as she looked down at the platforms and the tube-like pneumotrains sitting there facing the pressure doors of the vacuum tube. A special forces unit were unpacking their equipment on the platform and their commander called her over. "Miss Quilley, we have been ordered to proceed along this tunnel and take possession of whatever territory lies at the other end."

"But we don't know what it is."

He smiled. He was a coarse, ugly and unshaven man with broken teeth. "We were hoping you could guide us. You are the only person known to have visited that part of the facility."

"I'm not sure I can help you. I was rendered unconscious the moment the train entered the tunnel; or at least I have no memory of what happened to me after that point. The next thing I knew I was waking up in the middle of some woods in Canada."

"Is it possible you were not unconscious, but rather you remained conscious and your memory was erased?"

She shrugged. "I guess so."

"Then we should be alright. We'll make sure whoever does the memory erasure is neutralized before that happens this time."

"How do you plan to travel there?"

"On the train of course."

"Wouldn't it be better to walk?"

He frowned. "How; the tunnel is evacuated?"

"We could drill a hole though the door and fill it with air."

"We don't know how long it is, how much air we'd need, how far away the neighbouring segment of the base is. Time is of the essence. Still the majority of the military is backing Dealey and they'll be sending reinforcements. We need to take the entire complex before they arrive."

She looked at the train. "I feel... scared." she admitted.

The man looked at her with sympathy. "You don't have to do this you know. You're a reporter not a commando."

Siobhan recalled her father's frantic pounding on the walls of the train as it had glided away with her inside all those years ago. "No, I'll come with you."

Once the nine special forces operatives were all kitted up they boarded the train. Siobhan trailed behind them, training her camera on the men as they assumed defensive postures and waited. A crowd of onlookers stood on the platform to watch their departure. Once again the doors slid shut automatically, as if this were the New York Subway. The vehicle started moving, slowly and without any inertia. The huge pressure doors ahead slid open and the train entered the airlock. The view of the known world behind them was cut off as the doors closed and the interior lights of the train shone on the walls of a second set of doors ahead. The train's sidewalls creaked and popped as they expanded; the air surrounding the vehicle was being pumped out. The inner doors opened and the train inched forward, slowly at first, but accelerating fast. Strangely

Siobhan felt no momentum, as if she were aboard a spinning disk aircraft with its own gravitational field. The tunnel beyond was completely pitch black and the train was as silent as a greenhouse. The only perception of movement was the blurring rush of the tunnel's walls in the glow of the inside lights shining through the windows. It was impossible to measure their speed. Siobhan and the soldiers kept their eyes firmly on the forward panes, ready to spot whatever destination they were heading for. They did not sit down in the rows of seats. After twenty minutes a light appeared ahead. The train visibly slowed until a set of pressure doors appeared exactly like the one at the other end below Area 51. The men raised their weapons, their eyes transfixed on what awaited them. The inner doors parted and the train slid into another station very similar to the one they had just left. The side doors slid open. The commander shouted orders at his men and the special forces operative dragged all their equipment out onto the platform and then ran along the platform in three groups of three. "Stay here, Miss Quilley!" the commander yelled at her. There were a number of entrances leading off from the station and the men ran into them and disappeared from sight. Siobhan suddenly felt very vulnerable, left alone on the platform.

The station was not exactly like the one at Area 51; it was somewhat smaller and had a lower ceiling. It had a row of pillars along the platform, reminding her of a New York Subway station. She looked at her watch. It was eleven AM; less than forty-eight hours ago she had been working at Broadcast Center living her ordinary life. It felt like a fortnight ago. Change took a long time to wait for, but when it came it came very fast indeed. She remembered that Julian had once told her something similar about the revolution. Distant gunfire echoed from the entrances where the commandoes had gone; she couldn't tell which one, or all three, because of the reverberations. It was followed by loud voices and then silence. Siobhan's breath caught in her throat. She pulled the rifle out of her rucksack holster and pulled the slide to chamber a round. She flicked off the safety catch and raised the butt to her shoulder. With her left hand she bent down and reached into the bag of equipment the special operatives had brought with them. There were some hand grenades in there. She had never used that kind of weapon before, but she still shoved four of the little metallic pineapples into the pockets of her flak jacket. "Commander!" she shouted. There was no reply. Solid silence pressed down on her throbbing eardrums like lead weights. She decided to try and return to Area 51 and ran back inside the pneumotrain. There were no buttons to shut the doors and they stayed open. She jumped up and down as she tried to trigger whatever automatic function started the train; this is what happened at the other end. "Shut!" she commanded. "SHUT!" Nothing happened. Then a human figure appeared in the doorway directly opposite and walked towards the train. It was a tall thin bald man wearing a tuxedo. Siobhan levelled her rifle at him; he continued walking calmly towards her without flinching at all. When he was close enough to speak he said: "Miss Quilley?"

"Yes?"

"Could you follow me, please?" He spoke with an upper-class English accent. He walked away back towards the door without looking to see if she had obeyed. Siobhan hesitated, and then exited the train and walked after the man. The butler, which is what he acted like, walked precisely and stiffly, as if carefully calculating every step. His scalp was completely hairless; there was not even any stubble on his pale skin. It was as if hair had never grown there, not that he'd shaved it off. He had a large circular birthmark, about the size of a large coin, on the right side of his neck, just behind and below his ear. The corridor they entered was featureless white and square, like that of a basement. It had a row of lights on the ceiling in small cages. Siobhan jolted as she saw three men lying on the ground surrounded by a pool of congealing blood. They were some of the special forces soldiers she had travelled with; they were all clearly dead. She stepped over them gingerly. "Did you kill these men?" she demanded.

The butler ignored her. He didn't even break his precise stride. The corridor ended in a set of sliding doors that opened to reveal a lift. He entered and waited for Siobhan to join him, then he inserted a key into a lock before pressing a button, as if he were travelling to a restricted part of the facility. The lift moved upwards and the butler stood to one side of the control panel completely still with his arms at his side like a guardsman at attention. His eyes stared straight ahead at the far wall. He blinked. "Hey." Siobhan said. The man again did not react. His gaze was as vacant as a clothes shop mannequin. She waved a hand in front of his face and he showed no response. His eyelids didn't even twitch. She walked up to him and examined the side of his head. There were no features on it at all except for the birthmark, but it was a strange-looking birthmark. He was standing just six inches from the right hand lift wall and his back was in shadow, so she moved to his other side to get a better view of it. "What the...!?" It wasn't a birthmark at all, but a silvery metal device that looked electronic. From the way the butler's skin dipped down around it Siobhan could see that it was not just stuck on the surface, but actually embedded into his flesh. It was an implant of some kind. The man blinked again. Siobhan stepped back and decided time his blinks by her watch. The butler blinked once every half-minute, on the dot.

The lift stopped and the doors slid open. The butler stepped out and stood to the side. Siobhan followed nervously and found herself in a huge chamber the size of a school hall that was decorated like an aristocratic mansion. Her army boots sunk into the lush carpet on the floor. Red leather Chesterfield armchairs were placed around rosewood coffee tables. Every open space on the wall was hung with magnificent oil paintings. Gold leaf plaster shapes decorated the ceiling. At the far end of the room was a huge set of double doors made of polished chestnut. The sound of live classical music met her ears and she saw a string quartet playing a quiet minuet on a dais in one corner. She walked up to them and saw that they were all like the butler, dressed in a tuxedo, completely bald and with the same circular disk embedded in their napes. There were long windows on both walls of the hall and she went over to them to see what was outside. It turned out that the windows were actually the sides of an aquarium. Large fish swum lazily back and forth; the bottom was covered by decorative rocks and gravel. She then noticed that the inhabitants were not ordinary fish; in fact they were larger versions of the mutant undersea creatures that had attacked her father during the 1958 Area 51 invasion. There was an audible splashing sound from the aquarium. She placed her cheek against the glass so she could look up. The surface of the water was visible, but what was above it was hidden. A large object had just been dropped in and was floating. She saw immediately that it was a human body and it was dressed in military utilities. The creatures in the tank paddled upwards immediately and began tearing into the man like piranha fish. Siobhan screamed.

"Siobhan, please! That hurt my ears."

She swung round to see Henry Austin Dealey, the thirty-seventh and current President of the United States. "You!..."

"Who were you expecting?" He smiled genially.

She pointed out of the window at the body being devoured by the fish. "Is that one of the men I came here with?"

He shrugged. "I'm merely feeding my fish with whatever food source is available."

There was another splash and a second body plunged into the water. "For God's sake, Dealey! Those are human beings! You can't do this!"

"Why not? This is my facility, these are my fish and it is my staff who are carrying it out. Those men were part of an armed assault against my premises and were justly repelled by my automatic defensive systems."

"But they were fighting men of America! You are their commander-in-chief!... Will you not at least grant them an honourable funeral!?"

Dealey lifted his hand. He was holding a box that looked like a TV remote control. He pressed a button and the musicians stopped. They all stopped instantly and at the same moment. They lowered their instruments, sat bolt upright in their chairs and made no further movement. "This is a war, Siobhan. There is no cemetery or crematorium down here. We can't have dead bodies lying around to spread disease. I can't think of a more practical way to dispose of unwanted human flesh. Besides, I am no longer their commander-in-chief because those men are traitors and mutineers who are part of a criminal conspiracy to remove me from office by force... as are you." He looked at her severely from beneath lowered brows. "Do you really think that your boyfriend Kennedy is going to get away with this? Who do you think you are? General Lee?... Right now as we speak the legitimate forces of the United States are regrouping and preparing a counter-attack. We will take back Area 51 from your pathetic insurgents and execute every last one of you for treason, sedition and un-American activities... It's over, Siobhan." He grinned and picked up a bottle of expensive-looking brandy from a table. "Drink?... No?" He poured out a single measure into a crystal tumbler. He was dressed in the same light-blue wool suit he always wore on TV. "Very well. Come with me; I have some friends I'd like you to meet. Some of them you know already." He pressed a button on his remote control again and the two large chestnut doors opened automatically, smoothly and silently. He walked into the neighbouring room and Siobhan followed. The second room was similar to the first except the floor was covered by a wooden conference table; its top was as shiny as a brown-tinted mirror. A dozen people were sitting around the table. They turned their heads and gazed neutrally at Siobhan as she walked in. One of them was Leonora Dealey, the First Lady. To her left sat Dr Millicent Arbroath-Laird; for once she was not smoking. Dealey moved to the head of the table and remained standing. "Welcome, Siobhan Quilley. You are the newest member of our council."

"What are you talking about?"

"Oh yes, Siobhan." He flashed his basilisk grimace at her. "Why do you think we let you go last time? Why do you think we didn't kill you the moment you arrived here?"

Siobhan noticed for the first time that the wound in her arm was hurting. "What did you do to me when I came here last time?"

"We placed an object inside your arm."

"What does the object do?"

"Some of its functions are not ones I can explain to you right now, but one of its purposes was to monitor your... erm... various internal and external processes. It sent data back to us which we used as part of our project."

"What project?"

Dealey paused for a very long time. "I've been keeping an eye on you your whole life, Siobhan; just like I've been doing with your father. I've watched you grow from a girl into a woman." He smiled with an expression that was almost like that of a benevolent uncle. "And you have grown up so very very well, my dear."

"How do you know!?... Who the hell are you!?" She hissed between gritted teeth.

He chuckled. "Well, you and your nosy friend Dr Bulstrode managed to work out that I am not who I say I am... Are you sure you want to see me in my true form?" He straightened up and put his arms by his side. He gawped mindlessly as if he were doing an impression on one of his implanted bondsmen. Siobhan assumed she had passed out and was hallucinating as she watched his body expand and change colour. His head rose an extra foot above the ground. It warped into an elongated snout and his clothes disappeared to be replaced by a green scaly hide. It was his eyes that were the most shocking of all. They bulged and turned yellow; his pupils narrowed into slits. The being was a cross between a man and a lizard, standing upright; huge and horrific. "This is what I really look like, Siobhan." he said, but she heard no words. The voice was in her head as it had been two days ago when she saw the alien emerge from the giant white sphere.

The blast of adrenalin the spectacle caused made all her thought processes extra-fast. In a split-second she recalled a conversation she had had with her father two years ago, just before leaving for the Dubai summit: "*Did Dealey change in any way while you were talking to him? Did he get bigger? Turn a different colour?*" Clane Quilley was keeping many secrets, she knew that. He had not yet revealed all the things that had happened to him during Saucer Day and what happened immediately before and after. Her next move was instructively to raise her rifle and pull the trigger. She braced herself for the recoil as she fired on full automatic at the grotesque vision in front of her... but nothing happened. "Your weapons will not function in this room." Dealey's voice in her head instructed her quietly. "We have ways of rendering them useless." The aberration in front of her opened its mouth and let out a warbling gargling sound, almost like human laughter. All the other figures around the table did not react at all, as if they were used to such spectacles and had seen them many times. Despite the bizarre nature of the creature that used to be Henry Dealey, some of its features were no different to familiar reptilian species. Its eyes were just like a normal snake's; its mouth and teeth were like a lizard's. A second later the entity transformed again back into human form. Its eyes became a normal man's, its scales became skin and cloth, and it shrank back down to about six feet. The smart lounge suit it had been wearing rematerialized on its body. However the man who now stood before her was no longer Henry A Dealey. Siobhan felt her jaw go slack. "Gerald!?"

"Hello, Siobhan, old girl. You're looking damn fine, what! How's the old family getting along?" Gerald Caxton smiled his broad, toothy British grin. His neat black hair, beady brown eyes and wire glasses were unchanged from when she'd last seen him.

All the memories she had of Gerald Caxton time-lapsed through her brain. Back in Ireland he had been one of her father's closest friends, but it had turned out he was a part of the Truth Embargo and had been using her father to try and prevent Disclosure. He had disappeared on Saucer Day and had never been seen again. "Gerald... what the hell...!?"

Caxton sat down at the head of the table. "Won't you take a seat, Siobhan? It's not very welcoming of us to keep new council members standing." He gestured to an empty chair at the other end of the table.

Siobhan felt her legs give way as she released their muscles and she fell more than sat into the chair. She had difficulty speaking; she felt out of breath. "You've messed with my head, Gerald. You have, haven't you? None of that was real, what just happened."

347

He looked at her sympathetically. "I'm afraid it was, Siobhan. I know that's not an easy fact to accept, but it is the truth."

"Where's Dealey?"

"There is no Dealey. Henry Dealey is me. He always has been."

"What the fuck are you!?"

Caxton took a sip of brandy. "I, and people of my kind, are a group of concerned individuals who dislike the way the world is going and wish to change its course."

"People?"

He smiled thinly. "However you wish to define that term... Either way, we have been a part of life on planet earth for a very long time, before human beings even existed in the form of your present species. We have been... guiding you for most of that time; however it was only in the last few millennia that you have submitted to our guidance. Our goal is the creation of a society engineered and organized from top to bottom, specially to make it the ideal and optimal form of human civilization. This society would cover the entire world and every single man, woman and child would be a part of it. We estimate that we will be able to complete our Great Work of the Ages, our ten thousand year mission, within the next few decades. We suffered a major setback at the last hurdle, Disclosure and Saucer Day, but we have recovered most of the ground we lost."

Siobhan had recovered her wits somewhat. She remembered that her camera was still recording. "What if we don't want your guidance? Why don't you just ask our permission before you start pushing us around?"

"No. You would have inevitably made the mistake of refusing it. You are very infantilized species. You never really cease to be children your entire lives. A father does not ask his baby son if he *minds* being taught how to walk and speak does he?"

"Where do... your kind of people... come from?"

He laughed. "Now that is one question I could never answer in a way that would lie within your powers of comprehension."

"What will happen to us if we don't accept your... guidance?"

"Then humanity will descend into chaos and barbarism, a state from which you will never reemerge."

There was a long silence. "So where do I fit into all this?"

"You are going to help us build the New World Order. That is why we have invited you to join this council. This is why we have never killed you."

"I'll never join you!"

He leaned forward and put his hands on the table. He spoke slowly for emphasis. "Yes, you will."

"No I won't!" she shouted.

"You say that now, but you don't know what you're talking about. You think that your mind is your own. You believe it is the impenetrable keep of your fortress, but it is not. It is as weak and malleable as all the other functions of your body; and we have one of the world's greatest mind sculptors as a part of our team." He looked to his right and exchanged a glance with Dr Millicent Arbroath-Laird.

Siobhan chuckled darkly. "Oh yes, I know all about your plan now. I know how Millicent trained *you*." She directed her gaze at Leonora Dealey. "I know you've been infecting the hearts of young people with hatred. I know Millicent also trained the mother of the man I loved. Drove him into a frenzy!"

"Correct, Siobhan." said Leonora Dealey. "As I believe Tanya Spencer told you at that New Year party, we're all inside the lobster pot now. There is nothing else we can do with our lives except keep moving forward until the end. This is so important that not even her poor Julian could be spared."

Caxton's beaming face widened even further. "Siobhan, you already know that we sent Dr Arbroath-Laird into your life to break down your morale, your will to resist. It worked perfectly. We do it collectively with society in the same way we do it with individuals."

"Joanne, go and read Erich Fromm when you get the chance." added Millicent.

"We've carried out a long march through the institutions." continued Caxton. "And the final step was to plant our boot firmly within your skulls." His face took on a glint of triumphant glee.

"Why me, Gerald? Why not get somebody else who is easier to break down?"

He gave that affectionate familial smile again. "Partly for sentimental reasons I must admit. Your father was a wonderful friend and I regret having to leave him behind when I went underground. I hope to be reunited with him again very soon... The main reason though has a lot to do with balancing the natural moral forces that govern the universe."

"What do you mean?"

"Your father also had a lot of trouble understanding that concept. Basically what it means is that in order to keep our project on the projected pathway we have decreed, we need the help of the people who worked to destabilize it in the first place, and that means Clane Quilley and his bloodline."

"Well I don't want to give you my help, Gerald. I'm refusing."

Caxton tittered as he looked at her, as if she were a little girl who had just said something foolish. "Well, as I said, Siobhan, you don't have the option to refuse." He stood up. "It is time... Siobhan, we will now need you to accompany Dr Arbroath-Laird to our infirmary for treatment. Our procedures are perfectly painless and we will endeavour to keep your mental and physical distress to a minimum. You've seen my servants; they have been altered too and they do not suffer at all."

"No!"

"I'm afraid... I must insist." He pressed a button on his remote control and a door behind him opened. Three large men dressed in white coats marched in.

Siobhan felt horror rise within her. Again the adrenalin gave her brain a boost and she remembered the hand grenades she has stuffed into her pockets. Caxton had told her that her weapons would not work in this room, but did he just mean her guns? Maybe he didn't know she had the grenades because they were hidden in her pockets. There was only one way to find out. She lowered herself so that her body was partly hidden by the table top; then she seized one of the grenades and pulled the pin out. She had seen this done a few times in the movies and so was pleased to find that they worked the same in real life. The object hissed as its fuse ignited. She reached down under the table and rolled it along the floor like a bowling ball.

"What are you doing?" asked Caxton. He had not seen her actions.

Siobhan jumped to her feet and dived behind a nearby settee. *BOOM!* The explosion reverberated around the entire underground room. She saw the heavy tabletop rise into the air. It was split like a log into several pieces. Screams of pain echoed off the walls as soon as soon as the explosion dissipated. Siobhan jumped up to see the remains of the table scattered across the floor like firewood. The members of the council she had been pressed-ganged into joining were lying on the floor, most with grievous leg wounds. Blood was everywhere and Leonora Dealey's severed foot lay on the rug in the corner. Gerald Caxton was the only one still standing. He stood as still as a statue surveying the scene, his face blanched with shock. Then he turned and bolted from the room.

"Joanne!... Joanne!... Help me." Dr Millicent Arbroath-Laird was lying closer to where the table had been than the other people. She had somehow escaped the explosion with no visible injury, although the terrible smell rising from her, even worse than usual, along with the brown stain on the front of her skirt, indicated that she had lost control of her bowels. She was reaching out for her walking stick that lay a few feet away on the floor. Siobhan knelt down beside her and removed another hand grenade from her pocket. She pulled the pin and then reached up Millicent's skirt between the old lady's legs until she came across the crotch of her panties. She pulled the diarrhoea-soaked textile to one side and shoved with all her might. The loose ragged cellulite of her perineum eventually yielded and Siobhan inserted the weapon firmly into either one or the other of Millicent's melena-lubricated orifices; she couldn't tell which. "MY... NAME... IS... SIOBHAN!"

Millicent bellowed as she felt the grenade enter her body.

Siobhan only just had time to take cover behind the sofa before the grenade detonated. An unspeakable shower of dry wrinkled flesh, nicotine-stained blood, osteoarthritic vertebrae and semi-fluid excrement rained down upon her. When Siobhan stood up all that was left of Dr Millicent Arbroath-Laird, of St Andrews University and the Brentwood Institute, was a pile of pink mincemeat with some eviscerated bones sticking out of it. There was a cracking sound from the windows. The walls of the aquarium had been badly damaged by the two explosions and were about to give way. Siobhan sprinted for the door and just as she reached it the glass split. Spurts of water lanced across the room and there were renewed screams from the surviving occupants as they either drowned or were attacked by the hungry mutant fish. Water poured out of the door as Siobhan ran along a corridor leading off from the conference room. She prayed she would find some way of climbing to a higher floor because the aquarium was so big it might well flood the entire level. To her relief she came across a flight of stairs. As soon as she reached the first landing she looked behind her to see water lapping at the bottom step. A metal door stood before her. Siobhan pushed it and it opened. The water appeared to have short-circuited whatever security system controlled the doors. Inside was the last thing she expected to see. A corridor ran straight along between two walls made of barred sliding doors. It looked like a cell block in an old-fashioned prison. She walked forward and looked inside the cells and saw dozens of rows of crude bunk beds. On them were lying children, several hundred of them. They were aged between about five and nine years old, boys and girls in equal number, they were of all races, and they were all completely naked. They all sat up in shock and stared at her. "What are you doing here?" she asked.

None of them replied. They just looked at her with blank neutral eyes.

A sloshing noise behind her made her look back. Water was seeping under the door by which she had just entered.

"We need to get out of here! How do you open these gates?"

They still remained silent and motionless.

"You're prisoners here; you're hardly going to know that." Siobhan grabbed one of the sliding barred doors and pulled, hoping that the electrical damage to the facility also meant that the locks on these were broken too. It slid easily to one side. "Get out! Hurry up!" She moved to the next one and opened it too, imploring the young inmates to move. By the time she had opened all ten of the cells water an inch deep covered the floor. "COME ON!" She grabbed the arm of one of the boys and dragged him. "How do we get out of here!?" The sight of one of their number being extracted from the prison by force seemed to galvanize the children. They gave a juvenile cheer and jumped off their bunkbeds. Siobhan opened the door to the stairwell and ran up a second flight. The water was rising slower now. It was only about three inches deep. Perhaps this meant it had spread out and found a new level on the floor where the conference room was. It might even be draining into lower storeys such as the pneumotrain station. She hoped that three inches was too shallow for the killer fish to swim in and they would stay deep. The feast of the dead she had left behind should also be enough to lure them. She pounded up the stairwell with the children right behind her. It looked fairly ordinary with concrete steps and tubular steel rails. It was similar to the one at Area 51 which hopefully meant there would be a door at the top. After five flights the stairs it did indeed end with a door, but it was completely sealed and had no handle or latch. She groaned in frustration, punching and kicking the door, but then she remembered her hand grenades. "Go back down! Go back down!" She ordered the children. She placed a grenade on the floor by the door and pulled the pin, and then she ran down and joined the children on the floor below. "Cover your ears!" She demonstrated with her own hands, just in case the children didn't speak English. They copied her. After the explosion she ran back up and saw to her consternation that the weapon had not even dented the door. It had merely made a black mark on it. Then she remembered another scene from a war film that gave her an idea. She needed to have some kind of mass behind the grenade to deflect the explosive force in the right direction. She headed back down to the prison block and took two of the mattresses from the bunk beds. She braced these between the far wall and the sealed door and squeezed the hand grenade in between. She prayed that it would work because it was her last one. She pulled the pin and took cover. *BOOM!* The door was blown half out of its frame. She vaulted up the stairs with the crowd of children behind her, cheering and whooping at their success. She burst through the door and found herself in a bright chamber that was so full of stimuli that her head reeled. There were people everywhere, all dressed in normal clothes. Ahead of her was a wall painted with some horrific murals. Dead children lying in coffins, monsters wearing gas masks and other macabre artworks. Above her was a huge white vaulted ceiling that looked like some kind of fabric, as if they were under a giant circus tent. However, all that mattered was that she could see sunlight and blue sky. They had escaped from the subterranean darkness and were on the surface. The crowd of naked children poured out of the door, or the hole blown in the wall; rushing past her shoulders like a waterfall. They cheered and waved their arms with excitement. A crowd of people were standing and staring at them, not believing what they were seeing. A man dressed in an airline pilot's uniform approached her. "Excuse me. What's going on here?"

"Where are we?"

"Denver. This is Denver International Airport."

Chapter 25

Siobhan switched on the television and selected CBS News. Her former colleagues Don Mitchell and Breya Lollard were presenting. Don said: "*And finally yesterday evening, travellers at Denver International Airport had a bit of a surprise when the East Colorado Scouts and Guides Association put on an impromptu pageant in the departure hall of Concourse B. They dressed in skin coloured suits and performed their new Gang Show routine for all the waiting passengers. Unfortunately spirits got a little too high and the area had to be closed for several hours while the airport authorities cleared up the mess.*" He laughed and turned to his co-host. "*The playful young scamps!*" "*Yes indeed!*" said Breya, also laughing. "*I'm glad to say that my own children were not involved!... Now it's time for the news, travel and weather where you live.*" Siobhan sighed and turned to John F Kennedy who was lying back on an armchair with a can of beer in his hands. "Is there anything they can't cover up?"

He smiled at her sardonically. "Do you miss your old job?"

"Fuck off!" she chuckled. They had to laugh; if they didn't they would have sat around crying continuously. Martin Luther King and Dr Jenny Bulstrode were sitting at a table playing cards. She left the lounge and walked along the corridor to the bedroom where her mother was being kept. Gina Quilley was lying on the bed being tended to by a Navy nurse who was also named Georgina. Luckily they had an adequate supply of Gina's antipsychotic drugs. Clane sat in a chair in the corner of the room. He looked sadly at his wife as she lay on the bed staring at the wall like one of Gerald Caxton's slaves. Brendan was playing with a toy train on the floor beside the bed. The special forces unit that had evacuated him and Brendan from Boulder City had also broken into the mental hospital and released Gina Quilley. Siobhan was overwhelmed with relief that they were all safe. When Siobhan explained, her father accepted the new situation very calmly; and Brendan was just pleased to get some unexpected time off school. "I can't believe you've met Caxton again." Clane shook his head.

"I'm sorry I let him escape, dad."

"You did your best. I'm glad you've seen them too; proves I'm not crazy. I have wondered all these years. I watched the video... Is it still up?"

She opened her matchbook and called up the YourScreen video sharing board. The playing pane was blank and there was a notice on it that said: *This video has been removed by YourScreen for violating community guidelines.* "Damn! It's gone again. Still, I got six hours out of it this time." She got to work setting up a new account and reuploading the video. Because of its length this took over three hours each time. She urged users to download it and file-share it as soon as it appeared so that it wouldn't be lost. Some other YourScreeners scoffed and claimed in the comments boxes that she faked the whole thing. Conversely Kennedy admitted that he wouldn't have believed her about the shape-shifting part unless it had been captured on film. Siobhan wondered if she would have believed it herself under those circumstances. She put on a kapok jacket and woolly hat and opened the outside door. Cold air washed over her like iced water. She stepped outside and looked at the ice-covered mountains that lined the bay. In front of her was a jetty where several small ships were tied up and beyond them was the sea. The water was the colour of chocolate yoghurt where it poked out between the greyish-white ice floes. They had flown directly to Tarr Naval Base in Alaska after the established government had counterattacked Kennedy's occupying forces at Area 51. Over five hundred men had been killed before the senator ordered a retreat. JFK then told his surviving troops to return to their respective units and go covert in the hope that they would not be identified. Gerald Caxton, now back in disguise as President Dealey, had initiated a purge. Thousands of servicemen had been arrested and there were a number of defections from Kennedy's cabal back to the government. This was probably done out of genuine fear; or as part of deal, leniency in exchange for information. Department of Defence investigators were roaming from base to base across the land. It was only a matter of time before they had sanitized all of them. This left fewer and fewer options for Siobhan and her collaborators. How long would it be before the commandant of Tarr opted to turn them in in order to save his own career? He was only a rear admiral- lower half with ambitions to rise higher in the ranks. Although he had welcomed the senator and his accomplices in the previous evening, there were now signs that he was vacillating. Siobhan had to face the possibility that she and her family would be arrested, probably within just a few days. What would happen to her? She wasn't worried in the way she would have previously expected to be. She had trouble contemplating the future in the same way that the past now felt like part of a dream or a previous life; even though just three days ago her life had been very ordinary. Her recent experiences had dragged her into a world of the eternal present, a state many philosophers defined as paradise; free from worries of the future and regrets of the past. It wasn't quite like that. However she felt no regrets or guilt, not even for her brutal murder of Dr Millicent Arbroath-Laird. She felt proud of the way she had freed the children kept in their gloomy prison beneath Denver International Airport. She didn't dare to think about what purpose Caxton/Dealey had for gathering large numbers of your children and incarcerating them. She had heard no news of the young escapees since she had fled, but she hoped they were alright; returned to their parents who must have given them up for lost. Either way it looked as if Caxton/Dealey would prevail; Kennedy's plan to depose him was in ruins.

Her roamphone bleeped and she shook off her mittens to pull it out of her pocket. It was a special encrypted one given to her by a Kennedyite mole inside the Signals Intelligence Agency. Nevertheless they kept electronic communication to a minimum. "*Siobhan. Got an idea. Urgent we talk. Kerry.*" She went inside and showed it to JFK. He shrugged. "What have we got to lose? Go check it out."

Jenny had brought the Quicksilver 7 with her and allowed Siobhan to use it. She had to wait until night fell because it wasn't safe to fly in daylight, even in a spinning disk craft. At dusk she wheeled the aircraft out of the shed where it was being stored and took off northwards over the Canadian border. The landscape below her was completely uninhabited, unless Bigfoot was real and he was down there somewhere. She looped round through the heart of Canada with nothing below her except mountains and forests. She only saw a few lights from small villages and moving cars. She flew close to the ground to avoid military radar; this inevitably meant she had to fly slower to avoid crashing. It took three hours for her to reach eastern Ontario where she turned due south back into the United States and towards the safe house in New York where they had left to begin the coup three days ago. She landed on the gravel driveway outside where Kerry and, the doctor, whom she found out was called Dr von Pflenzmann, were waiting to greet her. They told her about their idea and what they had found out and Siobhan was enthralled. She contacted the man they had been speaking to and arranged to meet up with him. Despite her instructions to minimize communications she couldn't resist texting Kennedy: *"Jack. May have found a way to turn this around. Siobhan."*

....

The following day Siobhan caught the bus and train to New York City and flew to Milwaukee, Wisconsin by a scheduled airline. It was too risky to take the Quicksilver because she couldn't be sure she could land unobserved and hide the unusual vehicle from prying eyes. She booked a hotel to stay overnight under a fake identity created for her by another colleague in the Central Security Agency. She left the hotel at eight PM and headed down the street to the bar where she was told to go for her meeting. She wore a 1930's style headscarf and sunglasses, partly to prevent any government agents recognizing her, but also so that her contact would know who she was. She entered the bar and took a seat in a booth, ordering a beer first. She waited. The man was ten minutes late. He walked in and ordered a drink from the bar, then took it over to the booth. "Siobhan Quilley?"

"Yes." She looked up at the large middle-aged man.

He called himself "John" and she got the distinct impression that this was not his real name. He was an airline pilot who flew for TWA and was worried about both disciplinary action and criminal prosecution for revealing what he did to Siobhan. He explained for over an hour the secret operation he had been involved with. "We were told it was all about climate change; 'solar radiation management', they called it." he said. "The government are terrified about it but they don't want to come clean and say how bad it is, because then there'll be mass-panic. They said it was a secret plan to reduce the effects of global warming, but when I saw what they were doing I knew it couldn't be. It didn't take long for me to find out more. I discovered a real secret behind a fake secret." He handed her a piece of paper. "Keep that safe and show it to whoever has the means to put a stop to all this."

"Thank you, John." she replied fervently.

"Everybody knows something's going on." he said. "The news isn't saying anything. President Dealey has been on TV talking the same-old-same-old... but we surf the Mesh and see differently. We see AAF fighters in the sky all the time. Our flight plans are reset to avoid certain areas. Things are not normal and we all realize it even if we don't know what it is."

"You're not wrong, John."

"Whatever it is, Miss Quilley, I hope you get it fixed."

"We'll do our best."

....

Five days later Siobhan was back in the New York safe house with Dr Jenny Bulstrode. Both women had dressed from head to toe in black suits making them resemble anti-fascist protesters from a riot. They had also wheeled the Quicksilver into the garage and resprayed it black. It looked sinister, like a bat, as it sat on wooden blocks with newspaper taped over the windows, the paint slowly drying. They sat at the kitchen table having a last cup of coffee. Dr von Pflenzmann placed a plastic bag in front of them. Inside were four large silver cans with pop-off lids. "There are eight pounds of the formula in there. That's all I have had time to synthesize without a proper laboratory. That will probably be enough... I hope it will be enough."

"Thanks, doc." Siobhan had only just learned the name of the surgeon who had removed the implant from her arm.

"Here are your instructions." He handed them a sheaf of papers, printouts of meshpages. "This is everything we know about TCT Industries in the public domain. You may need to do your own reconnaissance when you arrive."

"We've read those over and over already." said Jenny.

"Take them anyway." he insisted.

Siobhan picked up a teaspoon. "So, remind me of the amounts again."

"Roughly two spoonfuls of formula for every hundred litres of additive."

"How will we know how much to put in when we get there?"

He rolled his eyes and sighed. "Take a look at the container's label and see how much is in it; then work it out... Are you ready to go?"

The Quicksilver was parked in the back garden for added security. "Siobhan, do you mind if I drive?" asked Jenny quietly.

"Sure, Jenny."

"And are you OK to do the other stuff?" She sounded embarrassed.

Siobhan smiled and in the dark she was positive Jenny couldn't see her. "I'll be fine."

"It's just... I'm too old to do all that." She got into the driving seat and Siobhan sat down beside her. Von Pflenzmann passed her the bag and she put it on the floor between her ankles. "Don't forget the spoon!" he hissed. He passed it to Siobhan just before she closed the door. He and Kerry waved as Jenny switched on the engine and the antigravity field built up. The craft rose into the air and the landscape surrounding North Branch village became visible as the dark shadows of the hills. Jenny opened the throttle and the vista vanished beneath them. It was completely dark and the only light came from the dashboard. "Which one first?" asked Siobhan.

"Baton Rouge?"

"Sure. Might as well start with the closest." The lights of towns and cities wheeled by underneath as they flew low and as fast as they could southwards. The TCT Industries complex was a few miles from a large oil refinery on the outskirts of New Orleans. This made sense seeing as the oil industry was its principle client. It was a square estate of about four acres surrounded by a high security fence. CCTV cameras were placed at various intervals on poles along the fence. Inside the fence was an opaque screen to hide the interior from ground level view. From the air, of course, everything was visible. There were a series of ugly buildings that reminded Siobhan of the power plant in Pennsylvania that she'd helped get restarted. Also there were huge cylindrical tanks that were clearly for storing chemicals. They stood upright around the main buildings like silos. Dr von Pflenzmann had told her to expect these and to ignore them. The thing to look out for were smaller portable storage vats because these were the ones filled with the completed chemical ready for immediate use and would be shipped out much sooner. Sure enough she spotted these. They were set up in the courtyard by the gate in rows on pallets, presumably waiting to be loaded onto a lorry. Siobhan winced as she saw human figures on the ground; security guards on duty. However they were all clustered around the main gate. Clearly they were expecting any trouble to come from intruders trying to break in at ground level. That was the direction the CCTV cameras were pointing too. That was perfect. "Jenny, drop me off behind that oblong shed there." she pointed. "Then get back up high again. I'll text you when I'm done."

"OK." The manoeuvre would have been impossible in any other kind of aircraft. A helicopter could technically have achieved it, but only if all the security guards happened to be deaf. The Quicksilver gave off only a very low buzzing sound that could be reduced to almost nothing under a low throttle and was infinitely quieter than the rattle of a helicopter. Jenny guided the craft down; Siobhan picked up the plastic bag, opened the door and jumped out. She landed on the ground neatly, ducked behind the wall of the shed and waited until Jenny had risen back to a couple of hundred feet where she hovered. Siobhan sat still with her ears wide open, but heard no sound except crickets in the grass. She peeked out from her hiding place and ran forward to where she had seen the vats from the air. They were egg-shaped plastic containers about five feet high. She shone her penlight on the label and saw lots of warnings that what it contained was "*TOXIC*!" and "*HAZARDOUS TO THE ENVIRONMENT*!" Then she found the capacity: eight hundred litres. The lid was firmly sealed by a plastic tear strip and she had no choice but to break that seal and hope nobody noticed. Secrecy was essential for this operation. If TCT got even a hint that their product had been tampered with they might decide to withdraw the entire batch, even if just as a precaution. She took her teaspoon and a tin of the formula out of the plastic bag and scooped sixteen spoonfuls onto the vat; then she replaced the lid and wrapped the seal around it. She used glue to repair the seal at the spot where she'd ripped it. By the time it had dried it would not at first glance look as if the seal had been disturbed. They would just have to hope whoever opened it next would not detect anything amiss. She then moved on to the next vat and did the same, then the next one. She had to hide once when somebody walked past. She dove into the shadows and held her breath as he strutted past, his boots echoing on the surface of the concrete yard. It took an hour and a half, but eventually she had added the formula to every vat. She crawled silently back to the shed and sent Jenny a text: "*Finished. Pick me up where you dropped me.*"

The dark black saucer descended with its door open. Siobhan leaped into her seat and Jenny pulled hard on the vertical power level to drive the craft upwards as quickly as possible. They both laughed with amusement, excitement and relief. "That wasn't too bad." said Siobhan. "This evening will be more fun than scary... Ballycoolin next?"

When they had cleared the eastern seaboard they were free of radar and so could increase speed and altitude for their transatlantic crossing. They were approaching the west coast of Ireland just forty-five minutes later. "Possibly a record." quipped Jenny. They were still in high spirits from their success at the first depot. The second TCT Industries plant was on an industrial estate in the outskirts of Dublin.

This was going to be Siobhan's third and briefest visit to her ancestral homeland. The plant at Ballycoolin was just a stone's throw away from Dublin airport and Jenny had to be careful where she hovered to avoid being in the path of aircraft taking off or landing. It was three AM in Ireland so the TCT security guards should be less alert than their colleagues in Louisiana where it had been early evening. The layout of the facility was very similar to the first and had buildings of a similar design. When Jenny had dropped her off Siobhan heard the sound of drunken laughter coming from the gatehouse. The security staff were clearly taking advantage of the absence of their boss to indulge themselves with some on-duty drinking. Siobhan giggled to herself at the presence of the Irish stereotype. For her it was excellent that they were drinking because while they were inebriated they would not be doing their job properly and she could work with relative impunity. She heard the noise of aircraft engines from the neighbouring airport as she tiptoed around the depot. She had more trouble than before finding where the chemical vats were stored. They were not kept in the open but were instead lined up in a warehouse with a large door. She found a small postern set in one side of the doors and luckily it was unlocked. Once she was in the warehouse she repeated what she had done in Louisiana and then called Jenny down to pick her up from just outside the door.

The final stop of the evening was a location in South Africa at a suburb of Johannesburg called Roodepoort. Johannesburg was a huge city and so there was far more chance of them being seen from the ground. The sky was also brightening slightly as they arrived there an hour after leaving Dublin. The architecture of this TCT Industries compound was also slightly different. There was little open space and just one large compact building. "Do you think we should leave it for now?" asked Jenny as they cruised above the plant at four hundred feet. "We could come back tomorrow night."

Siobhan thought for a moment. "No, let's go for it. We don't know how long we've got before they find out and we

363

need as much of the formula as possible in the air when that happens."

It was obvious this time that Siobhan would actively have to break into the building. The security guards looked far more intimidating. These men were completely sober and were armed; they carried submachine guns as they strutted back and forth by the gate in a highly professional manner. Jenny dropped Siobhan off on the roof. The top of the building was flat with a low wall running around it and its surface was covered with creosoted gravel. The air was far warmer here and Siobhan immediately began sweating profusely inside her black suit. There were skylights and air-vents at odd intervals and it took Siobhan a few minutes to find a trapdoor leading down into the building. It was sealed with a strong deadlock. Siobhan cursed and poked at the lock in a futile manner; it was fully shut. She walked further along to the edge of the roof and found a fire escape. It was made up of a series of narrow ladders and landings and she felt vertiginous as she descended it from the roof which was seven storeys up. She eventually found an open window and sneaked inside. Then she had no choice but to search the building. She had no weapons if she were caught; and also, even if she did escape, it would alert the company and they would find out about the formula; the whole mission would then be a failure. Later on, after reflection, she realized she had made a mistake and it would have been better simply to have aborted and come back the following night, as Jenny had suggested; but then and now she felt she had come that far and there was no turning back. Hopefully at that late... or early... hour, very few people should be about and she could hide from those who were. The interior of the building was air conditioned and pleasantly cool after the night heat outside. There were direction signs on the walls written in English and Afrikaans. One of them said: "*Storeroom*" and she followed the arrows down a few flights of stairs until she came to a heavy door which was unlocked. She opened it and sighed with relief as she saw the now familiar rows of plastic canisters containing the fuel additive. She switched the light on and got to work immediately. She had completed three vats before the door suddenly opened. She threw herself to the floor.

"Hello?" a voice said in a thick accent. "Anybody in here?" She heard footsteps walk in along the dusty linoleum floor; the same floor she had her cheek pressed against as she bit her tongue and struggled to control her breathing. She peeked through the gaps between the vats and saw a large black man wearing a peaked cap. He had his submachine gun slung across his chest. She suddenly realized how stupid she had been to switch the light on. The security guard walked down one of the aisles between the canisters into the middle of the chamber. He muttered something into a walkie-talkie in a strange language and got a reply immediately in the crackling speaker. A minute later a second guard joined the first one. They stood and talked for a few minutes in their own language then moved further into the room until they reached the far wall where they stopped. To her utter horror Siobhan saw that she had left the can of formula and the spoon in the middle of the back aisle. She had forgotten to hide it as well when she took cover. One of the guards had the heel of his boot less than an inch from it. If he looked down, he would see it easily. The man was rocking back and forth on his heels as he chatted to his colleague. She expected at any moment he would take a step back and knock his foot against the silver can and notice it. For the first time in many years, Siobhan recited the Hail Mary, albeit silently in her head. Eventually the two men moved to a safer distance. It was obvious they were not searching the room otherwise they would have done it by now and found her. They had only come in at all because the light was on and anybody who worked there could have accidentally left that on during the day. A few minutes later they walked out of the door and switched off the light. Siobhan exhaled with a gasp and sat up, struggling to calm herself. There was no time to sit around getting over the shock; she still had most of the vats to work on. She took out her torch and forced her hands to stop trembling as she measured out the spoonfuls. When she had finished she was careful to take the empty cans of formula with her. As she left the room she heard multiple voices.

She wondered for a moment what was going on and then realized how much time had passed. She looked at her watch. It was eight-twenty AM local time. People were coming to work. She now had to escape from a fully-staffed daytime chemical plant. She stomped down hard on her rising panic and tiptoed as quietly and quickly as she could to the stairwell. It was empty. She sprinted up the steps two at a time to the floor where the fire escape was. There were more voices there, including in the room with the open window. She ducked into a cleaning cupboard and waited. It was over ten minutes before the people in the room finally left it empty allowing her to run to the window and climb out onto the fire escape. She ascended as quickly as she could. She didn't look around herself as she climbed. It was broad daylight now and the sun was well above the horizon, but there was nothing else for it except to move as fast as possible and hope that Lady Luck would bless her one more time, and prevent people on the ground looking upwards and spotting her. When she arrived safely on the roof she almost laughed aloud with relief. She took out her phone. "*Finished. I'm on roof.*"

Jenny's reply came after longer than usual. "*Thank God you're OK. Negative. It's daytime now. Will be seen. Parked in trees hundred yards to north. Will wait all day, pick you up tonight.*"

Siobhan groaned, but she accepted Jenny's point. She would have to spend the entire day hiding out on the roof of the building. This was not particularly dangerous because it was unlikely anybody would come up there. There were also plenty of hiding places if they did. It was just the boredom she dreaded.

Siobhan managed to sleep for about an hour, but eventually it got too hot. She kept having to move to follow the patches of shade cast by the air-vents and other structures as the sun moved. She looked at her watch. It was only ten-thirty AM. She cursed and ripped the watch off her wrist. She shoved it into her pocket and promised herself to leave it there. She took off her outer clothes to keep cool. Thirst began to build in her, but there was no way she could obtain water without returning down the fire escape into the building which was too risky. She tried to let herself daydream, keep herself entertained with her own thoughts as she had when she was a child. It wasn't easy as her lips became drier and her tongue got stickier in her mouth. Her head started to ache and her mind wandered enticingly to images of cool mountain streams, glasses of icy beer and bottles of chilled tonic water. Slowly, ever so slowly, the blazing South African sun ascended to its highest point and equally slowly it descended down the opposite side of the building. Siobhan could clearly hear the sound of workmen in the yard down below. Machinery roared, voices shouted and boxes thumped. Once she crawled over to a gap in the eaves where the gutter emerged and peaked out. Lorries were parked in the yard and men were loading them up with cargo. She hoped some of that cargo was the tainted additive vats. She looked over at the clump of trees where Jenny was also waiting, but she couldn't see her. It remained hot as the sun sank lower and the light changed to that of late afternoon. Her roam beeped. "*You OK*?" asked Jenny.

Siobhan had trouble focusing her eyes as she thumbed a reply. Her hands were trembling too. "*Yrah. Thrstyy. Wannt to get oit of here.*"

"*Hold on. Won't be long now.*"

The activity at the depot eventually slowed down and stopped as people went home. The sound of frogs and other exotic nocturnal fauna broke out as the sun finally dipped below the horizon. The sky darkened from blue to purple to grey to black. Streetlight coming up from below was the only illumination. Siobhan's thoughts were in complete disarray. Her headache had thankfully stopped, but it had been replaced by confusion as the fluids slowly drained out of her brain like a squeezed sponge. She lay on the floor and stared blankly up at the stars. It took her a moment to react when her roam's text alert sounded. "*Siobhan. Coming for you now.*"

A moment later the stars were blanked out by a dark circle. She heard a voice calling her name. "Siobhan! Where are you? I can't see you."

"Here, Jenny." She weakly raised her hand.

367

A few moments later she saw Jenny crouch down beside her and grasp her shoulders. "Come on, Siobhan! Get up!" Siobhan's legs felt like two strips of spaghetti and her friend almost had to carry her over to where the Quicksilver was parked on the TCT Industries depot roof. Jenny pushed her into the passenger seat and then went back for all of Siobhan's clothes and equipment. She got into the driving seat and slammed the door. "Right, we need to get you home quick. We've got to get some fluids inside you." Jenny gunned the throttle and the vehicle took off.

"Have you been alright?" mumbled Siobhan.

"I've been better than you." Jenny laughed with relief. "I hid the disk in those trees beside the fence, but I had to leave it to find some water. I got thirsty too." She was texting furiously as she drove. "I wandered up the street and came to a cafe. Of course I've got no local money, but I managed to nip into the bathroom and drink from the washbasin tap before anybody saw me."

It felt like a few minutes, but it must have been about an hour, when their trip completed the last side of the irregular rectangle of their track and they landed at the safe house in North Branch. Dr von Pflenzmann and Kerry were waiting for them. Before Siobhan even had a chance to exit the vehicle the doctor had placed a cup in front of Siobhan's mouth and she tasted water. In her semi-conscious state she could barely feel the much-needed compound flowing down her throat. "Sip it slowly, Siobhan. Don't gulp." he said.

"You did it!" Kerry was bubbling like an excited schoolgirl. "You really did it!"

Chapter 26

Kennedy was on the phone to the commandant of Tarr Naval Base. As predicted, the commandant, Rear Admiral Granger- Lower Half, had developed cold feet over the mutineers using his base as a sanctuary. Siobhan picked up her coffee mug and went outside onto the patio to where Dr von Pflenzmann was standing and looking up at the sky. The white lines of the chemtrails made a crosshatch pattern on the blue heavens overhead as jet airliners traversed the skies above New York State. Siobhan had first noticed them many years ago and they had been so common since then that they had become normalized in her mind as well as everybody else's. "Still nothing." she said.

The doctor nodded grimly.

"It's been nearly a week now. How long will this take?"

"I don't know. We must be patient."

"Do you think we were sprung?"

He shrugged. "The additive stock into which you mixed in the formula will need to be distributed to the various refineries, maybe stored there for some time, mixed in with the kerosene, moved to the airports. I don't know how quick the fuel cycle of the airlines is, but it might take time to get our tainted product to the point where it is loaded aboard aircraft and actually dumped... After that, there may be further processes that will cause delays. The existing chemicals already dispersed in the atmosphere will not stop working straight away. It will take time for our formulated chemicals to replace those already in aerosol suspension. But if nobody intercepted the products there is no reason why they will not work eventually given enough time. We must be patient."

"It's difficult. Dealey... or rather Caxton... is bearing down on us, rooting us out, rounding us up. We're about to lose our outpost in Alaska. If they arrest us all before the formula works..." She looked back at the house and saw JFK still on the phone. She went back inside and looked into the kitchen where Kerry was studying a matchbook. "What are you looking at, sweetheart?" asked Siobhan. She went into the kitchen and looked over Kerry's shoulder. The monitor displayed a picture of a stone statue of a reptilian humanoid. It looked exactly like what she had seen Caxton/Dealey turn into beneath Denver airport. "Where did you find that?"

"I've seen them myself of course." said the teenager. "I saw them all the time when I was a kid in Area 51. But this is a statue that's almost five hundred years old."

"Where is this statue?"

"Magdalen Collage in Oxford, England. You see, they've known about them for a long time. I've been reading stories four thousand years old that talk about a race of people who are not really people. They're 'the serpent race' in disguise."

"And soon everybody is going to know about them again."

"Do you think?"

"Yes." lied Siobhan. They were on standby. There were three Quicksilvers in the garage that Jenny had flown in so that they could move out immediately when the hour struck. Like pilots on scramble alert, they sat around in the safe house, waiting for the call. At Tarr and several other military centres still supportive to Kennedy, there were aircraft on the runway fully-fuelled. However these fortresses of Kennedy's potential revolution were becoming fewer in number by the day as Dealey/Caxton's purge continued. It was a race against time. If it took too long for the formula to work, then by the time it did, Kennedy would no longer have the manpower to respond and chaos would ensue. Everything depended on him being able to get to Washington DC as soon as possible when the time came. The senator's voice took on a pleading tone as his head was bowed over the telephone receiver. "Admiral, please! Give me just another few days... No, I cannot guarantee that... You know what's at stake here, man! You agreed that Dealey has to go... Really!?..."

"Hey!" Martin Luther King suddenly ran down the stairs. "Switch on the TV, everybody."

"Which channel?" asked Siobhan, reaching for the remote control.

"Any news one... There's a breaking story in DC, something about a large number of alligators escaped from the zoo!"

The television came on. "Hold the line a moment, Admiral." said Kennedy. They all stared at the screen. Smiles broke out on their faces. Kennedy lifted the receiver and spoke in a forced subdued voice while he grinned. "Sorry to keep you, Admiral, it's just the situation has changed. For a start, you've just been promoted... Yes, I am serious... The thing is, you are no longer taking your orders from President Dealey; you are taking your orders from me as head of the new provisional government."

....

The three Quicksilver spinning disk craft headed towards the nation's capitol. At the same time Kennedy's forces were mobilizing all over the country. "Dr von Pflenzmann, you're going to get the Congressional Medal of Honour for this." said Kennedy.

"It was easy, senator." said the doctor. "Once we realized the purpose of the chemtrails we had the key. You see, the reptilians disguise themselves using a method that only the most upcoming physicists are just beginning to understand. That the universe works like a hologram; it is actually a projection of digital information processed at the quantum level. It works like a very complicated computer. We see each other as we do because of the coding that says we are humans. This is not a problem because we *are* humans. The reptilians take advantage of that knowledge to patch false codes into the projection system so that they appear in human form even though they are not human. We don't know exactly how they do this, but they have achieved it. They became worried a few years ago when they discovered that the Schumann cavity resonance was increasing; this could be because the earth is in the middle of a magnetic pole shift. This is the low frequency standing tonal within the earth's magnetic field. It has more than doubled since 1925. It appears that the previous Schumann cavity resonance level of about four and a half Hertz was very important for the reptilians' ability to keep these false human codes open... We don't know why. However now it is approaching ten Hertz. Therefore since the Schumann cavity resonance has increased it is more difficult for them to keep themselves disguised. They decided to inject

371

chemicals into the lower atmosphere to dampen down the effect of the increasing Schumann cavity resonance level. The best way to do this was to use high altitude aircraft. The only way to achieve this secretly was to co-opt existing airliners into unknowingly distributing the chemical."

"Although there is a dedicated chemtrail fleet as well." added Jenny.

"Hence their front organization, TCT Industries." continued the doctor. "In three plants around the world they distributed a chemical additive that they said was to increase fuel efficiency. Over fifty commercial carriers joined the programme and were used as unwitting hosts to change the chemical composition of the earth's atmosphere into one in which the reptilians could remain disguised in human form amidst a Schumann cavity resonance of over ten Hertz."

"Until we sabotaged their plan." said Siobhan.

"Yes, once we had the details of the chemical composition of the additive it was very easy to concoct an antidote, a formula we could mix in with the additive that would neutralize its effect. We managed to do that in all three manufacturing plants, thanks to Dr Bulstrode and Siobhan. The result is, the reptilians' human mask has now fallen and everybody can see them for what they really are."

"That's going to make people pretty scared." said Siobhan with a frown. She wondered what scene would await them as they descended into Washington DC.

The Capitol area was in turmoil yet again. Hundreds of people wearing suits were fleeing from the White House and the Halls of Congress. Traffic was blocking all the streets and horns were blaring. The three craft landed on the White House Lawn. The insurgents exited the craft and ran up to the building's main entrance, pushing past the panicking staffers who were running the other way. There were a group of about ten reptilians standing on the steps. Their teeth were bared and their tails swished angrily behind them. Their forked tongues periodically flicked in and out like a snake's. Kennedy blanched visibly. It was the first time he'd seen one of them in the flesh. He struggled to keep his composure as he spoke. "Which one of you is President Dealey?"

One of the beasts lifted its green clawed paw to elbow level.

Kennedy bravely took a step forward until he was just a dozen feet from the creature. He grinned momentarily, as if appreciating the darkly comedic way this scene might be regarded from a place of detachment. "Mr President, I do hereby relieve you of office in accordance with the Declaration of Independence, July 4th 1776, as a usurper to the Executive; one who has found your way there in contravention of the law and opposition to due electoral process, and in so doing is in direct violation of Article 2, Section 1, Clauses 2 and 4; of the Twelfth Amendment to the Constitution of the United States of America... It's over, Dealey. Everybody can see you now for what you are. Everything you did depended on secrecy and now your secret is out..."

The nightmarish beast lunged forward towards Kennedy; its mouth was open, its yellow gums glistening with saliva. Rapid-fire gunshots rang out, echoing off the white stucco walls. The reptilians all fell to the ground with patches of blood welling on their segmented underbellies. The US Marine guards who had fired the shots ran up the steps towards them. "Are you alright, senator?" one of them asked.

"Yes. Thanks to you." JFK was panting. "Nice shooting, fellers. And thanks for staying at your posts through all this."

Siobhan looked down at the Caxton/Dealey reptilian. Its baleful lemon irises were fixed on her eyes. "Siobhan." She heard its voice in her head again. "You think this is all over? It isn't! This is no victory for you. This is your ultimate destruction." Its eyes closed and it lay still.

Chapter 27

John F Kennedy refused to use the Oval Office. "No, that is for the President only, and I am *not* the President." he insisted. Instead he sat behind the desk of one of the miscellaneous offices beside the vice-president's office next to the West Wing's lobby entrance. The first thing he did was arrange for a TV camera to be brought in so he could address the nation. His broadcast was patched into every terrestrial channel, the emergency broadcast channel and a livestream on WorldMesh. "My fellow Americans." he began. "I sit before you today following the most extraordinary and unbelievable events that have ever befallen our nation. A non-human intelligent species from an unknown location, one resembling huge lizards, have taken over our nation, and several other nations of the world, by disguising themselves as humans. As I describe this situation to you I can't quite believe the words that I myself am saying, but it is true. However I am pleased to tell you that the illegitimate rule of these creatures has now come to an end. The story of how this was achieved will be told in full many times, but suffice to say it is as a result of the bold and ingenious machination of a group of people who will no doubt become national heroes. As I have said many times before; ask not what your country can do for you, but ask what can you do for your country? What I need you to do for your country now, my fellow Americans, is keep calm, remain steadfast, work with me and my executives to hold America together... The first problem that faces our nation is that every single individual within the Federal Government, including every one of the sixteen people listed on the Order of Succession as dictated by our great constitution, is one of the reptilian shape-shifters. Therefore, acting under the authority vested in me by the Declaration of Independence of July Fourth 1776, I do hereby form a provisional government until such times as the current state of emergency is resolved, the Federal Government can be restored and that a new presidential election cycle can be initiated. Once this is completed the provisional government shall be completely disbanded. When that time comes I will *not* be one of those running for

President. My current political office I believes disqualifies me as such. My title shall be Chief Executive Officer of the United States Provisional Government. I shall be appointing an assistant who will be known as the Deputy Chief Executive Officer of the United States Provisional Government. I can tell you now that the person appointed will be Congressman Dr Martin Luther King jr. My third appointment will be a board of secondary assistant Executive Officers; these shall be, Siobhan Quilley, Clane Quilley, Dr Jennifer Bultrode and Dr Wolfgang von Pflenzmann. The latter two shall also be designated official scientific advisers to the United States Provisional Government. Siobhan Quilley will double up as official adviser on media matters to the United States Provisional Government. My first executive order is the immediate recall of Congress. For those congressional districts whose representatives were among the shape-shifters, and those states for whom one or both of your senators were shape-shifters, officers of the United States Provisional Government shall be appointed by me until such time as a new Congressional election cycle can begin; and I intend this to be as soon as possible. With this foundation in place I wish to move forward to restore and rebuild our country. There will be more broadcasts by myself and my government in the coming days, weeks and months. May God bless you all, and may God bless America. Goodnight."

The camera cut and JFK leaned back in his seat with a groan of relief. He turned to a military officer standing next to him. "What's the situation on the streets, colonel?"

"Your units are all in place, senator. The acting Chief of Naval Operations says that the military is reporting for duty to the United States Provisional Government..."

Siobhan left the room and went for a walk along the West Wing corridors. She couldn't relax. She knew something was wrong. She was haunted by the last words of the Dealey/Caxton reptilian, transmitted telepathically into her head: "*This is no victory for you. This is your ultimate destruction.*" There was a vainglorious tone in that voice, as if it knew something she didn't. It was gloating, anticipating its own triumph.

Chapter 28

She and Jenny hovered in one of the Quicksilvers three hundred feet above the column of reptilians. "Nobody expected there would be so many of them." muttered Jenny grimly.

"What's the latest count?"

"Well over a million."

"Really? More than one in every two hundred people in the country was a reptilian?"

She nodded. "Most of them can't have known what they were. They didn't realize they weren't ordinary humans like the rest of us."

"They can't all have been in positions of power."

"They weren't. Most held some kind of authority; heads of companies, senior police officers, school principles and things like that, but I heard on the news yesterday that some kids were saying their elementary school teacher turned into a rep. It happened in the middle of class. She just transformed in front of their eyes. They said she was the kindest sweetest teacher that community has ever had."

Siobhan shook her head. "Strange days."

"Where are they all headed?"

It was two weeks now since what had been nicknamed "R-Day". The news programmes had returned to normal schedules, mostly thanks to Siobhan visiting the studios personally and driving them into restating, as she had the power plants and waterworks in Pennsylvania after Saucer Day. She threw her weight around as an executive officer of the Provisional Government and it was quite amusing to see Bill at CBS running around to do her bidding. She didn't overstretch her authority and bully him, although she was tempted. She scolded herself for even feeling the urge. The millions of reptilians all over the world had gathered together and left their former homes. They began walking in formation for reasons nobody knew. They stretched out in long well-ordered lines across the countryside, and sometimes through towns as well, although these lines did not form along existing road networks. However, reports from Europe said that some of the reptilian columns were marching along old Roman roads. Then somebody who ran a New Age spirituality meshboard posted a page declaring that the reptilians were following "ley lines", alleged threads of spiritual energy that span the entire earth. Others disputed this, including a few within the New Age movement. Either way, the actions of the reptilians seemed organized and purposeful. Whenever a reptilian column came near somebody's home they would flee. Entire communities had been abandoned by the residents when these bizarre cold-blooded interlopers came to town. Then a new report came of a conglomeration of reptilians forming in a certain place. About a hundred thousand of them were converging on the town of Abbotsford in western Canada close to the border. When Siobhan heard this news her memory was inexplicably stirred, but she couldn't remember why. The reptilians were moving slowly, walking less than two miles a day. They never seemed to tire. They didn't eat, drink or sleep.

When she returned to her office in the White House she had an E-gram marked "*URGENT!*" She opened it, read it and read it again. She dialled the number in the E-gram and spoke to the person on the other end for over an hour. Then she dashed out of the White House and ran over to her Quicksilver as fast as she could. She once again recalled the dying words of the lizard president: "*You think this is all over? It isn't! This is no victory for you. This is your ultimate destruction.*"

....

She landed on a patch of grass in the centre of Abbotsford. Prof. Wesley Harrison was waiting for her. "Thank you for coming, Miss Quilley, it's good to see you again." He shook her hand warmly. She remembered her visit to the CCRN a few years earlier when she'd made a report on it for CBS. The Canadian Organization for Nuclear Research and the Wilbert Smith National Laboratory was the home of the SQEC, the Superpositioning Quantum Electron Collider. The enormous particle accelerator was buried in a tunnel underground below the laboratory. She recalled how Prof Harrison had been dragged out of the lecture on the subject by the orders of the arrogant young Prof. Bertrand Lampson. He had been warning about the danger the machine posed because it could create micro-black holes and strange matter that could, in his opinion, destroy the planet. Siobhan had read Harrison's meshboard, wmn.ccrndanger.co.ca in detail. "I hope you can help, Miss Quilley. The reptilians have taken over the entire laboratory!"

She told him to jump aboard the spinning disk and together they flew to the CCRN complex just outside the town. Columns of the tall green creatures were marching purposefully into the white faceless buildings.

"They started arriving here yesterday, a whole army of them. Everybody in the facility just bolted, understandably. They escaped out of the gates on the other side."

"What are the reps doing in there?"

"Good question. Do you fancy walking in there and asking them?" He raised his eyebrows.

"Oddly enough, I might give that one a miss... But maybe we can fly over the top of the laboratory and see if we can see what they're up to from the air."

"Good idea."

She floated the Quicksilver low over the pale roofs of the CCRN complex and looked downwards.

Harrison pointed to a structure with a row of large windows. "I see movement in the control centre."

She moved the craft closer. The large windows allowed her to see inside a big modern room filled with electronic consoles and complex coloured wall-screens. Sure enough, a number of reptilians had taken up positions in front of the control terminals. They were far too big to sit on the chairs, so they had ripped them off their mounts and were crouching in front of the active displays with an air of expertise, just like human operators. "What the hell are they doing?" asked Siobhan.

"Oh my God!" The colour left Harrison's cheeks. "They're powering up the collider to initiate collisions!"

"Why?"

"Because they want to destroy the earth!"

It all fell into place. The last words of the Dealey/Caxton reptilian finally made sense to Siobhan.

"In warfare it's known as a '*Götterdämmerung* manoeuvre', sometimes called a 'scorched earth policy'. Basically if they can't rule this planet then they would rather wipe it out completely than let free humanity have it."

"How spiteful they are!... How are we going to stop them!?"

"We need to shut down the SQEC."

"How?"

"I'm not sure. I hate to say it, but we need Prof Bertrand Lampson's help."

"Do you have his phone number?"

"I think so." Harrison flicked through his roam. He pressed a button and held the device to his ear. After two minutes he gave up, shaking his head gloomily. "He's not answering."

"Can't we just cut off the electricity supply to the place?"

"It has its own generator."

"Where?"

"No idea."

She seethed and thought frantically for a moment. "Right, I'm going to land on the roof over there. The reps seem to be focused on the control building. There may be some information in that place that can tell us where the generator is, a sign with a map or a blueprint or something."

"Alright, but we must watch out for the reps."

She landed the vehicle on the roof and got out. She and Harrison explored the roof until they found a trapdoor similar to the one she'd found on the roof in South Africa a few weeks ago, except this one was unlocked. It led to some stairs that ended in a door to a major office. Inside the office were desks, computers and filing cabinets. "Ah, this looks like the place." said Siobhan. There was a door with a window at the far end. She peeked through, but there were no reptilians in sight. "Right, let's get searching."

"Wait!" said Harrison. "What's that noise?"

She stood still and she heard it too. It was a whimpering, whining sound, like a dog in pain. "Where's it coming from?"

"Over there!"

They eventually narrowed it down to a large cupboard. They opened it to find it was completely empty except for Prof. Bertrand Lampson. He was crouched on the floor trembling. His eyes were wide like a lunatic and his ivory-white teeth were clenched. His smooth black hair was knotted and matted against his skull by cold sweat. "Bert?" said Harrison.

Lampson continued to gawp in mad terror; he appeared not to recognize his old tutor. He mumbled incoherent nothings of panic in his choirboy voice.

"Bert! It's me; Wesley. Come out of there, man. We need your help."

Lampson didn't move.

Harrison reached into the cupboard, seized Lampson by his lapels and dragged him out onto the floor. "Come on, Bert! Pull yourself together! Snap out of it!" He slapped the man's cheeks. Lampson wailed in protest.

Siobhan grabbed Harrison's arms. "Wesley, steady on!..." She looked hard at Lampson's round eyes. "Listen, Professor. There are no reptilians in this room; they are all in the control centre. You are perfectly safe. We have an aircraft on the roof ready to take you out of here... But we urgently need you to tell us something. Where is the generator for the SQEC?"

He nodded his head and his mouth appeared to be trying to form words.

"Tell us, Professor! Where is the SQEC generator?"

"B... b... b... b... Build... Building... N... N... N... Nineteen!" Lampson stammered.

"Thank you." She stood up and went to a computer console. Eventually by clicking links and tabs she came across a page on the CCRN network that gave a plan of the entire complex. The buildings all were numbered and she soon came across Building Nineteen. It was labelled: *SQEC powerplant and transformers*. She called up Kennedy's number.

"Hello. Siobhan. Where are you?"

"In Canada. Listen, Jack. I need you to call in an air-strike." She explained the basics.

"Siobhan, I can't go sending AAF bombers to attack targets in Canada; that's an act of war..."

"Oh to hell with that, Jack! The world will be destroyed if you don't! Can't you just call Ottawa and make an excuse? I'm sure they'll understand in the long run."

Eventually he agreed.

"Make it as quick as possible." added Harrison. "If the reps start collisions at full power it will be too late. We need to kill the juice before they can do it."

They both helped guide the catatonic Bertrand Lampson up the ladder and into the Quicksilver. Then they flew to a safe distance on a hill overlooking the complex and then landed to see what would happen. Harrison kept looking at his watch. "Where are these goddamn planes coming from? Pakistan?"

"I hope Jack chose the closest base with land strike capability. I'm not sure he fully grasped what I told him."

The sound of distant jet engines rose slowly in the east. They all turned round and saw the specks of two approaching jets. "Let's hope they're not too late." said Harrison breathlessly. The planes flew in low along the shallow valley, arcing over the white blocks of the CCRN. There were a series of blinding flashes from the general area of Building Nineteen. A few seconds later the sound of the blasts reached them like a rolling thunderclap and the aircraft departed westwards over Puget Sound. They got back into the Quicksilver and flew over to examine the laboratory. A huge banner of black smoke rose above the complex from Building Nineteen. To their satisfaction they saw that the lights in the control centre were off. The electricity supply to the SQEC had been completely destroyed. They both cheered. "They can't repair it, can they?" asked Siobhan.

"Oh no; and even if they could find an electrical source the sudden disconnection of power to the collider while it is operating will have done catastrophic damage to the magnets and vacuum tube. It would take years of hard work to get that thing running again.

Then Siobhan noticed something unexpected. The reptilians in the lines stretching across the landscape from

382

the CCRN were all lying down on the ground motionless. She flew in lower for a closer look. "What's going on? What are they doing?"

"I don't believe it." said Harrison. "I think they're dead."

Chapter 29

The reptilians all died at the same moment. A few minutes after the AAF air-strike successfully knocked out the SQEC, the reptilian hordes in every corner of the world keeled over and dropped dead. They did it quietly and without any struggle. They all seemed to realize at the very same moment that all hope was lost. They had lost the planet they had worked for millennia to rule, and also any hope for the all-encompassing revenge that they craved so badly. Perhaps, as some experts had theorized, they shared a collective mind. Some psychologists now believed that humans did too, albeit to a lesser extent. The bodies lay everywhere. They decomposed and stank. Birds and foxes came and picked the bodies clean until only lizard-like bones littered the land as if a new generation of dinosaurs had just become extinct. Eventually the smell wore off and the bones were cleaned up bit by bit.

Siobhan finished her report for the provisional government and E-grammed it to Kennedy. She leaned back in her seat and groaned with exhaustion, as he had done after his first television address as Chief Executive. JFK was a busy man, working to rustle up some candidates for the primaries of the presidential election in November. The 1962 presidential election would be very different to any other, not just because it was a break in the quadrennial cycle. It also marked a new beginning. Siobhan cringed a bit as she thought this. It was a corny cliché that had been used so many times in the last few years. In fact it was a very pat political slogan; but this time she felt it meant something real. She left her office and went out to the carpark where her Quicksilver was resting on its landing skids. She had to take more care flying these days because quite a few people in Washington had bought spinning disk craft since Jenny's factory had reopened. It was a warm sunny day and she savoured the blue sky above her, now free of chemtrails. The flight to Rockville, Maryland only took a few minutes. The family had been overjoyed to be able to buy back the house that they had once lived in many years ago when Siobhan had been a child. It was a lovely detached mansion set in a leafy street of side gardens and big old trees. The owners had both repped back in March and their next of kin didn't want the place, so they sold it to the Quilley family at a discount price. As Siobhan landed on the front lawn, a postman was walking up the garden path holding a large box. She greeted him as he rang the doorbell. "Something for your dad I think, Siobhan." he said.

Clane Quilley opened the door. "Ah! It's arrived!... Thank you." He put the box on the kitchen table and started hacking at the tape seals with a pair of scissors.

"What's this, dad?" she asked.

"Look." What he lifted out of the box was a white plastic and metal-cased object that looked rather like a sandwich toaster, although it was about twice the size.

"What's that?"

He grinned like an excited child. "Our own free energy generator."

"Really?"

"Yes, it only cost ninety dollars. I'm going to wire it up to the fuse box now... No more utility bills for us."

Clane brought out his toolbox; then he switched off the electricity in the house for a couple of hours while he installed the free energy machine beside the fuse box under the stairs. Afterwards he imitated a bugle fanfare with his lips as he flicked the switch back on. "Ladies and gentlemen, this house is now running off free energy!"

Later on in the afternoon Siobhan walked into the lounge and saw Gina Quilley sitting in an armchair. "Hi, mom." She waved.

"Hello, Siobhan." Her mother was a lot quieter than she used to be before her illness, but she had made a remarkable recovery. She was off the medication and had forgotten about her terrible obsession of a few months earlier. She had used Siobhan's real name every single time since she had come out of hospital.

Clane was in the back garden making some kind of wooden structure with the help of Brendan. Siobhan pulled apart the patio doors and greeted her father.

"Hey, Siobhan, look what we're doing!" he called enthusiastically.

"What is it, dad?" She was delighted to see her father active. The weakness in the left side of his body had now almost completely healed.

"A sled. Brendan and I have spent all this afternoon making it."

"I'm going to ride through the snow on it, Siobhan!" bubbled her younger brother.

"But it's May." she giggled. "You've got a long time to wait for it to snow."

"Be prepared! Isn't that what the scouts say?" said Clane. "Better too early than too late."

As she returned to the kitchen Brendan came in after her and approached her. "Siobhan, Boggin want to talk to you."

"Boggin?" She looked her little brother with a quizzical expression, but she could tell he was completely serious.

"Yeah."

"But you haven't seen Boggin for months. Why has he come back now?"

"He hasn't; it's just that old Indian guy asked me to pass that on from Boggin as a message."

"The... the old Indian guy? You mean Flying Buffalo? You've seen Flying Buffalo!?"

"He never told me his name, but I see him sometimes."

"When did you see him last?"

"Today on my way to school. He said: 'Tell Siobhan Boggin want to talk to her'. So I said I'd tell you."

Siobhan paused. "Alright. Where's Boggin then?"

"We've got to go to my room." He led the way up to his bedroom and jumped up onto his bed while Siobhan sat on a chair in the corner. Brendan sat up and looked at her with interest. Then she sat up and gasped. In the middle of the room was a cloud of mist, a circular balloon of smoke, smoke that kept its shape. A rough hewn face appeared in the centre that gradually solidified. The features of the face became more distinct, the skin took on a purple hue and its large protruding nose became visible. Its black marble eyes glinted and its thick lips curled into a smile. "Hello, Siobhan." It had a squeaky, lilting voice.

"Boggin! Are you Boggin!?"

"Yes." It was just a face. Although she could see there was more of it around the face this was hidden in the mist.

"My God!... You're real then?"

"Evidently."

"What... what...?"

"I can't stay for long. Can you pass on a message to Brendan for me?"

"Why can't you tell him yourself?"

"The medication he was given means that he can't see me anymore. I'm afraid he probably never will again."

She nodded. "I see."

"Could you tell him this?... I'm going away. I have to go back to where I came from. I will return to this world, but my job then will be to befriend to another child. I will still look after Brendan, but I won't be able to communicate with him."

"Alright."

"I might come back to Brendan if he really needs me; if that is the case then I'll pass him on a message via Flying Buffalo."

She nodded. "Got that."

"Tell Brendan that I love him very much. I miss talking to him a lot. He will always be my friend."

"I will."

"Goodbye, Siobhan; and thank you."

"Goodbye, Boggin."

Boggin's face merged with the bubble of smoke and the bubble faded like evaporating steam until it was gone.

Siobhan turned to face her little brother. Brendan was already looking at her and he was crying. She sat beside her brother on the bed, lifted him onto her lap and embraced him.

....

Siobhan was dreamily making her way through her correspondence in her White House office when she stopped and stared. There was an E-gram from Julian. The title line was "*Happy Birthday*". She panted hard, conflicting emotions collided inside her head. She had missed Julian terribly, but at the same time she never wanted to see him again. She had loved him and she had

387

hated him. He was wonderful and he was awful. She considered deleting the E-gram unread. She stopped herself an opened it. "*Hi, Siobhan. Wanted to wish you a very happy birthday. 27 eh? What's it like working for John F Kerensky? Julian x.*"

"One 'x'." she found herself murmuring. She wrote back: "*Hi, Julian. Not bad thanks. How are you? x*" She decided to sign her E-grams with the same number of x's that he used.

He returned her E-gram within the hour. "*Hi, Siobhan. Very well indeed. About to do something very exciting and wondered if you want to be involved. x*"

"*What kind of thing? x*"

"*Can't tell you by E-gram. Will you meet with me? x*"

"*Where are you? x*"

"*Ireland. x*"

The E-gram exchange went on into the evening. Her mood changed. She recalled all the anguish she had suffered after their parting. "*Hi Julian. I'm very busy at the moment with the presidential election coming up. Jack needs me to work with him on that. I cannot just drop everything and travel to Ireland, especially to meet up with somebody who won't tell me WHY he wants to meet with me and the last time we spoke he called me one of the 'forces of reaction' who had come into his life to make him betray his cause and abandon his socialist whatever. And then told me to leave and broke my heart. So the answer is no. Anything else I can help you with this evening? Siobhan.*" She deliberately left the x off this time.

"*I'm sorry I said those things to you, Siobhan. I shouldn't have. I was unfair and too harsh. It turned out you were completely right about the WRSL. They really ARE a hate cult. You spotted their sectarian nature long before I did. Sometimes theory needs an outsider to look at it properly when an experienced scholar can't see the obvious. I am no longer following the false path of intersectional identity politics. I underestimated the proletariat and shouldn't have rejected them. Look, all I'm asking is if you want to do a bit of freelance journalism. That used to be your job didn't it?*"

"Julian, have you not got the message yet? How many times do I have to tell you? The answer is NO! No, no and a thousand times NO!"

....

The plane came into land at Shannon Airport. Siobhan could have made the journey in one hour using the Quicksilver, but she needed the time a conventional aircraft fight took to think, to adjust herself from her mindset of her existing life and prepare herself for what lay ahead. After a lot of begging, Jack had given her a week off; she hoped she would not need that long. Julian met her at the airport and drove her to the party headquarters at the seaside town of Tramore in County Waterford. His organization was no longer called the Workers Revolutionary Socialist League; it was called the Continual Red Army and was led by a very good-looking but rather aloof man from Argentina called Ernesto to whom Julian had clearly male-bonded very strongly. There were fifteen members of the group, including four women. They were all young, fit and aggressive. They wore dark green T-shirts with a red star on and a matching red beret. The equipment in their clubhouse included a formidable arsenal of weapons. "What is all this for?" asked Siobhan. She had her camera rolling continuously, but nobody seemed to mind. Ernesto in particular appeared very enthusiastic about being filmed. He posed for her camera with his chest puffed out and his sleeves rolled up so everybody could see his clenched biceps. "Tomorrow we depart to bring the revolution to Britain." he declared. "The bourgeois capitalist front that is the League of the World has controlled that island for too long. After decades of fascist rule, a genocidal onslaught and now total subservience to the forces of international reaction, the people of Britain will be freed to determine their own destiny via socialism."

"What if they choose their own destiny and that choice is not socialism?"

Ernesto gasped and raised his hands. "They will never do that! It is unthinkable!"

Siobhan had the good sense not to ask any of them about the reptilians or MFO's.

The following morning at dawn the Continual Red Army smuggled their military hoard down to the marina where they had a boat. It was a very old, but well-kept seagoing yacht. Ernesto took the wheel and they cast off the lines. They sailed along the south coast until they reached Carnsore Point, the south-eastern extremity of Ireland; then they turned northwest and headed out across the Irish Sea. At mid-afternoon they sighted land, a row of broken cliffs with clean yellow beaches in between. Small boxy houses could be seen inland from the beach. The yacht approached a mouldy old jetty and a group of people were waiting to greet them. These were also young people, badly dressed and visibly malnourished. There was a party atmosphere as the Continual Red Army disembarked and embraced their supporters. They began kitting up. Julian strapped a bandolier across his chest and an equipment belt around his waist including a holster for a sidearm and a scabbard containing a dagger. He lifted an assault rifle and thrust a magazine into it. She could see that he still had some difficulty in using his right hand; the injury he inflicted on himself had not completely healed. "Julian, be careful!" Siobhan found herself saying. She had been determined to remain a neutral observer, as a good press-woman does; but her poise was broken completely as she watched her former lover prepare for war.

"Why?" he answered deadpan. "What does it matter if I don't?"

"Because..."

He glared at her sarcastically. "Well?"

She felt tearful and looked away.

"Comrades!" yelled Ernesto. "It is time! Onwards together into the battle!" He continued in his native Spanish: "*¡Hasta la victoria siempre! ¡Viva la Revolucion!*" They leaped aboard a series of landrovers, galvanized by fervour, and the convoy drove away with the vehicles' tyres screeching on the broken road.

Siobhan did not go ashore at all. She sat in the saloon of the yacht. Her thoughts and feeling ground together like rusty gears. She distracted herself by reading a book she had brought with her, or viewing meshpages on her matchbook. She E-grammed her photographs to several newspaper editors. There was a particularly good one of Ernesto which she'd shot from below, looking up at his stern, beautiful face. He was staring into the distance with an intense expression. His long hair flowing from beneath his beret, his sparse beard neatly trimmed. One of the editors E-grammed her back: "*Nice snap, Siobhan. I can see a poster or T-shirt run with this.*"

It was getting dark when she heard the sound of the landrover engines on the dock. She ran onto deck to see the vehicles pull up. Ernesto jumped out of the driving seat and raised his rifle in the air. He let out a roar of triumph. The other got out and joined him in the action. Siobhan counted them; there were only fourteen. Where was Julian? "Oh my God no!"... Then she saw him. He climbed out of the back seat of the last landrover. She was running down the gangplank before she could stop herself, dashing across the quay to embrace him. His clothes were torn and spattered with mud, but he looked unharmed. He took her in his arms as she threw hers around him. They stared into each other's eyes for a few moments, and then Julian took her hand and started walking towards the yacht. She followed, powerless to resist. Everything around them was forgotten; Ernesto, their comrades, the celebration. Once on board the boat they headed below and entered one of the cabins. They kissed passionately as they used to during their happy times.

Chapter 30

The aircraft was furnished like an airliner and as comfortable as one in the front third, yet behind that it was like nothing Siobhan had ever seen. A row of steel dewars had been bolted into the cabin, filling up the whole space apart from a narrow aisle between them. Lieutenant Barry came out of the cockpit. "Miss Quilley, we are now at forty thousand feet and ready to begin spraying operations. Would you like to bring your camera and observe?" The crew opened the valves on the dewars by turning hand wheels. She found the old-fashioned and human scale of the job rather comforting. There was a master valve at the rear of the aircraft that was further down the pipes. As soon as that was open the fluid inside the dewars began running. She moved over to a window and looked out. White steamy vapour was issuing from the training edge of the aircraft's wing from four outlets. It spread out behind them as far as she could see. She felt very strange. This had been done in secret by covert operatives for many years now; and now it was beginning again in public.

It was the previous month that she had first found out. The Chief Executive had called her urgently. "Siobhan, we got a problem." Jack had said on the intercom. His voice sounded stern. She got up from her desk and left her office. It was a short walk along the main corridor of the West Wing to the Chief Executive's office. She knocked.

"Come."

When she entered she saw Dr Wolfgang von Pflenzmann and Dr Jenny Bulstrode sitting opposite him.

"Ah, Siobhan." JFK said in a far more cheerful and friendly voice than the one he had just used on the intercom. "Thanks for coming. We've got a troublesome little issue that's just come up. We're going to have to relaunch the chemtrail programme."

"What!?...Why?"

"Wolfgang."

The doctor cleared his throat. "It seems that we mistook what the chemtrail programme was actually doing. This was after we discovered a series of very powerful electromagnetic transmitters in northern Canada that were used by the government to radiate a massive amount of electromagnetic energy into the earth's atmosphere. The chemtrails were not just dampening the effects of the increasing Schumann Cavity Resonance, they were actually interfering with it, in the same way you might jam a radio signal. The chemical additive was actually a conductive material for the transmitters' energy."

"What does that result in?"

"Well, with the sudden removal of this interference signal the Schumann Cavity Resonance is restoring itself too abruptly. If left unchecked this will result in electromagnetic storms that will be a hundred times as intense as the world has ever seen. It might even destabilize the ionosphere to the point that it breaks down altogether for many years, leaving the earth naked and defenceless against solar radiation from flares and sunspots. The effects will the entire earth's surface being exposed to the same ionizing radiation that one would if one were standing a mile away from a one megaton nuclear explosion."

"That would kill us, wouldn't it?"

"Yes. This will all happen within a year unless we act. This is why we have no choice but to reenergize the reptilian's atmospheric grid."

"What? Forever?"

"No, no." von Pflenzmann shook his head. "We will eventually be able to switch it off, but only after reducing the power slowly over time to allow the ionosphere to adjust in line with the natural Schumann Cavity Resonance change."

"How long?"

"We don't know, but possibly several decades. Maybe for as long as a century."

"Holy shit!"

"It'll be OK, Siobhan. We know what we're doing." pacified Kennedy.

"But this means the reptilians could come back. They could disguise themselves as humans again."

"No. We know exactly how the active ingredient of the additive was responsible for the reps' shape-shifting powers. Von has devised a new formula. We are deliberately using this new formula in place of the old. It can heal the interference without allowing the reptilians to disguise themselves again."

The spraying took just over two hours and then the plane returned to its starting point and landed. Siobhan went for a walk. She stood by the fence of the Lockheed aviation centre at Ogden, Utah thinking what else she could add to her news story about the rebirth of the chemtrails. She had her camera trained on the row of aircraft. Most of them were old converted airliners. Some of them had just been commandeered and were being retro-fitted with the chemtrail delivery pipes by the company's engineers. The lack of a need for secrecy meant that they could now use this far more efficient distribution system all the time. She stopped the camera and walked back along the fence towards the press briefing centre. She watched the ground under her feet as she walked. It was summer now and the ground was dry. Coarse brown grass poked out from the sandy soil. She was daydreaming slightly so when the shadow of a man appeared in front of her she jumped back in shock. "Flying Buffalo!"

"Hello, Siobhan." he smiled. He was wearing casual summer slacks and a broad-brimmed hat.

She laughed. "It's good to see you again. Thanks for getting Boggin to give that message to Brendan."

"It was Boggin's idea. I merely facilitated... in fact that seems to be my primary function in this world."

She paused. "How did we do?"

"You did brilliantly. You people amaze me. There is no other species quite like you in existence that I'm aware of. You have achieved something that so many others fail at. Do you know that the reptilians are found all over the infinite universes? They latch on to any available consciousness they can. It is not unlike an adaptation of Jesus' Parable of the Sower. Fallow ground is everywhere for these parasitic beasts, but very few who start off as the fallow ground become the stones and thorns, and in doing so force the reptilians to leave. Well done, humanity... Very well done."

There was a long silence. "I saw Julian again last month. He's gone from my life now again. I don't know if it's forever this time. I doubt if he will even live much longer with what he is currently doing."

Flying Buffalo's eyes dropped to look at her lower body. "He has not completely gone from your life though has he?" He suddenly reached out his left hand and placed it against her abdomen. "Hmm... Twins. A boy and a girl. Congratulations to both you and Julian."

"Are you sure?"

"Am I ever wrong?"

She shook her head. "I only found out I was pregnant a couple of weeks ago."

"Now is the perfect moment. Your species, your planet and your nation are beginning a new life. What better time could there be for you yourself to produce new life?"

She looked at the horizon. "I want them to know their father, to be with their father."

"They might well."

"What kind of world are they going to grow up in?"

"That is entirely up to you. You have the brain and the hands to make of this world whatever you like. It could be a prison or a paradise. It could be heaven on earth or hell on earth."

She thought of Ernesto's belligerent and egotistical anger. "We have a nature though. You can't change human nature."

"No, but that nature can be a good or bad thing depending on how it is channelled. The same fundamental aggression of all human beings, especially males, can turn a man into a sadistic serial murderer, or a great and noble warrior or political leader. It's as much a choice as anything else." Flying Buffalo turned around and examined his surroundings.

"I guess you're going to tell me your work here is done, right?" she laughed, but felt sad at the same time.

He laughed as well. "So your father has been telling you all about me... No no, Siobhan. There will be no goodbyes this time. Those days are over. I am here and I am here to stay. We shall meet again; that I promise... But farewell for now." He walked ahead of her to the press hut.

Siobhan stood and watched his back as he walked over to the building and entered the door. She did not bother to go over and see if he had disappeared. She looked around herself, at the aircraft on the apron, the distant salt flats and the sandy mountains, the blue skies that would soon be filling with white lines again. "Never mind." she said to herself. "We'll make the best of it."

The End

If you enjoyed this book you might be interested in these websites:

http://www.paradigmresearchgroup.org/
http://www.richplanet.net/
http://www.ufotruthmagazine.co.uk/
http://www.disclosureproject.org/
http://www.exopoliticsgb.com/
http://www.exopolitics.org.uk/
http://www.stantonfriedman.com/
http://www.citizenhearing.org/
http://richarddolanpress.com/
http://www.checktheevidence.com/cms/
http://hpanwo.blogspot.co.uk/
https://thebasesproject.org/

Ben Emlyn-Jones' second novel *Rockall* is available free to read online at:
http://hpanwo-bb.blogspot.co.uk/2009/02/rockall-chapter-1.html

Ben Emlyn-Jones' first novel *Evan's Land* is available via private sale in limited numbers. Please email the publisher at:
bennyjay74@gmx.co.uk